CABAL OF CHAOS

CHRONICLES OF CAIN
BOOK 7

JOHN CORWIN

RAVEN HOUSE

LET CHAOS REIGN

The Oblivion Guard is trying to kill Cain.

That should be impossible. After all, Cain has a bargain with the summer and winter queens that keeps him safe from them directly or indirectly harming him. If they breach the bargain, then they'll lose considerable power.

Cain discovers that many of these would-be assassins come from Alpha and Beta dimensions, and they seem to have found a loophole that allows them to kill him without harming the queens. Anyone associated with Cain is fair game, and Aura and Layla are forced to hide out at Sanctuary with Cain.

But not even his secret hideout is safe anymore. The guardians are working closely with Eclipse, the assassination and bounty-hunting agency once run by Torvin Rayne. A cybermancer in their employ has found a way to triangulate the location of Sanctuary. The clock is ticking down, leaving Cain no choice but to go on the offensive.

But he soon discovers that rogue guardians are the least of his worries. There's a new player in town, a being known as the Winged God. And they seem to be pulling the strings. Their goal is to kill Cain and take Hannah for their own.

There's only one way to stop the threat, and that's to go straight to the source of the problem and kill everyone. But going up against an army of trained killers isn't a walk in the park even for Cain. He'll have to use every trick in the book to pull this off and make up a few along the way.

But soon they'll learn that no one, not even a god, is going to get between Cain and his mangoritas.

BOOKS BY JOHN CORWIN

Join the Overworld Conclave for all the news, memes and tentacles you could ever desire!

https://www.facebook.com/groups/overworldconclave

Or get your tentacles via email: www.johncorwin.net

Fan page: https://www.facebook.com/johncorwinauthor

CHRONICLES OF CAIN

To Kill a Unicorn

Enter Oblivion

Throne of Lies

At The Forest of Madness

The Dead Never Die

Shadow of Cthulhu

Cabal of Chaos

THE OVERWORLD CHRONICLES

Sweet Blood of Mine

Dark Light of Mine

Fallen Angel of Mine

Dread Nemesis of Mine

Twisted Sister of Mine

Dearest Mother of Mine

Infernal Father of Mine

Sinister Seraphim of Mine

Wicked War of Mine

Dire Destiny of Ours

Aetherial Annihilation

Baleful Betrayal

Ominous Odyssey

Insidious Insurrection

Utopia Undone

Overworld Apocalypse

Apocryphan Rising

Soul Storm

Devil's Due

Overworld Ascension

Assignment Zero (An Elyssa Short Story)

OVERWORLD UNDERGROUND

Soul Seer

Demonicus

Infernal Blade

OVERWORLD ARCANUM

Conrad Edison and the Living Curse

Conrad Edison and the Anchored World

Conrad Edison and the Broken Relic

Conrad Edison and the Infernal Design

Conrad Edison and the First Power

STAND ALONE NOVELS

Mars Rising

No Darker Fate

The Next Thing I Knew

Outsourced

1

The first longshot nearly took off my head.

My sigils tingled at the last possible instant. I ducked and a car window behind me cracked and puckered inward. I rolled forward to cross the narrow street and pressed my back against an old blue sedan. White-hot energy bit into the asphalt to the left and right of where I'd been, and another blast took out the driver-side window of the car I was using as a shield. Four assassins had just tried to end me.

They weren't ordinary assassins. They were Oblivion Guard.

I wasn't safe here. I pulled out my emergency escape plan—Panoptes, the all-seeing ring, and slid it onto my finger. Black worms crawled across my vision. A wave of dizziness slammed into me. A honeycomb of multiple views sprang up before me, but they were too blurry to bring into focus. The black worms squirmed madly, blinding me until I couldn't see where to go.

Let the madness consume you, Cain. Nurture the seed.

The voice in my head was all too familiar. I'd had a nice chat with the owner during my time in Hel. How in the hell was Nyarlathotep in my head? Was it real, or was I going completely mad?

I wrenched Panoptes off my finger and the dizziness faded. The black worms grew thinner until they faded from sight. But the veins in my hands pulsated with darkness. I'd borne the full brunt of the gaze of Cthulhu after he'd risen on Gaia Beta. Somehow, my mind had survived the encounter, but the symptoms of madness were getting worse. Prolonged use of Panoptes also caused madness and apparently stirred up whatever Cthulhu had left rattling around in my skull.

Fitzroy Simmons, my personal witch doctor, had promised to diagnose me when he returned from cleansing his soul. He'd dirtied himself with dark magic at my behest, extracting memories from Aura Beta and destroying her mind so she'd no longer be an existential threat to Dimension Prime. I hoped he planned to return home soon because if I survived this encounter, I'd need his professional help.

There was nothing left to do but take cover. I shoved Panoptes back into my utility pouch and slid beneath the car. The scopes on my would-be assassin's oblivion staffs would allow them to see my infrared signature through the metal. Even if the car was warm enough to cover my body heat, aura mode would reveal me just as easily.

The assassins were cloaked or well-hidden, giving them an unfair advantage. Thankfully, the first thing they taught in the Oblivion Guard was that life was unfair to the extreme. Someone always had an overwhelming advantage and was willing to use it against you. I'd killed plenty of entities for the Guard. Most of the time it had been like shooting fish in a barrel. Sometimes, the fish shot back.

I was more than capable of shooting back if given the chance but allowing myself to be ambushed just outside Voltaire's had put me at an extreme disadvantage. The moment I'd stepped far enough out of the fae safe zone, I'd been targeted. The border for the safe zone was a good fifty feet away across open space. There was no way I could make it back inside. Anyone who attacked me within its confines would be tagged and immediately tracked down by fae enforcers, namely the Oblivion Guard.

My attackers might be former members of the Oblivion Guard, but that didn't make them immune to the brutal punishment earned for breaking the sanctity of a safe zone. These particular assassins weren't even from my dimension. They'd been sent from Feary in Beta and Alpha—a specialized new task force assigned to eliminating me.

I'd learned of them after dropping off brain damaged Baura with Erolith. They'd tried to kill me before I planeswalked back to Gaia. I'd used Panoptes to escape, but not before eavesdropping on their conversation. I hadn't expected them to hunt me down on Gaia, and that had obviously been a stupid assumption on my part.

They weren't working directly for the high fae, that much was certain. If they were, attacking me would break the bargain I'd bound in blood with the queens of summer and winter. Breaking the bargain would cause severe damage to the power of the queens and all high fae. No, these people were working for someone else.

Their next move would be volleys of longshots in an effort to pierce the car all the way through, so I cast a shield sigil in the narrow space between me and the car's underbelly. I didn't think it was possible for even the powerful burst of a longshot to penetrate cleanly through the metal, but I didn't want to take any chances.

Metal creaked and the car shook as longshots pummeled it from all sides. Sparks flew and the odor of gasoline stung my nose. I looked toward my feet and saw a wet stain creeping and pooling toward me. If the blasts didn't ignite the gas tank directly, they'd certainly turn the automobile into a blazing inferno with one well-placed shot.

I had to get out of here or charbroiled Cain was next on the menu.

Peering out from beneath the passenger side, I gauged the distance to a two-story house just beyond the sidewalk. The narrow slit between the concrete curb and the bottom of the car provided marginal safety from an assassin's shot, but it also blocked me from sliding out from under the car on that side.

The transmission hump for the rear wheel drive likewise blocked me from retreating that way. If I went back the way I'd come, I'd only open myself up to all four assassins again. Protocol dictated that two of those assassins were creeping upon my position right this very moment while the other two kept close watch in case I tried to make a run for it.

The only way to stand a chance of coming out of this alive was to squeeze beneath the front axle housing and only open myself up to a shot from three directions. First, I needed a distraction. I reached into my utility belt and found a small windup car. It wasn't as good as the remote control one I kept in Dolores, but it might suffice.

I cast a camouflage blind over myself, then cast a shield in front of the sedan to give myself an extra two percent chance of surviving. I wound up the mechanism on the tiny car, powered the sigils, and let it go. The car vanished, replaced by a human-sized blur consistent with someone hiding behind a camouflage blind. It also generated a false aura and heat signature. It was fae-level glamour—enough to fool their oblivion staffs, but there was nothing I could do to cover my own aura or heat signature. My only hope was that they reacted as instantly as they were trained to do.

The instant I released the windup car, I powered the sigils on my legs and thrust myself out from beneath the front of the car. Asphalt bubbled and sprayed as longshots blew through the illusion provided by the windup car. It generally took most guardians one second to power up another longshot. Even the best took half that time. As for me, I knew a trick to powering multiple shots in much quicker intervals.

I hoped none of these assholes knew that trick, or I was toast.

By now, the assassins were seeing two distinct heat signatures or auras, depending on the mode they used for their scope. They already knew the one they'd fired at three times wasn't me because there was no blood or brain matter sprayed on the road. I threw a layer of shields to my left and right as I ran toward the house where one of the four assassins was likely hiding on the roof.

Shields shattered like glass around me as I sprinted with every-thing I had toward the house. I threw out another layer of shields while adding a juke to my movements to keep from having my head blown out from behind. I dove toward the hedges on the left side of the house and rolled until my body was flat against the brick.

Two more longshots from opposite directions burst the shields an instant after my dive. Another longshot splintered the bushes at the corner of the house. By now the assassin on the roof was creeping to peer over the edge. Five shots from each assassin so far. The energy expended was tapped into their cloaks as well, meaning the fae glamour hiding them from me was about to fail.

I summoned my staff and flicked into aura mode. The world looked grayscale through it, but the auras of living beings would show up in color. Unlike their staffs, mine could penetrate fae glamour. I'd upgraded my orb with one from the lost armory of Hephaestus. Even if the assassin closest to me still had their cloak active, it wouldn't matter.

The glowing outline of a head poked over the side of the roof an oblivion staff aimed at the ground. My longshot struck the forehead dead center. Black matter sprayed into the air and the body slumped forward, falling halfway off the house before sliding the rest of the way off and thudding to the ground.

I looked at the face and recognized the drow as one of Torvin Rayne's loyal followers. Their name wasn't important anymore. I just wondered which dimension she was from. I yanked the cloak from her corpse and put it on. It was a tight fit, but that wasn't an issue. As long as it was on me, its enchantments would protect me. The seam sealed at a touch from my finger. I activated the cloaking sigils. The glamour flickered unsteadily but turned on.

I took the drow's oblivion staff and stuck it through my belt, then put my back to the wall and slid toward the backyard. The other assassins knew their friend was dead, but they wouldn't be deterred. They were already converging on me from three directions.

The attackers who saw their friend die knew I'd take the cloak and use it. They'd take extra precautions when approaching since they couldn't see through fae glamour with their staffs. Now I had an advantage they didn't. I was cloaked and could see through their cloaks. This was going to be a walk in the park.

A flicker drew my attention to the fence about twenty yards from my position. The glamour invisibility fizzled out on my borrowed cloak at the same time one of the assassins leaped over the fence, their oblivion staff sweeping the backyard. They must have seen me out of the corner of their eye because they spun, ducked, and fired.

The magical bullet barely chipped the brick exterior, probably because the assassin had fired so many shots and they were getting tired. I sprinted sideways, powered my brightblade, and slashed it down at her. She blocked with her staff, thrust a foot at my midriff. I jumped back, gripped her ankle, and yanked.

She fell to her back. Rolled to the side. I gave her no quarter, lunging with my brightblade, keeping her off balance. This was the elf, Tisha, who'd given me a ride south of Faevalorn after I'd spoken with Erolith. Her body language had given away the first assassination attempt by this crew.

My body sigils tingled. I blocked a longshot with my brightblade as the assassin from the other side of the road came into range. My brightblade glowed marginally brighter as it absorbed the energy. It was one more perk of the upgrade from the lost armory. If I blocked enough spells, I could retaliate with a large burst of power.

Tisha used the diversion to jump to her feet and ignite her bright-blade. She assumed a defensive position. The fear in her eyes told me she didn't dare try to take me in a fair fight. The drow who'd nearly shot me in the back earlier flipped her staff, gripped it by the hilt, and activated her brightblade. Blade humming with energy, she crept closer.

"Hello, Ena." I smirked. "It's awfully strange seeing you here considering you're dead in this dimension."

"You will soon share the fate of my alt, Cain." Her drow accent hung heavy on her English words. "And after you, we will find your Alpha alt and slay him as well. It is time to halt your meddling."

"Would you have gotten away with it if not for those meddling kids?" I feinted toward Tisha. The elf jumped back several feet, confirming my estimation of her. "Want a Scooby snack?" I pretended to reach into my utility belt.

Tisha looked puzzled, probably because the translation enchantment on her cloak didn't know what to make of Scooby snacks. Most guardians learned a handful of Gaian languages since they regularly visited safe zones and magical communities to ensure no one challenged their fae overlords.

English apparently wasn't a language Tisha had learned.

I assumed that by now, the fourth assassin was creeping along the back or front of the house, trying to determine if they could take me by surprise without their cloak active. I felt confident at this point that there weren't more of them lurking nearby or they would have blown off my head.

There had been at least eight of them who'd tried to kill me in Feary. Why they felt less than half that number was sufficient here was puzzling. They must have thought ambushing me would be quick and easy.

That question could wait. The only thing that needed answering now was whether I could take on three guardians by myself. Ena was highly skilled. I'd seen her spar with Torvin, and she'd scored points regularly during practice bouts. I knew little to nothing about Tisha or the assassin I'd killed moments earlier.

The fourth assassin finally walked around the corner of the house, apparently having reached the conclusion that he didn't need to employ stealth for the three of them to end me.

"Look, it's your buddy, Anair! Did you bring the smores for the campfire?"

The male drow stared unflinchingly at me. Like Ena, he'd been a hardline supporter of Torvin. Like Ena, his alt in Prime had died in the Dead Forest, consumed by a dhole worm. Even without Tisha, my chances of defeating the pair of them were slim.

"Why didn't you bring the whole crew again?" I changed from a defensive to a neutral stance, standing almost casually. My sigils didn't tingle as they were enchanted to do when an unseen danger prepared to act against me. They were my magical Spidey sense, given to me by Caolan the druid. If anyone else was lurking nearby, they'd start to tingle.

My opponents had options besides the brightblades. If just Ena and Tisha engaged me, Anair could target me shotgun style, no long-shot needed. As much as I wanted to murder them and put a stop to this threat right here and now, dueling three guardians would be a death sentence.

2

Ena sneered. "If you're fishing for information, Cain, it'll have to wait until you're dead."

"Fair enough." I gave her a friendly smile. "Maybe you'll tell me when I start cutting you to pieces, limb by limb." I glanced at Tisha. "I've killed Torvin in two different dimensions. It'll be my pleasure killing off the rest of his little minions."

"Minions?" Anair snarled. "Ena is Torvin's right hand!"

"*Was* his right hand." I shrugged. "Tell me, did Torvin masturbate with that hand?"

"Mock all you wish, human filth." Anair's eyes glowed with anger. "The God Hand will have its revenge."

I frowned. "God Hand? Did you guys start a new band without me?"

Ena held up a finger to shush Anair before he blurted a retort. "Do not let the human provoke you, friend. We have the advantage. Let us end it now."

I looked at Tisha. "Are you really in with this crew? You look way too frightened right now."

She stiffened, but her defensive stance remained unchanged. "I am a loyal member of the God Hand."

"Elves are taking orders from drow?" I shook my head. "What's the world coming to?"

Anair's brightblade powered on with a hum. Ena began circling to the side. "Elf, you will remain in place until I give the signal. Her fingers twitched in the secret language of the Oblivion Guard. The signs seemed random which told me they'd adopted a code so I couldn't eavesdrop. I didn't need to understand what they meant because I already knew they wanted Tisha to take a longshot the moment she recharged.

I tried one last gambit. "You realize that by attacking me unprovoked, you'll break the bargain I made with the fae, right?"

Anair scoffed. "No, little human. There is a loophole."

A loophole?

Ena was nearly in position, so I decided it was time to bow out. My brightblade hadn't gathered much extra energy, but it was enough to do what I needed. I swung the blade and willed the collected power to flow out of it. A weak salvo flashed out and caught Anair in the chest. The only reason I caught him unprepared was because ordinary brightblades didn't do that.

The impact knocked him on his ass. Ena and Tisha flinched in surprise and that was enough time for me to fling flash bombs at them. My targets threw up their hands as the flashes ignited. I was already turning away, leaping over the fence and making a beeline for salvation.

I could have run back into the fae safe zone and sheltered at Voltaire's with an endless supply of mangoritas and Aura for company. It was the safest option, but also inconvenient. I didn't want to have to hide. I wanted to be somewhere I could plot my next moves against the God Hand, as they so melodramatically called themselves. Torvin had called himself the Black Hand, and it seemed his former followers had created their own little cult to continue the tradition.

"Why is it always a hand?" I muttered. "Right hand, Black Hand, God Hand. How about the Foot Up Your Ass?"

Torvin, like many drow in the Oblivion Guard, had been an arrogant, sadistic bastard. He'd been banished from the guard thanks to me, and then joined the supernatural assassination agency, Eclipse, where he'd continued being an utter bastard.

It seemed he'd had a side gig going as well. Had he thought of himself as a god? Did his minions still think he was a god even though he was dead as a doornail? It just didn't add up.

I sprinted around the neighboring house as my sigils tingled in warning. The enemy was in hot pursuit. Drow and elves had a physical advantage over humans. They were faster and stronger, meaning they'd catch me if I ran in a straight line. Thankfully, Little Five Points offered plenty of twists and turns for me to use to my advantage. Dolores, however, was parked back in the opposite direction, and I didn't think they knew what she looked like.

I always used precautions no matter where I was going. I always parked far away from Voltaire's and always in different locations. I always cloaked Dolores with illusion, so she never looked the same twice. It was most likely the assassins had waited near Voltaire's since they knew I'd eventually show up for a mangorita even if they didn't know which direction I'd come from.

My weakness for girly drinks had once again gotten me into trouble. I should've known that the rogue guardians wouldn't give up after failing to kill me in Feary.

I ran through a neighborhood, cut through backyards, and jumped over fences. Dolores was only two streets over, and I was almost home free. I thought for sure I'd lost my pursuers, but Anair must have thought I might try to circle around and backtrack because he appeared from behind a house directly in front of me.

His eyes flared when he saw me, but the hesitation lasted only a moment before he ran at me, brightblade humming. It was a cold day, so not many pedestrians were out and about, but a few of them gawked at the display as Anair came at me, his cloak flowing behind him.

I met his attack with a parry. Sparks flew as the superheated energy blades crashed against each other. He pressed the attack, employing the advantage of drow reflexes against my slower human ones. It was one of Torvin's signature swordplay strategies, one that relied on pushing back a weaker opponent, tiring them, and keeping them off balance.

Anair bared his teeth in a grin as he drove me back while I barely fended off the flurry of attacks, fear and resignation filling my eyes. "Oh, Cain, you weak, pathetic thing." His grin turned to a sneer. "There is no doubt you had nothing to do with Torvin's death, because you fight like a child."

"Please, mercy." I continued backing off. "Why do you want to kill me so badly?"

"So, our god can finish his plan, worm." He spat at me. "Filth!"

"Your god?" I tried to muster a little more fear on my face. "Who could that possibly be?"

Anair chose to remain silent because victory was at hand. He added a double feint in the middle of his blitz to throw me even further off balance. My sigils tingled as Ena and Tisha found us.

Nubs—non magical humans—stood watching and gawking. Some recorded the fight with their phones, apparently thinking this was a street performance. They were about to get a very rude awakening.

Anair continued the blitz pattern attack without any of the variations his master used to win most of his duels. What made Torvin so formidable was his ability to weave several fighting styles into one cohesive dance that most beings had no chance to defend against.

Just as Anair finished the flurry of attacks that signaled a coming feint, I ghostwalked. My blade slashed. His head tumbled backward from his body and the brightblade fell to the ground, sizzling against damp grass. I snatched it and depressed the symbol on the hilt to deactivate it.

"No!" Ena shouted.

I quickly tugged his oblivion cloak off, made easier by his missing head. One could never have too many cloaks enchanted with fae glamor.

Nubs cried out in alarm or wonder, thinking this must be some kind of fakery. I deactivated my brightblade and whirled mine and

Anair's staffs in either hand. I took a bow. "The Jedi order will never prevail against the power of the Sith." I cast a sigil and a weak wave of magic flowed out around me, frying the electronics of any phone within fifty feet. My phone was safely tucked into a hardened pouch, protected from such hexes.

As nubs shouted in alarm, throwing down their phones or cheering my victory over the evil Sith, I flipped the finger at Ena and Tisha, then dashed away. I dodged around a house and cut across the next street. I didn't know if they'd stop to pick up their fallen comrade, or if they'd chase me, but it was better if I avoided them.

Ena alone would be a challenge. She was a fierce fighter, quick with the blade, and able to adapt against opposing fighting styles. She was far superior to the copy and paste fighters like Anair who learned by rote. She might not be as good as Torvin, but she was a close second.

Dolores was only a few blocks away, but I didn't want to risk giving away her position. She was disguised, but Ena could see through the illusion with her oblivion staff. Even the smallest amount of information could help her track me, and I wasn't about to help her in any way.

A dark house on the left provided an opportunity to hide and observe. I ran into the backyard and tested the back door. It was locked, so I pushed my brightblade into the jamb, slicing wood and metal latches. I banished my staff, opened the door, and stepped inside. Like most abodes in this area, the house was old but remodeled with an open floorplan.

The kitchen and family room were one large space. Nothing blocked the view from the kitchen all the way to the back door. I hoped the top floor offered a bit more concealment.

I took the stairs to the second floor and entered a bathroom with a window facing the street. Toys in the tub and the children's toothbrushes on the edge of the sink told me the owners had a boy around the age of six, and a girl about a year younger. Hopefully they were out for the day since I didn't want any collateral damage if Ena and Tisha found me.

Ena ran down the street alone, presumably because she left Tisha to take care of Anair's corpse. She peered through the scope on her oblivion staff, sweeping it back and forth along the rows of houses. If she so much as glanced this way, she'd see my aura by the window and know it was me since it glowed brighter than a nub's.

Even without my Ekhsis heritage, my aura shined differently due to my magical usage and because of the enchanted devices I kept in my utility pack. The oblivion cloak was the only thing that wouldn't show up, but it and the one I'd taken from Anair needed to recharge.

The primary disadvantage of using aura mode was that it couldn't penetrate dense surfaces like the plaster walls in these old houses. I ducked across the hallway into the children's room and got in the closet, putting several plaster walls between me and Ena. I gave to the count of fifteen, then went back to the window. Ena banished her staff, then took off running down the street.

She might have seen me before I went to the closet. She might run down the street, around a house, and double back. On the other hand, she might have assumed I was far enough away to evade being scoped and taken a wild guess as to where I'd gone.

"Always assume the worst," I muttered, repeating Torvin's oft-used phrase when addressing the "scum" as he'd called trainees.

Torvin might have been a sadistic, evil son of a bitch, but he'd also been a strategic genius.

I opened the window, slid down the front roof, and landed on the grass. Then I bolted across the street and ducked behind another house. I summoned my staff and peered through the scope. A moment later, Ena's glowing aura slipped through the back door. She'd probably glimpsed me just as I left the bathroom to hide in the closet.

She held her staff at the ready, prepared to ignite the brightblade at the last minute to catch me off guard. She flipped up the scope and swept it up and around the ceiling, looking for me. I ducked back behind the house and sprinted across the backyard. I jumped up and slid over the tall wooden fence.

I ran through another backyard, reached the next street, and turned left. An old blue beetle was parked not far away. I ran over to it, gripped the door handle hidden beneath the illusion, and opened the door to my beloved Dolores. The blue beetle shimmered since the illusion size didn't match the car it was hiding. Dolores was a nineteen-seventy Dodge Coronet Super Bee station wagon, a good deal longer than a Volkswagen Bug.

I ignited the liquid mana engine and waited for a car to pass so I could pull onto the street. Resisting the urge to gun the accelerator, I casually drove to a stop sign, looked both ways, then turn right. Moments later, I was far enough away that I felt comfortable dispelling the illusion.

The nub in a car next to mine did a double-take as the beetle vanished and Dolores in all her dark beauty appeared. I'd upgraded her enchantments, inscribing an illusion sigil on her hood so I could change the appearance while driving. Before, I'd had to get out, trace a sigil, and then activate it. Ever since a clone assassin had tried to kill me, I'd decided to enhance my defenses.

But now I had other chinks in my armor to worry about. Layla and Aura knew where I lived. The rogue guardians likely knew about them since even the legitimate Oblivion Guard knew about my acquaintances and probably tracked them from time to time. Aura and Layla were seasoned professionals, able to detect and evade most stalkers, but the Oblivion Guard was another matter altogether.

I created a group text for Aura, Layla, and Hannah. *Ambushed by rogue guardians outside Voltaire's. Escaped. Use extreme caution.*

Aura responded immediately. *Inside the safezone?*

I didn't like driving and texting, so I waited for the next traffic light to respond. *Meet at Sanctuary for details.*

Hannah texted a moment later. *Rogue guardians here?*

I didn't respond.

Another rule I adhered to was to never travel straight home from Voltaire's. Now was especially not the time to break that rule. I took a meandering route while constantly checking for tails, then pulled behind a building where I disguised Dolores with another illusion. I pulled onto the road and took another random route.

After a few more miles of evasive driving, I stopped at a shopping center and got out of the car. Using the scope on my staff, I swept Dolores for magical trackers. As expected, she was clean, but it paid to be thorough.

That still wasn't good enough. I went to the rear of the station wagon and took out a tool kit. Inside was a nub bug detector. This took considerably longer since I had to scan from front to back, along the sides and the bottom just to be safe. My heartbeat calmed once I finished the scan and found nothing.

I put away the toolbox and got back into the car. Before leaving, I took a few minutes to think about my next steps. I'd terminated two rogue guardians, but how many more were in the so-called God Hand? Most importantly, how had they been able to directly attack me without breaching the bargain I'd made with the fae?

The loophole mentioned by Anair was obviously so big that the high fae felt confident risking their immense power to have me killed. I'd been extremely thorough in crafting the bargain with the fae, so I couldn't even begin to guess how they thought it could be bypassed.

The Oblivion Guard could arrest or detain me for crimes as part of their normal duties, but they couldn't assassinate me under orders from any high fae. They couldn't even so much as attack me without breaking the bargain unless I attacked them first.

What they were doing now fell far outside of their duties, and I had to find out how and why these rogue guardians were able to do it before it was too late.

3

Hannah was waiting outside when I arrived at Sanctuary. She ran into the garage and hugged me before I was fully out of the car.

"Cain, what happened?"

"The same rogue guardians who tried to take me out on Feary were waiting outside Voltaire's when I left." I gave her a breakdown of events.

"A loophole?" Her nose wrinkled. "What loophole could they possibly mean?"

"That's the million-dollar question." I left the garage and went inside the former church that was now my home. The strange structure had once belonged to the Cult of Nyar, a splinter group of Ekhsis who worshipped the Elder Things instead of the Elder Gods. I'd been born here and should have been sacrificed to Nyarlathotep, but a young cultist had murdered everyone and saved me.

He'd sent me to Oblivion to live with Ekhsis there. They'd been all that remained of the original humans from a former iteration of the universe. Now I was the only one left. Despite the horrific history of this place, it was very well protected with both fae and druid magic. It was probably at least as secure as a fae safe zone.

My former pet octopus, Fred, stood inside, looking up at me with his big alien eyes. He'd grown marginally taller, but he was still very much a baby Cthulhu. I squeezed out of the oblivion cloak I'd taken from the dead guardian and dropped it and the stolen oblivion staff in my room.

"Cain, are you okay?" Fred's speech had improved remarkably, but he still sounded like a child. A mouth tentacle touched my arm and his more mature voice sounded inside my head. *How can the rogue guardians attack you?*

"Hannah, you can tell him." I went into the kitchen and pulled a loaf of homemade bread from the breadbox so I could make a sandwich.

Hannah told Fred and then they began throwing out random theories.

"Maybe they're not following orders at all," Hannah said. "These Handers are rogues like Torvin was and can do whatever they want."

"Handers?" I snorted. "Is that what we're calling them now?"

"Well, they're not really guardians anymore, are they?" She mulled it over. "Since they're not in the Oblivion Guard, they can attack you all they want."

"First of all, no one simply leaves the Guard, especially not with their oblivion staff and cloak. The queens would never allow it." I sliced a tomato and placed it atop the thin-cut turkey. "I was able to keep my staff because I had enough leverage with the Beast War. Unfortunately, my cloak was destroyed during my rebellion, and they refused to give me another one."

"If that's true, then it sounds like these Handers are playing for two different teams." Hannah bit her lower lip. "You'd think the queens would know something is going on and put a stop to it. But if they're coming from another dimension, then maybe their queens don't know what's going on."

"That brings up my second point," I said. "How did Handers from another dimension reach Prime without a Tetron? I have the ones from Prime and Beta, and we destroyed the one from Alpha."

Hannah frowned. "Remember that portal Baura used to escape

back to Beta? That wasn't made by a Tetron, and we never really figured out who put it there."

"A god of chaos most likely."

"If that's true, wouldn't their interference have caused another splinter in the timelines?" She nodded to herself. "Maybe there are other beings who can make interdimensional portals."

"That's true," I conceded. "Direct intervention by a god causes more dimensions, but history proves they can come to the aid of someone without risking another splinter event. Perseus and Hercules are two examples."

Hannah narrowed her eyes in thought. "But those gods were blood related right?"

"Hmm." I nodded slowly. "That might be a mitigating factor."

She snapped her fingers. "Then how could they directly help Baura and enable her to launch an eldritch invasion of Prime without splintering the timeline?"

"You're right. It doesn't make sense." I added some salt and pepper to my sandwich. "They tried to change a major event when they interfered with our fight against the Firsters. Instead, they created Alpha and Beta dimensions. They knew aiding Baura could lead to the destruction of Prime, so that should have been another splinter event."

Fred chimed in. "We need Fate. She knows."

I pressed my lips together. "Yeah, unless I go after Alistair again, I don't think she'll just drop by."

Hannah drummed her fingers on the table. "You've used the Tetron recently so you would have seen the newly formed dimensions if that had happened."

"Unless they were dying branches like the ones Fate told me about before." I'd done a tour of duty as Death incarnate. Some of my actions might have led to splinters in the timeline, but they'd been minor enough that the newly formed timelines withered and died. If I'd murdered Alistair the necromancer while performing the duties of Death, then that could have caused a full-on split.

"No, helping Baura would be major." Hannah's gaze went distant. "We're missing something."

"Baby god." Fred's mouth tentacles quivered. "A demi."

I picked up the top slice of bread and paused as his words hit me. "A dimension-shifting demi?"

Hannah nodded. "That's got to be it. There must be a demigod with that ability."

Full-fledged gods existed across all dimensions at once. There was only one Zeus, one Hera, one Loki. Lesser beings, even the mighty Cthulhu, existed individually in the various splinter dimensions, even though it seemed they shared some thoughts and memories. Demis and the rest of us scrubs were fully apart and distinct from our alts in other dimensions.

I put the final slice of bread on my sandwich and took a bite while I considered the ramifications. "All major gods who transcend dimensions are able to move across them freely. It's possible any child of Zeus could inherit that ability."

"I don't think it works like that," Hannah said. "Sigma and most of Zeus's demi kids have lightning powers and enhanced physical abilities. Those are his dominant inheritable powers, right? Something like walking across dimensions is a higher power intrinsic to being a god. Creation is another trait that doesn't seem to be inherited."

"You can create." Fred's mouth tentacles quivered. "You are different."

"Yeah, she's different, all right," I said. "And she's also right that most demis don't inherit non-dominant traits of gods—at least not that I've seen."

Hannah paced back and forth. "Then again, we could be wrong. Maybe Zeus and the others can't just walk into other dimensions whenever they want. Maybe they need a god who can do that for them."

"We don't know enough to make an educated guess about it, so this speculation isn't getting us anywhere." My cell phone buzzed with a text message. "Hannah, can you go get Layla and Aura? They're outside the gates."

She nodded. "Be right back."

While she saw to that, I ate my sandwich in silence, Fred's hungry gaze watching my every move.

"Can I have sandwich, Cain?"

"Don't you have a tub of popcorn somewhere?"

He nodded. "But I want sandwich."

I made him one and tossed it to him. He caught it in his tentacles, and it vanished with a slurp. "You don't even savor them."

"Sorry." He clasped his hands and made big eyes at me.

"Go eat your popcorn, you little glutton."

He hesitated. "Cain, the madness in you is worse."

I sighed. "Yeah, I noticed."

"My father did this to you. I want to help. I don't want to be a monster like him."

I walked around the counter and knelt next to him. "Fred, you're not a monster."

"I am. But I think monsters can still be good."

"You're different, but you're not a monster." I raised an eyebrow. "Are you just guilt-tripping me for another sandwich?"

A mouth tentacle touched my arm. *Sandwiches are wonderful, but that is not why I'm saying this. I have found other monsters who are different like me. We don't want to be eldritch anymore, Cain. We want to be human.*

"Being human doesn't solve anything, Fred." I patted his head. "You've got a whole set of gifts that no human has. Don't try to be something you're not. Embrace what makes you unique."

His huge eyes blinked. *I never thought of it that way.*

"We all have strengths and weaknesses. For example, you can see the madness in me."

His tentacles quivered. *It is a cloud of poison in your veins and in your mind. I want to help.*

"Well, unless you know how to siphon it out, we'll just have to hope Fitz can help." It was hard to tell what was going on behind those big alien eyes of his, but I sensed he was feeling out of place among all of us humanoids. He was a stunted spawn of Cthulhu, unable to grow much beyond his current size. He bore a curse that was his bane, but probably a blessing to the rest of us since we didn't want Fred to turn into a goliath monstrosity that could drive us all insane with a mere look.

I will help you Cain.

"Thanks, Fred." I freed my hand from his tentacle and went back to eating my sandwich.

Fred climbed onto the couch and dug into a large tin of popcorn.

Hannah, Layla, and Aura burst inside a moment later.

"How did you and Aura arrive at the same time?" I asked Layla.

Layla shrugged. "Don't ask difficult questions, Cain. The elf pulled up to the gate right after I did."

Hannah grunted. "I'm surprised you came so quickly. You took two days to respond to the last nine-one-one."

"If it had been about anything other than the Oblivion Guard, I probably would've just gone drinking." Layla dropped onto the couch. "But we're all connected, and those sneaky bastards know it. Last thing I want is to be stalked by rogue guardians."

"It's the last thing any of us want." Aura sat at the kitchen table. "It explains why I felt like someone was watching me the past few days."

"There were only four of them this time." I opened a beer since I didn't want Aura to be distracted with making mangoritas right now. "Only two survived."

Layla nodded. "Must have been some major noobs."

"One was Torvin's former right hand, Ena." I gave them the details of the encounter and Hannah told them about our discussion regarding loopholes and interdimensional portals.

Layla walked around the kitchen counter and plucked a beer from the fridge. She popped off the non-twist cap with her bare hand and took a sip. "The portal part is easy. We need to find a minor god of travel."

Aura snapped her fingers. "She's right. A god of travel probably has the capability of opening portals."

"But aren't those kinds of gods just to keep travelers safe?" I set my beer on the counter and twisted the bottle. "I don't recall any of them being about the act of traveling."

"Ganesha, Hermes, Abeona, Lugh, um..." Layla trailed off. "That's all I can think of off the top of my head."

"I've heard of exactly one of those gods." Hannah looked confused. "Who are the other ones?"

"Ganesha and Abeona are Indian. Lugh is Welsh." Layla shrugged. "It came up in a drunken conversation I had with someone at one of Bacchus's parties. Actually, I think it was with Lugh himself."

"I'm surprised you didn't drop names like Yachimata-hime or Yachiamati-hiko." Aura tapped a finger on the table. "If you want to really sound cultured."

Hannah looked at her phone and began reciting a long list of travel deities.

I waved her off. "Okay, wait. What we need to look for are Liminal deities specifically."

"Liminal." Layla furrowed her brow. "Yeah, we talked about them too, but I think that was during the orgy."

Hannah fake gagged. "Gross, Layla."

Layla just shrugged, skipping her normal snark. "One day maybe you'll start talking about ordinary things while someone's banging you. It's normal."

Aura checked her phone. "Liminal deities are gatekeepers."

"Yep." I picked up my beer and walked to the kitchen table. "I think we can narrow the search to Greek and Norse gods for now."

"How are we supposed to identify a single deity out of so many?" Hannah tapped on her phone screen. "And are we looking for their demi kids or the actual deity?"

"I don't know." I took a sip of beer and pulled out a chair. "It would have to be a minor god or a demi or else we'd have new dimensions popping up all over the place."

"Maybe Hermes had a kid." Hannah looked up from her phone. "I mean, I'm sure he's banged a few Earth women."

"In and out in a flash." Layla grimaced. "Talk about a bad sex partner."

"The Olympians are a horny bunch." I sipped my beer. "I'm sure Loki and gang have been collecting demis from all over the world to help them, so they don't cause more splinter dimensions. Someone who can open interdimensional portals would be especially handy."

"Let me put it simply," Layla said. "What's our objective?"

I turned my chair to face the kitchen. "Find the gatekeeper, neutralize them so the rogue guardians can't freely cross dimensions. Then we pick them off one at a time."

Aura leaned back in her chair. "You fought off eight total guardians in Feary?"

"We're calling them Handers," Hannah said.

Aura wrinkled her nose. "Handers?"

Hannah nodded. "Short for God Hand."

I waved off their tangent. "Yes, there were eight Handers total on Feary."

Aura seemed to mull over the new nickname, then just rolled with it. "Were all of them members of Torvin's inner circle?"

I gave it some thought. "I don't think so. Only a handful of hard-liners considered themselves Torvin's true disciples. Ena and Anair were the only two I'd say for sure were part of the cult of Torvin."

"He was quite the cult leader." Hannah shook her head. "Why did Erolith give him such free reign?"

"Erolith was ordered to keep a hands-off approach by the queens, so Torvin was considered the head of the Oblivion Guard until I had him exiled."

"He was exiled as part of your agreement with the fae?" Aura said.

"Yeah." I took a sip of beer. "I had the fae on the ropes with the Beast War, so I used it to fuck over Torvin."

"Then he came to Gaia and took over Eclipse." Aura tilted her head slightly. "He started the so-called Divine Council and framed Hera for the murder of countless demis."

"The Divine Council was really just Torvin and some of his hard-liners." The connection seemed obvious to me in hindsight. "Now they call themselves the God Hand, and I'd be willing to bet that instead of killing demis, they're now focused on recruiting them."

Layla clapped her hands. "Then let's invade Eclipse headquarters and kill the assholes." She turned to Aura. "Where might that be?"

Aura looked uncertain. "The office building that I operated out of was just a branch office used by handlers. There was a secret headquarters that housed their special operations, including a cocky cybermancer who liked making everyone's lives miserable. Despite all my digging, I never found out where the headquarters was or who else worked out of there, mainly because Elektrode thwarted most of my attempts to find out with my own cybermancer."

Hannah laughed. "Elektrode?"

"That's the cybermancer's name." Aura grimaced. "He'd send out memos telling us to be loyal because Elektrode was always watching."

"What a douche." Hannah scowled. "Sounds more like a cyber-bully than a cybermancer."

I yanked us back on topic before the conversation went off the rails. "Did Torvin ever go to the branch office?"

She nodded. "He was there all the time because lived in the penthouse of the same building. I think he moved some of our operations to the new building just because it was one of the tallest buildings in the city and he liked looking down on the city."

"Sounds like Torvin," I said. "You never told me exactly how that place worked or how you managed to worm your way into the organization."

"Yeah, Aura." Hannah stared at her accusingly. "Did you start working there before or after you met Cain and decided to use him for the Enders?"

Aura slapped her palm on the table. "How many times do I have to apologize for deceiving you? For gods' sakes, I ended up helping you and I even renounced the Enders! Baura taught me that killing the gods isn't worth the price."

I gave Hannah a warning look. "Let's lay off the accusations for a while, okay? I think everyone knows how you feel by now."

"You don't feel that way too?" Hannah turned her accusing gaze on me. "That's bullshit, Cain."

"Do I fully trust Aura? No. Do I trust her enough?" I nodded. "Yes. We've got enough cooperative ventures under our belts to at least give her the benefit of the doubt."

"Never underestimate the elf." Layla smirked. "Baura sure impressed me. That was one scary bitch. Our Aura, not so much."

"Aura gives me treats." Fred struggled to pull himself up onto a chair like a toddler might. "She is not evil."

Hannah rolled her eyes. "Okay, Aura. Tell us about Eclipse."

Aura stood up and took a beer from the fridge, then sat back at the table before talking. "I never planned on joining the Enders. They, however, planned on me joining. That's because my great-great-grandmother, Valindra, is the one who founded them."

Hannah's eyes widened. "Say what?"

"The Enders started as an anti-god cult sometime after the fall of Fyeth Elunore. It was just a fringe element that other elves preferred not to talk about. It wasn't until Valindra lost her mother that she became obsessed with killing the gods. She met with the cult leader and told them to join her quest. The cult leader didn't want to lose her power, so Valindra killed her."

"The woman knew what she wanted and took it." Layla held up her beer. "Cheers to hardcore babes."

Aura took a long gulp of her beer. "The others knew she was immortal, so no one else challenged her. Valindra took control of the cult and named it Dhedoni."

I grunted. "Alder for god slayers."

"Few outside the organization knew its true name. That's why it was referred to as the Ender faction by those who know of the various demi groups." Aura stared at the beer bottle. "Valindra had her twin girls, became mortal, and eventually died, but her leadership led to the discovery of the existence of the lost armory and other god killer weapons. She left it up to her successors to use that knowledge."

"How long is your line of ancestors going back to Fyeth Elunore?" Hannah asked.

"I don't know exactly. Much of our family history was lost over the centuries." Aura finished off her beer. "My grandmother wanted nothing to do with Dhedoni. My mother joined them for a brief time but killed herself after my twin sister and I were born. They sent an emissary some years later and asked me to assume leadership, but I knew nothing about them because neither my grandmother nor my mother ever told me about them."

She stiffened. "Then my grandmother had the talk with me when I was sixteen. She told me about the curse and what it meant for my life. I was devastated. Filled with burning rage and hatred for the gods. That was when I sought out Dhedoni and accepted their offer. We identified possible enemies and allies and targeted the Divine Council for infiltration. I trained to become an assassin from the age of eighteen and then applied to Eclipse when I was twenty-three.

"Torvin himself dueled me for the final interview. I lost badly but did well enough to earn a position." Aura wiped her eyes. "It was one of the most terrifying experiences of my life. I was assigned to low-level hits on various humans in the supernatural community. After a while, I realized the people I was killing were former human commanders and allies from the Human-Fae War."

Layla grimaced. "Torvin was a real piece of shit. The war had been over, and that asshole was still nursing a grudge."

"He saw humans as bugs who needed to be squashed." I shook my head. "When the bugs challenged their overlords, he saw it as an opportunity to wipe out as many humans in the magical community as possible."

And it sounded like the evil works of Torvin were continuing from beyond the grave.

4

Aura continued her story.

"We suspected the Divine Council was operating in cooperation with Eclipse or that they were maybe even one and the same. We recruited a skilled cybermancer to help me. He was able to hack into their systems and found files on dozens of demigods, most of whom had been killed by the so-called Divine Council or had been recruited by Humans First and other groups. Unfortunately, Elektrode discovered the hack and traced it back to my guy. He was assassinated, but my cover remained intact."

Hannah leaned forward on her elbows. "Okay, this is some heavy spy game stuff, like magical James Bond. I love it!"

Aura didn't look enthused. "Hearing the stories might be entertaining, but living that life was so stressful, it nearly drove me crazy. What if they discovered my deception? What if they destroyed everything I'd worked for? What if Torvin put me in a safe and dumped me in the ocean? I don't have super strength, so I might have been trapped inside, resurrecting and dying repeatedly until the curse kicked in. Then I'd become pregnant and give birth, dooming my surviving daughter to a life of torture."

"Ok, stop it!" Hannah squirmed. "I don't want to think about that."

"I didn't want to think about it either, but it was a real possibility that my cover would be blown, and I'd be subject to Torvin's tender mercies." Aura wiped the sweat from her forehead. "Look, the important thing is that my cybermancer only penetrated the outer layer of the onion where the jobs are submitted to the handlers. He compiled a list of all targets and categorized the tags that identified the type of target. Then Elektrode found him and had him killed."

"A list?" Hannah tilted her head. "Like vampires, werewolves, wizards, and stuff like that?"

"Yes. In almost all cases, the assassins were told what kind of mark they were after. But in rare cases, the mark's abilities weren't identified." Using condensation from her beer bottle, she traced a symbol on the table.

I looked at it. "The letter D?"

"They used Greek symbols," she said.

"Delta." I nodded. "For demi?"

Aura shrugged. "I guess. Anytime a mark was tagged with this symbol, the case was routed to an anonymous handler."

"They identified their handlers in the system?" I frowned. "Wouldn't it all be handled anonymously?"

"Every handler had a fake name in the database. This handler record was simply named Special Detail." She wiped the condensation from the table.

"Special Detail." I raised an eyebrow. "In other words, their special assassin was a demi like Sigma."

"Right. But back then I didn't know about demis." Aura got up and dumped her empty bottle into the trash. "They always assigned a Delta to this special assassin. In some rare cases, they had to assign trackers to first locate the targets. Even after they killed my cybermancer, I still had limited access to the database, so I kept an eye out for the Delta tag. The next time one popped up in the system, I immediately took a flight out to Minnesota to see the target in person."

Hannah's eyes widened. "Did you try to save them?"

"That was the plan." Aura sighed. "The target, a young boy, lived on a remote farm with his family. The mother was trying to fix a flat tire but couldn't get the jack to work. The boy picked up the rear end of the pickup truck with one hand and unscrewed the lug nuts with the other one."

"Must be handy to have a kid that strong," Layla said. "Was there a father figure on the farm?"

Aura nodded. "He went to town early that morning. The moment I saw how strong the boy was, I knew he was something much different and more powerful than anyone I'd ever seen. I immediately contacted my people and arranged an extraction. The plan was to whisk the boy and mother away and keep them where no one would find them. Then we could hopefully recruit them to our cause."

Hannah grunted. "How'd that work out for you?"

"I was observing the farm from a treetop at the far end of a cornfield. There was a whooshing sound and the corn stalks in the middle of the field flattened. A girl maybe ten years old just appeared out of nowhere. She had the most beautiful ebony skin." Aura trailed off as if entranced by the memory. "She leaped straight up, twenty feet in the air and rotated to get her bearings, then jumped fifty feet at a time until she reached the farmhouse. The boy's mother grabbed a rifle from the pickup and fired it at the girl. She hit the girl center mass and knocked her back a few feet."

Hannah gasped. "She took a bullet in the chest and didn't go down?"

"The mother fired again, but the girl pounded the ground with a foot. The ground shook like a miniature earthquake and the mother fell down." Aura took another beer from the fridge. "The boy looked confused but when he saw his mom go down, he rammed the girl so hard they plowed into the house. They fought inside for a while, until the house shook itself apart. Then the girl rammed the boy, and they flew back outside and hit the pickup truck. The mother shot the girl four more times, knocking her to the ground."

Aura grimaced. "The mother screamed at the boy to break the girl's neck, but he started crying. The girl gripped him from behind and squeezed until his head popped off. Then she threw it at the mother and crushed her skull. The place was a bloody mess, but the girl tried to make it look like an accident and flipped the truck onto the bodies."

"Yeah, but the house was demolished!" Hannah sputtered. "My god, I'll bet the cops didn't know what to make of it."

"The girl went back to the cornfield where she'd first appeared and made a phone call. Then she sat down and waited for nearly two hours before vanishing." Aura bit the inside of her lip. "That was the moment I knew I was up against a group far more powerful and capable than I could have imagined."

"How'd the girl appear out of nowhere?" Layla said. "Fast-travel node?"

"I thought that at first too, but there has to be a destination node within a few miles of the target location." Aura shook her head. "It was a different kind of magic. The fae purposefully limit fast-travel nodes on Gaia and the ones that exist are kept hidden."

I stood to get another beer. "Did you realize they were demigods then?"

"I arrived at that conclusion later when I showed the recording to members of my faction." She walked around the kitchen counter. "Despite what the fae propaganda claimed, we knew the gods were still alive. We knew horny old Zeus was still out there impregnating mortals because he doesn't know how to pull out."

Hannah chuckled. "I'm surprised there aren't tons of demigods out there if the gods are banging every mortal they come across."

"God DNA isn't typically compatible with that of mortals," Aura said. "It takes a special kind of human to conceive a baby with a god."

"Hardly seems possible at all." Layla shook her head. "You'd think getting pounded by someone as strong as a god would turn a body inside out."

Hannah wrinkled her nose. "I'm sure they go easy unless they're sadistic."

"Oh, they're all sadistic bastards." Layla's face paled. "I witnessed that firsthand."

"After seeing the fight, I knew that I had to save and recruit as many demigods to our cause as possible." Aura's lips pressed together. "But demigod targets were rare, totaling maybe one or two in a year. Every time a Delta appeared in the system, I'd fly out to their location only to find the girl had already killed them. It wasn't until two years later that I finally reached a demi before the girl did. The Delta came up in the system and I took a private jet to Nevada."

She shook her head. "Somehow, I reached the kid first. He lived in the middle of nowhere with his mom, and I found out why the minute I tried to drive onto their property."

Hannah leaned forward. "What happened?"

"The mom threatened me with a gun and told me to leave. I got out of the car and tried to reason with her, but then Junior shot a bolt of lightning at my feet. I'd never been more scared of a five-year-old kid in my life."

"Really?" Layla snorted. "Even after seeing those other demi kids get murdered?"

"I tried to explain that he was a target and would die without my help. I told her about Eclipse and the demi assassin who'd soon be there to kill them both." Aura sighed. "That only made them more afraid. The kid zapped me and nearly knocked me out, so I got in the car and left as fast as I could. But I still wasn't ready to give up, so I went to a hill about a quarter of a mile away and watched from there. This time I had an M82 Barrett fifty caliber sniper rifle. This time I planned to kill the girl, or at least try."

"A gun like that can blow out an engine." I nodded. "Good choice."

Aura nodded. "The girl didn't appear until early the next morning."

"Wonder why there was such a delay," Layla said. "And why there was a two hour wait for her after she killed that strong boy."

"We wondered that too, but never came up with anything." Aura leaned on the counter. "Whatever the reason, she girl showed up on the dirt road a few hundred feet from the doublewide trailer where the kid and his mom lived. I tried to take a shot, but she ran so fast toward the house that I couldn't aim. She knocked on the front door and the mom answered with a hail of gunfire straight through the door."

Hannah grimaced. "Ooh, bad decision, Mom."

"Yeah, the girl ripped the door off, then threw the mom about fifty feet into a boulder." Aura shook her head. "Then Junior screamed and ran at her. She tossed him as well. He landed in the dirt. Got up, screaming, and crying. The girl ran at him, so I had no shot. Then the clear desert sky suddenly went dark with clouds. The boy reached up and a bolt of lightning struck right in front of the girl. She screamed and went flying. Then the boy pummeled her with so many lightning strikes that I had to put my hands over my ears and close my eyes, so I didn't go blind and deaf."

"Gods be damned." Layla's eyes widened. "Did you record the fight?"

Aura nodded. "But the lightning was so bright it was hard to tell what happened. The boy eventually fell to his knees, exhausted. The girl was nothing but a charred corpse. I wasn't sure if I should scoop the boy up and make a run for it, or if he'd kill anyone in the vicinity when he woke up. Whoever sent the girl must have known she was dead, because someone else appeared on the road before I'd made up my mind about what to do. They took the boy, went back to the road, and vanished a few minutes later."

"Hang on." I narrowed my eyes. "Was that boy Sigma?"

Aura nodded. "Yeah, although he was much older when you encountered him."

"Well, now I know how they chose their demi assassins." I shook my head. "They just pick up whoever killed the last one. Trial by combat."

"It wasn't until Hannah's case came along that I was able to save someone." Aura shrugged. "The case needed a tracker because the mother had done such a good job of moving around and hiding. I managed to get Cain assigned to the case because he seemed like the perfect candidate for doing the right thing."

Hannah's face brightened. "That was my case?"

Aura nodded.

I raised an eyebrow. "Why did you think I'd do the right thing?"

"Because I'd been talking to you for years as your friendly bartender." Aura glanced at Hannah as if waiting for accusations to fly, but Hannah seemed eager to hear the rest of the story. "I knew you were carrying around a lot of guilt from the war."

"And ghosts." I looked at Hannah. "I almost didn't save her, though."

"But you did, and that's what counts." Hannah ran around the table and hugged me. "Now look at all the fun we've been having."

"Sure. Fun." I patted her arm. "It's a miracle any of us are still alive."

"Some of us *have* died." Layla's face darkened, but she shook her head and gulped down the rest of her beer. "I say we burn the hornet's nest and kill off Eclipse and the Handers. Problem solved."

I turned to Aura. "Do you still have access to Eclipse's database?"

She shook her head.

"Layla is right. Let's track them down, find their secret headquarters, and end this." I hadn't given it a lot of thought, but the path forward was mostly obvious. "We need to break into their database and use the information to find them and their allies. If they do have a gatekeeper demi, then we should try to recruit them or kill them so they can't transport assassins so easily."

"Agreed," Aura said. "There might be even more valuable information that could lead us to other demis."

Layla turned her beer bottle on its side and spun it. "You don't have remote access anymore?"

"No." Aura glanced at me. "When my cover was blown, all of my equipment was remotely deactivated and destroyed."

I raised an eyebrow. "Did you ever bring any of that stuff onto my property? Because I guarantee you, they could track it."

"No, I kept the laptop and other equipment at a fake residence when I wasn't in the office. My cybermancer created a virtual terminal so I could use everything remotely from anywhere without being traced." She offered a wan smile. "I know how to be careful."

I nodded. "Just making sure. Last thing I want is to step outside my safe zone and have a dozen longshots blow me to shreds because the Handers know where I live."

Layla spun her bottle again. "Gods be damned, I really don't need this in my life right now. Maybe I should sit this one out. The guardians can track me all they want but they'll be disappointed when I never meet with you."

"They'll never need Pornhub again either," Hannah said. "Once they see you at a party, they'll get all the porn they want."

"Maybe I should charge them." Layla turned to me. "I think it's for the best, Cain."

I said nothing, mainly because I trusted her to have my back in a fight. But as usual, this wasn't her fight. Layla used to come along for fun but dying and being trapped in the hellscape of Soultaker had dramatically changed her perspective.

She stood and tossed the beer bottle into the garbage can across the room without even having to bank it off the wall. "Good luck, Cain."

Layla Blade kissed me on the cheek, then left without looking back.

5

Aura gave me a look of disbelief. "You're just going to let her go?"

"Yeah, Cain, what the hell?" Hannah jumped up. "We need Layla!"

I stood up and dropped my beer bottle in the garbage can. "We do, but that's her decision, not mine, not yours."

Hannah stared daggers at me, then ran out of the door after Layla.

Aura frowned. "Can Layla even get out of the gates without you?"

"Hannah can let her out." I was still hungry, so I made another sandwich.

"You're awfully nonchalant about this, Cain." Aura leaned on the counter. "Do you really think just you and I can survive against a squad of rogue guardians?"

"Yeah." I spread mustard on the bread and topped the sandwich. "Won't be easy, though."

Fred watched intently as I took a bite of the sandwich. "Cain—"

"No, Fred." I nodded toward a large tin container. "Eat your popcorn."

Aura's forehead pinched. "Don't you prefer to eat fish, Fred?"

I snorted. "Oh, he'll eat anything, believe me."

"I want to grow." Fred flexed a blubbery arm. "Want to be big!"

"Then eat fish, not popcorn or sandwiches." Aura shook her head. "He really needs a nutritionist or else he'll be three feet tall forever."

"Cthulhu stunted him so I doubt he'll ever get taller." I took a bite of my sandwich. "And that's a good thing. We don't want another insanity-inducing monstrosity lurking in the ocean."

"I wish I could be big." Fred's big eyes somehow grew bigger. "I can be a good monster."

Aura shook her head. "You didn't meet your dad on Gaia Beta like we did. I don't think you have a choice but to be harmful to humans if you grow up like him."

Hannah burst through the door and slammed it behind her. "Fucking bitch!"

I raised an eyebrow. "The talk with Layla went well?"

"Oh, so well!" Hannah threw up her hands and dropped onto the couch. "She's got PTSD bad, Cain."

"Can't blame her." I took another bite of my sandwich. "Fighting and dying every day in the hellscape of Soultaker is enough to destroy the minds of even seasoned vets like Layla. Just give her time."

"As usual, we don't have time to spare." Hannah pounded a fist on the couch cushion. "Trying to convince her to do anything is like talking to a brick wall."

"Did you let her out of the gate?"

"I gave her my ankh and told her to come back when she was ready." Hannah stared at me defiantly. "I hope you don't mind."

"I do, actually." I sighed. "What if the Handers capture her? Then they can bypass my defenses without a fight."

"It only has one use left on it." Hannah looked somewhat abashed. "I checked it."

"One use is enough to lose everything." I'd given Hannah an ankh that served as a key to my kingdom, but it had limited uses before it needed a recharge. I wasn't comfortable with it being out there, but I had faith Layla would toss it before letting anyone else take it from her. It was also doubtful the Handers would know what purpose it served anyway.

"Well, what's our next move?" Hannah got up from the couch and leaned on the kitchen island. "Do we break into the Eclipse office where Aura used to go?"

"Aura and I might do that." I gave her a look. "You're not. And before you protest—"

Hannah waved me off. "Cain, it's fine. I'm not a super spy like you and Aura. But I can watch your backs or do something else that's useful."

I regarded her for a moment. "That's a very mature response."

"Dude, after Tokyo and Australia, I've learned that it's better to just listen to you." She shivered. "That fucking necromancer woman almost stole my soul."

"I can name three occasions since then that you've gone against my explicit instructions."

"One of those occasions was you telling me to stop giving Fred popcorn!"

"Wow." Aura snickered. "Serious violations, Hannah."

"Yeah, the worst." Hannah rolled her eyes. "Oh, and the second one was him telling me not to go after Shae."

"First of all, she's in another dimension and you're not taking the Tetron out for a joyride just to win back your girlfriend." I set down my sandwich. "Secondly, she broke your heart, and you need to get over it."

"That's good but harsh advice." Aura looked sympathetic. "Grace and I decided to take time apart since Caolan gets really annoyed when she's distracted."

"I notice you left out the third occasion." I picked up my sandwich and took a bite.

Hannah worked her jaw back and forth. "I located another necromancer that I thought was connected to Alistair, so I tried to track him down."

I gave her an expectant look. "And then..."

Hannah groaned. "I found him in a nightclub and beat his ass only to find out that he's an undercover mage guild knight who was looking for illegal necromancy."

Aura snort-laughed. "Gods, I hate the fucking mage guild knights."

"Yeah, I wasn't too broken up about it." I finished my sandwich and wiped my hands together.

"You laughed your ass off when I told you." Hannah huffed. "I'm getting better at listening, and that's the important thing, right?"

I nodded. "Yeah, little by little. Then again, you are a teenaged demigoddess, so a little immaturity is to be expected."

Aura took out her smartphone and opened the map app. She scrolled to Buckhead and put a marker on a building. "The Eclipse office is here. Getting to the building isn't an issue, but actually reaching the office inside without a special charm is nearly impossible."

I flipped the view to street level and rotated the camera to look around the high-rise. "Warded?"

"You might say that." She zoomed out. "They use maze traps."

"Oof." I blew out a breath. "Guess they're not too keen on nubs wandering in."

Hannah squeezed in beside me. "So, they have a labyrinth in the building?"

I shook my head. "It uses illusion and disorientation magic. If you enter without a charm, then you basically get turned around and exit the same door you entered without even realizing it. The more you try to beat the trap, the more confused you become."

"The disorientation magic works like alcohol, inebriating you until you can barely stand up." Aura quirked her lips. "It's very subtle fae-level magic."

"My true sight scope could probably see through the illusion," I said. "But I've got nothing to counter the disorientation magic. It's not like a mind trap. It's like you're being dosed with drugs the further in you go."

"Just wear gas masks," Hannah said.

"Gas masks wouldn't protect you. Trust me when I say some fae magic can't be beaten, and the last thing we need is to be staggering around like drunks while trying to infiltrate an office full of assassin."

"Sounds like a lot of security for just a branch office." Hannah looked perplexed. "Can't we find their secret headquarters another way?"

"I tried." Aura sighed. "My cybermancer was looking for network addresses connecting our office to the secret headquarters, but Elektrode had him killed before he could trace it."

I grunted. "Did you try to follow anyone like Torvin to see if they could lead you there?"

"Of course." She looked offended. "Do you know how hard it is to follow a member of the Oblivion Guard without them knowing? I gave up trying after nearly getting killed by one of his flunkies."

"It's real convenient how Layla suggested we burn the hornets' nest and then she bailed." Hannah huffed. "Now we've got to pull off a Mission Impossible in the hopes that something in the Eclipse database is going to lead us to their super-secret headquarters."

"I think Aura's cybermancer had the right idea." I looked through pictures of the building. "Maybe there's a way to trace the location using network information."

"My cybermancer gave me network tracing programs I could use if I ever broke into the server room, but there was no way for me to get in there without someone knowing." Aura smacked her lips. "Eclipse is a tough nut to crack, even if you have access to the building. If I could just download the database and the network logfiles that might be enough for the software to work."

"Where do you think the real HQ is?" Hannah said. "New York?"

Aura shook her head. "No, they'd keep it close. It's somewhere near Atlanta."

Hannah's brow pinched. "Why is so much in Atlanta?"

"Simple," I said. "It's because Faevalorn is its geographical equivalent in Feary."

"Also because of the concentration of mushroom portals in this area." Aura switched to a custom map view and dozens of purple dots appeared all across the metro area. "It's easy to go to Feary and take a portal halfway across the world if they need to."

Hannah still didn't look convinced. "Yeah, but if they have a gate-keeper demi, why use portals?"

"Because if they have a gatekeeper demi, they're only using them for the highest priorities like killing other demis." Aura turned to me. "That would explain why the assassin demis had to wait hours for a portal home."

I grunted. "Agreed. Atlanta is the place to be if you want to use mushroom portals for fast traveling. But it's also convenient to keep close to the unified fae court."

"Well, hopefully, we find some answers when we hijack their server." Hannah rubbed her hands together. "I always wanted to be a spy."

"This will take a lot of planning." Aura sighed and shook her head. "We need to think outside the box to stand a chance at getting inside the branch office, much less the secret HQ."

I rinsed my hands in the sink. "While you two plan the heist, I've got other business to attend."

Hannah blinked. "What other business could there be?"

I decided to keep it open and honest since not telling her would just be a pain in the ass. "I've had some issues since I looked Cthulhu in the eyes on Gaia Beta. When the assassins tried to kill me, I couldn't use Panoptes to escape. Putting it on literally disabled me. The only person who can diagnose and possibly treat me is Fitz."

Hannah's forehead wrinkled. "Really? I thought you were feeling fine."

"I have nightmares about Cthulhu every night, and if I use too much magic, then the madness starts to cloud my vision." I grimaced. "Panoptes nearly pushed me over the edge."

"I'm fine until I try to use the ring. And my dreams have been pretty consistently awful."

Aura looked aghast. "You dream about Cthulhu every night?"

"Yep." I leaned on the counter. "I see his eyes, giant orange suns of insanity trying to consume me whole. Then I wake up with worms crawling across my eyes, or tentacles on my arms. Sometimes I vomit black butterflies, or slugs."

Hannah sucked in a breath. "Like, real butterflies? Or imaginary ones?"

"Good question. I think they're imaginary since they vanish after a while." I shook my head. "Sometimes, I wake up choking and baby squids or frogs pour out of my mouth."

Fred looked up from his popcorn bucket. "Ooh, squids are yummy!"

"Gross, Fred!" Hannah looked appalled. "They're practically your relatives!"

"Yummy relatives." He smiled and rubbed his tummy.

"Gods be damned he's so adorable." Aura closed her eyes and shook her head. "And so damned disturbing."

"Thank you, Aura!" Fred's mouth shivered in pleasure. Then he flinched and looked at me. "See, I'm a monster. I say monster things and they make me happy."

"You just think differently than we do," I said. "You're not a monster."

Hannah gripped my arm. "Cain, are you really throwing up squids? Or are they imaginary too?"

"Everything seems so real, so vivid." I struggled to explain it. "And I'm definitely awake when it happens. But then it all disintegrates into nothing."

She blew out a breath. "Yeah, you need help. I don't want you melting down in the middle of the action."

"Me either. That's why I texted Fitz the other day. I'm meeting him tomorrow." I paused a moment to see if anyone objected.

Hannah rubbed my arm. "Well, we need you at a hundred percent. I can use Panoptes if you need me to."

I patted her hand. "We'll need every trick in the book to get into Eclipse."

"Not even the eyes of Panoptes can bypass their mind traps." Aura tapped her fingertips on the counter. "If anything, it's the perfect counter to something that relies entirely on sight."

"Ugh, you're right." Hannah held out her hand. "Give me the ring and I'll experiment with it."

"Not yet." I patted my utility belt. "I need Fitz to diagnose me while wearing it first."

"Makes sense." Hannah sighed. "Thanks for being open and honest about it."

"See, even Cain is learning to step outside his shell." Aura smiled. "So, the next question is, am I staying here for the time being so the guardians can't track me?"

"Yep." I motioned toward the guest rooms. "Make yourself at home." I opened a cabinet to reveal a bottle of tequila and some mixers. "Coincidentally, I also have the ingredients for mangoritas."

Aura rolled her eyes. "Are you sure you have everything?"

I pulled out a drawer and placed boxes of plastic pirate swords and toothpick umbrellas on the counter along with an assortment of colored curvy straws. Then I pulled various fresh fruit from the magic refrigerator. It kept everything inside fresh thanks to its preservation enchantments.

Aura stared at me blankly. "Message received, Cain. I'm going to clean up first." She walked into the guest room and shut the door.

Hannah opened her mouth, then shut it.

I raised an eyebrow. "What do you want to say?"

She pressed her lips together as if resisting, then explosively exhaled. "We need Shae."

I crossed my arms. "Agreed."

"And before you say no or say it's because I still love her and miss her, then yes, you're right!" Hannah wiped tears from her cheeks. "But we—" She blinked. "You agree?"

"She can see straight through most kinds of glamour. She has powers that would allow us to easily defeat the guardians." I shrugged. "We need her. But you'll have to deal with the emotional trauma of unrequited love if she helps us."

Hannah laughed through her tears. "I love when you get poetic, Cain."

"That's not poetic." I put a hand on her back. "I was planning on mentioning Shae when I got back from Fitz's. Since it's out there now, maybe you can use this time to get used to the idea of seeing her up close and personal again even if she doesn't feel the same way you do."

She shivered. "It's been so long. I wonder how's she's doing."

"I haven't spoken to Cain Alpha in a while, so I don't know." I sighed. "But be prepared for the worst. She might have another girlfriend by now."

Hannah took a long, deep breath and released it. "We need her to keep you safe, Cain. I can do this."

"Good." Teen angst was the last thing I needed.

Aura emerged from the bedroom wearing yoga pants that were too big on the backside for her. She held up the droopy cloth. "Can I please keep some clothes here? Layla's ass is ten times bigger than mine."

"Yeah. Remind me when there aren't rogue assassins after us."

Aura winced. "About that. I think it's worse than we thought."

"Worse?" I narrowed my eyes. "What do you mean?"

"When I was using the bathroom, I decided to look at the freelancer bounty boards. Your bounty has doubled."

"Doubled?"

Hannah frowned. "Wait, Cain still has a bounty on his head? I thought that was dropped after everyone found out he started the Beast War against the fae."

"It was dropped, but it's been reinstated by an anonymous client, and the amount has doubled." Aura turned her phone to show us the board. "And Cain isn't the only one on the list."

Hannah's mouth dropped open. "Hang on, I'm on there too? Why am I only worth fifty grand?"

I took the phone and scrolled down the list. "Oh, this isn't good."

"No, it's not good at all." Aura clenched her fists. "Someone wants to wipe the board clean."

"Cain, maybe we should visit Alpha and warn your alt." Hannah looked at the list and shook her head. "He needs to be warned. We need to go there anyway to get Shae."

"Yeah, you're right." I cursed under my breath. "I should have done that the moment I got home."

Hannah nodded. "You had a lot on your mind. Besides, I'm sure Acain can take care of himself."

Aura groaned. "See, that interdimensional naming convention of yours doesn't work."

"It worked fine for Baura."

"Yeah, but it doesn't work so well for Bcain or Bhannah, does it?"

Hannah wrinkled her nose. "They're dead anyway. At least Layla in Alpha has a different name already. It's confusing referring to Cain and his alt by the same name."

"Well, putting the first letter of their dimension's name in front of their name doesn't work." Aura tapped a foot. "We could call him Sthyldor."

"I don't think he'll like that." I waved off a rebuttal. "I need to get cleaned up and we'll go."

I just hoped it wasn't too late to warn Cain Alpha.

6

Hannah's eyes brightened. She'd finally get to see her beloved Shae—the girl who broke her heart. "I'll get changed too."

"You're looking too excited." I put a hand on her shoulder. "Don't get your hopes up about Shae."

She swallowed hard. "I'm trying, Cain, but it's hard."

"I know it's hard. But it'll be worse if you think she's going to be happy to see you and she's not. It'll hurt even worse."

Aura nodded in agreement. "Hannah, expect the worst."

Hannah threw up her hands and stalked away. "Fine! I'll expect to walk in on her banging my evil doppelganger!"

"Ooh, that'd be a real doozy." I gave her a thumbs up. "I like the way you think."

Hannah's mouth dropped open. "Shut up, Cain."

I took a quick shower and threw on some fresh clothes. I went to my underground vault to fetch the Tetron, and on a hunch, checked all the artifacts I'd recovered from Baura's lair. I hadn't taken anything from the duffel bag because there was a lot to sort through, and I hadn't had the time to do it.

I'd been keeping apocalypse weapons from Beta in a mysterious warehouse that was only accessible using Panoptes but had discovered they'd all been replaced with cheap fakes. Baura hadn't been behind it, meaning someone else had access to the warehouse. They'd taken the weapons and replaced them with fakes for reasons unknown. I'd been meaning to get to the bottom of it, but now I had another crisis on my hands that couldn't be ignored.

I opened the duffel bag and took out the Tetron from Beta. I'd just shoved it and everything on the shelves in Baura's creepy underground lair into my bag because the tunnels had been crawling with ghasts. Otherwise, I would have realized what I was realizing right now.

This Tetron looked like the real deal, but the parts on it didn't move. It was just a solid hunk of metal designed to pass muster to anyone giving it a passing glance. It even felt about the same weight, but the main parts of it, the Cubon, Spheron, and Pyron were welded on.

"You've got to be shitting me." I inspected everything else in the bag using my true sight scope to detect magical auras. The artifacts ranged from magical orbs to magical daggers, helmets, and even glass shoes. Some was authentic, but most of it was fake.

I couldn't imagine who would have access to the warehouse and Baura's underground lair, but they'd done a damned good job of stealing things right from under our noses.

The only reason I'd gone after Baura in the first place was because I'd thought she still had the apocalypse weapons and would use them on Prime. She'd thought that I had them and planned to blackmail me into giving them to her in exchange for Layla Beta's life. That obviously hadn't worked out. Despite that setback, she still had a plan to send an eldritch invasion to Feary Prime and I'd stopped her.

As I was inspecting the rest of the loot, I noticed tiny words etched on a dagger. I had to use my phone to magnify them.

Enjoy these lovely gifts, Cain. I told one of my minions that if anything should happen to me that they must replace my artifacts with these fakes and hide the real ones somewhere you'll never find them. Hugs and kisses —Aura

I backtracked on my initial assessment. Whoever had taken the apocalypse weapons from the warehouse was not responsible for these fakes—Baura was. She knew that if I captured her, I'd eventually get her to admit where her artifacts were. Technically, I hadn't done that, but Fitz had used dark magic to pry the secrets from her brain. Since she only knew the last location of the artifacts, that was the information Fitz had taken from her.

Baura had outsmarted me at almost every turn despite being completely off her rocker. And since Fitz had severely damaged her brain while prying information from her head, there was no way Baura could tell me where her minion had taken the real artifacts. None of them were as dangerous as the apocalypse weapons, but the Tetron offered the power of dimension hopping to anyone who wanted it.

I shoved the useless trinkets back into the duffel bag and dropped it on the floor. I would have to deal with this another time.

Then I grabbed my Tetron, ensured it was still the real deal, and met the others in the kitchen. I'd set an eye of Panoptes to watch the Voltaire's in Alpha, but only one of us could travel using it. I certainly couldn't use it thanks to the madness infecting me, so we'd have to travel with the Tetron instead.

Cain Alpha would usually be at Voltaire's drinking mangoritas at this time of the evening, but if he'd been targeted as I had, then it was more likely he was home at his version of Sanctuary.

"We've got to go outside the gate to use this." I tucked the Tetron in my utility belt.

"It doesn't work inside your safe zone?" Hannah asked.

"Doesn't work inside any safe zones." I went outside and slid into Dolores. Once the others were in, I drove down a dirt road to the western side of the perimeter and parked the car inside the fence.

"I haven't been here before." Hannah looked around. "Is this another one of your secret exits?"

"Maybe." I climbed out of the car and traced a sigil over a section of the chain-link fence. The fence looked like the typical weak stuff nubs used, but it was heavily enchanted and reinforced. It also sat just inside the ring of silver and other metals that encircled the entire compound, thanks to Caolan and the elemental spirit who presided over the land.

The section of fence folded open just enough for us to slip through. We stepped out into the unprotected wilderness surrounding Sanctuary. My home sat in the center of eight acres of mostly unspoiled land, giving me a buffer between my secret hideout and the nubs. I scanned the area with my scope to ensure there were no lurking assassins or other dangers before taking the Tetron from my pouch.

Hannah held my arm and took Aura's hand to connect us. I manipulated the three pieces of the Tetron, the Cubon, Spheron, and Pyron, and we shot up from the ground and into space. Gaia, Feary, and Oblivion hovered before us, each plane slightly phased out but occupying the same space. I took us out further and the local interdimensional array appeared, three Gaias, Fearys, and Oblivions orbiting each other.

Gaia Beta was easily distinguishable due to the crimson hues of its skies. Cthulhu, Shub-Nuggurath, and other eldritch horrors fought over the spoils of that world in the hopes of using it as a launching pad for a bid to take over Gaia Prime.

"How about Caina?" Hannah said. "We put the A at the end instead of the beginning."

Aura blinked and looked away from the spectacle of worlds spread out before us. "Sounds like a woman's name now."

I switched us to the Alpha dimension and willed us to go to Gaia. We sped groundward, hurtling at such immense speed, that it was difficult to resist reflexively throwing up my arms in a useless attempt to protect myself from being crushed like a bug.

We landed lightly on our feet just outside the fence. I suspected Cain Alpha had changed the wards on the perimeter. He and I might be the same person in many ways, but it didn't mean we trusted each other blindly. The phone system in Alpha was a strange mix of mechanist and nub technologies, so I'd brought along another phone I'd acquired here for communications.

I called Cain, but it rang through to voicemail.

"Either you called this number by mistake, or you're one of two people who has it. Leave a message or don't." The voicemail prompt beeped.

I ended the call and dialed Hemlock—the Layla of this world. She went by her fae name instead of the assassin moniker Layla Blade, which made it much easier than calling her Alayla. Although now that I heard the name in my head, it sounded kind of nice.

Hannah frowned. "Cain, why are you smiling?"

"Alayla."

She blinked. "Wow, I like that one." She spun on Aura. "See? My naming method for doppelgangers is the best."

Aura put her hands on her hips. "So, A-aura is my doppelganger's name?"

Hannah giggled. "You done messed up, A-a-ron."

"Good one." I ended the call since Hemlock didn't answer. "Something's definitely wrong. No one is answering."

"Maybe they're at the lake cabin?" Hannah suggested. "The cell reception up there is bad."

I shook my head. "The mechanists fixed all that."

"Try opening the fence." Hannah nodded at the fence.

Using the scope on my staff, I switched to aura mode and examined the sigils guarding the perimeter. They were different than the ones I used, meaning I had little chance of guessing the right combination and pattern direction. My security sigils used directional flow so tracing the pattern might involve starting in the middle and working outward, or it might mean using two fingers at the same time instead of one.

Trying to guess would only lead to literally knocking myself out. My wards started with gentle punishments that grew worse with each try, ending in a fatality on the fourth attempt. The avoidance wards and glamour protecting Sanctuary kept out the nubs, so four warning shots seemed very generous to anyone trying to breach the perimeter.

My phone rang. I looked at the caller ID and was relieved to see Hemlock's name. "Where are you?"

She got straight to the point. "Did you come to warn us about the assassins?"

"Did you already encounter some?"

"Some?" She paused. "How many are there?"

"More than I want to fight."

"Gotcha." She sighed. "I see you're at the perimeter. I'll come get you."

I looked around and spotted the glint of a wildlife camera in a tree. "Clever."

"My idea. See you in a minute." She disconnected.

Moments later, wheels crunched on gravel and underbrush as a pickup silently approached, headlights off. A figure stepped out, cast in silhouette by the moon.

"I'd recognize that badonkadonk even in the dark," Hannah muttered.

Hemlock stepped up to the fence and tapped an ankh against the chain-link. The fence peeled open, and we filed through.

"Where's your eye patch?" Hannah said.

Hemlock climbed back into the truck without a word, so the rest of us got in after her. I took shotgun and turned toward her. Her eyepatch was gone. Light reflected from the new eye like that of a nocturnal animal.

I liked it. "New eye?"

She nodded and put the truck into reverse. "Necrosurgeon crafted it for me."

"A what?" Hannah leaned forward from the back seat. "Sounded like you said necromancer."

"Necrosurgeon." Hemlock turned the truck around and headed toward Sanctuary. "It's a new field of research from the people who brought you Frankenstein's monster and nub medical technology."

Aura looked in the rearview mirror so she could see it. "Did they transplant a cat eye?"

"They took the eye from a dead cat, genetically spliced it with human DNA, and some other stuff, then stuffed it in my eyehole." She stared into the mirror. "Want me to stop so everyone can gawk, or should I get us to the church first?"

I grinned. "Good to see you again."

She smirked. "Yeah, I just wish it was under better circumstances. Watching you and Cain get drunk on mangoritas is more fun than I could have imagined."

"Does that eye give you better night vision?"

She nodded. "Yeah, but I have to close my other eye. Just my bad luck I didn't get fae eyes."

Some fae had reflective eyes for excellent night vision, but Hemlock was half-human and didn't have them.

"Is this an electric pickup?" It was as quiet as one we'd found on Gaia Beta, but it looked different.

"Liquid mana direct drive to electric motors." She turned onto the main drive and parked outside. "It's another hybrid project between mechanists and nubs."

"I love it." Hannah ran a hand down the back of the leather seat. "Most mechanist cars put style above utility."

Hemlock slid out of the truck, and we followed her inside Sanctuary. The interior had undergone serious renovations since the last time I'd been here. The floorplan wasn't quite as open, but it still felt spacious. The portrait of Hannah with the daggers in the eyes was gone. Fred's pool had been previously filled with concrete, but now was completely covered over with new hardwood floors.

"Whatever happened to Fred here?" Hannah asked.

"Don't know." Hemlock glanced at the place where his pool used to be. "So, shall I start, or you?"

I looked around. "Where's Cain?"

"He went to the lake cabin to check on the demis." She leaned against the kitchen counter. "I guess I'll start."

"I'm listening."

"Cain was at Voltaire's. He had a couple of drinks and was getting ready to leave when he sensed someone watching him. He didn't see anyone, so he assumed it was a cloaked member of the Oblivion Guard."

Hannah scowled. "Do they give this Cain a hard time like they do my Cain?"

She nodded. "Erolith died, so they have a new leader, Aeolus."

My eyebrows rose. "The Storm King?"

"Yep." Hemlock went around the counter. "Want a mangorita?"

Aura stormed over. "I'll make one, thank you very much."

"Still jealous, I see."

"Making the perfect mangorita is my thing!" Aura went to the liquor cabinet and took out the tequila. "You're cheating when you use rum, by the way."

"Rum tastes better with mango."

"Rum does not belong in a mangorita!" Aura gathered the supplies and began crafting the concoction.

Hemlock returned to her story. "Cain tried to duck out of one of the secret exits, but he sensed someone else waiting for him out there. He decided to take his chances and stepped out of the safe zone. Cain knew from the tingling on the back of his neck that the guardian was following him, so he led him to one of our trap buildings."

I frowned. "You guys set up trap buildings?

She nodded. "The mechanists make us anything we want. Plus, having extra safety measures is always good."

Hannah tilted her head. "Um, what's a trap building?"

"It's an easy way to lose a tail." Hemlock vaguely outlined a building shape with her hands. "The stalker follows you in, but the walls switch around the moment they enter, trapping them. You can delay them temporarily or lock them up."

"Wow, that's cool!"

"Cain sensed danger from other directions and realized he was being penned in on all sides, so he went into the trap building." Hemlock watched Aura with some amusement as the elf mixed the drinks. "They followed him inside, and then the walls trapped them. They're reinforced, so even a brightblade would have trouble cutting its way out."

She smirked. "Oh, and we gassed them. While they were sleeping, we took their cloaks. They apparently banished their staffs so we couldn't liberate those as well."

"Well, he did a lot better than me." I told her about my narrow escape.

"Yeah, but you don't have an army of mechanists helping you." She took a slice of mango before Aura could use it and popped it in her mouth. "We planned to interrogate the prisoners, but Cain decided to go to the cabin and make sure the demis are okay."

Hannah looked ready to burst with questions, so I gave her a warning look. She slumped and looked down.

"I'd like to interrogate the prisoners. The ones who attacked me are from Alpha and Beta."

Hemlock nodded. "Most of our prisoners were from Beta."

"They told you that?"

She shook her head. "A nub scientist came up with a way to differentiate the radiation signature of people from other dimensions and planes. The wars on Feary Beta mean that people from there have higher levels of something, something, blah, blah." She shrugged. "They explained it to me, but I didn't care. All I know is that Feary Alpha and Feary Prime are too close to tell apart, but beings from Feary Beta and Gaia Beta practically exude these different radiation particles."

"Makes sense." I nodded. "So, the prisoners not from Beta could be from Alpha or Prime?"

"Cain thinks they're from Prime because they hardly knew anything about the mechanist technology here."

"Makes sense," I said. "The fae from Feary Alpha probably know all about the major changes here on your Gaia, whereas those from Prime wouldn't have seen it before."

"Unfortunately, they somehow escaped from the trap house without cutting through the walls." Hemlock pressed her lips into a thin line. "Looks like we don't get to interrogate anyone."

"We think they have a demi who can make portals," Hannah said. "That's probably how they got out."

Aura stabbed an umbrella toothpick through a slice of pineapple and mango and set it carefully on the edge of the finished mangorita, then jabbed the plastic pirate sword through an orange slice. She plunked the curvy straw into the drink and sneered triumphantly at Hemlock.

"Here's your drink, Cain." Aura presented it to me as if it were the greatest moment in history.

"Thanks." I took a sip and sighed. "Damn, that's good."

Hemlock smirked. "I should make mine and you can compare."

"We've got bigger things to worry about than a mangorita pissing match," Hannah said. She turned to Hemlock. "How's Shae?"

I groaned. "Hannah."

Hannah kept talking. "Is she dating someone else?"

Hemlock pressed her lips together grimly.

A tear trickled down Hannah's cheek. "Please don't tell me she's with Esteri."

Esteri was Hannah's evil doppelganger who even now only followed Cain Alpha's instructions because she was a minion of Cthulhu. Just thinking about that chain of command made my brain spasm. The mechanists in Alpha had tried taking over the world by controlling Cthulhu's creatures with the Rlhala. Esteri, as a servant of Cthulhu, was then bound to their command.

Once we'd freed the world of mechanist rule and taken the Rlhala, I'd freed Shae and Hannah from Cthulhu's service, then given myself and Cain Alpha exclusive control over Esteri and the other demigods once controlled by the mechanists. Some of them had proven they could be trusted enough to be freed from Cthulhu, but I'd left that decision up to Cain Alpha.

I put a hand on Hannah's shoulder. "I thought we agreed that you weren't going to get personal about this."

"I can't help it, but I promise I'll do better." She wiped her wet cheeks. "I just want to know who she's with now."

Hemlock stared at her silently for a moment before answering. "When Shae came back after your breakup, she started training because she wanted to master as much as she could before going in search of her mother."

Hannah flinched. "She wants to meet Nyx? But isn't she trapped in Tartarus?"

Hemlock shrugged. "How the hell should I know?"

"Nyx is an Elder God, so she's in Prime. Why would Shae come to Alpha for training?"

"Because Cain cordoned off an entire island in Lake Lanier and dedicated it to teaching demis how to use their abilities." Hemlock glanced at me. "He's been a busy fellow."

"Hey, if it keeps him occupied, that's fine by me." I crossed my arms. "Shae is pivotal to our plan to counter the assassins and find out how they're able to attack us without breaking the bargain we struck with the high fae. For all we know, the queens from all three dimensions are plotting against us."

Aura stopped mixing another drink and narrowed her eyes. "Gods be damned. I think I just figured out their loophole."

7

W e watched Aura expectantly, but she went back to mixing herself a drink.

Hemlock glowered at her. "You don't just say something like that and then go quiet, elf. Spit it out."

Aura didn't even look up. "Who makes the best mangoritas?"

"Really?" Hemlock scoffed. "Can you believe this twit?"

"Oh, I can." Hannah shook her head. "She's petty sometimes."

I tuned out the conversation and considered what little we knew about the assassins. They were from various dimensions, presumably being commanded by the high fae, if not the queens themselves. Their orders were to kill me, my alt, and probably all our associates. That should be a violation of the bargain I'd struck, but apparently, it wasn't.

Then I latched onto the information that must have given Aura her epiphany. I met her gaze, and she seemed to realize that I'd figured it out.

She blurted it out before I could. "Cain struck a bargain with the high fae from Prime. Cain Alpha struck a bargain with the high fae from Alpha."

Hemlock snapped her fingers. "Those clever bitches. The queens giving the orders are from different dimensions than the Cain they're targeting. They're also using assassins from other dimensions just to be safe."

I nodded. "Attacking me should have violated the bargain. It might not have been enough to completely break it, but the queens would have known if their ploy would work. Once the guardians attacked me and nothing happened, then they knew they could freely kill me so long as the orders came from their alts in the other dimensions."

"Exactly." Aura finished making herself a drink and took a sip. "The fae are masters of making bargains and exploiting loopholes."

"Well, now we know, but that doesn't change much." Hannah shrugged. "We need to get Shae so we can kill these bastards and infiltrate Eclipse."

"Yeah, so that's the problem." Hemlock shook her head. "Shae left and went back to Prime two weeks ago."

Hannah sagged. "Why didn't you lead with that?"

"Between you and the elf, I could barely slip in a word edgewise." Hemlock turned to me. "And no, I don't know where in Prime she is. I'm surprised she didn't come straight to you since you've got connections with the underworlds."

Hannah turned to me. "Did she come to you Cain?"

I shook my head. "That's not something I'd keep from you."

"Great." Aura stirred her drink. "Having Shae would've made things so much easier."

"Maybe we can track her down, Cain." Hannah's eyes widened. "After she helps us, we can help her find her mom."

Hunting down Shae while rogue guardians hunted us wasn't an option. Her glamour-piercing abilities and other powers would've more than evened the odds in our favor, but we could still do it without her.

Since that option was off the table, I moved onto other pressing topics. "What are Cain's plans for avoiding the guardians?"

"We're going to lay some traps and hunt them. Nothing definite beyond that, though." Hemlock pressed her lips together again. "Cain did overhear something important when the guardians were following him. One of them said that if the cybermancer did his job and triangulated the location of Cain's secret lair, then they wouldn't have to go through so much trouble following him."

Aura hissed. "Elektrode is trying to find Sanctuary?"

"Impossible." I shook my head. "That's not something you can just use a computer to find."

"No, but if he uses locational data from places you've been seen in Atlanta, then he could start to form a pattern." She grimaced. "This is bad news. We need to stop him before he finds Sanctuary."

"Just great." Hannah sighed. "There's no telling how much time we have before an army of Handers shows up outside the gates."

"Handers?" Hemlock looked confused. "Sounds like porno."

"The rogues are members of an organization called the God Hand," I explained. "Handers is our nickname for them."

"This is what we need to do." Aura nodded to herself. "We can break into the Eclipse office here instead of the one on Prime. It might be an easier option."

"Buckhead was completely demolished when the mechanists attacked." I shook my head. "The area has been built over already, and it's unlikely Eclipse used the new building. They probably just relocated everyone to their secret HQ."

"Damn." She pursed her lips. "What about the one on Beta?"

"I doubt there's anything left of Atlanta in that dimension, but I can check."

Hannah shivered. "Do we really want to go back to Beta?"

"Most of the eldritch infestation was in Greece." Aura shrugged. "The Atlanta area might be safe to visit."

"It's not a great idea, but it's not bad either." The Eclipse offices on Prime were a guaranteed hard target. If by some miracle the office building on Beta were still standing, we could probably get all the information we needed with a minimum of fuss.

"You're considering it, aren't you, Cain?" Hannah didn't look pleased. "Just thinking about going back to Beta makes me ill."

Hemlock leaned against the kitchen island. "Have you had time to find out what happened to the apocalypse weapons from Beta?"

"That was first on my list until this assassination attempt." I sipped my mangorita. "As of yet, no one has claimed responsibility or started wrecking Gaia with the missing weapons."

"Let's hope that continues to be the case." Hemlock shook her head. "Cain and I have a bad feeling that whoever took the weapons is just biding their time."

"I think the caretakers of the warehouse took them," Aura said. "Since they're the only beings with access to the warehouse besides Cain, that seems like the most logical explanation. If they've safeguarded other dangerous artifacts, then the weapons are in good hands."

"I hope you're right." Hemlock crossed her arms. "So, is there anything else I can help you with, or do we have to drag out this conversation even longer?"

Hannah smirked. "Aw, I thought you loved small talk as much as our Layla."

Hemlock turned to me. "Where is my alt, anyway? Is she still playing the victim after her Soultaker adventure?"

Hannah's smirk soured. "Maybe you should try a little stint in Soultaker and see how you handle it."

"It's just embarrassing to see myself act like that."

"She was embarrassed when you started calling yourself by your fae name." Hannah shrugged. "Guess you're even now."

I decided it was well past time to head out. "If you and Cain come up with a way to handle our current situation, let me know. I'm open to suggestions."

"I will." Hemlock nodded toward the door. "I'll give you a lift back to the fence."

Hannah headed to the door, then stopped and turned. "Hemlock, if you hear from Shae, can you let me know?"

Hemlock pressed her lips into a thin line. "I'm going to do you a favor, girl. Shae is too obsessed with finding her mother and her origins to even think about settling into a cozy relationship. Just let her go. Learn to be happy with someone else."

Hannah's forehead pinched in pain. She closed her eyes and slowly turned back to the door, shoulders sagging. "I know you're right, but it hurts." She opened the door and went outside.

Hemlock blinked, a flash of remorse crossing her face. "Guess I forgot what it's like to be young, dumb, and in love."

"I think we all have." Aura gulped the rest of her drink, then left.

I sipped my mangorita. "From a tactical perspective, Shae is invaluable. Are you certain there's no way to find her right now?"

"Ask your friend, Death." Hemlock shrugged. "Like I said, I'm surprised Shae didn't come to you for help. I guess she wanted to avoid Hannah."

"Yeah. Then again, I haven't exactly been available lately." I took a long draw off my drink, sad that I had to rush it.

"Don't look so sad, Cain." The corner of her lips curled into a lopsided smile. "You can take a few minutes to finish your drink."

I shook my head. "I've got to travel to Seattle and get my head checked."

Hemlock raised an eyebrow. "Still having Cthulhu issues?"

"Yep." I set the unfinished mangorita on the counter and sighed. "That's what I get for trying to stare down Cthulhu."

She put her hand on mine. "Don't waste too much time. If a cybermancer has your scent, it's only a matter of time before he triangulates the location of Sanctuary. I know you and my Cain have been beyond careful to keep this place hidden, but those pencil-necked bastards have a way of accumulating data and analyzing it."

"Believe me, I know all too well how to track down an elusive target." I took another gulp of my drink. "It's never about following someone in a straight path. It's about learning their history, their patterns, and using it to narrow down the possibilities. I try to keep my patterns as random as possible, but even I have my habits. Once Elektrode filters the static from the signal, he'll have Sanctuary in the crosshairs."

"I'll have to see if Elektrode exists here. With any luck he died when the mechanists annihilated Atlanta." She pursed her lips. "The building they use in Prime is in Buckhead?"

I nodded. "That entire area was leveled. Let's hope he died so we're only dealing with one of them." I finished off my drink and stood. "Let's go."

Hemlock drove us to the same hidden gate we'd arrived at earlier, then turned the truck around and left without so much as a goodbye once we were outside the perimeter. I used the Tetron and took us into the interdimensional array. Instead of dialing us back toward Prime, I took us to Beta.

We hovered in space over the same geographical location we'd just left in Alpha. The skies over this desecrated version of Gaia burned red. The oceans were sickly green, and other major bodies of water were almost black. Cthulhu had risen, and the entire world was showing the effects.

He wasn't totally to blame. Shub-Nuggurath and other Elder Things had invaded, waging war on Cthulhu's minions so they could have control over this shadow copy of Gaia. Gaping craters all along the eastern seaboard gave evidence that Chthonian worms had opened wormholes in the area. If Atlanta was teeming with monsters, then this option would be off the board.

We hung suspended far above the world. From this distance, it was impossible to make out many details, so I willed the Tetron to take us in closer until we were as close as I could get us without actually traveling to the world. As far as I knew, we were safe in this inter-dimensional limbo.

Rotating the Spheron changed our relative location until we hung about a thousand feet over Buckhead, or at least what remained of it. Many buildings had collapsed during the first phase of Baura's apocalypse when earthquakes from Earthmaker had shaken the globe.

The skyscrapers that still stood were pockmarked, cracked, and looked as if civilization had ended centuries ago, and not just months prior. Aura pointed to one of the few standing buildings. Though all the buildings around it had been reduced to rubble, it was still standing, if just barely. Most of the windows on the lower floors were gone, and the structure was leaning dangerously.

The Sovereign was one of the newest and tallest skyscrapers in Buckhead. The rectangular lower half rose about twenty stories, graduating into a cylindrical shape where it continued skyward another thirty levels. The name seemed fitting for an organization like Eclipse to operate out of since Torvin and those who ran it seemed to think they had supreme authority over all they surveyed.

"Looks like the building's protective enchantments held." Aura turned toward me. "Can we get any closer?"

"Not without actually traveling there." Holding us in this position was already a strain since it wasn't our original location. When I used the Spheron to take us to different locations, it was like pulling a rubber band wider and wider, increasing the resistance. That resistance was also a useful way to gauge how much energy it would take to travel that far.

Using the Tetron to transition from one dimension to the next required very little energy, provided the geographical location was the same. I'd nearly knocked myself unconscious when using it to travel alone from Sanctuary to Greece. Traveling with a group had benefits since it would take energy from everyone.

Aura put a free hand over her eyes to peer at the landscape below. "Can you set us down on top of the building?"

I rotated the Spheron to take us over the precise location, but we remained over the street instead. "The safe zone around it won't let me get directly over it."

"The streets look clear." Hannah shrugged. "We might as well go in for a look."

Aura nodded. "Agreed."

The city looked completely dead and deserted but spending a couple of days on Gaia Beta had taught me valuable lessons about the eldritch. There could be countless horrors lurking just below the surface or hiding inside the building. Since the monsters had devoured anything and everything they could get their claws on, it was possible they'd starved to death.

It seemed worth the risk to go in for a quick look. "Okay. Just brace for the power draw." I gave them a second, then willed us to travel to the street below. We hurtled toward the ground and landed.

We gasped in unison as the Tetron took its pound of flesh.

Hannah's knees wobbled. "Whoa, I felt that."

"I'm surprised it affected you at all." Aura took a moment to steady herself. "Letting that thing use us like living batteries can't be a good thing. Is it draining our souls?"

"Maybe, but it's better than walking." I shrugged. "Might have been smarter to drive over here in Prime first. Then again, I wasn't planning on traveling here right now."

Hannah wrinkled her nose. "God, it smells like rancid farts out here."

I glanced at a nearby manhole cover. "No telling what's in the sewers."

Aura looked up at the leaning tower. "Guess where we have to go."

Hannah winced. "The penthouse."

Aura nodded. "The handlers' offices are on the thirtieth floor, but Torvin's suite is at the top."

"Hold up." I knelt and closed my eyes, letting my body sigils have a moment to detect any dangers.

Hannah mussed my hair. "Do you need a nap, Cain?"

Ignoring the question, I took out my staff and scanned the area with the scope. The range was limited by rubble and concrete walls, but it was better than going in completely blind. I didn't see any auras or heat signatures, confirming that the area was as dead as it looked. Just before I put it away, I spotted a slender glowing line running several feet underground from the street surface. The glow was faint and weak, but something was there.

It might simply be an underground power line that somehow still had a charge despite there being no electricity, but it seemed wise to give it a wide berth. I checked the area for similar signatures but didn't find anything. I stood and started walking down the broken sidewalk in the opposite direction of the anomaly, then crossed the street.

Hannah paced alongside me. "Did you see something, Cain?"

"Yeah." I described what I'd seen. "Might as well steer clear just in case."

"I agree a hundred percent." Hannah glanced back at the area as if something might pop up and chase us.

I kept my staff at the ready, using the scope to scan for dangers.

Hannah wrinkled her nose and abruptly stopped as we rounded a pile of concrete and twisted rebar. "I think I know what stinks so bad."

A sickly green mushroom about knee height jutted from the broken asphalt. Countless others dotted the broken street. A glaze of putrid green slime covered their tops and dripped from the edges. I took out my staff and looked at one with aura mode. It glowed gently, not because it had an aura, but because energy emanated from it.

Powerlines beneath the road flickered and glowed in synch with the glow of the mushroom. I'd never seen a fungus like this on Feary, and it certainly wasn't native to Gaia. The spores from another world must have hitched a ride on the invasion force sent by Shub-Nuggurath or one of the other Elder Things.

"Can I see?" Hannah took the staff and looked through the scope. "Dude, those things are electrical."

"Looks like it." I took my staff back and swept the area. The gaseous and electrical discharges from the mushrooms clouded the view, making it impossible to see very far past them. "Whatever you do, don't touch them."

Hannah grimaced. "Why would I want to touch a nasty slime-covered shroom?"

Aura picked up a piece of rubble and tossed it at the nearest mushroom. It hit the top and splashed slime before slowly sliding off and landing in the puddle of slime on the road around it. "This must be part two of the invasion. Alien plant life."

Gaia's ecosystem was slowly being replaced, rotting it from the inside out.

8

Gaia Beta was quickly morphing into something horrific and alien.

I examined our surroundings more closely and noticed black and green mold covering the areas around the mushrooms. Zooming in with the scope revealed tiny worms wriggling in the slime. Dark beetle-like insects with spiky shells crawled across the mold. "I don't think this place will look anything like Gaia within a few months."

Hannah shivered. "Cain, this is giving me the heebie-jeebies. Can we hurry up and do this?"

Keeping my staff out, I moved toward the building, trying to keep away from the fungus and mold. Though the entire bottom floor was blown out, we had to climb over piles of concrete to get inside the building lobby. The stench was even worse inside. Mold covered the walls, and mushrooms nearly four feet tall grew from cracks in the foundation.

Hannah covered her nose with her shirt. "God, this reeks!"

I located the stairwell entrance. The bent and twisted metal door blocked it, so I ignited my brightblade and carved off the hinges. Even then, it was jammed tight, so I had to cut it in half to finally dislodge it. A tangle of rebar blocked the other side, so I took several more minutes hacking through it.

The stairs, thankfully, were mostly intact. There was mold along the walls, but none of the mushrooms. Even so, the smell was unpleasant. I stopped to inspect one of the mold insects. It was about as large as a dung beetle, but that was where the similarities ended. The exoskeleton was covered in spines, almost like a sea urchin. Tiny tubules extended from its body and into the mold.

"That thing looks poisonous." Hannah picked up a piece of rebar and gently prodded the insect. Black liquid oozed from the spines as the rebar touched them, giving credence to Hannah's theory. The insect lost its grip on the mold and fell on the floor. She crushed it with the rebar, leaving a stain of dark ichor.

"I hope that doesn't trigger a stampede of shoggoths." Aura cupped an ear. "Didn't killing bugs in the Dead Forest do that?"

"Those were shoggoth or facehugger larvae." Keeping away from the moldy wall, I started up the stairs. "These are just bugs."

"I hope so." Aura glanced at the dead insect once more, then followed me.

The mold receded to nothing by the time we reached the second floor, leaving us in gloriously fresh air, and giving us hope that the climb wouldn't be as miserable as anticipated. Aside from cracked and broken stairs, the climb for the first few floors was easy and unimpeded.

Our luck held until the sixth floor where we reached our first obstacle. The ceiling had collapsed and blocked the steps. The hole in the ceiling wasn't large enough for us to squeeze through, and my brightblade couldn't easily cut through so much debris.

I opened the door leading into the sixth-floor hallway. It led past office suites with broken doors and shattered windows. A skeleton dangled from electrical wires in the ceiling. Torn clothing and bone fragments littered the floor below it.

"I wonder what his story was." Hannah glanced up at the remains as we skirted beneath them.

"Probably hid in the ceiling." Aura touched claw marks gouged deep into the drywall. "Looks like a horde of shoggoths came through here."

Holes in the walls and splintered doors told the story of what had happened here. Baura's use of Earthmaker, Tidebringer, and other apocalypse weapons had released eldritch creatures from their prisons beneath the world's crust. According to Horatio, the mechanist leader from this dimension, it was likely that an invasion force had landed here eons ago only to be buried alive by the Titans and other Elder Gods.

Some of them had survived in caves, or in pocket worlds. Once freed, the ravenous creatures devoured everything in sight. The nubs had been caught off guard by the destruction of their cities. Being swarmed by shoggoths, malgorths, and other monsters soon there-after had been the final nail in this world's coffin.

Keeping alert for any signs of movement, I continued down the hall and to the stairwell on the other end. The door hung off broken hinges. Sunlight spilled into the stairwell, probably from a hole in the side of the building. The sickly odor of mold reached my nose a few feet before I stepped inside.

I peeked inside the door. The entire outer corner was gone, exposing this section and the one above it to daylight. The stairs ended at the landing above, leaving a gap of several feet to the next set of stairs. Mold covered the walls, floor, and ceiling. The area echoed with the grinding sound of mandibles feasting on it.

My boot crunched several insects as I stepped inside, gingerly testing the moldy floor to see if it was slick. Though it looked slimy, it was actually tacky like slightly dried glue. The other bugs remained unfazed by the deaths of their comrades, so I stepped inside with the other foot, crushing several more. The soles of my boots smacked wetly as I pulled them off the sticky floor.

I put up a hand as Hannah tried to follow me in. "Wait here a sec." I went to the gap at the corner. A sliver of concrete was all that remained of the landing, but it was enough to edge around the corner and reach the next set of stairs. There was nothing but open air between this floor and the second or third story landing far below.

The broken section continued up for several stories where the rest of the building seemed intact.

The climb would be dangerous and difficult, but doable. I went back to the hallway and wiped my soles off on the carpet. "We can continue from here, but I want to check the other stairwells." I walked down the hallway and looked at a diagram with the emergency exits listed. The lower rectangular section of the building had eight stairwells spread out along the outer hallways.

The cylindrical section of the building had six. It meant we had plenty of options for hiking our way to the top of the building, so there was no need to risk traversing an exposed section. The next stairwell was about a hundred feet down the hallway. The door was gone, but rubble blocked the entrance.

A thick metal door blocked us from reaching the next section. Bulges in the metal were proof that the shoggoths had tried to break it down and failed. A few slashes with the brightblade severed the hinges and the lock. A quick kick with the bottom of my boot sent the door crashing to the floor.

The hallway continued for another fifty feet and ended in open air where a giant gash in the side of the building had obliterated a section of the floor. It didn't look like we could jump the gap, but I walked over to inspect it anyway. A thick black cable hung from somewhere above. Provided it was firmly rooted to something, it could provide a way to swing across.

I stopped at the edge of the gap, grabbed a piece of exposed metal beam, and leaned out over the void. There was a drop of several stories onto twisted rebar. Judging from the human skeletons below, it appeared that some people had taken that way out rather than be torn to shreds by shoggoths. They'd still been eaten, but they'd at least been dead.

My sigils tingled.

Hannah gasped. "Cain, look out!"

The dangling black cable snapped toward me and that was when I realized it wasn't a cable. Sticky flesh wrapped around my arm before I could jerk back. It hauled me up several feet in a violent surge, paused, and then yanked again.

"Cain!" Hannah tried to grab my boot, but I was out of reach.

I looked up. The tongue was pulling me toward an undulating tooth-filled maw several stories above. Bulbous eyes stared down at me from what appeared to be a giant froglike head. The creature's body was slender, the skin translucent. Raw muscle and organs were visible through the skin. Its three-toed feet held it to the ceiling of a stairwell far above.

My arm and staff were tangled in the tongue. Yanking hard, I tried to free myself, but it was like trying to break free of a spider web. I tried to ignite the brightblade, but my finger couldn't move to depress the section that turned it on. My right leg was also bound, leaving only my left side free.

Hannah continued shouting my name from below, but unless she sprouted wings, she wasn't going to do anything.

My right arm was twisted and slightly bent so I couldn't even use it to pull myself up higher so my left hand could reach the staff. Even if I managed to turn on the brightblade and sever the tongue, I'd drop to my death.

I had a couple of choices. My dueling wands were holstered in concealed pockets on my pants. I could probably blast the monster in the face, but that would again result in falling to my death on the rusty rebar below. There was a gap of about fifteen feet between me and the exposed hallway on each level, but it might as well be a hundred feet away for all the good that would do me.

Or maybe this tongue gave me the perfect way to escape. I began rocking my body back and forth. The monster's eyes rotated wildly. It croaked and the tongue retracted toward its mouth even faster. Trying to remain calm, I continued rocking steadily, increasing the range of my swing each time.

The edge of the building came tantalizingly close, but still too far away for me to reach. I waited for the backswing to reach its apex, then rocked again. This time, my fingers latched onto rebar. The tongue yanked and my shoulder felt like it was going to come out of the socket. I lost my grip and swung back out into the void.

I had to be close to the eighth floor by now, and the tongue creature was only two or three stories higher. I'd lost momentum, so the next swing wasn't even close to the building. Trying to keep my movement steady, I rocked again, missed the building, and rocked once more.

The monster gurgled and croaked in seeming anger or frustration. Instead of grabbing the rebar with my left hand, I used my right foot to fling the tongue below against the rebar. It tangled through several bars and stuck just like it was designed to. The flesh yanked taught as the creature continued pulling.

It croaked in alarm and the tongue above me went slack. I looked up and nearly croaked in alarm myself. The creature had pulled so hard it had lost its grip and was falling. In about ten seconds, it was going to fly past. Since my arm and leg were still tangled, that would jerk me upside down and possibly dislocate a few joints. I frantically reached up with my left hand and closed my fingers around the hilt of my staff.

The brightblade hummed to life. The monster fell past me. Frantically twisting the trapped staff, I manage to slice partway through the thick tongue. The flesh went taught. The partly severed section snapped, and the creature plummeted several stories before being impaled on the rebar below. It cried out with a piteous final croak and went still.

A roar echoed through the streets. A roar that most definitely hadn't come from the tongue creature. The world went eerily silent once again and I hoped my skirmish hadn't attracted an unwanted visitor.

I hung upside down since my leg was still firmly trapped. I deactivated the brightblade and wormed the staff free from entanglement, then banished it to get it out of the way. With the tongue severed and no longer taut, I was able to unwrap it from my right arm. The tongue was not only sticky but was covered in tiny directional bristles that prevented prey from jerking loose, much like barbs.

On the upside, it kept my leg locked in place, so I didn't fall. On the downside, it made freeing my leg much harder while hanging suspended from it. I leaned upward, straining my abdominal muscles until my hands closed around the section of tongue stuck to the rebar. I bent forward until my head was against my leg and managed to grasp the rebar with a hand.

There was no way to get my other leg up and over the rebar, so I'd have to do this the hard way. Powering my body sigils for extra strength, I pulled up with my left hand until I could reach the rebar with the right. Pulling up another inch gave me enough slack to do what I needed. I let go of the rebar with my right hand, letting my left arm hold the entire weight of my body. Gritting my teeth from the strain, I twisted my leg and pulled the tongue away from it with my hand.

My bicep burned with fatigue. My shoulder felt ready to pop free of the joint. But at long last, my leg came free, leaving my tired left arm the only thing between me and a long fall to my death. I reached up with my right hand and grasped the rebar, sighing in relief to take the strain off my other arm.

That, however, was only a small part of what I needed to do. I still had another five feet to go to reach the inside of the building. The severed tongue hung in my way, so I swung my feet up and kicked until it fell free.

My left arm was crying for relief, but I was almost home free. Using the rebar like monkey bars, I moved hand over hand until there was nothing else to grasp. Then I swung back and forth a few times, building momentum, and released the bar. I flew forward and landed heavily on the carpeted floor inside just a few feet from the ledge.

Sighing heavily, I lay on my back for a moment to rest. I took out my phone but there was no signal. So, I crawled to the ledge and looked down. Hannah's worried face peered up at me from far below.

She cupped hands around her mouth. "Cain, are you okay?"

"I'm doing great. How's the weather down there?"

"Shut up!" Hannah made a fist at me. "We're coming up the broken stairs, okay? Wait for us."

"See you there." I scooted back from the edge, climbed to my feet, and began talking to myself. "Eight floors down, forty-two to go." I blew out a breath. "Breaking into Eclipse on Prime would've been easier at this point."

Going to Gaia Beta without a plan had been an idiotic idea. I just hoped it didn't cost us dearly.

9

The floor I was on was configured differently than the sixth. There was no hallway, just a giant room with the jumbled remains of cubicles. A pile of human bones and broken desks filled the center of the room. The monsters that had devoured the people here had apparently turned their remains into a nest. The far corner of the office space was covered in mold and large mushrooms, but this side was clear.

I walked down the side of the room to the stairwell entrance and looked inside. A large number on the wall told me this was actually the ninth floor, not the eighth. The floor was covered with mold and insects just like the one a few floors down. I walked to the edge of the landing. Hannah and Aura were already edging their way up and around the sixth-floor landing. They vanished beneath me, then appeared a moment later on the seventh floor.

Aura looked up at me with worried eyes. "This was a terrible idea, Cain."

"We've come this far. Might as well keep going." I watched as they navigated the narrow ledge of the seventh and eighth floors and finally reached me.

Hannah groaned. "Fine, let's keep going." She walked past me and examined the broken landing leading to the ninth floor. "We're almost past the bad section anyway."

Aura scoffed. "I think this entire building is bad."

Another roar echoed in the streets outside, followed by a distant but constant thudding.

Hannah hissed. "I think your fight with the licker must have attracted something."

"Licker?" Aura frowned. "It wasn't licking him. It was tonguing him."

"That sounds nasty."

"So does licking." Aura shuddered. "You don't call frogs lickers, so why would you call that thing a licker?"

I shook my head. "Is this really the time to have this conversation?"

"It needs a name, Cain." Hannah motioned upward. "Let's think up something on the way up."

I started climbing to the next landing. This section was still mostly intact so by the time we reached the tenth floor, the stairwell was fully enclosed again. The mold hadn't grown above the landing. Since I'd only seen it in areas exposed to sunlight and the outside, that led me to believe it needed sunlight to grow.

Mold usually didn't need sunlight or any kind of light as far as I knew, but I wasn't a botanist. The otherworldly mold and fungus probably had its own set of alien conditions for thriving. I was just relieved to have a break from the odor and the strange insects.

Our climb continued uninterrupted until we reached the top floor of the lower section of the building. I exited the stairwell first to check out the hallway. The windows were still intact on this floor, and the offices looked untouched aside from a few bloodstains on the carpet or the walls. The building diagram on the wall of the stairwell showed another set of stairs leading up and into the cylindrical section of the building.

"I think the roars stopped." Hannah stopped at a window. A broken and battered Buckhead spread out below, its roads jammed with unmoving cars and debris.

I scanned the area with my scope but saw no signs of life. "Whatever it was must have calmed down."

"Let's hope so." Aura walked down the hall and toward the elevator lobby where the next stairwell door was located.

The doors were smashed open on two of the elevators. Bloodstains and broken suitcases were all that remained of whoever had been attacked. Clothes littered the floor. Another suitcase held nothing but expensive-looking shoes. A golden watch and a smartphone with a diamond-encrusted case lay a few feet away.

A familiar thick black cable hung down one of the elevator shafts. I drew my staff and slashed the cable with my brightblade. Flesh sizzled and croaking shrieks echoed from above as the wounded tongue monster reacted.

Hannah grimaced. "How long are their freaking tongues?"

"And where do they keep them when they're not fishing for food?" Aura poked her head into the elevator shaft and looked up. "It's on the wall about twenty feet up."

"I've got so many questions." Hannah peeked inside and quickly ducked back out. "Is there really that much prey in the elevator shafts? Why isn't this thing sticking its tongue in a pond instead?"

"There's mold further down the shaft." Aura pursed her lips. "Maybe it's eating the bugs if there's no larger prey."

The creature croaked in pain, raising a ruckus as it ran around on the wall inside the elevator shaft. I drew a dueling wand and looked up and inside. Tongue dangling and dripping black blood, the thing stopped when its bulbous eyes spotted me. I fired a quick blast at its feet, hoping to knock it loose.

It shrieked in pain, lifting the hit foot, then charged down the wall at me. I ducked back into the hallway "Back up."

Hannah's eyes widened. "Is it coming for us?"

"Yep."

Aura snatched a high-heeled shoe from the floor and brandished it like a weapon.

I sheathed the dueling wand and drew my brightblade just as the creature leaped into the hallway, its froglike mouth hanging open.

The bleeding tongue snapped back into the mouth then lashed out so fast, it was a blur. The shoe in Aura's hand vanished into the mouth.

"Holy shit!" Hannah picked up a suitcase and threw it at the licker. The tongue slapped it out of the air and sent it banging down the elevator shaft.

I stepped in front of Aura and Hannah before they resorted to fighting the thing with underwear. The tongue shot out and tried to snatch the brightblade. Flesh sizzled and burned. The licker shrieked and shook its head violently as if that might soothe the pain.

That left it wide open. A quick lunge and jab, and my brightblade stabbed into the thing's head. It collapsed twitching onto the floor, dark blood oozing from the smoking wound on its head. I gave it another good jab in the head to make sure it was dead, then walked around the corpse.

As with the other licker, the skin on the body was translucent, revealing hints of muscle, bones, and organs beneath. It was like trying to make out details blurred behind frosted or warped glass. I turned off the brightblade and poked at the skin, expecting it to be paper-thin but it was tougher than it looked.

Hannah knelt and looked inside the mouth. "I kind of want to see where the tongue goes, but I also don't want to touch it."

"Me either." Aura shuddered.

The head was wide and froglike whereas the rest of the body was more like that of a lizard, albeit with translucent skin. Its bulbous eyes were each as large as a human head. I used the bottom of my boot to push the creature onto its side. The head flopped over, revealing its underside. Flesh sagged on its chin. I used the brightblade to slash open the chin and throat.

"Looks like the chin acts as a pocket for the tongue." I cut until I exposed where the tongue was rooted deep in the neck. "It probably coils up inside there."

"Crazy." Hannah cocked her head to look inside the neck. "It just seems impractical."

"It's probably very practical wherever this thing came from." I shrugged. "Its natural habitat is much different from ours."

"I guess." She stood and brushed off her hands. "I just don't want to get eaten by one."

The licker measured about eight feet in length from the tip of its nose to the puckered anus on its backside. Its four legs looked eerily similar to human arms, but the feet had three toes covered in fine bristles that probably helped it walk up walls and hang from ceilings.

Aura stared at it. "Why does this thing look like a mutated human?"

Hannah frowned. "It does look like a deep one hybrid, doesn't it?"

"A little." I checked the other elevator shaft for a dangling tongue, but it was empty. "Let's get to the stairs."

The stairwell in this section of the building had a metal railing and a square open space between the landings. I looked up the center shaft. Daylight shone from all sides through cracks in the stairwell, but I couldn't quite see all the way to the top. Lights flickered off and on, though the emergency batteries had to have died long ago.

I suspected there were more of the strange electrical mushrooms somehow giving power to the lights. There was enough sunlight to navigate the stairwell, but I drifted a few light balls to the top for a better look at what lay ahead.

Tongues lashed out as the glowing orbs floated past some of the floors above. The lickers apparently weren't limited to hanging from the ceilings or walls.

"Wonderful." Hannah made a sour face. "There's a ladder in the elevator shaft. Maybe we should climb that instead."

"Good idea." I went back to the elevator and sent light balls floating up. Once again, tongues snapped at the orbs as they passed the floors above. "Or, maybe not."

"The stairwell is easier to fight on," Aura said.

"Agreed." I looked around for something they could fight with, but there wasn't anything more effective than suitcases or high heels. I considered my options and went with my brightblade over the dueling wands. More and more often, I was going this route, it seemed.

Dueling wands were effective in the right situations, but they didn't deliver enough bang when it came to the eldritch. But they still came in handy with close quarters encounters of the humanoid variety.

"Maybe we should just go and come back with weapons." Hannah bit her lower lip. "There's no telling how many more lickers are up there."

"We're halfway there already." I used the scope on my staff to scan for heat signatures and auras. A pair of lickers became visible two floors up. Too much concrete was between us and the others for the scope to reveal them. "If we leave, we'll have to go all the way back down and out of the safe zone because I can't use the Tetron or make portals here."

"All right." Hannah sighed. "Wish I had a clockwork rifle at least."

I headed up the first flight of stairs. "Stay here and float some more light orbs up the stairwell when I give the signal."

She nodded and preconditioned a sigil.

Using a muffling spell to quiet my footsteps, I went up the first flight, walked along the landing and crept up the next one. I held my hand over the railing and gave Hannah the signal. She tossed a pair of light balls up. Right when they reached the level with the lurking lickers, I dashed up the stairs.

The lickers hung from the ceiling side-by-side, their bodies casting distorted shadows as they vainly tried to capture the glowing orbs hovering in the center of the stairwell. The ceiling was ten feet tall, making it difficult to stab them with my brightblade, so I switched to longshot mode, aimed at the first creature, and fired.

Blood spattered on the ceiling and the licker went slack, dangling from the ceiling by its legs. Another longshot pierced the head of the second one before it even knew its comrade was dead. This one flinched violently, lost its grip on the ceiling and flopped to the concrete floor, twitching.

I went to the railing and looked up the center shaft. Nothing stirred, so I sent another light ball drifting upward, stopping it as soon as a tongue tried to claim it, revealing a single licker three levels up. I motioned for the others to come to this level, then continued up to confront the next monster.

The licker's tongue lashed out several times before the creature realized it couldn't catch the light. It crept across the ceiling until it reached the edge of the stairwell shaft, then slowly extended its tongue toward the glowing prize. This one's belly was swollen grotesquely.

I punctured its skull with a longshot. The licker dropped limply and flopped over the railing. A gelatinous mass spewed from its backside then it rolled over the railing and fell down the shaft. Its body slapped wetly against another railing then flipped into the void as it reached a broken section of building far below. It thudded hard several stories down as it reached its final resting spot.

Tiny fishlike creatures squirmed in the goop that had spewed from the corpse. I leaned closer and realized they resembled tadpoles. That licker had been pregnant.

A faint croak echoed from above, answered by a chorus. I assumed the noise startled the other lickers, probably putting them on guard. More croaks answered back. Not from above, but from below.

I looked over the railing. The center shaft seemed to drop into an infinite spiral, working its way down past the broken sections of the stairwell where sunlight shined through the gaps of missing building.

Hannah and Aura poked their heads over the railing and looked down. Pale bodies appeared and disappeared as they climbed up and over the landings. Others crawled up the stairs, croaking and shrieking. They hadn't reacted that way to the deaths of their other comrades. It seemed killing a pregnant one had drawn their attention and now, a horde of lickers was rushing up the shaft toward us.

Unhindered by the large gaps in the stairwell, they'd be on us in minutes.

The others ran up behind me.

Hannah gripped my arm. "Cain, what the hell is happening?"

"No idea."

Aura glanced down the center shaft. "I don't know why they're coming up here, but we need to get moving."

"What about the lickers above?" Hannah said. "We can't just run upstairs."

I gave Hannah my dueling wands. "Watch my back."

She flicked the wands through the motions. "Cain, I only know a couple of spells with these."

"Yeah, well put them to good use. That's why I told you to keep practicing."

She nodded grimly. "Let's go."

"Close formation, okay?"

She gave me a thumbs up.

I cast muffling spells on hers and Aura's shoes, then readied long-shot mode on my staff and began working my way up the stairwell like the leader of a SWAT team, Hannah close behind me, her hand on my back.

A licker crawled over the railing above us. I struck it between the eyes, and it fell with a final croak, bouncing off railings below on its way down. The shaft filled with excited croaks from above and below. We were going to be sandwiched between hordes of lickers.

A pair of lickers crawled down the stairs above. I downed them with two quick shots. Another one right behind them nearly got me with its tongue, but Hannah zapped it with a wand, and it snapped back in pain. I dropped its owner with another blast.

Hannah scribed a sigil behind us and cast a layer of shields over the center shaft below us.

"Good idea." I didn't know how long it would delay the lickers, but every little bit helped. The space was too large to adequately cover with shields, and I needed to conserve my efforts for longshots.

I increased the pace and downed another licker two stories up. Hannah tossed more light balls into the shaft and sent them soaring up, attracting the attention of the creatures above us, so I could ventilate their skulls.

We continued the climb, killing lickers more frequently as they crowded down the stairs. But the next section decided to throw us for a loop. The landing was partially destroyed, leaving a gap we'd have to jump. Several lickers dropped from a hole in the landing above, piling up right where we needed to go.

I killed two with longshots but there were simply too many of them. This was the end of the line.

10

I flipped my staff and ignited the brightblade. Turned and slashed the stairwell door off the hinges. Hannah kicked the door with the bottom of her boot and knocked it over. We scrambled into a hallway lined with numbered apartment doors.

Several of the doors hung open. Suitcases, clothing, and other personal effects littered the floor. I ran down the hall. The first apartment was large. The entire back wall, once a giant window overlooking the city, was broken and open to the elements. Curtains billowed in the gusting wind and paper littered the floor.

The next apartment was more of the same.

The third door led to a studio apartment with a large concrete pillar for a back wall and only a narrow window. If we were going to be cornered by a horde, this was the easiest place to defend. I kept my brightblade at the ready and cast shields and sigils around the doorway to prepare for the onslaught.

Hannah did exactly what I'd trained her to do. She rummaged through the kitchen drawers and slapped a pair of large knives on the counter. "Aura, grab these just in case." She went into the bedroom and emerged a moment later with a pistol and a box of bullets. "Or use this."

"I'm really impressed right now." I peered into the hallway. "You're doing much better than you did in Tokyo."

"I told you I'd do better next time." Hannah positioned herself at the window. The glass was intact, but that wouldn't stop the lickers from coming in.

Aura loaded the pistol. "Tokyo was the necromancer woman?"

"Yeah." I looked down the hallway toward the stairwell entrance, but so far, no lickers had emerged.

Aura frowned. "Are you still hunting necromancers? I thought Fate told you to lay off."

Something wasn't right. I put a finger to my lips and extinguished the brightblade.

The croaking and shrieking continued unabated from the stairwell, and then the sounds faded. I held up a finger telling the others to wait, then crept to the stairwell and peered inside. It was empty, but the licker noises weren't far away. I looked up and around, saw nothing, and stepped to the railing.

Lickers swarmed the area below, bodies worming between each other in a tight crush on the level where I'd killed their pregnant comrade. It was hard to see exactly what was going on, but they seemed to be all over the place where the tadpoles had been. The bodies of the lickers I'd killed a moment ago lay unmolested where they'd dropped. The monsters apparently weren't cannibals, but they had no problem eating their young.

Or maybe this was something else entirely.

Killing the pregnant licker had probably released a concentrated dose of pheromones into the shaft, drawing the attention of every monster in the vicinity. Had the death of the pregnant female unleashed a mating frenzy? The squirming and writhing could very well be sexual, or maybe they just wanted to eat some tadpoles.

The important conclusion, however, meant there were probably no more of the creatures above us. Provided we could jump over the broken landing above without drawing attention to ourselves, we could continue the climb unhindered.

I went back to the others and motioned them to follow. We crept into the stairwell and up to the broken landing. I cast a camouflage blind over the gap to block the view of the lickers below in case any of them were looking up. Hannah jumped the gap first, easily reaching the other side. Aura and I followed.

We went up the stairs and skirted the hole in the next landing. The outer wall was gone for the next few levels. Sunlight glinted off black mold and the spiky insects feeding on it. We couldn't hug the wall unless we wanted to find out just how poisonous the insects might be, so we moved closer to the railing and hoped we didn't reveal ourselves to the monster mash below.

A loud boom shook the building. Metal creaked and dust rained down, sparkling in the shafts of sunlight. The licker croaking and shrieking continued unabated, but the three of us froze in place, unspoken questions on our faces. I shook my head and pointed up, then jogged up the stairs.

The building shuddered again. A block of concrete broke loose from a landing above and plummeted down the shaft. I picked up the pace, keeping away from the mushrooms and moldy wall. My legs burned from the steady climb, but it was better than having to fight lickers every step of the way. The structure continued to shake, the tremors growing stronger and more violent.

I risked a peek over the railing and spotted the source of the quakes. A massive white worm was squirming up the shaft, bashing through the concrete stairs like they were paper. It was an eldritch dhole, one of the biggest I'd ever seen. Its conical nose tore through concrete and metal with ease, every impact shaking the building to its bones. The thing was twenty stories below us, and massive as the fuselage of a jumbo jet.

Hannah gasped. "Holy fuckballs."

"Holy fuckballs, indeed." I shook my head. "We're not going down that way."

Aura gripped the railing. "Is it going after the lickers?"

The lickers weren't the brightest creatures, but even they were starting to scatter and panic as the structure shook and rattled apart around them. Several fell over the railing. The dhole opened a gaping maw of splintered teeth and swallowed them whole.

"Does that answer your question?" Hannah said.

"Let's go." Throwing caution to the wind, I ran up the stairs, taking two at a time. The violent quakes nearly caused me to stumble against the wall. Insects fell from the walls and crunched underfoot as we ran over them. One of them landed on my shoulder. I instinctively cast a shield and brushed it off.

The tilt of the building was more noticeable here near the top. It was only ten degrees or so, but it made footing treacherous with the violent quakes from the dhole.

We finally reached the top landing and encountered an obstacle that would have stopped us dead in our tracks if the building hadn't already been so damaged. A mithril door designed to slide into the wall blocked the entrance, but there was a huge hole in the thick concrete wall next to it. We bypassed the nearly indestructible door, slipped through the hole, and into what had once been Torvin's inner sanctum.

The spacious penthouse beyond had few walls. The open design boasted a panoramic view of the city I would have found amazing if not for the dhole shaking the building apart. Ornate furniture, a double king-sized bed, swords, guns, and even a few pots and pans were heaped against the far window, having slid across the polished concrete floor thanks to the tilt of the building.

Cracks ran through the windows and the glass ceiling, but none of them had broken despite the pummeling this building had taken. That made perfect sense. Torvin wanted to look down on the city of nubs, but he also wanted top-notch protection for his little empire. The glass was enchanted. It could probably take a direct hit from a rocket launcher without breaking. But even enchanted glass had its breaking point and the dhole ravaging the bowels of the Sovereign was testing those limits.

More items slid toward the far window as the quakes from the dhole rattled everything loose. A portrait of Torvin fell off the wall next to the door and flopped facedown. Bottles of liquor rattled from an open cabinet and shattered on the floor. I winced at the destruction of several bottles of rare drow brandy.

Granite countertops and ornate wooden cabinets occupied the center of the room. There was no stove, no microwave, no refrigerator, no appliances of nub design. A fae preservation chest and a magic pot were the only items Torvin deigned necessary for cooking and keeping his food fresh.

I didn't even see a bathroom or a closet, but there was a thick wooden arch affixed to the floor near the pile of furniture on the downward slope side of the room. Judging from the symbols carved into the frame, it was a pocket dimension doorway, like the kind my fae tent used to give it a larger interior. Torvin probably had a nice little sanctuary on the other side where he could shit in the woods.

Balancing carefully, I let my feet slide across the slick floor toward the kitchen. I gripped the counter and guided myself closer to the pile of furniture. The building shook.

"Where would Torvin keep a computer or database?"

Aura pointed to a desk piled up with the other furniture across the room. "Probably there."

I drew my staff and ignited the brightblade, then slid toward the desk. My boots were grippy on dirt and mud, but not so much on damp, polished concrete. If I lost control of my slide, I could dig the brightblade into the floor and slow myself. Being eaten by a dhole seemed preferable to crashing through the window and plummeting fifty stories to the ground.

I reached the desk without incident. A sigil slate on the side of the desk told me the desk was usually locked. Tracing a combination of sigils would open it. But when I pulled on the handles, the drawers opened without resistance. I already knew the desk was empty before I checked the other drawers, but I did it anyway.

"It's cleaned out." I braced against the desk as the building rocked even more violently than before. Metal creaked and groaned. The enchanted windows and glass ceiling cracked and splintered. The building tilted another five degrees, another ten degrees.

Hannah and Aura cried out and fell hard against the kitchen counter. The magic pot slipped from its hook and hurtled toward me. I ducked and it flew overhead, smashed into the window behind me. Cracks spread across the wide pane. The building shuddered, and the window bowed outward from the crush of heavy furniture.

Hannah shouted in alarm. "Cain, watch out!"

The window exploded. Furniture poured through the opening. My pants snagged on a desk drawer. I stabbed my brightblade into the concrete floor. The surface shimmered and repelled the blade because it was hardened with magic—just like the windows. Unable to stop myself I slid through the window, flipping head over ass in freefall. The ground rushed up to meet me and—

I gasped and blinked. I was still in the building.

Hannah and Aura were still braced against the kitchen counter. The magic pot slipped from its hook and hurtled toward me. I ducked and it flew overhead, smashed into the window behind me.

"Oh shit." I already knew what would happen next. I reached down and freed my pants from the snag in the desk and banished my brightblade. The building tilt was so severe that the sides of the furniture had become the tops. I walked across the front of an ottoman, jumped to an upended nightstand, and reached the massive bed.

"Cain, watch out!" Hannah shouted.

I ran along the headboard of the bed and dove toward the only thing that could save me. The window exploded. The furniture funneled through the opening and started its journey earthward. My hands found the only thing anchored to the floor—the fae arch. My right hand slipped off. My left barely held on by two fingers. I swung my legs and reached with my right hand. It gripped the wooden arch just as my other hand lost its grip.

I dangled above the broken window, nothing but freefalling furniture between me and the street below.

I reached up with my left hand and secured my hold on the fae arch. I was safe for now, but how in the hell were we going to get out of here? The grappling hook in my utility belt could anchor us to the kitchen counter, but there was no way in hell to use the stairwell. The only other way out was the private elevator on the far side of the room.

With the grappling hook, we could reach it, but it'd be tricky.

Far below where the cylindrical section of the building met the rectangular base, glass shattered and concrete fractured. The building shook and the cylindrical section began to break free of its moorings, swaying.

"Cain!" Hannah reached into her utility belt and tossed her grappling hook line toward me. "Grab hold and I'll pull you up."

I grabbed the hook. Straining and bracing against the kitchen counter, she began to pull me up. Aura leaned over and helped her. I hoped whatever anchored the cabinets to the enchanted floor was strong, because she and Aura were putting all their weight on them.

A distant rumbling told me that we didn't have time to reach the elevator shaft, and even if we did, it wouldn't matter. The building toppled and jerked to a halt. Hannah lost her grip and I fell, landing heavily on the arch.

"I'm sorry!" She pulled frantically once again.

I hauled myself up, but the thin cord didn't make it easy without gloves. Aura reached down and pulled me the rest of the way up. I slid over the counter and joined them on the back. The wood was so solid it didn't even creak.

Hannah looked at me expectantly. "What now?"

I took out my grappling hook and tossed it toward the countertop on the other side of the kitchen. It latched onto the granite. "We need to get to the elevator shaft. Hopefully, it hasn't completely collapsed. If the ladder is intact, we can take it down."

"That's a big if!" Aura grabbed the cord. "Let's hope for a miracle."

Metal shrieked and the building leaned over another few feet before jerking to a stop. A bag of flaming hot cheezy balls fell from a cabinet and smacked me in the face. I pulled it away and shook my head. "What other dirty secrets are you hiding, Torvin?"

"Shit!" Aura lost her grip and fell on top of Hannah.

"Oof!" Hannah shoved her off. "Damn, that hurt! How much do you weigh, Aura?"

Apparently too much, because with one last metallic cry of anguish, the building began to topple in slow motion, and we had nowhere to run.

11

Hannah gripped my arm. "We're fucked!"

It was like watching a disaster movie on the big screen, except that big screen was the real world right in front of you and you couldn't look away. The Sovereign was so tall it looked like we were going to collide with the much shorter building across the street, whatever it was. If the other building had been another twenty stories taller, it might have been enough to arrest the momentum and give us a chance to survive.

But that wasn't the case. We were going to hit it hard. Our bodies would slam against the cabinets or fly over them. Our internal organs would be crushed to paste. Aura would resurrect, but Hannah and I would be a licker feast. Provided any of them survived the dhole.

We had a chance, but it was a slim one. It all depended on just how good the enchantments were in this place. I stood up. "Follow me if you want to live."

"You're quoting Terminator now?" Hannah rose unsteadily. "Where are we going?"

I aimed for the center of the arch. "Let's hope to a really good pocket dimension." I jumped. The momentum of the falling building was slightly slower than mine. There was probably a mathematical calculation to tell me just how hard I was going to hit whatever was on the other side of the arch, but I was too busy trying not to lose my shit to calculate anything.

I went through the arch. Hit something hard and rough, and rolled until another hard thing stopped me, knocking the wind right out of my sails. I gasped for breath just as a body slammed into me, and nearly collapsed my lungs. Another impact followed immediately after, but I braced myself just in time.

Hannah stood and pulled me to my feet as I gasped, trying to reinflate my lungs. "Where are we?"

I looked around despite the burning agony in my chest. We stood on a circle of stone pavers with a large pool of dark water in the center. A lip of gray granite had stopped me from rolling into the water. A forest of leafless snow-covered trees surrounded the stone patio. The air was frigid, but the stone was warm, and steam rose from the pool.

The bag of cheezy balls floated in the water along with an assortment of other odds and ends that had fallen through the arch instead of joining the furniture against the window.

Hannah dipped a hand in the water. "Cain, if this is a pocket dimension like your tent, why isn't it tilting along with the building? How is it normal?"

"Because it's a high fae enchantment, like my tent." I blew out a breath. "The arch is connected to the real world, but this place operates on its own principles."

I went to the forest and tried to squeeze through the thick branches and brambles, but an invisible force blocked me. There was a path on the other side of the pool, so I walked down it and found a small stone chair with a hole in it. "Well, I found Torvin's shitter." It was hard thinking of that stone-cold drow taking his morning constitutional on this stone throne.

Hannah's mouth dropped open. "Can you imagine Torvin taking a dump while looking at memes on his phone?"

"It is hard to imagine, but everybody poops." Aura looked around the toilet. "What did he wipe with?"

"It probably squirts cold water on his butthole." Hannah peered into the hole. "I don't want to touch it much less test it out, though."

"Drow don't need to wipe," I said.

Hannah wrinkled her nose. "Ew, are you serious?"

"No, he's not." Aura rolled her eyes. "Their buttholes need wiping too."

"If this is a tiny self-contained dimension, wouldn't his crap pile up?" Hannah looked into the toilet again. "It's solid matter, right? Matter can neither be created nor destroyed, so it has to go somewhere."

"Pocket dimensions are created from real matter, but they exist in a void." I shrugged. "I guess the shit goes into the void."

"And floats forever?" Hannah looked disgusted. "My god, think of all the piss and poop orbiting around this mini-planet."

"Can we talk about our next steps instead of Torvin's bowel movements?" Aura walked back toward the arch and stood in front of it. "Do you think the building has finished falling?"

As if in answer, a chunk of granite countertop whistled at high velocity through the arch, narrowly missing her head, and crashing into the trees. Aura dove out of the way as more debris, concrete, wood, and several more bags of flaming hot cheezy balls sailed through the arch.

Hannah gasped. "Cain, what if the arch is destroyed? Are we trapped forever?"

That was something I hadn't even thought about, but suddenly became the most important topic of our lives. "Not forever." I gave her a grim look. "We'll starve long before that happens."

The arch shuddered as concrete and debris rammed into the sides, but it held. Apparently, it was magically hardened because no ordinary wood could have survived the abuse. Then again, we were only seeing this side of the arch. If the other side collapsed, would we be able to get through?

The rain of debris stopped. Most of it had fallen to the ground immediately after coming through the arch. Some of it had ended up in the pool, and the rest collected against the trees on the other side of the water.

I gave some thought to the trajectory of the building and considered another option. The top floor would be well outside the safe zone now. If that was the case, I could probably use the Tetron to safely get us back to Prime.

Hannah reached the same conclusion a second later. "Cain, can we just use the Tetron to leave?"

"Gods, I hope so." Aura touched a wound on her forehead where a chip of stone had grazed it. "I don't want to have to pick my way through a destroyed building infested with lickers and a giant worm."

I took the Tetron from its pouch and rotated the Cubon until it clicked and hummed. I pulled out the Spheron until it snapped into place. The Tetron began to whine. "Hold onto me."

The others gripped my arms.

I pressed down on the Pyron. My body left the ground and soared into a void. Hannah and Aura floated next to me. A tiny white star twinkled just above a cube of stone. Dozens of ice-covered rocks floated around the cube, like miniature asteroids.

"Where are we?" Hannah looked up and around. "Where is Earth?"

"We're outside the pocket dimension." I scanned left, right, up, and down, but the cube and the tiny star were the only things visible in an endless void. I rotated the Spheron, but nothing happened. Manipulating the Pyron likewise did nothing.

Aura grimaced as one of the floating rocks drifted past. "That is one-hundred percent frozen shit."

"Well, now we know where it goes." Hannah tried to touch one, but her finger passed through it. "Mystery solved."

Aura gagged. "Gods be damned! Did you just try to touch Torvin's frozen crap?"

The Tetron apparently couldn't take us to the multidimensional array because wherever we were was completely separate from it. I willed us back into the pocket dimension and we landed back near Torvin's toilet.

"It was floating toward my face, Aura." Hannah released my arm. "I was trying to push it away from me."

"Gods be praised we're not solid while using the Tetron." Aura shuddered. "Hannah's got some strange kinks, Cain."

I gave them both a look. "Are you seriously talking about Torvin's feces right now? The Tetron can't get us out of here. We've got to use the arch and pray it's functional." I marched over to the wonder of fae magical engineering. It was clogged with all manner of debris, so I had no way of knowing if it still worked.

The rubble jammed inside was a mix of twisted rebar and concrete. I took out my brightblade and began slicing through the rebar first. The attached chunks of concrete fell and rolled across the ground. Hannah and Aura hauled the chunks away while I continued working. As I cleared one large chunk of concrete, another slab slipped through the opening.

The arch operated similarly to a portal, except without the bubbling effect. I couldn't see through to the other side. All I saw were the trees on the other side. That meant I couldn't see what else might be resting atop the arch waiting to fall through. For all I knew, it was covered by ten tons of rubble, and we'd have nowhere to go even if we could go through it.

I began cutting at the newly arrived slab, then stepped to the side as it fell free. Rubble poured through and filled the gap again.

"Fucking hell." I deactivated the brightblade and began scooping rubble with my hands, tossing it out of the way.

The others helped clear it, but every time we cleared the arch, more rubble poured through.

Hannah threw up her hands. "At this rate, we'll fill the entire pocket dimension with concrete."

"Keep digging." I cast a wide shield and used it as a shovel to hoist another load out of the way. "This is actually a good thing. If this stuff can flow in, that means nothing big is blocking the other side."

Hannah's eyebrows rose. "Oh, that's a good point."

Aura hefted a chunk of concrete and tossed it into a pile at the edge of the trees. "Worse comes to worst we can dump the concrete in Torvin's toilet and let it float in the void."

Hannah's face brightened. "That's a great idea!"

After a good hour of moving rubble, the inflow finally stopped. I shoved the brightblade through the hole and waved it around. It encountered resistance to the sides, but not directly in front. Trying not to get my hopes up, I put my head through the arch. A massive tangle of metal beams, rebar, concrete, and wood surrounded the arch.

I turned to the others. "Wait here. I'm going to see what we're up against."

There were tons of debris between us and the open air. On the bright side, it looked like we might be able to squeeze through the openings, provided none of it collapsed. I climbed through the arch and into a small nest of twisted rebar. The Sovereign Building had collapsed against the shorter neighboring structure. According to the remnants of a sign on the side, it was the Gilbane Building.

The penthouse, or what was left of it, jutted over the other side of the roof. Some of the walls were still intact, but it had turned into a giant jungle gym of metal and concrete that we'd have to navigate. Or, maybe we wouldn't. The building had fallen well outside the safe zone, so using the Tetron should make it easy.

I just had to find a place with enough room for us to touch. The broken concrete and rebar made it difficult. There was barely enough room to squeeze through in most places and certainly nothing large enough for the three of us to link together.

The first thing to do was find a path through the mess. The rooftop of the other building was at least fifteen stories away. Trying to make it there was impractical. I needed something closer. Using my brightblade, I sliced through rebar, freeing chunks of concrete to fall to the street below.

I continued my assault, carving a path toward an oasis of space about two stories below the penthouse. Howls echoed in the streets below. A pack of shoggoths raced into sight, stopping below and looking up. I wasn't worried about them. Even if they ran up the stairs in the other building, there was no way they could reach me out here.

"Cain?" Hannah's voice came from somewhere behind me, but I'd lost sight of the arch.

I wormed my way through the narrow spaces and back toward the arch until I could see her. "What?"

"Is it safe?"

"Safe enough." I pointed toward the platform of concrete about a hundred yards away. "We just need to get there so the three of us can link and use the Tetron."

"Want me to get Aura?"

My arms ached from cutting a path. "Not yet. I'm going to come back and take a breather."

"Okay." She dropped back through the arch.

I climbed back over broken concrete and carefully navigated sections with nothing but rebar and a deadly drop below. I slid back into the arch and sat on the ground.

Hannah brought me a bag of flaming hot cheezy balls. "Hungry?"

"Yeah, a bit." I opened the bag and tested one. It was spicy but not unpleasant. Winter drow were known for their love of spicy and dangerous foods. Torvin had been no exception. Packages of ramen lay around the rim of the pool. I was hungry enough to eat them dry.

Something else caught my eye—a glint of highly polished metal stuck between two stones. There was a lot of metallic debris lying all around, but this looked different. I walked over to the edge of the bathing pool and knelt at the stone wall around the rim. I pulled a pair of needle-nosed pliers from my utility belt and worked them into the crack.

I was able to open them just enough to grip the mystery object, then worked it free. It was about the size of a credit card and shone like stainless steel, but both sides were blank.

"What is that?" Hannah crouched next to me. "A credit card?"

I shook my head. "No, it's a random sigil generator."

"Like a sigil keycard?"

Aura knelt next to Hannah. "This is magic tech developed by humans, most notably those supporting Humans First."

Hannah frowned. "Is it magic or tech?"

Aura nodded. "Yes."

I rotated the metal card. "It was developed during the Fae-Human War. It basically generates a random combination of sigils that are used to unlock sigil slates."

"But couldn't you just use your revealing mist to see what sigils had recently been used?" Hannah traced a simple sigil on the stone. "Because the oil left from their fingers basically gave you all the info you needed."

"Right." I picked up the bag of cheezy balls and sat down on the stone wall. "The humans were so outmatched that they never had a chance to propagate the tech. The people who invented it were taken into custody by the Oblivion Guard. I assumed they'd been executed, but it looks like Torvin might have used them for his own ends."

"I'm sure the rabbit hole of Torvin's treachery and deceit runs deep." Aura took the card and ran a finger along the surface. "I'll bet this thing generates the sigil codes for the slates guarding this place and maybe even the secret headquarters."

"Yep." I ate a cheezy ball. "The problem is, how do we activate it?"

She sighed. "It probably needs a fingerprint or a sigil combination to activate it."

Meaning, with Torvin dead, this thing was useless.

12

Even though it probably required the fingerprint of a dead drow, I held out hope that there was another way to use this sigil plate.

I took out my revealing mist and sprayed both sides. It glommed onto the oily residue left from fingers and gently glowed, revealing a mishmash of fingerprints on both sides. There were random lines in the oil, either from other objects brushing against it, or from someone swiping a finger.

Hannah squinted. "So, um, any clues? Because it looks like someone put their grubby hands all over it but didn't do anything else."

"Maybe it's proximity activated?" Aura said. "Once you get near the sigil slate, then it turns on and gives you the sigils."

"Maybe." I looked closer at the fingerprints, but there was no pattern to them, nothing indicating the user had to press a finger to the card to unlock it. There was a sigil slate near the stairway entrance to the penthouse, but I didn't know if it still worked. "Maybe we should test it. If this thing works in Prime, we might have the key to Eclipse's kingdom."

Aura grinned. "Just when I thought this misadventure had been a complete waste of time."

Hannah rubbed her hands together. "Oh, I hope this works. It was such a letdown not finding anything."

"Yeah, major bummer." I put the card in a pocket on my utility belt, then tucked the mister and the pliers away.

Aura tilted her head. "Is there anything you don't carry in there?"

"Girl Scout cookies." I ate another cheezy ball. "Nathaniel Church warned me about those little devils."

Hannah blinked. "Say what? You have Thin Mints in your freezer."

I went back to the arch. "I found an ideal spot for us to Tetron out of this hellhole and it's not far from the sigil slate I noticed in the stairwell earlier. Follow me there."

The others nodded, so I poked my head through the arch, gripped the rebar on the other side, and pulled myself up into the broken body of the Sovereign. Despite my efforts at making the way easier, it was still like navigating a gauntlet. We crawled through tunnels of concrete, wormed around bent beams, weaved through tangles of rebar, and finally reached the sad remnants of the stairwell.

The slate was still on a section of wall that hung for dear life by a bent metal beam. I had to crawl across another beam, drop down to the top of the wall, and hang over the side just to reach the slate. I took out the card and held it as close to the slate as I could reach. Nothing happened. I tapped the card against the slate. Still nothing.

Hannah hung upside down from rebar for a better look. "There's no electricity, Cain."

"These don't hook into the power grid. They use liquid mana." I pointed to a slot on what had formerly been the inside wall. "Just one disc lasts for years."

"Maybe it didn't survive."

"Maybe." I dangled over the side and looked inside. There was a tiny metal disc similar to a watch battery inside the slot. I pushed on it. It popped out and fell.

Hannah gasped. "Cain!"

I reached out, attempting to cast a shield to catch it. Instead, I felt my fingers grasp it, even though it was well out of range. The disc stopped and hovered in midair. I pulled it toward me. It drifted to my other hand. I released it from my kinetic grip and grasped it with my real hand.

"Holy shit, Cain. You're getting good at that."

"I don't even know how I'm doing it." My new telekinetic abilities had sprung up recently. Despite plenty of practice and attempts to control it, it only seemed to work randomly. A subconscious part of my mind clearly activated it, but I had yet to discover the key.

I carefully inserted the mana disc into the slot and pressed it in. It clicked into place. Then I leaned back over the other side and held the card near the sigil slate. A series of sigils lined up lengthwise along the card. The mechanism the slate once controlled was destroyed, so I didn't bother testing the sigils.

I balanced myself back atop the wall. "It works."

Hannah, still dangling upside down, clapped her hands and laughed. "Yes!"

I pocketed the card and motioned toward Hannah. "You're in the way."

"Why don't we just stand on the wall and Tetron out of here?" she said.

"Are you kidding me?" I pointed to the thin beam of metal barely supporting the wall, then bounced to show her how much it swayed. "I don't think it'll hold up two of us much less three."

"Oh." She quirked her lips. "Maybe we could hang upside down from here and grab your hand."

"I really don't think—" The side of the Gilbane Building exploded in a shower of concrete and glass. The dhole worm burst from the hole like a belly buster in Alien and twisted up toward us. It seemed my activity had not only drawn the attention of shoggoths but this monster as well.

"How in the hell did that thing survive when the building collapsed?" Hannah shouted.

I didn't know or care. We were about to be worm food if we didn't get the hell out of here. "Jump to the wall!" I shouted. "Jump!"

"But you said—"

"I don't give a shit what I said! Get your asses over here!"

Hannah grabbed a bar below her, swung down, then jumped over to the wall next to me. It swayed and bobbed. The damaged beam creaked with the strain.

"Aura!" I shouted. "Get over here!"

Aura's head appeared in the gap of concrete. Her eyes flared wide at the sight of the giant worm winding out of the Gilbane and into the Sovereign's exposed guts. "Gods be damned!" She clambered out of the hole, slipped, and barely caught a metal bar with her fingertips before she fell. Gritting her teeth, she grabbed hold with her other hand, then swung over to us.

The metal groaned and bent. The wall began to slope down. The worm burst from the side of the Sovereign. Its mouth flared open, revealing a maw of needle teeth.

I grabbed Hannah's hand. "Grab Aura!"

She flinched from her stupor and grabbed Aura's hand.

"Jump!"

"Are you fucking—" Aura's words cut off as I jumped and dragged them off with me.

The worm chomped the wall an instant after we leaped.

We plummeted earthward at a much faster velocity than I'd expected. I linked my arm through Hannah's to free up my hands. Took out the Tetron, and quickly manipulated it. Shoggoths on the street below looked up hungrily at the fresh meals about to be delivered to their doorsteps.

We were hurtling downward so fast, the wind threatened to tear the Tetron from my grasp, and my eyes watered. My fingers fumbled while pulling on the Spheron. It snapped into place. The ground was only feet away. The shoggoths leaped up eagerly, mouth tentacles writhing, salivating for this unexpected treat.

I jammed down the Pyron.

A tentacle brushed my face. Hannah screamed. Aura unleashed a nervous fart.

Our descent abruptly stopped and reversed. We shot into space and the multiverse array spread out below us.

Aura leaned on Hannah. "I think I pissed myself."

"Me too," Hannah said.

"Are you sure you didn't shit yourself, Aura?" I looked over at her. "That was one hell of a fart."

"A tentacle nailed me in the stomach, Cain." She grimaced. "I'm afraid to check my pants."

Hannah patted her arm. "For once, Aura, I don't blame you."

I was too drenched with sweat to know if I'd soiled myself. I was just ready to go home. I navigated us to Prime. The Sovereign and Gilbane buildings sparkled in the sun, untouched by the destruction that befell their alts on Beta. I was too tired to attempt traveling anywhere else with the Tetron. Our arrival location would be the same relative place we'd left on Beta—the northeastern side of the Gilbane.

Hannah looked worried. "Um, Cain, do you think we'll arrive in midair at the same velocity we left Beta?"

I blew out a breath. "Damned good question." It was a theory I didn't want to test. If we materialized ten feet above the ground still hurtling at terminal velocity, then we'd make a huge mess. I twisted the Spheron to change our location to the sidewalk around the corner from the Gilbane Building and hoped it was enough to negate our previous trajectory and speed.

It also ensured that if Eclipse had surveillance around the Gilbane Building in addition to the Sovereign, then we'd be out of sight just around the corner. Even this tiny change of destination was going to hurt once the Tetron exacted its due from us.

I willed us to travel, and we dropped lightly onto our feet, much to the surprise of a couple walking in our direction. They stopped and stared, wide-eyed while we collapsed on the ground as the Tetron drained energy from us for the short distance we'd traveled.

"Jesus, are you okay?" The two women knelt next to Hannah and Aura and patted their hands.

"They're absolutely filthy!" The brunette wrinkled her nose. "And they stink to high heaven."

"Where did they come from?" The other woman looked around. "They just appeared out of nowhere."

"We're fine." Hannah pushed wearily to her knees. "Thanks for checking on us though."

The brunette took her hand. "Is this man abusing you?"

Aura groaned. "Oh, you have no idea."

"No, he's not." Hannah scowled at Aura. "Don't give these nubs any ideas, you idiot!"

"Nubs?" The brunette stood and backed off. "What's going on here?" She took out her phone. "I'm calling the police."

I finally recovered from the jolt and stood. I put the Tetron away and cast a sigil to hex the woman's phone. It sparked and smoked. She shrieked and tossed it to the ground.

Her companion jumped up and gripped her arm. "We need to go. Something's not right."

"Nothing is ever right," Hannah said. "And I peed my pants!"

The women turned and ran, much to the confusion of other pedestrians.

"Great." I sighed and looked for a taxi, but there wasn't one nearby. Plus, other people were starting to take notice of the bloody, bruised, and filthy trio that had magically appeared in this wealthy section of town.

A taxi stopped at a nearby traffic light. I opened the door and we piled inside.

The driver flinched in surprise as three filthy passengers crowded his backseat. "What is wrong with you people?"

I held out a wad of cash. "Just drive, please. We were in an accident."

He blinked. "To the hospital?"

"No. We need to go to Decatur."

He shook his head and pushed the money away. "Get out! You're stinking up my cab!"

I had a feeling he was about to make a scene, so I drew my

dueling wand and gave him a jolt to the neck. He slumped in his seat. I got out of the back and went to the driver's side. There were too many people around for me to avoid notice, so I unbuckled the man's seatbelt, then carried him out of the car and leaned him against the side of the nearest building.

People watched me in confusion and dismay. I tossed out a hex, smoking some nearby cellphones and their confusion turned to panic. People shouted and tossed burning phones to the ground.

"Watch out, it's gonna blow!" a boy shouted as he ran and ducked for cover.

The diversion worked, but then I saw the two women from earlier pointing us out to a police officer on a Segway. He narrowed his eyes, drew a whistle, and, well, he whistled with it.

"Welcome home, chumps." I climbed back into the driver seat and gunned the accelerator. The rear tires squealed, and we took off.

Hannah buckled in. "I'm ready for a nap."

Aura looked back. "Cain, slow down! You're going to draw too much attention. Besides, that cop on the scooter won't catch us."

A siren whooped twice in quick succession and a police SUV screeched out from behind other cars and started chasing us.

Aura sighed. "Never mind."

Hannah leaned her head on Aura's shoulder. "Wake me up when this is over."

I veered around a corner to take us away from the Sovereign building since I didn't want to raise a ruckus near a place we might soon break into. While I could probably just stop and deal with the single police car chasing us, I didn't want to expose us to traffic cameras or other surveillance.

Tired as I was, I cast camouflage sigils on the windows that would blur the view of anyone or anything looking in. Then I steered us down Peachtree, ran a red light, and took us south on Piedmont. Dodging cars, veering back and forth over the median, I managed to put some distance between us and the cop. But it wouldn't be long before more cars joined the chase. This had to end quickly.

The three lanes ahead were blocked by slowpokes and a line of cars trying to turn left. I bumped the left rear corner of the car in the center lane. It spun out and I dodged around them.

I couldn't help but grin.

Aura snorted. "You enjoyed that didn't you?"

"I absolutely despise slow assholes who don't stay in the right lane." I accelerated down the road, then slowed, and turned left. Cars screeched to a halt as I crossed their paths. One of them didn't stop in time and bumped the rear end. I twisted the steering wheel to keep it from spinning out of control and raced down Miami Circle.

The road was a dead-end, but there were several clubs, stores, and other places to hide in. I drove about halfway down, then turned into a narrow delivery entrance that took us to the parking lot on the backside of a dance studio. I jumped out of the car and traced an illusion sigil on the hood, then powered it.

The yellow taxi morphed into a white car of the same make and model with heavily tinted windows. I got back in the car and leaned back the seat. Sirens wailed in the distance. Moments later, an Atlanta Police car veered into the parking lot and stopped. There were only two other cars in the lot, so it didn't take the officer long to decide the lot was clear. He spun the car around and left.

I closed my eyes for about five minutes, listening to the sirens come and go. I looked around the parking lot for security cameras and didn't see any, but in this day and age it was hard to spot them all.

"This feels familiar." Hannah climbed out of the back and into the front passenger seat. She buckled in. "It's like the time you kidnapped me."

"Yep." I checked the time and figured fifteen minutes was enough.

"Good memories." Hannah patted my arm. "We should get into police chases more often."

Aura groaned. "You're up there reminiscing, and I'm sautéing in my own juices."

"Hey, I wet my pants too, Aura, so chill." Hannah looked at a wet spot on her jeans. "Gross."

"We're all a bit gross right now." I started the car and pulled out of the parking lot. Another pair of police cars raced past, heading toward the far end of the street.

Flashing lights at the end of the street told me the cops had it blocked off while they searched. I quickly traced a sigil on my forehead and cast an illusion mask. Turned around to Aura. "Lie down and stay absolutely still."

If this didn't go perfectly, we'd have every nub cop in the vicinity chasing us.

13

Aura laid down without hesitation. I cast a camouflage blind over her, and she blended into the seat. If she so much as moved, it'd be obvious, but it was the best I could do on short notice. Then I cast an illusion mask on Hannah, turning her into a young, bearded boy with long hair. Then I drove casually down the street until I reached the blockade.

A cop held up a hand to stop me while two others watched, hands on weapons.

I rolled down the window. "What's going on? Are we in danger?"

The cop looked inside at Hannah, then at the back seat. "We're looking for three suspects, a middle-aged man and two women." He stepped a little closer and made a sour face as he apparently got a whiff of us. "Jesus H. Christ you stink."

"Are they dangerous?"

He backed up a step. "We think so. Where are you coming from, and did you see anything?"

"I was just down at the dance studio trying to find out about their classes, but they weren't open." I shook my head. "I didn't see anything."

"What about you?" The officer looked at Hannah.

I hadn't told Hannah she looked like a man, so I dropped a hint. "Did you see anything Oscar?"

She blinked. "No?" Then abruptly got the hint and tried to deepen her voice. "No, I sure didn't, Uncle Billy Joe."

The officer frowned. "Billy Joe, huh?"

I nodded. "My family is a bunch of hillbillies."

"That would explain the smell." His nose wrinkled. He backed up and waved us on. "You can go."

"Thanks, officer." I drove between the other police cars and had to stop at the red traffic light.

"Billy Joe?" I glanced at Hannah.

She checked herself in the mirror. "Why didn't you tell me I was a boy?"

"I was in a hurry." I shrugged. "My mistake."

The seat in the back moved as Aura sat up. "At least you didn't have to pretend to be a seat."

I dispelled the illusion since it was a little distracting. Before I turned back around, I noticed one of the cops waving the others over urgently. I lowered my window, flicked my fingers in a sigil pattern, and cupped my ear so I could listen in.

"Hey, that car has the same license plates as the one we're looking for." The cop shook his head. "It's even the same make and model."

"But it's a different color." Another cop looked back and forth between the monitor in the police car and us. "No way they could change the color that fast."

"It's gotta be the same car!"

"But there were only two people inside, and both were male." The third officer rubbed his eyes. "Maybe we should detain them just in case."

The second one blew out a breath. "Yeah. Something doesn't add up. We didn't search the trunk, so the others could be hiding in there, and that kid in the front might be a hostage."

Two of the cops climbed into a car.

"Cain, the light's been green for twenty seconds." Hannah grabbed my arm.

I turned back around and gently pressed on the accelerator, trying to act casual even as the police officer gunned it to catch up to me. "Lie back down, Aura."

"It's lay back down, not lie," Hannah said.

I glanced at her. "No, it isn't, Terry Lee Joe Bob."

"Yes, it is, Billy Joe Bob Baxter!"

Aura groaned. "Are you two really arguing about grammar right now?"

I didn't have time to hide her with illusion again, so I turned left and thought about how I was going to prevent another damned police chase from happening. The cops caught up and whooped their siren twice. I put on my blinker and turned right into a bank parking lot. I drove to the back and parked.

"Hannah, put another illusion on Aura."

"I'm not very good at that yet."

"I don't care. Just do something." I got out of the car and walked around the back, glancing at the license plate number, OU812. I flicked my fingers behind my back and imagined the eight turning into a three. Then I walked toward the police car. "Did I do something wrong, officer?"

They pulled their guns. "Put your hands up."

I did as they asked. "You're scaring me. What did I do?"

"Walk backwards to the trunk, then open it while still facing us."

I tried to look frightened. "Why am I opening the trunk? What's in there?"

"You tell us." They approached slowly, pacing me as I backed up.

I stepped to the side so they could see the license plate, then pressed the trunk release with a finger. It opened. Inside was a spare tire, motor oil, and an assortment of clothing.

One of the officers stepped closer and looked inside while the other held me at gunpoint. "Nothing." He closed the trunk and blinked when he saw the license plate. "Hang on, you said it was Oscar, uniform, eight, one, two. This is three, one, two!"

The other cop squinted. "Wait, what? I swear to God that was eight, one, two."

"Oh, you ate one too?" I grinned. "Nice."

The first cop blew out a breath. "Fucking rookie mistake and you've been on the job three years."

"No, I swear it was an eight. There's no way—" The other cop stopped talking and stared blankly, his gun still trained on me.

"Um, can he lower his gun?" I trembled. "I don't like it pointed at me."

"Lower the gun, Buck." The other office sighed. "I'm sorry, sir. We thought you had the same license plate as the car we're after."

"Same make and model. The license plate is identical except for one number." The other cop holstered his gun. "Something is severely fucked up. I looked long and hard at the license plate."

"What's fucked up is your vision." The other cop shook his head. "You can go, sir."

I got back in the car, drove around the other side of the building, then got back on the main road.

"Cain, you just made that cop look insane." Hannah giggled. "I need to practice my illusions."

Aura sat up, a strange patchwork of colors flickering along her body. She held out her arms and looked at them. "Gods, Hannah, if this is the best you can do, you suck. I look like an argyle sweater."

Hannah giggled again. "I know, right?" She bit her lower lip, waved a hand, and the illusion melted away. "Cain just has me practicing too many things at once. Wizard magic, fighting, dancing, and as usual, trying to dredge up the trigger to make my own magic work."

"Progress takes time." I steered us onto the highway. "It takes years to master illusion and other magic."

"Yeah, it takes forever." She leaned back and closed her eyes. "Wake me up when we get home."

"We're not going straight home." I pulled into a shopping center and parked. "Taxis usually have GPS locators on them, so I'm not taking this thing anywhere near Sanctuary."

"Okay." Hannah got out of the car, looked around, and pointed to an old pickup truck. "That one looks ripe for the taking."

I dispelled her male illusion. "You sure?"

She paused. "Well, it's close to the store, so someone might see us take it."

"Yeah." I found a late model compact car with keyless entry and used a wand to send a jolt of power into the door. Nothing happened the first time, so I repositioned my wand to align it with the door controls inside and tried again. This time, the power window dropped open, and the door unlocked.

"Nifty." Hannah raised an eyebrow. "I don't remember seeing that spell before."

"It's a new one so we don't have to hunt for keys or smash out windows."

Aura shook her head. "Did you lose your lockpick kit?"

"It's in Dolores because it's too bulky for my utility belt." I shrugged. "And it doesn't work all that well anyway." I slid into the driver's seat. Like most modern cars, there was no key slot, just a push-button start. The key would usually send a signal allowing the starter to start it. I pressed my wand to it and released another jolt of power.

The car hummed to life.

"How'd you bypass the security?" Hannah said.

"This spell is like hotwiring, but without all the inconvenient wire stripping." I backed out of the parking lot and headed home. "The only downside is that the spell will short-circuit some cars or burn out the starter. I just know that the spell works almost perfectly on this model of car."

"Really?" Hannah made a thoughtful grunt. "Maybe tell me that next time we're looking for a car to steal."

When we arrived at Sanctuary, I parked outside the garage so I could use the scanning kit from Dolores. It took a matter of minutes to confirm the stolen car didn't have a tracker on it.

"You can never be too paranoid," Aura said.

"It's called being careful." I put away the scanning kit. "We can ditch this car back at the shopping center again when I get back from Seattle tomorrow."

"Dude, I'm so tired." Hannah yawned and walked toward the church. "At least we didn't come home empty-handed."

I took out the sigil generator card and examined it. "Yeah. Now we just need to figure out how to reach the penthouse without being shredded by security."

We went inside and stopped in our tracks.

A blood-spattered Layla sat on the couch eating a sandwich. She turned down the volume on the TV. "These reality dating shows are brutal."

Hannah shook her head. "I'm going to bed. You can tell me about this later."

Aura went straight to the guest room.

Layla wrinkled her nose. "Did Aura shit herself?"

I was tempted to say nothing and go to bed myself, but I was also hungry, so I washed my hands and made myself a sandwich. "I take it the assassins found you?"

"They've got mercs working for them now." Layla snorted. "Mercs! Can you believe they think they can capture me with low-level trash?"

I sat down next to her. "Tell me what happened."

"I needed to know if they cared about me or if I could live in peace, so I went to Voltaire's." She picked up a glass of milk and drank some. "The minute I got close to the safe zone I noticed some thugs watching the place. They looked human, but they didn't even bother hiding their smell."

"Glamourized goblins?"

She nodded. "Glamourized goblins. Looks like the fae gave them some fancy rings that made them look human. I have no idea why they didn't cover the smell."

"Goblins have a very distinct odor, and you're half-fae with heightened senses." I shrugged. "I probably wouldn't have smelled them."

"Yeah, you're right." She finished her sandwich and leaned back. "I turned around and walked away. They followed me. Three of them trapped themselves in an alley with me."

I chuckled. "You always have an interesting perspective, Layla."

"They asked me where you lived and threatening to hurt me if I didn't cooperate." She giggled. "It was adorable."

I grunted. "Yeah, totes."

"I ASKED them who their evil overlord was, but they didn't feel like talking at first." A malicious grin spread across her face. "So, I used the old call an ambulance routine?"

"The what?"

"When they drew their poisoned daggers and came at me, I started crying and shaking."

I nodded. "The little lamb routine. Makes them overconfident."

"Yeah, but this one has a fun twist." Her eyes brightened. "Right when they got close, I said, call an ambulance! Call an ambulance!" Then I drew my daggers and threw them while shouting, "But not for me!"

I laughed. "Gods, Layla. That's the stupidest routine I've heard."

"But it's fun!" She took another drink of milk. "First two goblins went down fast. I pinned the last one to the ground and ripped off his ring so I could see his butt-ugly face. Then I promised I'd let him live if he spilled his guts about who sent him." Layla shook her head. "He didn't know anything, so I spilled his guts for him."

"Did you keep the ring?"

She nodded. "But it doesn't work on me. I think it's spelled to only work on either goblins, or the ring owner."

I grunted. "Well, I'm glad you're okay, but I'm going to bed."

She glanced at my room. "I'll sleep on the couch if that's okay."

"It's fine." I kissed her cheek. "Love you."

Layla smiled and kissed my cheek. "Love you too. Why do you stink so bad?"

"I'll tell you tomorrow." I finished my sandwich, then went into my room, locked the door, and took a shower. Tomorrow was going to be a very long day.

Black worms crawled into my head the moment I closed my eyes. Cthulhu's glowing orange gaze stared down at me from a void of darkness. Waves crashed against a distant shore, and shoggoth howls echoed in the night.

I wasn't even asleep yet and the dreams were already starting. Then again, I might be asleep and just not realize it. Either way, I needed to know what was wrong with me and if there was a cure. Because if Fitz couldn't help me, then I was well and truly fucked.

A distant voice called to me. "Cain, I hope you can hear me. I'm very disappointed in you. You are not nurturing the seed. You're stunting it. Do better, or I will take matters into my own hands."

I tried to wake up. Tried to shout back at the voice. My madness was deepening if Nyarlathotep could speak to me so easily. And his words filled me with cold dread.

14

I woke up in a cold sweat the next morning, my body covered in dark slime crawling with slugs. Grimacing in disgust, I rolled off the bed and tried to wipe the sludge away. A shadowy figure watched me from the entrance to my closet. The silhouette was shaped like a humanoid worm. A face appeared in the light, mouth grinning maniacally, worms squirming from the orifice.

I reached back to summon my staff and the world shimmered. The sludge was gone and so was the specter of Nyarlathotep.

"Fuck." I rubbed my eyes and shook my head. This was going to be a hell of a day.

I checked my bank account before chartering my flight to Seattle. My balance had once been in the millions. Now it had dwindled to just under a million. All these capers and hijinks were costing me a pretty penny, and this little adventure promised to cost even more. Without my high-paying jobs from Eclipse, or side jobs from the bounty boards, I was going broke.

It was high time to replenish my funds by any means necessary. Flying commercially made more sense, but the schedule didn't work. So, I booked the charter flight at a bargain price of only five grand per flight hour.

When I arrived in Seattle, I put on an illusion mask since there was a standing order from the vampire overlords to kill one Cain Sthyldor. Then I took a taxi to my witch doctor's house. Fitzroy Simmons opened the door with a look of mild displeasure.

"All I want to know is how you managed this Cain. How does someone let the same thing happen to them twice?" He stepped out of the door and closed it behind him, then led me around the front yard to the gate in the backyard fence.

"It's not the same." I frowned. "How come you never just lead me through your house to the back?"

"Because I don't want you in my house, Cain. You're bad luck." He opened the hidden door to his root cellar and motioned me downstairs. "I've also started having vampire troubles again. It seems they're not entirely convinced my security is up to the task."

"I can help with that." I walked toward the workbench and stopped. "I thought you used the money I gave you for enhanced security."

"Yes, I hired a private company." Fitz plucked ingredients from a shelf and began mixing a concoction. "There's also a strange power struggle throwing the local vampire community into chaos. There are more shakedowns in the magical community, and those who don't pay are dying."

"Strange?" I sat on a mithril chair used to restrain powerful entities. "What's strange about that? Vampires are always infighting."

"Not like this." He frowned. "Rumors have it there are two Bergstroms fighting each other for the top position."

"Two Bergstroms?" I frowned. "Aldus Bergstrom is still the vampire kingpin of the northeast, right?"

"That he is. And he seems to have multiplied." Fitz crushed the ingredients with his mortar and pestle then silenced further discussion so he could chant.

While he did that, I gave some thought to what he'd said. Bergstrom never had a twin brother and he'd murdered all his siblings long ago. He was also a major reason why it was dangerous for me to come to Seattle without wearing an illusion mask. He still hated me because I'd assassinated a goodly number of his lieutenants and other loyalists during the Human-Fae War. I'd continued killing his minions who came after me once they'd discovered I was in Atlanta.

He'd eventually given up trying to take me out on my home turf, apparently content that I rarely came to Seattle or got in his way these days. I'd had a run-in with his people during my first encounter with Fitz. That had led to Fitz becoming a target. As a witch doctor, he wasn't protected by the local mage guild despite the membership fees they forced him to pay.

I'd given him a large sum of money to help him with his problem since I'd been the one to put him in the sights of some very dangerous people. He'd continued to help me despite his misgivings, so I owed it to him to keep helping him.

I had a slight problem, however. I'd made great money with Eclipse and accumulated a small fortune. But without that supplementing my income, it was time to turn back to other methods to support my lavish lifestyle. Of course, it was only lavish in that I spent an inordinate amount of time and money trying to keep the world out of Cthulhu's hands.

It seemed that while I was in town, I needed to make a pit stop to replenish my funds.

Fitz dipped his fingers into the gunk he'd made and spread it beneath my eyes as he chanted. He dragged his fingers from my temples toward my eyes, then stopped chanting and slapped a mound of the gunk on my head.

I grimaced. "How much of that do you need on my head?"

"Oh, the last part wasn't necessary, Cain." He smirked. "I just thought you deserved it."

"Great, thanks."

He took a patch of grass and wiped beneath my eyes, then dropped the soiled grass in a jar of clear liquid. Dark veins snaked through the water, coalescing into a dark cloud. Orange orbs glowed in the darkness. Images of my nightmares flickered into existence, morphing into all the variations I'd had since looking Cthulhu in the eyes. Even Nyarlathotep's grisly visage made a brief appearance.

Fitz groaned and shook his head. "Cain, you damned fool, you're sick again. And this time it's even worse."

I watched the nightmares with sick fascination. "Is it magic cancer again?"

He rinsed his mortar and pestle and began putting ingredients back on the shelves of his root cellar. "No. It's not like the sickness from the cursed pearl of Cthulhu. You were exposed to an intense source of psychotic energy, and it has saturated your mind."

I wasn't sure if I should be relieved or not. "So, no magic cancer? I'm not going to need a unicorn heart?"

Fitz glared at me. "Cain, did you listen to anything I said? Your mind has been poisoned beyond comprehension. If not for your extraordinary heritage as an Ekhsis, you would be consumed with madness already." Fitz gripped my wrist. "You need rest and relaxation for a full month."

I took out Panoptes. "I can't even use Panoptes anymore. The moment I put it on, I get weak and have visions."

He snatched the ring. "I'm going to mix a potion that will help expel the toxins in your brain, but you need to rest. Go to a beach somewhere and just relax far away from the people you usually associate with. There is nothing else I can do to help you, unfortunately."

"But I need Aura to make my mangoritas. And I need to keep training Hannah."

He groaned. "Cain, are you going to listen to me or not?"

I sighed. "Okay, so let me explain. Assassins from another dimension are trying to kill me. But once I solve that problem, then I can relax."

His mouth hung open. "You're already insane, aren't you? What is the matter with you?"

"You know how you said there are two Bergstroms fighting over the same territory? It sounds like the Bergstrom from another dimension somehow got here. Someone is using the alternate dimensions to spread chaos and confusion in Prime."

"The gods of chaos are still at it." Fitz worked his jaw back and forth. "Let me make your potion. It will help, but it won't cure you. Only resting your mind can give it the chance to purge the madness."

"Thanks, Fitz." I sat back down in the mithril chair. "Maybe you should move to Atlanta. It might be safer, and it'd be a hell of a lot easier to help me."

"I don't want to be closer to you, Cain." He shook his head. "If anything, I want to be further away."

I nodded. "Fair enough."

"I should move to Australia."

"Please don't."

He glared at me a moment. "Every time you visit, I'm tempted to pick up and leave."

While Fitz made my concoction, I checked my various bank accounts and calculated my total funds. My past adventures had put a serious dent in my savings. For years I'd done nothing but work and save. The only thing I'd spent money on was mangoritas. I'd been a wanted man. A hated war criminal. There hadn't been much to do with my money until I'd met Hannah and fallen down a rabbit hole of eldritch adventures. I'd discovered that the gods still lived, and that Cthulhu had poisoned me with a cursed pearl.

Replenishing my funds was unavoidable.

"Can I get Panoptes back?"

Fitz looked up from his work. "If you continue to use it, the damage to your mind might become permanent."

"Hannah can use it. Someone took the apocalypse weapons I'd stored in a secret warehouse only accessibly with Panoptes and we have to solve that mystery before someone else tries to rule the world."

He tossed the ring to me. "If it drives you insane, don't come running to me."

"If I do come running to you, it means I'm too insane to remember you telling me this."

Fitz poured his anti-madness potion into a jar of transparent beads and shook it. A moment later, the fluid was gone, absorbed into the beads. He dumped them into a plastic pill bottle that looked like something you'd get from a local pharmacy.

He plucked a single bead from the bottle and held it out. "Swallow one of these once a day. Don't bother increasing the dosage since it will cause too much strain on your body."

I popped the pill. "How do they work?"

"The psychotic energy is akin to radiation saturating your tissue." Fitz held up a hand. "Sometimes you may notice dark veins rising to the surface of your skin. This physical manifestation means your body is under stress and the saturation levels are rising. The potion will negate this energy a little at a time and cause you to expel it in one of many ways."

"Many ways?" I frowned. "Why do I have a bad feeling about this?"

"Sometimes you may vomit, other times it will come from your digestive system."

My frown faded. "That doesn't sound too bad."

"Other times, the energy may come from your pores or other orifices."

My frown returned. "Okay, that sounds bad."

"The more physical and mental stress you endure, the greater the chance the toxin levels will increase." He began putting away his things. "You need to take these pills and rest until you go five days without any expulsions."

I tucked the bottle into my utility belt. "Once I stop the interdimensional assassins, I'll be sure to do that."

Fitz rolled his eyes. "Yes, Cain, you be sure to do that." We went upstairs to the backyard. He closed the root cellar door, and an illusion hid it from sight. Then he opened the gate and motioned me through.

My body sigils tingled as I stepped through. The reasons for the warning were standing across the street from Fitz's place. I was still in disguise, so I acted as if I didn't even notice a flock of vampires glaring at us. It was sunny outside, but the vampires apparently had no issues. That was probably due to enchanted articles of clothing or jewelry.

The Mages Guild frowned on such things because they didn't want magic users giving vampires the ability to day walk. It seemed in Seattle that things were different.

Fitz groaned. "Why are there so many of them?"

"Haven't they been harassing you?"

He nodded. "Yes, but only one or two at most. Not six of them."

"It's because of me." I nodded toward his house. "Go inside. I'll take care of this."

"So much for your rest and relaxation." He continued toward the driveway. "I'll not hide from these bastards."

"You're only going to piss them off more." I reached the end of the driveway and met the glares of the vamps. "Can we help you with something?"

A vampire in plaid pants and a cardigan turned to his companions. "He's wearing an illusion mask."

"Reveal yourself, stranger." A tall vampire with thick black hair stepped into the residential street. "Once I see your real face, you can go about your business."

"Oh, how kind of you." I stopped at the end of the driveway. If memory served, Fitz's private security company had created a boundary of wards around the property to keep out vampires. They couldn't step onto the property without permission. "Who are you to interfere with Mages Guild business?"

"I'm Decker, Aldus Bergstrom's right hand." He walked up to the curb and stopped. "My sources would have told me if the Mages Guild was doing business with this witch doctor."

"Which Bergstrom are you talking about? The one from Prime, or a different one?"

He blinked. "How did you—" His gaze narrowed. "That's not common knowledge."

"Oh, for the Mages Guild it is." I crossed my arms. "Which Bergstrom are you working for?"

"That is none of your concern." He bared his fangs. "Now, kindly remove your disguise or this will get ugly. Just because we can't come onto the property doesn't mean we can't do some serious damage." He snapped his fingers. A vampire threw something that looked like a quarter toward the house. I instinctively cast a shield. The quarter smacked into it with a resounding crack just a few feet away from smashing Fitz's large picture window.

"By serious damage, you mean petty vandalism?" I shook my head. "Clear out of here before I call down an army of guild knights on your heads."

The vampires looked at each other and started laughing.

"Funny." Decker smirked. "Anyone in the Mages Guild knows that we control their moves. This is vampire country."

A car came around the bend and slowed due to the vampire blockage in the middle of the road. The driver honked his horn when no one moved out of his way. A vampire went to the door and motioned for the man to lower his window.

The driver cracked the window. "What's going on? I need to get through."

"You need to get out of the car." The vampire said.

The man's eyes glazed over, and he got out of the car and stood there. "Hey, why did I get out of my car?"

"Keep walking until you get to your destination," the vampire told him. "When you arrive, you'll remember your car was stolen."

The man nodded. "Yeah, I'll do that." He turned and started walking.

"Are you really free to use compulsion on nubs?" I shook my head. "The Mages Guild is really falling down on the job."

Decker nodded, and the vampires ripped the doors off the car and threw them at the house. They bounced off windows and brick without doing damage but tore up the hedges in the front.

"Hardening spells?" Decker chuckled. "Let's see how they do against an entire car."

The other vampires picked up the car and rocked it back and forth, preparing to heave it.

Fitz narrowed his eyes. "You're lucky I'm a man of peace!"

Decker snorted. "As if a witch doctor could do anything to us."

I held up a hand. "Fine, I'll reveal myself. But you have to promise to leave this man alone."

Decker held up a hand and the vampires set the car down. "No promises. Do as you're told."

I sighed. "Well, this just got messy." I dropped my mask.

"I knew it was Cain!" the plaid pants vampire said.

Decker smirked. "You win the prize, Angus."

Angus sneered. "I told you watching this house was worth it. Cain and this guy are in cahoots or something."

The other vampires laughed.

"Cahoots?" Decker rolled his eyes. "Who even says that anymore?" His smile faded as he looked at me. "Cain, as I see it you have one option. Come with us, or we'll starve you and your witch doctor out."

"That sounds like two options." I folded my arms. "Why would I go anywhere with you? Bergstrom wants me dead."

"I mean, we all want you dead, you traitorous son of a bitch. But the boss gets to have his fun with you first."

"How many of you do I have to kill to get you to leave Fitz alone?" I pretended to count them. "I think five should do. Angus can run back to Bergstrom and deliver the message for me."

Decker's smirk returned. "Not even you can take on six of us, Cain."

"Can't I?" I drew my staff and the brightblade hummed to life. I really wished I had the oblivion cloak with me to even the odds, but this would have to do. "I guess you don't remember much about the war, then."

"Oh, I remember plenty." He and the other vampires drew guns.

15

There were seven guns trained on me since one of the vampires decided to be a hotshot and sported two pistols.

Decker smirked. "You're not bulletproof, Cain."

I shrugged. "I'm working on it."

He leveled the pistol at me. "Don't make us shoot you and voodoo man to bloody pulps."

"Voodoo?" Fitz huffed. "I'm from Jamaica, you ignorant fool."

"Back in my day, vampires didn't use guns." I scoffed. "What has the world come to?"

"Guess you're about to find out." Decker leveled the gun at me.

"Last chance, Decker." I readied a shield spell on my fingertips. "Only Angus is walking out of here if you don't leave."

Angus laughed nervously. Some of the vampires looked uncertainly at me. A few bared their fangs. Emboldened by their numbers advantage.

"Not a chance, Cain." Decker's hand blurred and a gunshot rang out. The air laced with cracks when the bullet hit my shield.

I threw out a layer of small shields, then ghostwalked right behind Decker. He spun inhumanly fast, but his head rolled to the ground even faster. I ducked, slashed the legs off another vampire, ghostwalked behind the next one, and impaled his chest. Flesh sizzled. A scream died on his lips, and he went down.

The next one fired a barrage of shots from his pistol. I swung my brightblade to deflect some of the projectiles, but one got through and smacked into my enchanted jacket. It kept the bullet from penetrating, but it still hurt like a bitch. I ducked, cast a shield to the vampire's right. He tried to juke right and rammed into the shield. I slashed off his gun hand.

The fancy watch on his wrist must have had the day walking enchantment because his skin turned bright red, and an agonized scream tore from his throat as his body burst into flames. I let him burn and ghostwalked to the next vampire. Two quick slashes removed his arms and an inferno claimed him as well.

I threw up a layer of shields and turned to face the lone survivor —Angus. He fired until his weapon went empty. Dark worms crawled at the edges of my vision. My legs felt weak from so much ghostwalking. A giant rose on the horizon, blotting out the sun and replacing its light with the glow from his eyes.

Cain. Cthulhu glared down at me. *You are mine.*

This isn't real.

Gunshots rang out distantly. Something punched me in the gut and the shoulder. Cthulhu growled and the sound sent chills snaking down my spine.

"Cain!" Fitz leaned over me. "You fool, I told you to rest and relax, not kill five vampires!"

I blinked and the world returned to normal. "Angus?"

Fitz sighed. "I strung him up."

"Huh?" I pushed up on my elbows. Angus stood awkwardly, arms and legs cocked like a puppet being pulled in all directions. His eyes rolled madly in his head, and his tongue lolled. "What the hell?"

"He was shooting you, so I used a spell that is handy for controlling unruly children." Fitz shrugged. "I may have overdone it."

I pushed slowly to my feet. "Thanks."

"No problem."

I walked over to Angus. "Can he hear me?"

Fitz nodded.

"Which Bergstrom do you work for, Angus?

The strings seemed to relax because Angus went limp and the crazed look in his eyes faded.

He shivered in fear. "The original, not the doppelganger."

"Tell him to leave my friend alone, or I'll hunt you down one by one." I leaned closer. "Understood?"

Shaking, he nodded.

"Good." I pointed to Decker's head. Apparently, the enchantment protecting the rest of the body from the sun stopped working on his head once it was separated, because it was blackened and burned, the skull showing through patches of hair. "Take that with you, okay?"

He gulped. Nodded.

I slapped his cheek. "Good boy. Let him go, Fitz."

Fitz murmured and Angus slumped. The vampire took one horrified look at his dead comrades. He picked up the smoldering head and sprinted away in a blur.

Fitz stared at the corpses littering the road in front of his house. "My HOA will be most displeased with this mess."

Ghouls were handy for cleaning up corpses, but not when they'd be out in the open. I cast a camouflage blind, but that wouldn't do much good if another car came along and bumped over a body, and it also didn't hide the smoke still rising from the burning clothes.

I looked around to see if there were witnesses. Luckily, Fitz lived around a curve and there weren't any houses with a direct line of sight onto his property. That was probably why he'd chosen this house for a home. "Do you have a potion for dissolving bodies?"

"Why would I keep such a potion around?" He pressed his lips together. "We'll have to move them."

"We could use Panoptes." I held up the ring. "Maybe you can—"

He shook his head. "Absolutely not, Cain. I just finished the ritual for cleansing the darkness from my soul for what you had me do to Baura, and I'm not about to invite more darkness in."

"It won't drive you mad right away."

"The answer is still no." He blew out a breath. "I'll be back in a moment."

"What about the car?"

He didn't answer. A moment later he returned with a wheelbarrow. I started tossing vampire body parts and bodies inside of it.

A car came around the curve, slowing as the driver rubbernecked the destroyed car parked on the side of the road. He rubbed his eyes as he passed, probably because the bodies were blurred with the camouflage illusion, and he thought his eyes were going bad.

I waited until the car passed before picking up another body. "You don't get much traffic here."

"I placed aversion wards at the nearest intersections, so most people turn there instead of coming this way."

"You could have just bought a house on a dead end."

"This location was ideal for other reasons." He shrugged. "It works." He took the wheelbarrow to the backyard, emptied it, and returned.

We loaded another couple of bodies, took them to the back, and then returned for the rest. I dispelled the camouflage blind and looked around for loose body parts. A hand and an arm became visible. I tossed them in the wheelbarrow and then gathered a watch, some rings, and the pistols.

The vampire blood had burned, leaving black marks on the road. It might arouse suspicion if a supernatural investigator came here, but the nubs would just think it was normal asphalt discoloration.

I picked up the car doors and slid two of them into the backseat. The others went into the trunk but jutted out so I couldn't close it. I started the car and drove it down to the next intersection where I left it on the side of the road. The owner was still walking down the sidewalk a few hundred yards away. He'd keep on walking until he reached his destination and there wasn't anything I could do about it. The exercise was probably good for him.

I used a cleaning mist to remove my fingerprints, then walked back to Fitz's place. He was looking at his mangled hedges and the gouges in the grass where the car doors had struck it.

"What are we doing with the bodies?" I asked.

Fitz gave me a deadpan stare. "I'll take care of them, Cain."

"With a body dissolving potion?"

He rolled his eyes. "I don't think so. Such a potion is just as dangerous to the living as it is to the dead. And it doesn't dissolve bones."

"I'm sure ghouls would be happy to eat them."

"That's my thought as well, though I'm loathe to invite such creatures onto my property, but perhaps I can take the bodies elsewhere." He stared at the pile of bodies. "Cain, you have serious issues."

"Tell me about it."

"Please, go."

I nodded. "I'm sorry about the hassle, Fitz. I'll make it up to you."

He laughed softly. "Oh, I'm sure you will."

I waved goodbye, but Fitz wasn't paying attention. I walked around the side of the house and went to the street. The vampires had been an unwelcome diversion, especially since I had another task to take care of before heading home. On the upside, they had left me a gift that might make my task easier.

I walked down to the intersection. The doorless car was still on the side of the road, although it was getting looks from passing motorists. I traced a sigil on the hood and waited until there was no traffic, then powered an illusion to make the car look as if it was undamaged. Then I climbed in and drove.

During my early days of living on Gaia, I'd been forced to make money in unorthodox and morally questionable ways. Once I'd started taking assignments for Eclipse, I'd been able to live mostly honestly. Unfortunately, I'd now have to resort to crime.

ATM machines were easy pickings, but the amount of money in them varied wildly depending on how much had been withdrawn during the day, or the policy of the ATM owner. It was usually easier to go straight to the bank. I also tried not to rob banks anywhere near me. There were so many cameras these days that it was nearly impossible to avoid being recorded.

The maps app displayed nearby banks. I chose a branch

belonging to a large company since they normally carried more cash, and I knew from experience that their customer service was awful.

I had special bags that worked great for heists, but I hadn't brought them along since this hadn't been part of the plan. I went into a sporting goods store and found a bag that was made of thin nylon and easy to fold into my pocket. I purchased two of them, then went back to the car and drove a short distance to my target.

I parked at a neighboring fast-food restaurant and walked over to the bank. It was a mid-sized single-story building with a typical design. There were rows of teller stations, most of which were empty. There were offices along the left wall and cubicles on the right side where people applied for loans and other fun bank stuff. I headed left toward one of the counters where people filled out deposit slips. In this day and age, nearly everything was done by mobile apps or online, but there were still enough old farts who wanted paper.

I stood at the end of the table and noted the signs on the doors. The one at the far end belonged to the branch manager. There weren't any public bathrooms by design. This place was designed to make people wait mindlessly in line and leave. The only way to approach this was with all the confidence of a person who knew exactly what they were doing.

There were at least six visible cameras and two security guards. I flicked my fingers and cast blurred illusions in front of the cameras as I walked beneath them. They weren't meant to blind the cameras, but to prevent them from recording in high definition. I did the same for the security guards.

They squinted and rubbed their eyes, unable to figure out why their vision had suddenly gone bad. Then I walked boldly toward the branch manager's office, casting illusions over the lenses of the two cameras down that way.

The three working tellers were too busy with customers to look my way. Other customers were waiting in lines or sitting in chairs awaiting an appointment, and none of them so much as glanced up from their phones as I walked by.

I stood outside the manager's office a moment later. There was muffled conversation inside, but I turned the knob and entered anyway. The manager's desk faced the door. He looked up from his computer monitor the moment I entered. The placard on the desk read, *Kevin Reynolds*. I closed the door behind me.

"Oh, I'm sorry to interrupt, Mr. Reynolds."

"Bob, hang on for a moment." Kevin hit a button on his desk phone. "Who are you?"

"I'm here for my three o'clock appointment."

He blinked. "It's two o'clock and I don't—"

"Hey, do you like Harry Potter?" I took out a wand. "Look what I got."

His mouth hung open. "What in the hell is going on here?"

I flicked the wand and a jolt of electricity struck him in the forehead. He spasmed and slumped in his chair. I quickly walked around the desk and slid him out of the chair and onto the floor, concealing him from anyone else who walked in.

Most bank vaults operated on a timer, opening the outer door only during business hours. There was a teller vault, and the main vault, the second of which required either codes from two people, or keys. Sometimes they required both. Since Kevin was napping and since I couldn't read minds, there was no way I was getting his code.

Thankfully, I didn't really need it.

Kevin was too short for his clothes to fit me, so I'd have to do this the riskier way. He wore business slacks and a white shirt with a red tie, so I first traced a sigil on my clothing, then powered an illusion so my clothes looked like his. Then I stared long and hard at his face and cast an illusion mask mimicking his appearance.

I looked in a mirror on the wall. The illusion flickered slightly, but hopefully most people wouldn't notice. I took his keyring, but nothing resembling a vault key was on there. I used one of his keys to unlock the top drawer on his desk and found a security keycard inside. It was probably one-half of the equation to getting inside the main vault.

Getting the other keycard would be tricky, especially since I wasn't particularly good at impersonating people and since I didn't have a spell that would help me do it. But I took the keycard anyway. I sprinkled a sleeping potion on Kevin's upper lip to keep him down a little longer, then locked his office door and closed it behind me.

I walked casually down the hallway between the teller's area and the offices where a locked door guarded the back rooms. A swipe of the keycard unlocked the door. I stepped into a hallway. There was a conference room on the left, a break room further down the hall, some restrooms, and a corridor between them.

Casting blurring illusions over the cameras, I continued down the hallway and turned left into the corridor. The vault foyer was just on the other side. A quick flick from my wand jolted the lone security guard into submission. I sprinkled sleeping potion on his upper lip and then inspected the vault.

The thick outer door was open, but a barred gate blocked entry. I focused on the area behind the bars and ghostwalked inside. My knees wobbled and the room darkened as if something were draining the light.

The fight with the vampires had required too much energy. Waiting a few hours or a day would have been smarter, but I also didn't want to hang out in Seattle for much longer. The light levels slowly returned to normal. That had nothing to do with my ghost-walking and everything to do with the toxic psychic energy poisoning my brain.

Judging from the denominations of the stacks of bills, there wasn't more than a hundred thousand dollars inside the vault. I unfolded the duffel bags and stuffed them with the stacks of bills. They filled up quickly since they weren't very large, but it was enough money to tide me over until the next time.

I cast camouflage illusions over them, turning them to blurs. Then I ghostwalked out of the vault. This time the effort dropped me to my knees. Dark veins crossed my eyes, and the light faded to almost nothing. Thrumming filled my ears and I felt myself falling into an endless void.

16

Darkness faded into light faded into darkness faded into light faded into—

"Oh my God!" High heels clicked across the floor. "Kevin, what happened? Did someone try to rob us? Roy's unconscious!"

The light returned.

I blinked until the dark veins in my vision receded.

A woman I recognized as one of the tellers stood in front of me. I assumed Roy was the security guard I'd knocked out.

She regarded me uncertainly. "Kevin, are you okay? Your face is dark red."

I groaned. "I think those donuts Roy brought in this morning are bad. I'm about to shit my pants."

She flinched. Frowned. "Donuts?"

I pushed slowly to my feet. "Yeah. I think Van Wilder made them."

"Who?"

I flicked my wand and she slumped. I caught her before she toppled to the floor, then gently laid her atop Roy. They'd have an interesting conversation when they woke up. I picked up the camouflaged bags and walked down the hallway. I continued past the offices, the teller stations, and out of the front door. The security guards were still in position, but constantly rubbing their eyes. The illusion blurring their vision would fade in another ten minutes or so.

Hannah had been ecstatic the first time we'd robbed a bank together. She'd had zero moral compunction about it even before I'd launched into my spiel about how robbing a bank didn't hurt the customers or the bank. Banks were insured, so the FDIC paid back any losses from a robbery. I also took great care not to kill anyone, leaving behind nothing but questions and a mystery they'd think about probably for the rest of their lives.

As far as I saw it, I was doing those people a favor.

I strode confidently across the parking lot and over to the fast-food restaurant. Once I was in the car, I dispelled my illusion mask and clothes, then did the same for the duffel bags. I figured I'd gotten away with at least a hundred grand, maybe more. Not bad for an hour's worth of work.

I started the car and drove toward the airport. Wind whistled through the cabin since there were no doors. It wasn't an ideal ride, but it was more convenient than taking a taxi. I thought about dropping the illusion and revealing the state of the car to other drivers just for laughs, but that would draw too much attention.

When I reached the small regional airport, I gathered my duffel bags and boarded my chartered flight. I was just glad they didn't charge me to be on standby. The flight attendant served me a drink and a snack after takeoff, but I was exhausted and quickly fell asleep.

The nap did me some good because I felt refreshed when we landed at Dekalb-Peachtree Airport in Atlanta. I loaded my duffel bags into Dolores and headed home.

Hannah glanced at the duffel bags when I walked inside and immediately jumped off the couch. "Did you rob a bank without me?"

"Yep." I dumped the cash on the floor. "Want to help me count it?"

She glared at me, then sat on the floor and started sorting the denominations into stacks. "I want to rob a bank with you next time."

Layla came up the basement stairs, sweat dripping from her forehead. She'd probably been using my training room. "What was this about robbing a bank?"

"I needed cash." I shrugged. "Things are expensive."

She pursed her lips. Nodded. "Yeah, I wondered how much longer you could keep up the spending pace. That operation in Romania probably cost an easy five hundred grand."

"Almost nine hundred." I blew out a breath. "We're going to need a lot of equipment to break into Eclipse. And if we find their hidden HQ then we'll probably need more."

Layla nodded. "I could kill you for the price on your head and we'd have plenty to spare."

"Might as well." I frowned. "Too bad Cain from Beta didn't leave behind a corpse."

"Ooh, that would have been amazing." Layla dropped onto the couch. "I could've made some serious bank with that."

"Why do I keep hearing about banks?" Aura came out of the guest bedroom.

"Cain robbed a bank without me." Hannah pouted. "I love robbing banks!"

"Maybe when your illusion game is on point you can rob them solo." I sat on the floor and started counting the Benjamins.

"Don't think I won't." Hannah stared at me. "You look exhausted."

"I slept well on the flight. I'm fine."

"What did Fitz say about your condition?"

I set aside fifty thousand dollars and started on the next stack. "He gave me some pills and said to get some R and R for a solid month."

Layla guffawed. "Like that's going to happen."

"Yeah." I shrugged. "But the symptoms are getting worse. I'm afraid I'll start having visions in the middle of a fight or while infiltrating Eclipse."

Hannah patted my hand. "Maybe we can find a unicorn heart for you."

"This is different." I put aside another fifty grand. "It's not magic cancer, it's psychotic toxicity."

Layla snorted. "Sounds like a fancy way of saying you're insane."

"Exertion triggers visions of Cthulhu and physical manifestations of the poisoning." I stood up and walked toward the kitchen. "I'm going to ghostwalk and let you see."

Layla stood. "Can I get some popcorn first?"

"Maybe you shouldn't do it, Cain." Hannah grimaced. "You're just going to exacerbate the problem."

"Please do it, Cain." Layla rubbed her hands together.

I ghostwalked a short distance. The light in the room dimmed and dark veins crawled across my vision. I distantly heard Hannah gasping and calling my name, but the words were overwhelmed by a deep thrumming and moist chewing as if thousands of tiny mouths were feasting on a bloated corpse.

Cthulhu's eyes brightened in the darkness, rising higher like twin suns until he looked down at my pathetic human form. Pain radiated from somewhere to my right. More pain from the left. The darkness faded into light.

Hannah looked at me, aghast. "Don't you fucking do that again, Cain!"

Layla knelt by my side. "Cain, I'm sorry. I shouldn't have encouraged you."

Aura stood behind them. "I don't know how we're going to pull this off."

"Was it bad?" I asked.

"Bad?" Hannah scowled. "I slapped you ten times to snap you out of it."

Aura held out a phone. "I recorded everything."

I took the phone. In the video, I stood near the kitchen. I vanished in a trail of dark vapor and reappeared a few feet away, immediately dropping to my knees. Dark veins crawled across my face and into my eyes, clouding them until they were pitch black. Orange pinpoints glowed in the center of the darkness, growing larger and larger. Hannah started shouting my name. She slapped my cheek. Shook my shoulders. Slapped my other cheek. I continued staring blankly, the orange glow filling my eyes.

Hannah began slapping me repeatedly, alternating cheeks until at last I blinked. The orange glow faded, and the darkness receded from my eyes, my face, my neck, until I was normal except for slightly reddened skin and glowing cheeks from the slapping.

I looked up at Hannah. "I'll bet you enjoyed that, didn't you?"

"Any other time, yeah." She shook her head. "But this was scary."

Fred waddled from behind the couch, water dripping off his body. "Cain, you're back!"

Layla frowned. "Did Fitz actually do anything to help you, Cain?"

"There wasn't much he could do." I sighed. "He told me to take some pills and get plenty of rest."

Fred stopped before me. "You are worse than before, Cain, but I can help."

"No offense, but how are you going to help?" Hannah patted his arm. "Cain needs less madness, not more."

"There are others like me." Fred looked at her with soulful eyes. "Others who don't want to be monsters."

"Hold up." I stared at him. "Others like you? Are they spawn of Cthulhu too?"

He shook his head. "No, Cain. They are eldritch like me."

"Not to state the obvious, but the eldritch don't cure madness, they cause it." Aura grimaced. "You'll just make it worse."

"No, I can be a good monster." Fred gripped my arm with his little hands. *Trust me, Cain. You said I can be more. I found other eldritch who also want to be more than they are.*

I regarded him for a long moment. "I trust you, Fred." I also didn't have much choice but to try something, anything that would put me back in top fighting condition again.

"Um, look, I totally get that Fred wants to help, but what if he accidentally makes things worse?" Hannah gave me a pleading look. "It's not worth the risk. Why don't you take a couple of weeks to relax and then we can go after the Handers?"

"We might not have two weeks." I blew out a breath. "Right this very moment, Elektrode is sifting tons of data and narrowing down the possibilities of where I live. The closer he gets, the harder it'll be to hide. We might have an army of Handers waiting outside the gates by the time two weeks is up." I pushed to my feet. "I'm going to trust Fred."

Layla bit her lower lip and looked back and forth between me and Fred. "If he's so confident, I say let him try. It's not like Cain has a choice, really."

Aura folded her arms. "Elektrode is relentless when he has someone's scent. My former cybermancer was one of the best and even he couldn't hide. I say we let Fred try to help."

"Fine!" Hannah threw up her hands, then knelt next to Fred, a soft white glow in her irises. "Fred, you'd better not fuck him up worse than he already is."

Fred's eyes grew huge. "I would never hurt Cain. I promise."

She wiped tears from her eyes. "Then fix him. Please."

Layla gripped Fred's arm. "Don't pull a mini-Cthulhu mind fuck on him, or I'll slice you up and sell you as sushi."

Fred gulped. "Layla why do you think I would do that?"

"I know you wouldn't do it on purpose, but don't do it accidentally or it's sushi time, okay?" She mimicked slashing with knives complete with accompanying sound effects.

"I'll be right back." Fred waddled to his pool and dove in.

Three pairs of eyes watched me quietly as I eased myself into a chair.

Layla broke the silence. "So, how's the weather in Seattle?"

"Raining vampires." My hands felt stiff, so I flexed them to get the kinks out. "There's a turf war going on."

"Not surprising." Aura shrugged. "Vampires are always infighting."

"This time it's Aldus Bergstrom versus his alt from Alpha." I cracked my knuckles one at a time. "Sounds like whoever is helping the Handers is also taking the opportunity to sow more chaos."

"There are two Bergstroms?" Aura whistled. "That's two too many."

"I had to kill a few of them just to make them leave Fitz alone." I shook my head. "Things are getting out of control."

"Nothing new there," Layla said.

There was a splashing sound and Fred popped out of his pool, his stubby, chubby body leaping gracefully and landing with a wet plop. "I'm back!"

"And?" I raised an eyebrow.

"My friend is ready." He motioned me toward the pool. "We can go meet him now."

I took off my shirt, shoes, and socks, then walked over to the pool of dark water in the corner of the den. The construction workers who'd originally built it for me probably wondered what kind of nutjob wanted a thirty-foot deep swimming pool with salt water in their den. They probably couldn't have imagined it was for the pet octopus swimming in the aquarium.

I sat down on the side of the pool then slid into the water. It was cool, but not uncomfortably so. Fred dove in and his tentacle grabbed me by the ankle.

Hold your breath, Cain.

How long will I be under?

Long enough. Take a deep breath.

I didn't like the way that sounded, but I took a deep breath. The tentacle tightened and yanked me down. I plummeted into darkness. Water rushed past me, bubbling, boiling and suddenly calm. I drifted in the watery void, anchored by a tentacle. My lungs should have been starving for oxygen, but I felt oddly contented, unconcerned.

A shadow approached in the void.

Stay calm, Cain.

Why don't I need to take a breath?

I am breathing for both of us.

How?

Remain calm, Fred replied.

The shadow grew larger until it hovered before me. The massive eye of a malgorth became visible in the gloom and I suddenly understood why Fred told me to stay calm. Because the last thing I wanted to do while trapped underwater was look even more madness in the eye. The gaze of a malgorth was nothing compared to Cthulhu, but in my condition, every little bit pushed me closer to the cliff of insanity.

Fred, that's a fucking malgorth.

He is my friend. He wants to be good like me. Fred floated in front of me. *I would never harm you, Cain.*

I would have blown out a breath, but since Fred had told me to hold my breath, I didn't want to mess that up.

I trust you.

His mouth tentacles quivered. *I'm glad.*

A gentle light glowed around us, and the massive creature became visible. It was the strangest looking malgorth I'd ever seen. Its skin was white and not the usual gray. The eye wasn't black as pitch. In fact, it seemed to be the source of the light. I felt oddly calm. At peace. My eyelids grew heavy, and I began to drift off.

No! I forced myself to stay awake.

Don't resist, Cain. The voice wasn't Fred's. It was the malgorth's. Thick, white tentacles caressed my head. The eye emanated a softly glowing warmth. I could resist, but maybe I shouldn't.

What are you?

I am what could be. I am a possible future for the eldritch, thanks to Fred.

I blinked. *That makes no sense.*

Yes. The tentacles massaged my temples. *Some of us are born different. Some of us see a different path. We have Fred to thank for that.*

I tried to respond, but my mind was too relaxed. I was comfortably numb.

Oily darkness seeped into the water, clouding it.

I must have drifted off for a moment. When my eyes opened, the malgorth was turning away. The water bubbled and boiled. Tentacles gripped my arms and pulled me at an incredible pace. I blinked and saw Fred, his tiny body looking graceful and lithe in his natural element.

Fred, you're beautiful.

He looked back at me, eyes filled with happiness. *Cain, you are still high, but thank you.*

High? I broke the surface of the pool and landed on the stone floor with a thud. I sucked in a breath of air. It felt harsh to my lungs after a small eternity of calm in the ocean depths.

"Finished!" Fred declared proudly.

Aura, Hannah, and Layla crowded around me.

"I thought for sure you drowned him!" Hannah knelt next to me. "You were gone for over an hour!"

The peaceful haze faded from my mind, taking with it the happiness and calm I'd felt from the touch of the malgorth. I pushed wearily to my knees. My shoulder ached where I'd landed on it. "Fred, how is there a malgorth that doesn't cause madness?"

Fred's mouth tentacles stretched out and gripped each of us by the wrists. *He was born that way and outcast. I found him on one of my adventures and helped keep him hidden from others who wanted to harm him.*

Layla hissed. "He was born here on Gaia?"

Yes. There are eldritch living deep in the oceans, waiting for the day Cthulhu awakens.

"Wait, he took you to see a malgorth?" Hannah shuddered. "Fred, what were you thinking?"

I held up a hand. "It was a white malgorth, and he was actually quite nice."

Layla blinked. "I think Fred did a royal mind fuck on Cain. He's lost it." She made cutting noises. "Sushi time."

No, Layla! Fred's tentacles quivered. *He is a good malgorth.*

I watched Fred carefully. "Did he cure me?"

He removed much of the mind poison. But there is too much to take all at once, so it will take many visits to fully heal. Also, you need rest.

"Great, now you sound like Fitz." I had to admit I felt a lot better, as if an invisible weight was lifted from my shoulders. "How are baby malgorths made?" The image of mating malgorths flashed unpleasantly in my mind.

I have not had the opportunity to watch them mate, but hopefully soon.

"Hold up." Hannah shook her head. "Fred, how are you having adventures in your little swimming pool?"

"He has a deepway." I looked into the dark water. "I don't know how, but he does."

I do not need a deepway. Fred looked at us with his huge eyes. *The water is all connected, so I can follow it. I can take others. I discovered this when I was sad and lonely one day. Malgorths and other eldritch cannot do this, so it is probably because I am a spawn of Cthulhu.*

"You can take us anywhere there's water?" Layla's eyes brightened. "Like through city pipes?"

Hannah giggled. "Oh, we could pull a Harry Potter and pop out of the toilets at Eclipse!"

Fred blinked several times. *I cannot take anyone through pipes. That water is too clean and untouched by the world.*

"That makes no sense," I said.

It makes sense. It is unnatural water. I tried to go there but it rejects me.

"Damn." Hannah sighed. "I really wanted to jump out of the toilets at Eclipse."

"What if someone was on the toilet when you appeared?" Layla said. "Would you ram your head up their ass?"

Aura snickered and quickly covered her mouth. "That's not really funny. It's just stupid."

Hannah burst into giggles. "What if you smacked into a turd?"

I shook my head. "Fred, I need to know more about this malgorth. It reminds me of something."

His powers remind me of Hannah's. The glow is similar, but it is peaceful and calming, not deadly.

"Yes, exactly." The connection snapped into place so naturally that I had few doubts about it. "Your malgorth friend doesn't have destructive powers?"

No. He is harmless and defenseless, I'm afraid. I took him to a safe place where I take all my new friends.

"This is freaking me out, Cain." Hannah chewed on her upper lip. "Fred, I want to meet this malgorth. I need to know if he's really like me."

Gladly. Do you want to go now?

I snapped my fingers. "Wait, what other friends do you have, Fred?"

A whale I rescued from spears. Some sea turtles who were trapped in nets. Dolphins that were beached. And lots more. Would you like to meet them?

Layla snorted. "Great. We've got the eldritch version of Aqua-Man on our team."

"Nah, Fred's way cooler than that." Hannah patted his head. "Can we go see the malgorth now?"

I nodded. "I think it's important that you meet."

Let's go! Fred released us from his tentacles and waddled toward the pool.

"Um, let me go put on a swimsuit." Hannah went into her room.

"You don't have any other eldritch friends like the malgorth?" I asked while he waited.

He touched my arm with his tentacle. *My friends have heard of others, so I have gone looking. But sea life is always on the move. It is hard to follow rumor to a specific location. Thurgle thinks we are all capable of being what we want.*

"Thurgle?"

My malgorth friend.

Hannah came out of her room in yoga pants and a sports tank top. "Let's go!"

Fred took her hand with his tentacle, and they jumped into the water. There was a rush of bubbles and they vanished into the depths.

17

I stood over the pool for a moment, unable to stop thinking about the white malgorth. Was Thurgle an anomaly, or just a new possibility, a new direction for the eldritch? He might just be a random mutation, but I had a feeling there was more to it. If he was connected to Hannah somehow, then that might bode well for humanity, or it might mean our doom.

Layla took my hand. "How are you feeling, champ?"

I closed my eyes and concentrated. The murky madness was still there, but fainter. Even so, I wasn't about to test things with another ghostwalk. "I feel cleaner." I opened my eyes and offered her a wan smile. "This malgorth is a Christmas miracle."

She snorted. "Maybe I ought to give him a try. It'd be nice to clear my mind after Soultaker nearly consumed it."

"That's a good idea." I was still feeling a little high from the treatment, so I impulsively leaned forward and kissed her.

Layla pulled me closer, sighing in pleasure, then abruptly shoved me away. "None of that nonsense right now."

"Oh, don't stop on my account." Aura sat on the couch watching us. "I was about to get some popcorn."

"I'm in more of a slaying mood than laying." Layla blew me a kiss and dropped onto the couch. "Now that Cain is better, I'm ready to kick some ass."

I sat on the opposite side of my sectional couch. "Let's talk Eclipse. Is our newly acquired sigil keycard enough to get us past the traps?"

"Let me walk you through the process of entering the building." Aura crossed her legs. "Every day I'd walk into the side entrance and take the elevator to the forty-eighth floor. Anyone without a charm who stepped into the elevator lobby would become disoriented and trapped in an illusion maze. Those of us with a charm would walk from the lobby and into the security area guarded by bridge trolls."

"Bridge trolls?" Layla laughed. "Did they wear suits?"

"Actually, yea, they did. Black suits. They would scan us for magic and for nub devices. No cell phones or outside technology or magic was allowed. Only our work devices." Aura's gaze went distant, as if reliving the process. "The only way up to the penthouse was from another elevator in the back of the office, this one also guarded by illusion traps and sleep magic. Another charm was required to make it through there without falling unconscious within seconds. I only caught glimpses of the area, but there's a sigil slate securing the elevator as well. The sigil keycard we found might work for that."

Water splashed and Hannah flew up and out of the water, landing gracefully on the stone. Fred landed beside her.

"That was amazing!" Hannah laughed and hugged herself. "Thurgle is so cool."

I knew how she felt. "I take it he gave you a taste of his power?"

"A little, but it's so strange." She looked at me in wonder. "I felt connected to him somehow. Almost like we're related."

Layla grimaced. "Uncle Thurgle?"

"No, not like that." Hannah went into her room and emerged wrapped in a towel. "It's like our powers are connected somehow. But he's a malgorth, and I'm a human. It doesn't make any sense."

"I'm sure it does, we just don't know how." I tried to formulate a connection but I just didn't see how a being so alien could be related to Hannah. "Surely you don't have the same father."

"Ooh." Layla grinned lasciviously. "Or maybe he's into some really kinky stuff."

"Tentacle porn is a thing, Cain." Aura shrugged. "Although I can't imagine which god would be able to successfully mate with a freaking malgorth."

"Loki could." Hannah shivered. "My god, what if Loki is my dad?"

Loki had birthed a giant worm and even Odin's eight-legged horse, so he was a likely candidate for impregnating a malgorth. The question was, why would he do it?

"That doesn't explain your powers." I shook my head. "From what I know of Loki, his skillset is nothing like yours."

"Well, it could be another god like Loki." Aura shrugged. "That makes some kind of sense."

"But not enough." I turned to Fred. "Any suggestions?"

Fred shook his head. "No. I'm sorry."

"Maybe we should shelve this discussion for another time," Aura said. "I think we have more pressing matters."

"Flying through the water was so cool." Hannah patted Fred's head. "You're amazing."

He clapped his little hands. "Thank you, Hannah!"

She grinned. "Fred, are you sure we can't do the toilet thing? I really want to pop out of a toilet and shout, surprise!"

"I wish I could." Fred's tentacles quivered with a sigh.

"Well, there goes my toilet surprise one-liners." Layla huffed. "Look out daddy, momma brought home the toilet paper!"

Aura's eyebrows arched. "That's what you were going to say after popping out of the toilet?"

"Pretty good, right?" Layla sighed. "Fred, don't come back to me until you figure out how to make my dreams come true."

"Jumping from toilets is your dream?" Fred tilted his head in confusion.

Hannah giggled. "Fred, it's the ultimate dream."

I took a long look at Layla. "Are you in all the way now? You seemed pretty eager to get out of this mess earlier."

Layla stared at the wall, a smile spreading on her face. "When I killed those fucking goblins, it just made everything feel right again. They're dead for good. This isn't Soultaker's hellscape where they'll be back tomorrow to rip out my guts, you know? That was when I realized that Layla Blade doesn't hide from anyone. She takes them out."

"Well, at least we know what to get Layla for her birthday," Hannah said.

Aura looked confused. "What would that be?"

Hannah grinned. "A big plate of murder sauce."

Layla wrinkled her nose. "Did you just try to come up with a one-liner?"

Hannah winced. "Ugh it sucked, didn't it?"

"Yeah, it was bad." Layla shrugged. "But you're trying and that's what's important."

Aura snorted. "It's so much better than look out daddy, momma brought home the toilet paper."

I picked up the cash off the floor and shoved it back into the duffel bags. "How about we come up with a plan instead of one-liners?"

"I'm with Cain on that one." Aura looked at the fridge as if she wanted to go get a drink, but then changed her mind. "We still don't know how to reach the top floor through all of Eclipse's security."

"Didn't you say they illusion and sleep traps?" Hannah finished drying off and sat on the other side of the sectional couch. "Why didn't we run into any on Beta?"

"Because the enchantments were destroyed." I put the duffel bags on the kitchen table, then turned to Aura. "You're certain the sigil keycard won't disable the traps?"

"Yes, I'm positive." She huffed. "I already described all the layers of security. You need a charm to get through the traps, and even if you somehow made it without one, then you have to face down a pair of bridge trolls. Once you're past them, then you've got another trap guarding the only elevator that goes to the penthouse."

I nodded. "What about the stairwells?"

"The stairwells are blocked off by mithril doors and more sleep, stasis, and illusion traps." Aura shook her head. "The keycard will let us through the doors, but we'd still need charms to pass through the stairwell. I guarantee you that not even you can just waltz through two stories of fae-level traps."

"Agreed, but at least we could bypass the security in the lower office." I mulled over it. "We need to lay our hands on a charm."

"They'll still see you coming. You won't make it to the top before they send assassins down to take you out." Aura pressed her lips together. "We need a charm and oblivion cloaks for each of us."

"Oh, is that all?" Layla rolled her eyes. "Let me order those online."

I looked at the images of the Sovereign building. The lower office occupied the two stories below the penthouse, essentially locking down all access to the floors above. It was a very tough nut to crack, even with oblivion cloaks and charms.

AURA TOOK out her phone and displayed a detailed three-dimensional map of the top three floors. "My cybermancer made this rendering of the building and I labeled the danger zones." She tapped the screen to check a box. The stairwells and elevator lobbies shaded red. Another tap displayed labels detailing the spells guarding those areas. She checked another box and tiny trolls appeared in key guard locations.

Hannah stared at the diagram. "I guess the elevator shaft is out of the question."

"There's a shield spell in the elevator shaft that only the elevator can pass through. Anyone climbing the ladder will be blocked. Anyone riding on top of the elevator will be crushed." Aura set the phone on her lap. "We'll have to ambush four people leaving the office and take their charms. If we can't get oblivion cloaks, we can at least fight our way to the penthouse."

I gave it some thought. "Maybe I can disable the illusion, sleep, and stasis traps. Ambushing four people who are probably trained assassins in their own right would be extremely difficult."

Aura raised an eyebrow. "Can you dispel fae-level magic?"

"No, not without help." I shrugged. "Maybe Erolith can help me."

"Yeah, somehow I think he won't help you since the Oblivion Guard is involved in all this." Aura rotated the rendering. "This is going to be very tough."

"Is Elektrode there?" Hannah asked. "Or is he at the secret office."

"The secret one."

I made a raspberry. "Okay, so let's go over this ambush plan. Do you know who to target?"

"Sort of." Aura waggled her hand. "We had to wear facemasks to hide our identities the moment we got into the express elevator to the forty-eighth floor. We weren't allowed to ride together—only one at a time. So, I waited on the bottom floor and snapped pictures of everyone who came out of the elevator, because they usually took off the mask so as not to alarm the nubs."

"Great." I clapped my hands. "Let's see the pictures."

"Yes, but there's a slight problem." Aura flicked on her phone screen and turned it around to display the image of a woman with a blurred face. "The charms we wore also prevented nub cameras from recording our faces."

I stared at the feminine body in the picture. "So, we have to go by what their bodies look like?"

"We have height, build, and some idea what style clothing they preferred. I think we can identify them easily enough like that."

"I guess." I tapped a finger against my chin. "Do they walk in the front entrance of the building like everyone else, or is there a secret entrance?"

"Normal entrance."

"Did you record their voices? The way they walked? Anything useful?"

"I could only take pictures. Recording video was too risky." Aura flicked through more pictures. "I think this is enough. You've identified people based on less information."

"Yeah, but there will be hundreds of people entering a building that size on any given day." I shook my head. "We'll need to case the building and identify possible marks. What kind of security is on the outside of the building?"

"Eclipse has cameras of its own with facial recognition software." She turned off the phone screen. "But nothing magical as far as I know. The safe zone around the building also dispels basic illusions and other magic."

"Great." I blew out a breath. "We'll have to observe from across the street then."

"I told you it wouldn't be easy, Cain, but it's the only way in." Aura sighed. "Things have probably changed there since Torvin's death, so there are probably factors I can't account for."

"What are our objectives inside the building, exactly?" Layla looked perplexed. "We're just stealing a database and some other info so we can locate their secret headquarters?"

"That's part of it," Aura said. "That database will probably identify all the demis in their crosshairs and might have other valuable information. It might even tell us how they're crossing dimensions. The real treasure trove will be in their secret headquarters, though."

"And the other part?" Layla said.

"We kill as many of them as possible," I said. "Put a massive dent in their operations. Let them know they can't just attack us and feel safe."

Layla didn't look convinced. "Are they really going to have much of a presence in this building?"

"Since Torvin isn't living in the penthouse, it's likely someone else of importance is living there," Aura said. "Either way, if we plan this correctly, they'll never see us coming. We hit them hard and fast, then get out."

"And alert their secret HQ that we're coming." Layla crossed her arms. "If you track their network addresses, then it sounds like this Elektrode will see us coming a mile away. They'll know that we know their location."

"Not if I can use the tracing program from the Eclipse office." Aura turned off her phone screen. "Those two places exchange network traffic all the time, so it won't look out of the ordinary if I do it from there."

I nodded. "We might stir up the beehive by killing everyone at the Eclipse offices, but they won't have any idea that we know their location. And if there are Handers there with cloaks, we can take those for our own use. It's a win-win."

Layla still looked unconvinced. "Yeah, provided we ambush four handlers and steal their lucky charms without anyone knowing. We can't afford to enter the building with any fewer than all of us if we plan to fight our way to the penthouse. This whole idea feels sloppy and rushed."

Aura shook her head. "It's not a bad plan."

"It's a horrible one," Hannah replied. "We're looking at this from the wrong angle. What if we went in from the outside? We could scale the building at night and break into the penthouse quietly and murder everyone in their sleep."

"The penthouse is guarded by magically hardened glass." I challenged her with a look. "How would we get inside?"

"With your brightblade?" She made a humming noise and mimicked cutting with a sword.

"You saw how tough that glass was on Beta. Besides, anyone inside would see the brightblade before I even got started." I chuckled wryly. "Believe me, members of the Oblivion Guard are light sleepers."

"Okay, then how about we use the bathing pool in Torvin's pocket dimension?" Hannah turned to Fred. "That water is in a stone pool, so it's natural right?"

Fred shook his head and touched her arm with a tentacle.

Her smile faded. "Oh, I guess you're right."

"What did he say?" Aura asked.

"Pocket dimensions aren't connected to this water." Hannah sighed. "Damn, I thought I had something there."

Aura nodded. "I never would have thought of that."

Hannah's demigoddess DNA gave her the ability to think outside the box, but sometimes it was just too far outside. However, her original plan gave me something to think about. Ambushing four handlers and then fighting our way to the penthouse was extremely sloppy. Layla and I might be skilled fighters, but we operated best using stealth and misdirection. If we were going to survive this, then we needed to use our strengths to guide us.

The enchanted glass on the penthouse might be magically hardened, but what if there was already an opening? Torvin wasn't the kind of person who was content to look down at the ants from behind a pane of glass. He'd want to go outside, spread his arms, and have a narcissistic king of the world moment with a nice glass of drow brandy.

I turned to Aura. "Is there a balcony on the penthouse level?"

She frowned. "I never saw one. The pictures of the building on the internet aren't accurate because Eclipse heavily modified the top three levels. I'm sure there's also some fae illusion at work on the exterior."

Hannah's face brightened. "Why are you asking about a balcony, Cain?"

"Because the Torvin I knew and hated wouldn't have a penthouse without a balcony." I nodded to myself. "He'd want to go outside and look down upon the inferior humans."

"Well, we can do an outside recon with a drone," Aura said.

"And if there is a balcony, then what?" Layla said.

I held up the sigil card. "This might open it. And if that works, we can use stealth to murder as many assassins as possible before they even know what hit them."

Layla grinned and smacked her lips. "I like that part, but how are we getting up there?"

"I was thinking we could do a pendulum maneuver," Hannah said. "Just like in Mission Impossible!"

"First of all, no." I shook my head. "And second of all, there aren't any buildings tall enough to make that come even close to working."

Hannah took out her phone and looked at the street level view near the Sovereign with her maps app. "I guess you're right. And I suppose climbing it with suction cups is unrealistic."

I had a sudden burst of inspiration. "We'll parachute in."

The others regarded me with wide eyes.

Fred jumped up and down. "Fun!"

"Cain, I don't know about you, but I'm no expert with parachutes." Layla laughed uneasily. "There's no way I can nail a landing on a building without a ton of practice."

Aura shook her head. "My training included a lot, but certainly not pinpoint landings with parachutes."

"I'm willing to try," Hannah said with a grin.

Layla gave her a look. "That's because you're stupid."

I leaned back and crossed my arms. "I've never used parachutes, but I did have extensive training with Icarus wings."

"Icarus wings are completely different." Aura flipped a hand dismissively. "And impossible to get unless you're in the Oblivion Guard."

Hannah tilted her head. "Aren't those the wings that the Anubis shifters used on Alpha?"

Aura nodded. "But they're extremely flimsy and dangerous. They don't call them Icarus wings for nothing."

"Infiltrating Eclipse from the ground floor is even more dangerous and stupid." I shrugged. "Why not bypass all those challenges and go straight for the top? Besides, there are ways to mitigate the dangers of Icarus wings."

"Assuming we could even get four pairs of them, how, exactly, does one mitigate the dangers?" Aura stared at me expectantly.

"We use them like gliders. No active propulsion except for landing." I stared back at her.

"What about clockwork wings like Esteri and the others used?" Hannah said. "They might be easier to control, and a lot easier to find."

I snapped my fingers. "Even better idea. We have connections on Alpha who can supply us with them."

Aura looked uncertain. "Are you sure clockwork wings are better than Icarus wings?"

"They're easier to get." I shrugged. "I have no idea if they're safer."

Hannah turned to Aura. "Obviously, we'll have to train with whatever we get, but I think we can agree wings are probably safer and easier to use than parachutes."

"Agreed." Layla glanced at the money bags. "Do you have enough money to buy clockwork wings?"

"We should be able to get them at no cost," I said. "After all, we know all three Horatios on Alpha."

"True." Layla pursed her lips. "I say we go get them ASAP. I need to see how they handle."

"First thing in the morning." I yawned. "I'm exhausted."

"Sleep, Cain." Fred's mouth tentacles stretched toward me. "You need rest."

"That's for sure." I rapped my knuckles on the kitchen table. "Can one of you procure a drone and scope out the top floors of the Sovereign? I need to know for sure if there's a balcony."

"I'll do it!" Hannah raised her hand eagerly. "I just need some money."

"You'll have to make sure you don't violate nub laws," Aura said. "They're picky about who can fly drones in the middle of the city."

"I'm going to take it to the roof of a neighboring building and launch it from there." Hannah shrugged. "Should be easy enough."

Aura nodded. "I'll go with you."

"I'll go with Cain tomorrow to get the wings." Layla stretched, bones cracking. "I'm going to bed too."

"Sounds like a plan." I went downstairs to my meditation room first. A good fifteen-minute session in the small room would be a real test of how much madness remained in me. Small glowing white flowers grew from cracks in the walls, the floor, and even the ceiling. They were the strange byproduct of Hannah's meditations.

Not always, but sometimes when she meditated, these other-worldly flowers would sprout despite there being no nutrients or even water in the stone floor. I'd also seen her grow monstrous flowers with gaping jaws, humanoid flower babies, and worse. Sometimes her creations were wondrous and sometimes they were terrifying. I hoped that one day my training would pay off and she could control her powers.

That day, it seemed, was still a long way off.

My meditations were mostly calm, but Cthulhu's orange eyes lurked over the horizon of my mind. It seemed Thurgle had worked wonders for me. I went back upstairs to my room and locked the door. Whatever the albino malgorth had done to me had made me even more tired than I'd been earlier. I brushed my teeth, showered, and got into bed.

As I started to drift off, I felt the darkness creeping up on me. The twin orange suns of Cthulhu's gaze rose on the imaginary horizon. But the sensation was weaker than normal. Less pronounced. The nightmares commenced, but they were noticeably weaker than before.

The malgorth, it seemed, had helped me more than I could have hoped. And if I was going to get through this, I'd need all the help I could get.

18

Breakfast the next morning was a loud, busy affair as we discussed the day's plans over pancakes and bacon. Then Hannah and Aura left to find a drone for scouting the Sovereign building, and Layla and I prepared to go to Alpha.

The mechanists in Alpha were headquartered near Voltaire's. The once secret watering hole for the supernatural community had risen from the ashes into a hub for mechanist inventors and magic users alike. The evolution of Gaia Alpha had taken a sharp turn away from that of Prime's, where the nubs still knew nothing of vampires, were-wolves, wizards, and the like.

Layla and I got into Dolores and headed out. I planned to get as close to our Voltaire's as possible before using the Tetron to take us to Alpha. The Handers were probably watching both establishments, but there wasn't much we could do except to be careful.

I parked near the Vortex a few streets over from Voltaire's, then we got out of the car and walked to the back of the parking lot where there were few eyes to watch us. We linked arms and I took us into the multidimensional array, switched to Alpha, and dropped us in the same relative place. In this case, it was on a sidewalk next to a personal rail station, since Little Five Points, like most of Atlanta, had been demolished during the mechanist attacks and rebuilt in this dimension.

There were multiple mass transit options in this dimension, but the personal rail station was the easiest. It consisted of small rail cars with enough room for four passengers. Each car moved quickly until they reached a micro-station where they stopped long enough for passengers to disembark, and for new passengers to climb in. Any cars coming behind would slow on approach and queue up.

We hopped into the next car, and it accelerated, zipping down the sidewalk to the next station a few blocks away. We got out at the station near Voltaire's, then quickly walked into the safezone before any lurking guardians took a potshot at us.

Layla frowned. "Are safe zones even safe anymore? If the fae from other dimensions are trying to kill us with the cooperation of the local fae, then they could just ignore the safe zone rules, right?"

"Maybe." I shrugged. "Be ready for anything."

"Except we can't fight back while we're inside the zone." Her eyes scanned the area. "I hate that they get invisibility, and we don't."

"I have one cloak, but I haven't had time to recharge it yet." I took out my staff and looked for auras through the scope. "We need cloaks for our assault on Eclipse to achieve maximum efficiency."

"I can't wait to have my very own cloak." Her eyes brightened. "Now I'm really looking forward to fighting."

"There's your silver lining." The Voltaire's here looked like a giant Victorian mansion. Aura Alpha lived in the penthouse at the top. It was a grand looking place, but it certainly didn't have the character of its original format.

I knocked on the front door.

The speakeasy panel slid open and Durrug Alpha peered at us. He opened the door without asking for the password then showed me a romance novel with a shirtless troll fondling a female cecrops on the front. "Other Durrug read this one yet?"

"I don't recognize it, but I also haven't been able to go there much lately." Durrug and his alt like trading book recommendations, though it had also turned into something of a competition. The smuttier, the better. I was just amazed there were so many romance novels with trolls and cecrops in them.

He closed the door behind us and sat back down to continue reading. Aura Alpha locked eyes with us as soon as we entered. The frown on her face flattened into hopeful expectation. We went to the bar and sat down.

"Cain?" Aura began mixing a mangorita without asking. "Why are you here? I thought this place was too hot to visit."

I shrugged. "Cain Alpha filled you in on the situation?"

"Hemlock called." She glanced around nervously. "There are people watching this place for the Oblivion Guard. They've probably notified them that you're here."

"It's all good." I looked upstairs where mechanists in blue jump-suits drank and made merry with their companions. "We're here to procure some supplies that we can't get on Prime."

"Mechanists supplies, I'm guessing?"

I nodded. "Clockwork wings."

Aura's brow furrowed. "Those are very expensive and heavily regulated. The nubs went crazy for all things mechanist during Reconstruction. Clockwork wings were a major hit, but so many people were dying and committing crimes with them that they had to regulate their sale."

"You seem to know an awful lot about clockwork wings," Layla said.

Aura rolled her eyes. "Because I hear everything here. I have eyes and ears of my own. This world might look like it's transformed into a perfect mechanist Utopia, but the underbelly is far worse than it ever was now that nubs know about supers and have access to magic."

"Jealous nubs don't like supers." I sighed. "Are there many hate crimes here?"

"Tons, but the nubs usually come out on the losing end." Aura waved away the issue. "Anyway, I can point you in the direction of clockwork wings." She set down a frosty mangorita with all the fixings. "But they'll cost you a lot."

Layla snorted. "But this is Cain, the man who saved this pathetic world. Shouldn't he be able to get them for free?"

"There's still a lot of goodwill for Cain, but there's also a faction of mechanists who despise him for ruining their plans for world domination." Aura rapped her fingers on the bar. "And they're the ones who control the patents and regulations for clockwork wings now."

"What about Horatio and his alts?" I rapped my knuckles on the counter. "I was hoping to speak to one of them."

"They're on the outs in the mechanist community." She shook her head. "He and his loyalists set up shop on the opposite side of Atlanta since the Futurists took over this side."

"Futurists?" I groaned. "Gods be damned. Give people something good and it takes them no time to fuck it up. So now there are competing mechanist factions?"

"Two of them so far. The Futurists made friends in the government and new patent laws were passed, granting their faction rights to already existing inventions even though Horatio and the Traditionalists argued they're the ones who originally created them."

"But due to the destruction of civilization, they don't have proof, right?" I took a sip of the mangorita and relished the sweet taste with the bite of alcohol. "Karma sucks sometimes."

"Exactly." Aura turned to Layla. "What do you want to drink?"

"Goblin rye."

Aura looked impressed. "Branching out, are we?"

"It's my go-to when I'm mentally prepping to kill some fuckers." Layla locked eyes with a pair of people across the room. "We're going to have a fight on our hands the minute we leave the safe zone."

I nodded. "Where can we find these Futurists, and do you think they'll do business with me?"

"They'll definitely do business with you because they have to." Aura lifted a bottle of dark green alcohol from the top shelf and poured some into a glass for Layla. "Cain still controls the demis, and if he's not happy, nobody's happy. He's also built himself a small army of free demis, although that's not what he calls it."

"Hemlock mentioned his training camp on an island in Lake Lanier."

She nodded. "The nub government doesn't like it, and neither do the Futurists, but they don't dare mess with him."

Layla smirked. "I think I'm more impressed with Cain Alpha than this guy right now." She took a sip of rye and hissed. "Damn, I love that burn."

"It is pretty impressive." I had no desire to train or take on the responsibility of housing and caring for superpowered kids. Cain Alpha could deal with that. Maybe he needed it as insurance in this dimension. It certainly meant he had a better chance of surviving the Oblivion Guard than I did.

I took another long sip of mangorita. "Tell me where to go."

Aura took out her phone and dropped a pin on the map. "It's just down the street, shaped like a giant flying saucer."

"Like their secret underwater base?"

She nodded. "Yep."

Layla laughed. "Does this one have legs too?"

"Probably." Aura leaned on the counter. "Just go inside. They'll recognize you and someone who can help you will make themselves available."

"I was hoping to get something for free." I blew out a breath. "Guess I should've brought along some extra money."

"Yeah, the Cain here was pretty peeved that he can't rob banks anymore." She shook her head. "The nubs know about magic, so now they use wards to protect their money. The Mages Guild has been making serious bank with their magical security business."

Layla gave me a sly glance. "We have options."

"Well, use caution, because this isn't the wild west anymore." Aura walked to the other end of the bar to help another customer.

"Maybe you can't use Panoptes, but I sure can." Layla took a gulp of goblin rye and sighed with contentment. "Let's go case the Futurist complex and find out where they keep the clockwork wings."

"Good idea." I finished my mangorita quickly and left cash on the counter.

Aura hurried back over to us as we were getting up. "Is this Prime cash?"

I nodded.

She pushed it back over to me. "I can't use it anymore. All money is minted with magical ink to prevent counterfeiting now." Aura pulled a crystal from behind the counter and held it over the money. She produced a dollar bill from her pocket and set it next to mine. Hers glowed slightly while mine didn't.

"Just fucking great." I groaned. "I can't use my money over here?"

"I'm afraid not." She reclaimed her dollar bill and gave me mine. "I don't mind your drinks on the house, Cain. But the Futurists might not feel the same."

"Wonderful." I stuffed my money back into my wallet.

She put her hand on mine. "One more thing I've been hearing a lot about cross-dimensional interference. Apparently, some of the supers in this world aren't happy about the nubs knowing about them and decided to move onto greener pastures in Prime. There's word of an underground railroad for people who want out of Alpha and into Prime."

"Aldus Bergstrom's alt is in our Seattle," I said. "But we have no idea how he or anyone else from this dimension is getting over there. Unless the mechanists have come up with a way to cross over."

"When nubs found out Seattle was overrun with vampires, they revolted. It's no longer a vampire stronghold, and that's probably why Bergstrom Alpha made the move to Prime." She glanced down the counter to make sure no one else was nearby. "The mechanists are working on interdimensional travel, but they're not making progress."

I pshawed. "Why am I not surprised they're working on it?"

Aura leaned closer. "The Futurists and Traditionalists are in a race to make the first working prototype with the blessing of the nub government, but my sources say they're nowhere close to success."

"Thank the gods." Layla wrinkled her nose. "We don't need any more contamination from this place than we already have."

"That technology would be unimaginably dangerous." I scowled. "Travelers from Alpha might not be too bad, but what if they decide to go to Beta and open a gateway from that hell world?" I waved my arm around. "You can kiss all this goodbye."

"Point made." Aura smiled wanly. "Let's just say there are plenty of high beings that don't want that to happen, fae included."

"Good." I blew out a breath. "We need to find out who's helping travelers now before a world-ending event happens."

"I'll let my Cain know if I hear anything. He can pass the information along."

"Thanks." I turned to go, but Aura grabbed my arm. "By the way, we had some interesting visitors here not long ago. They came looking specifically for you."

I raised an eyebrow. "People come looking for me all the time, and it usually means trouble."

"In this case, I think it was good. Specifically, it was a certain snake-haired lady who wanted to thank you."

I blinked. "Dusa?"

"Medusa, her sisters, and a number of descendants." Aura shook her head. "This place emptied out so fast, I thought we were being invaded by Shub-Nuggurath."

"Medusa herself came looking for me?" I paused to take it in. "She knows that I don't even live in this dimension, right?"

"She was hoping you might stop by and visit sometime." Aura shrugged. "I told her it didn't happen that often."

Layla slapped my back. "Nice, Cain. You ready to tell her you fucked her daughter on Prime? Maybe you can get her in the sack too."

"No, thanks." I gave the situation some thought. Not because I wanted to be thanked by Medusa, but because she could be a valuable asset. "How long ago was this?"

"Few weeks ago." Aura let go of my arm. "They're gone now, back to Feary, I think."

"Thanks for telling me."

"Uh-oh." Layla patted my shoulder. "Are you thinking about asking them for help?"

"Yeah. On Prime at least." I glanced at the people watching us. "We've got other business to worry about first."

"It might be better if you take my secret underground exit," Aura said. "Go into the back toward the restrooms, go up the stairs, and to the elevator. I'll meet you there." She turned and went into the kitchen.

I took another look around the room, then went to the end of the bar, around it, and into the back. A troll wearing a chef's hat emerged from the unispecies bathroom and went into an employee's-only door. Layla and I walked up the stairs, looking back to see if anyone was following us.

Aura stood next to an old-school elevator with a cage door in the upstairs lobby. She traced a complex series of sigils on the gray slate next to it, and the door opened. "Use the sub-cellar button to go to the lowest sublevel. Walk to the end of the second aisle and pull on the fourth wine bottle from the wall on the lowest rack. That will open a secret door to my clockwork chariot. There's a map on the dashboard. Touch the pin at the intersection near the address I gave you, and it'll automatically take you there."

"Fancy," Layla said. "Now get back out there and pretend you're not helping us."

"Already on it." Aura went through a secured door and closed it behind her.

We got into the elevator and the cage slid shut. Layla pressed the button, and we began to descend just as the people who'd been watching us came up the stairs. We ducked before they saw us, but they'd likely realize the elevator was in use and assume it was us.

I just hoped they didn't have a way to follow us. They didn't look like Oblivion Guard, but if they were, it was likely they could attack us in the safe zone while we could do nothing except run.

19

The lift descended slowly, dropping past several levels filled with wine racks, alcohol, and food supplies. It creaked to a stop in a wine cellar with stonework that looked far too old to be part of a newly constructed building.

"I think we're safe." I looked up the shaft through the caged top of the lift, halfway expecting to see a brightblade carving open the elevator door far above. Seconds ticked past, and there was no sign of pursuit, so I stepped out of the elevator. The door closed behind us.

"I think these sublevels existed at the old Voltaire's." Layla ran a hand along old brickwork. "You think our Aura has a secret escape tunnel too?"

"Probably." I walked to the end of the second aisle and pulled the wine bottle as instructed. The brick wall slid aside, revealing a long sewage tunnel that was too clean to have been used in recent history. "This is too far underground to use for sewage and water runoff. Why is this even here in the first place?"

"Maybe they tried to create another Underground on this side of town." Layla touched the stonework. "It's old, but not that old."

The Underground had been exactly what it sounded like—an underground town built by goblins and other beings who'd been exiled from Feary and forced to live in a world where they couldn't simply pass as humans without serious magical help. It had naturally turned into a haven for criminals of all varieties even as it functioned as a home for non-humans.

It was likely they'd tried to expand since some of those groups didn't get along very well in close quarters. I'd had to venture there on a number of occasions to locate fugitives and tag them for Eclipse. Its denizens liked to think it was a convoluted warren of tunnels where even the vaunted Oblivion Guard would have problems locating people, but they apparently didn't understand the power of tracking sigils, like the ones I'd used in the labyrinth of Minos. I'd once set up an entire network of echo-location sigils just to help me map out a section of the Underground.

We walked down a ramp to a set of narrow rails where a brass chariot with four wheels and a plush seat was parked. A footlocker on one side of the chariot contained an assortment of clockwork rifles and pistols.

Layla whistled. "Our sweet little elf doesn't play around, does she?"

"I think she intentionally lets us underestimate her abilities." I examined the embossed map on the brass dashboard. It was circular and displayed several city blocks in a radius around Voltaire's, giving the user plenty of directions to escape in. The place we wanted to go was at the outer edge of the radius to the north.

I pressed the button at the nearest intersection and the clockwork chariot ticked to life, rolling down the tunnel toward the destination.

"Do you think the safe zone extends all the way down here?"

I nodded. "A safe zone forms a sphere of protection extending up into the sky and down into the ground for nearly half a mile."

"Fucking fae." Layla sighed and leaned back against the cushioned seat.

"You seem more like yourself." I regarded her for a moment. "I like it."

"Yeah, me too." She leaned over and kissed me on the lips. "Thank you."

My lips tingled pleasantly. "For what?"

"Everything you did to get me out of that hellhole." She kissed me again. "I wouldn't have done the same for you."

"I know." I pulled her closer and kissed her lips, her neck, her ears. "I'm a masochist like that."

"I know." She sighed and slid away from me. "I should be drunk at a party right now, not gallivanting around with you, and certainly not making out like a teenager with you."

"Unfortunately, your association with me has made you a target." I gazed at the stone wall. "I also don't know why I just stated the obvious."

"Well, be happy I'm here. And maybe I'll get a sweet little oblivion cloak out of this mess."

"Yeah, wouldn't that be nice?" I summoned my staff and scouted ahead with the scope. It was unlikely we'd encounter anyone down here, but there was no such thing as being too careful when it came to the fae and the Oblivion Guard.

The chariot ticked to a halt on a circular platform. The platform rotated slowly until the chariot faced back the way we'd come. We got out and the vehicle rolled away, presumably back to its starting point. A ladder on the tunnel wall extended up into a shaft. I examined the hole with my scope but didn't see anything suspicious.

This was apparently the only way out, so I grabbed the first rung and started climbing. I'd gone about fifty feet when I realized just how nice it was to climb up a dark shaft without worrying about some eldritch creature trying to snatch me with its tongue.

A horizontal tunnel about eight feet in diameter intersected the ladder at the top. I climbed out and walked forward to a metal door at the end, Layla close on my heels. There was no latch on the door, but it swung open when we reached it. I stepped out and into an alley. Once Layla joined me, the door swung shut, vanishing seamlessly into the brick wall.

Layla searched the wall. "This is seriously good craftsmanship. Like dwarf level if I had to guess."

"Agreed." I noticed a dark blemish to the left of where the door had been. "This is probably where you trace the sigils to get back in."

"That bitch didn't even give us the codes." Layla ran her hand along the brick. "Well, at least we have the Tetron."

I walked to the end of the alley. Clockwork vehicles ticked past on the busy avenue. There was a hubbub of conversation from people eating, drinking, and talking on patios outside restaurants. There were brightly lit stores offering clockwork wares alongside stores selling nub technology.

To the north was a wide plot of concrete, and in the center was a shiny chrome saucer that looked as if it could have been plucked from a vintage sci-fi movie. The avenue split in two directions, circling the massive structure. A huge neon sign in front of the building boasted, *The Future is Here.*

"Crazy mechanists." Layla shook her head. "Looks like there's plenty of foot traffic through the area, so I don't think they care who walks through."

I strode onto the sidewalk and toward the building, keeping an eye out for anyone or anything suspicious. The aroma of pizza from one of the restaurants threatened to derail my concentration even though it was far too early to be thinking about lunch. It also made me wonder why they were making pizza in the middle of the morning.

As we neared the Futurist building, I noticed that some of the foot traffic on their property consisted of shiny chrome automatons. The clockwork robots approached pedestrians as they entered the perimeter and spoke with them for a short time. Sometimes, the bots escorted people toward the building. Other times, they simply let them go on their way.

Layla noted the same thing. "Interesting."

"Yeah." I was impressed with how smoothly the bots walked. They were at least as good as some golems I'd encountered. Mechanist technology had come a long way in a very short period of time on this world. Or maybe all these inventions existed long ago, but never saw the light of day on a world dominated by nubs who knew nothing of the supernatural.

We reached the perimeter and continued onward toward the building. A bot just ahead of us came to life and approached. "Good day. I am here to help if you need it. What is your destination? Your options are, just passing through, I'd like to visit the retail store, I'd like to visit the factory, or I'd like to talk with a representative." It stood still, the flickering camera eyes watching us.

I chose the best answer. "A representative, please."

Clockwork ticked audibly in the bot's metal skull. The shutters on its camera lens eyes clicked shut. It remained motionless for a moment then sprang to life again. "Parameters bypassed. Entering Cain protocol." It stiffened. "Please follow me."

I tilted my head. "Cain protocol?"

"Yes. You are a priority individual." It rotated smoothly on a heel and pointed to the building. "Please follow me."

"How do these things even work?" Layla whispered. "They don't use computers, do they?"

"No idea." I watched the shiny chrome bot walk smoothly away from us. "Must be some kind of magical programming."

Layla shrugged. "Are we following that thing?"

I nodded. "Might as well."

"The Futurists sure love chrome," Layla said as we followed our guide. "Don't know if I like it better than the Traditionalist brass though."

I shielded my eyes from the sunlight reflecting off the saucer dome. "I think both sides could mix it up a little instead of going with the same look for everything."

"Yeah. At least antique brass doesn't completely give away your position on a battlefield."

The bot led us past long lines of people waiting to enter the main doors of the complex to a side entrance. Its eyes flashed in a sequence and the door slid open. We continued into a large circular lobby with polished white floors, walls, and ceilings. The furniture was retro, minimalist, and bright white.

"Chrome and white." Layla nodded. "Got it."

"I'm beginning to wonder if the Futurists are actually run by Apple."

Layla snorted. "Sure looks like it."

A bot standing behind a counter clicked to life. The eyes on the bot guiding us flashed a sequence of lights and the other bot went inactive again. Aside from the door we'd just entered, there didn't seem to be a way out of the room. There were no doors, no hallways, no stairs. My hand itched to summon my staff, but my sigils weren't tingling.

The floor vibrated and gravity increased. The entire room was an elevator, and we were going up.

Layla sensed it too. "Let's hope their Cain protocol doesn't involve dumping us into an incinerator."

"At this point, nothing would surprise me." I turned to the bot. "Where are we going?"

Its eye lenses flickered on. "I am taking you to the representatives who can best help you, Cain." Its lights dimmed, and it went still again.

"Unhelpful." Layla cracked her knuckles and wiggled her fingers. "Someone might get a dagger in the throat if they don't tell us what's going on."

The room jolted to a halt. Latches clicking into place boomed in the emptiness of the shaft below. The room rotated with a mechanical whir, gears ticking smoothly until more latches engaged to halt it. A long length of wall slid open to reveal a conference room where a lone man in a white business suit sat at the head of the table. He was a silver fox, handsome, probably in his mid-fifties, and with a commanding presence about him. The bot came to life and walked into the room.

"Your guests have arrived, sir." It bowed deeply.

"Standby mode," the man said in a deep voice. He sipped the rest of a green liquid from a plastic cup and turned to another bot. "Fetch another matcha tea latte, no sugar for me."

Our bot turned, walked to the side of the room, and went still.

The other bot took the empty cup and walked to the wall. A section slid open, the bot exited, and the wall closed seamlessly.

The walls of this room curved to form an oval space. The outer wall was one large window, giving a wide view of the city beyond where cranes and workers were still rebuilding the city.

The man remained seated. "Cain Prime, this is an unexpected pleasure. We've dealt extensively with your alt here in Alpha but haven't had the chance to acquaint ourselves with you."

The way he phrased the statement made it sound like familiarizing themselves with me was more akin to a science project than a social visit. "I wasn't even aware the mechanists had split into factions." I pulled out one of the curvy chairs and sat down. It was even less comfortable than it looked. "Who are you?"

"Sato, at your service." He nodded ever so slightly as if to indicate just how much he was at my service. "I am on the Futurist board of directors."

"You must be an inventor, then."

He shook his head. "I'm the head constable, though we don't use that outdated phrase anymore. Now we are peacekeepers."

"You people are really shaking things up." Layla sat down and drummed her fingers on the glass tabletop. "What caused the split?"

"We were strongly against the attempted takeover of nub civilization." He clasped his hands together. "We wanted a peaceful union of mechanist and nub technology, much like it is now. But Horatio and his twisted cohort of Traditionalists had the power and the opportunity to destroy and did so with little thought to consequences."

"Ah, so you're the good guys." Layla smirked. "Got it. Is that why you stole all their patents and drove them out of this side of town?"

"We seized that which they had willfully misused." Sato shrugged. "I know to an outsider this must seem rather cruel, but I can assure you that we fully intend to follow Cain Alpha's plan for reconstruction. There will be no more wars in our future."

"It's awfully naïve to assume that." Layla shook her head. "By booting out the other mechanists, you're giving them a reason to fight back one day."

Sato shook his head. "Cain enforces the peace with the threat of his demis. I don't think anyone dares go against that kind of power."

I really wasn't here for a lesson in the new world order of Alpha, so I skipped to the point. "We're here because we need some hard-to-find equipment. I was told you can help us."

"I am happy to help." He crossed his legs. "Tell me what you need."

"Clockwork wings."

His eyebrows rose slightly. "Those are restricted items, per the provisional government's rules."

"Well, surely they can be unrestricted for me." I held my gaze on him. "I would hope that I warrant an exception."

"Cain Alpha made it clear there were to be no exceptions to the provisional government's rulings." Sato cleared his throat. "We would need to submit requisition forms to the Special Requests Committee—"

Layla smacked her hand on the table. "We saved your world. We're not subject to your stupid laws. Make a phone call and get us our clockwork wings."

Sato ran a finger around his collar. "I don't make the rules. If I authorize the sale of restricted inventory to anyone, even you, then I'll be committing a crime. I'm happy to submit a request on your behalf. The wait time is only four to six weeks right now."

I worked my jaw back and forth. "I don't mean to be a Karen right now, but I want to talk to the manager."

"There is no one here who can—"

"Maybe you aren't clear on who controls what here." I leaned toward him. "Cain Alpha controls the demis only because I let him. I have priority and could easily call a couple of them to come visit your lovely establishment to ensure I get exactly what I'm asking for."

His calm, assured demeanor faltered with a gulp. "I was not aware that was the case." Sweat beaded on his forehead. "But I can't help you."

"How about this?" I stood. "Take us to the clockwork wings. We'll take what we need, and you can tell anyone who asks you that it was under threat of force. No crime, no foul."

He rose to his feet. "I'd prefer you not do that."

I shrugged. "Great. Now that we've settled that, take us to the clockwork wings, or Esteri and pals will come pay you a visit." It wasn't a bluff, but I also didn't have a direct way to communicate with her or the other demis that remained under Cthulhu's control. I also assumed Cain Alpha wouldn't appreciate me messing with the peace, no matter how fragile it really was.

"Cain, I'm going to have to ask you to leave." Some of his self-assuredness returned. "We're not entirely helpless even against Esteri and her thugs. In fact, we've made arrangements to protect our interests."

"Yeah, with whom?" Layla produced a dagger and twirled it in her fingers. "The Mages Guild? Mother Theresa?"

He smirked, and I knew in that instant who his new allies were just as my body sigils tingled madly in dire warning.

20

Sato backed away, his smirk broadening into a grin. "They're all yours, guardians."

Layla spun and threw three daggers at once. One of them smashed into the automaton as a pair of gun barrels extended from its chest. The bot toppled over. The other two daggers bounced off thin air, eliciting grunts from the cloaked guardians.

"Wow, slow reactions." Layla grinned. "I thought guardians were quicker than that."

Close quarters combat with cloaked assassins wasn't high on my list of favorite things, so I ghostwalked toward Sato. The wall behind him opened and he slipped through. The opening closed before I could grab him. Rather than draw my staff in the small space, I unsheathed my dueling wands and traced sigils to either side of me. The patterns glowed, one frost white, the other red.

The air around them heated and cooled, causing fog to billow across the room. The fog wasn't thick. It wasn't meant to hide us. It was meant to reveal hidden objects in enclosed spaces. Volumetric displacement spells were handy like that. Fog swirled as a pair of cloaked guardians moved toward us.

Layla's eyes brightened. "Only two of you? Hot damn, Cain, I can see my new oblivion cloak already."

The guardians seemed to realize we could see them due to the spell and dropped their cloaks. Brightblades hummed to life. Layla jumped back onto the table as humming energy slashed downward. She whirled, leg kicking out. The guardian blocked with a forearm and slashed with the brightblade at her other leg.

Layla flipped forward, grabbed the guardian by the head and twisted violently. The assassin spun in the same direction, narrowly avoiding a broken neck. Layla lashed back with a foot and knocked the guardian to the floor.

The other assassin, a gray-faced drow, lashed out at me with his oblivion staff. I dodged back, sheathed my wands, and drew my staff. Our weapons clashed. He tried to kick me, but I blocked it with my knee, spun sideways, and sent him off balance. He fell against the table. Threw off his hood and pushed upright, teeth clenched in anger. His brightblade ignited.

I didn't especially like using a brightblade in such tight quarters but followed my attacker's example and powered mine as well. We exchanged a flurry of strikes, each of us parrying the other, backing up, then pushing forward on an offensive. It took one cycle of exchanges for me to find the attacker's weakness.

Like most guardians, he'd been taught how not to telegraph his moves. How to account for patterns. How to avoid being predictable. But like most living beings, there were minute flaws in his mechanics. Despite the anger on his face, he maintained a calm demeanor and balanced fighting form. But he overextended his jabs, putting too much weight forward of his front leg. It delayed his retreat by a fraction of a second more than it should take.

It wasn't much, but I'd take it.

I drove him back toward the window, feinted with an overextension of my own, and drew back from the jab with a slight hesitation. His eyes narrowed ever so slightly as he took note of my mistake, just as he was trained to do. It was difficult to tell if he'd believed it, but I'd find out a in a minute.

He went on the offensive, driving me back, then faltered just enough to give me an opening for a counter-offensive. At that moment, I knew he'd believed my mistake to be real. He was trying to make me think I'd found his weakness, so I'd overcommit with another jab. Ironically, that was exactly what I was trying to do to him. He just didn't realize that yet. I flared my eyes dramatically and lunged, seemingly with everything I had. His eyes narrowed with satisfaction as he dodged to the side and drove his brightblade deep into my ribs.

At least that's what he meant to do. I used my momentum to roll forward. Since he believed his blade would pierce me, he'd given a little extra thrust to his jab. That turned his overextension into a stumble. I rose to my feet and delivered a quick slash. His head rolled, neck smoking as the white-hot energy from my blade cauterized his flesh.

Layla slow clapped behind me. I turned around. She sat on the table, legs crossed, a smirk on her face. Her would-be assassin lay in a puddle of blood face down on the floor. Their cloak sat on the table next to Layla.

I'd seen her fighting an instant before, so it was obvious she'd defeated her opponent only seconds before me. I tugged the cloak off the guardian I'd killed, then picked up his head and examined the face.

"Alas, poor Yorick?" Layla said.

"I don't know this guy." I dropped the head. "Or the one you killed. Looks like they're sending in whoever happens to be nearby."

Layla tried on the cloak. It was a little tight on the arms but wasn't a bad fit. The one I'd procured was a little baggier but better than the one I'd taken before.

"How do you work this thing?" she said.

I traced sigils on the front, and she shimmered out of sight. I did the same with mine, then reached out and found her arm. I held on for several seconds, allowing the cloaks to pair. A ghostly shadow version of Layla appeared next to me.

Layla whistled. "Freaky. So, this is how they see each other even when no one else can?"

"Yep." I let go of her arm. "Every time you uncloak, it resets."

"How do I activate my own cloak? I don't want to have to rely on you to do it every time."

"Behave yourself and I might tell you."

Her shadowy face grinned. "Cain, don't ask for the impossible." Her grin turned lascivious. "Have you ever had sex in one of these things?"

"Less talking, more stealing." I looked around the room. "We need to find the clockwork wings and get out of here."

Layla bent down and picked up the oblivion staff of her fallen opponent. "Should we take these with us?"

I nodded. "Never hurts to have backup staffs."

"You have Panoptes with you?" Layla picked up the other oblivion staff. "I'll spirit these over to the warehouse."

I took it out of a pouch and gave it to her. She slid it on and winced. "Oh, fuck. What's wrong with this thing?"

"What do you mean?"

She vanished. A few seconds ticked past, and she reappeared without the staffs. Pain etched on her face, she tore off the ring and threw it at me.

I caught it. "Mind telling me what happened?"

"The instant I put it on, it was like I had worms in my eyes. It hurt my head so bad, I wasn't sure I could use the ring."

I grimaced. "Like black worms crawling across your eyes?"

She nodded. "Did—did you infect the ring?"

"Holy shit." I blew out a breath. "I must have. I didn't even realize that was possible."

"Well, Panoptes is nothing but eyes. If you saw Cthulhu when you put on the ring, so did the eyes on the ring." She shook her head. "It's usable, but just barely. What if it infects anyone who uses it?"

"Then we've got one more issue to worry about." I sighed. "We might need to use it to steal the clockwork wings."

"Can't we just grab them and use the Tetron to take them with us?" Layla rubbed her eyes. "I don't want to risk Panoptes again."

"That's the plan, but Panoptes is the backup." I touched the wall where Sato had vanished, but there weren't any visible levers, switches, or buttons. The Futurists seemed to have done away with all Traditionalist designs except for the clockwork mechanisms.

Layla ran her hands along the wall. "Let's just use the Tetron to get out, then we'll come back cloaked."

"Might be the easiest option." I took out the Tetron and manipulated its components. While it didn't work underground, it had no problems operating inside buildings, even if we were several stories up. But when I activated it, nothing happened. A slight pain pierced my temple, and that was when I knew our options just narrowed.

Layla's shadow leaned closer. "What's wrong?"

"This building is protected by a safe zone or something similar."

"Why am I not surprised?" Layla scowled. "How are we getting out of this room? How did the guardians get in here without us seeing the walls open?"

I gave it some thought. "I think they were already here waiting. The Futurists are aligned with the fae, or at least cooperating with them."

"Seems like willful cooperation," Layla said. "Sato looked happy at the thought of us dying. That entire show he put on was just an act."

"Yeah." I tapped my fingers on the wall. It felt like the same kind of material used for the transparent hull on mechanist submarines. It was at least as tough as titanium, meaning slicing through it with a brightblade wasn't a good option. The door slid into the wall, driven by clockwork cogs and gears. There was no good way to spring it open.

I tested the transparent wall and confirmed that it wasn't glass, but the same stuff as the wall. "This place is a fortress."

"Not even a little surprised." Layla sighed. "I guarantee you it has giant crab legs too, just like their secret underwater base."

A faint ticking drew my gaze to the downed automaton. Its head had been dented by the dagger, but it didn't seem to be otherwise damaged. I knelt in front of it. "Bot, I need you to open a door for me."

"C-c-c-command?" The bot stuttered. "Initiate...protocol."

I didn't know any of its commands, so I just winged it. "Door unlock protocol."

"Command not recognized."

"Emergency escape protocol."

"Processing." Clockwork whirred. The bot's limbs jerked as if trying to move, but the damage to its head apparently affected its motor control. "Emergency escape protocol activated." Its eyes flashed a sequence like the one I'd seen opening doors earlier.

I hefted its torso, but it was heavier than it looked. I turned to Layla. "Help me with this thing."

She gripped the bot from the other side, and we lifted it. Its eyes continued flashing in different sequences with a pause between each. It was probably programmed with codes for most of the doors in this place. I just hoped some were the doors we needed.

We dragged the bot to the wall Sato had opened. There was nothing visible like a slate or anything to open the door, so I let the bot keep flashing and hoped for the best. The best happened a moment later and the wall slid open to reveal a corridor.

A squad of automatons stood in the hallway, gun barrels extending from their chests. Their eyes lit the moment the bot appeared in front of them, but they didn't open fire.

One bot in the front spoke. "Friendly protocol engaged."

"They can't see us with the cloaks on," Layla whispered.

The lead bot's eyes flashed and rotated, searching for the source of the voice.

I whispered back. "No, but they can hear us."

"Anomaly protocol engaged," the lead bot intoned in its friendly butler voice. "Searching."

I didn't see how we'd lug the heavy bot down the hall and through its comrades, so I motioned Layla to set it down. We dropped it and it thudded heavily on the floor. This drew the lead bot's attention, but it still took no action.

We squeezed through the blockade of bots, causing some of them to shift sideways. Our movements caused no reaction since their sensors, visual or otherwise, couldn't detect us through the fae-level glamour.

Layla's shadow grinned. At least one of us was having fun.

The corridor curved out of sight ahead. The left side was a window, offering a view of the outside but no way out. I knew from experience with mechanist submarines that the material could take a heavy beating without breaking.

Voices echoed from ahead. We rounded the curve and found Sato marching toward us with a group of people in black uniforms, a fresh cup of matcha tea in his hand. The dress code had obviously changed since the factions split, but it seemed safe to assume that these were constables, the law enforcement wing of the mechanists. Their outfits resembled business suits like Sato's, most wearing black diamond-shaped insignias on their chests.

Sato wore an insignia with three white diamonds joined at the corners. Most of the rank-and-file constables had only one black diamond, though at least one had two diamonds. The man with two diamonds stopped and turned to face the wall. It slid open a moment later, and a pair of the lower ranking constables went inside and began handing out shiny chrome rifles.

How did he open that door? He hadn't spoken a passphrase, used a keycard or even touched the wall. He hadn't flashed lights at it like the bot either. It didn't seem like the mechanists to use nub-based biometrics readers, but maybe they'd implemented optical readers, or facial recognition.

"Lieutenant Astor, a word." Sato motioned the double-diamond guy over.

Astor, a straight-shouldered no-nonsense looking kind of guy strode over. "Yes, sir."

Sato crossed his arms. "It's doubtful they survived but take no chances. Shoot to kill."

"Yes, sir."

Judging from the red tags on the magazines jutting from the sides of the weapons, that was what they'd already planned to do. If their ammunition marking system was anything like that of the Traditionalists, they were going all out with incinerator rounds instead of the less lethal shock rounds.

If we didn't get past them undetected, they'd light up this hallway with a barrage of gunfire.

21

Layla and I could have probably taken out Sato and most of his crew right then and there, but that would be counterproductive. It would be much better to navigate the corridor and slip past silently. There were probably hundreds more constables and bots that could trap us in the confines of the hall. Unless and until we figured out how to open doors, there was no way out.

Invisible or not, I didn't know how we'd get past the crush of constables ahead of us. I wasn't even sure this was the best direction to go. Unless they formed a single file line when they started moving toward the conference room, there was nothing we could do but push through the throng and hope nobody realized it wasn't their fellow constable who'd bumped into them.

Layla and I looked at each other. She motioned for us to run ahead. I nodded and approached the constables milling about in the hallway while they waited for a rifle to be handed to them. Those who were armed had formed another group on the opposite wall, so I hugged the wall closest to the armory and slid down it until I reached the door.

I peered around the doorway to see if that room might be a good place to hide until the constables left, but decided it wasn't feasible.

Once the door closed, we'd have no way out. Layla could use Panoptes to spirit herself away, but since she couldn't take anyone living with her, I'd be stuck.

So, right after the next constable took his weapon, I slipped past to the other side of the doorway. Layla timed her passage the same way, and we weaved our way through the rest of the constables until we were finally in the clear.

Sato stood near the back with Astor, the pair talking in conspiratorial tones. I stepped closer to hear their conversation.

"...guardians were very clear. Only their Beta squad is allowed to engage. Alpha and Prime must remain out of it unless we are absolutely certain the target is from a different dimension than they are." Sato pressed his lips together. "That's why we have to hold them here until reinforcements arrive."

"Understood, sir." Astor shook his head. "I thought we were done with the fighting."

"We are done when the fae say we're done." Sato frowned. "And I would very much like to have Cain and his allies dead here and on Prime. He is too dangerous. Too controlling."

A constable approached the pair. "Sir, we're loaded and ready to go."

Astor nodded. "Be ready to move out." He walked to the armory door and faced it for a few seconds. The door slid shut. Then he walked back over to Sato.

Layla tapped me on the shoulder and motioned urgently down the hallway. I held up a finger. It was nice being able to eavesdrop invisibly just like the old days when I'd been in the Oblivion Guard. The light glinted off Astor's insignia, causing me to take a closer look at it. It was oddly thick for something that should be a simple piece of metal.

"Let's get underway, Lieutenant." Sato started pushing his way through the crowded corridor. Seized by a sudden impulse, I slid into the throng sideways behind him to keep my profile down. It was so crowded the constables didn't seem to notice an invisible force was slipping past right after him.

As Sato turned sideways to squeeze through, I reached out and lightly tugged on the insignia on his uniform. It was pinned on. He didn't notice my attempt since the insignia was rubbing against the other constables. There was no gentle way to remove it since I couldn't very well undo the pin clasp. So, I resorted to a little bit of chaos, and shoved a constable hard into Sato.

That caused a domino effect.

The constable I shoved knocked Sato over backwards. The constables behind him fell over, causing a pileup. As Sato fell, I gave the insignia a hard yank and it popped free. Then I shoved the same constable again and he fell on top of his leader.

Slipping back out was easy since everyone was trying to help their comrades up while also clutching their rifles. It was a good thing they'd practiced trigger discipline or a few of them might have ended up with incinerator rounds burning through their guts.

Layla watched me with confusion, mouthing something along the lines of, "What in the hell are you doing?"

I held up the white three-diamond insignia and hurried past her down the corridor. We reached a dead-end moments later. I held Sato's insignia about chest high and waited. Nothing happened. Then I remembered the cloak, and turned off the glamour, revealing myself.

I held up the insignia again. After a pause, the wall slid open revealing more corridor beyond.

"That's what opens the doors?" Layla whispered.

I cloaked myself again and touched Layla to pair our cloaks so we could see each other. "I wasn't sure, but it was worth the risk."

"I'll say." She tapped a finger on her chin. "I'll bet we could get to their restricted inventory with that thing."

"I think you're right. Problem is I don't know where it is."

She pursed her lips. "Ask a bot to take us?"

"Surely there's a diagram around here somewhere. Mechanists love diagrams."

"We might have walked right past rooms full of diagrams, but it's impossible to tell where the doors are in this place." Layla touched the seamless wall as if to make the point. "And this place is huge, so I don't think we'll find it just by walking."

I imagined the outside of the facility. The retail area had likely been right on the front where people had lined up to go inside. The gadgets inside wouldn't be on the restricted list, and it was unlikely the mechanists would store such items anywhere close to retail customers. The manufacturing facility was probably on the side where I'd seen the loading docks. That would also not be the place to store restricted items.

If anything, such inventions would be kept somewhere secure, and yet where they could show them off to potential buyers. Just because they were restricted didn't mean that they didn't sell them regularly. In fact, it seemed likely that the government was one of their biggest customers.

That meant there was probably a high-security warehouse with a showroom attached to it. It wouldn't be on the upper floor, but on the ground level where items could easily be loaded onto trucks and shipped out.

"We need to find another elevator."

Layla quirked her lips. "How anyone finds anything in this place is a miracle."

"It's part of their security." I nodded to myself. "And it's actually brilliant. They're not tracing sigils on anything, so there's no oily fingerprint residue for me to find with my mist. They're not using passphrases or biometrics, either." I held up the insignia. "These totems allow contactless access based on rank. Even if you steal one, you'd have to know the layout to actually get anywhere before you're caught."

"Sato is going to realize his insignia is gone anytime now." Layla motioned toward the newly opened door. "We need to go somewhere and go fast."

"Agreed. Scout ahead and see if the corridor is clear. I'm going to reveal myself and start opening doors."

She nodded. "Be right back."

I dispelled the cloak and walked down the hallway holding the insignia toward the inner wall. The first door that opened led into an apartment lavishly adorned with nub furniture and electronics. Whoever owned it apparently didn't care for the minimalist design I'd seen elsewhere.

"Executive living quarters?" Layla said from behind me.

"Yeah." I closed the door and moved down the hall. The next area was a Roman style bathhouse with pools of steaming water and a well-stocked bar. "Well, they certainly know how to live it up."

"I want to live here." Layla sighed.

"I assume the corridor is clear?"

"Yep. No signs of life." Her invisible hand touched me. "Are you uncomfortable with an invisible assassin at your back?"

I glanced where I imagined she stood. "Not with you guarding me."

She laughed softly. "You're cocky. I like it."

I returned to the hallway and continued the search. Four more doors opened in the corridor. Two were living quarters. One was a game room with pool tables and virtual golf. The last one was a closet of supplies. Time was ticking and we were no closer to finding an elevator.

"This isn't going well." I backed away from the last door.

Layla made a thoughtful noise. "Open the door to one of the apartments again."

"Why, you want to take a nap?"

"No. Think about it. This isn't just a regular office building, it's a fortress." Her finger tapped invisibly on the wall. "Do you really think the people who live on this level are going to run to one elevator and wait on it while the building is being attacked or burning down around them?"

"Ah." I got her point. "They might have their own personal elevators."

"Yep."

I walked back down to the closest executive suite and opened the door. It was as large as the others, but not as lavishly adorned as the first. A giant nub television took up one wall. Four gaming consoles sat on the glass shelf to the side. The mechanists obviously loved nub technology as much as the nubs loved theirs.

The doors inside the room were normal, with handles and hinges. A door opened by Layla's invisible hand revealed a master bedroom attached to a huge bathroom and walk-in closet.

"If there's a secret elevator, it'll be in here." Layla snorted. "Never mind. It's not secret at all."

I walked into the closet. At the far end was a single metal door. The button depressed at Layla's touch and the door slid open to reveal a small elevator.

"Mom, why is the door open?" a child's voice said from the den.

"Joseph?" a woman called out. "Joseph, are you here? We're back early."

I motioned to the elevator and stepped inside. Layla took my hand to let me know she was inside. The button panel was round and covered in buttons with letters and numbers. There were so many that I didn't know which one to push.

"Pick one, dammit," Layla hissed.

I hit one at random. The door slid shut silently and we began to descend. The lift slowed, stopped, and then started moving laterally.

"Oh, of course it moves sideways." Layla's hand tightened on mine. "I wonder where it's taking us."

I examined the panel and realized it was round because it was a diagram of the building. A red button at the bottom was probably for emergency escapes, but it seemed this lift could deliver us anywhere we wanted to go.

"This one," Layla said.

"You're invisible. I can't see what you're pointing at."

"Shit, we're stopping."

The door slid open silently. The room beyond was full of the hustle and bustle of people in business suits with light-blue insignias on them. Large computer screens hung from the ceilings, many of them displaying complex clockwork diagrams. A woman near the elevator door stiffened as a subordinate often did when their boss entered the room.

This elevator system was likely used by the inventors to move about the building without walking. She looked mildly confused when she saw me. Then her gaze moved to the black oblivion cloak and her confusion turned to concern.

I gave her the severe look that struck fear into the hearts of most when they saw a guardian. Her eyes flared. She backed up a step. Then I grinned and gave her a thumbs up. She nearly fell over backwards trying to get away.

Layla pressed a button and the door closed. "This will take us to the warehouse."

I touched her and dispelled the cloak. "Show me which button."

She pointed to a series of buttons labeled with the letter W and numbers, then dropped her finger lower and pointed to one labeled W-S without a number. "Probably means special or secure warehouse."

"Or water storage."

She flashed a smirk. "Yeah, that's probably it."

I activated my cloak and hers, then paired them to make us visible to one another. "I'm positive Sato knows his insignia has been missing for at least the last fifteen minutes."

"At least. Unless they're still standing outside that conference room door."

"I'm surprised they don't have cameras in there." I shook my head. "They certainly use a ton of nub technology."

"I think most mechanists would rather die than openly use nub tech." Layla pressed her lips together. "That's why there aren't nub cameras everywhere."

"Yeah, but mechanists have their own versions of cameras." I gave it some thought and hit upon another idea. "I think they just don't have any recording devices on the executive level."

"Because they don't want any record of what goes on up there." Layla nodded. "Makes sense."

"I'm more surprised their families live with them." I watched the buttons on the panel light up as we passed their locations. "You'd think they'd have estates somewhere outside of town."

"Why not both?" Layla shrugged. "These people are making big bucks."

"True." I noticed a series of buttons in the middle of the circular diagram. One was labeled with an *H*. Another was labeled *CC*. "They have a command-and-control center here. That must be where they activate the crab legs."

"You're joking, but I'm positive this place can walk like the underwater lair on Alpha. Soon as the shit hits the fan, this bad boy is gonna rise up and start shooting." She pointed out the one with the *H*. "Helicopter pad?"

"I think so." I pointed out three *D* buttons that circled the *CC* one. "I think these are airship docks."

"I wonder if Cain Alpha has any idea what's going on here." Layla blew out a breath. "The Futurists are prepping a war machine."

"They don't stand a chance against him and the demi squad. Not even the Oblivion Guard can fight them, especially with—" I came to a sudden realization.

"With what?" Layla said.

"Cain doesn't have Shae anymore. She abruptly left to find her mother because someone gave her new information about where to find her."

"Someone told her where to find Nyx?" Layla's brow furrowed. "I thought she was in Tartarus."

"Normally she is, but Hemlock told me that she'd heard Nyx can leave at certain times of the year and when she does, she goes to some ancient temple in Greece." I whistled. "Shae can see through any kind of glamour, meaning the Oblivion Guard couldn't get close to the demis without being seen. She's the reason they killed an entire squad of guardians."

"With her gone, that means the Oblivion Guard can sneak up on the others."

I nodded. "Yeah. I think a shit storm is about to be unleashed against Cain's island."

And his best weapon had left for parts unknown.

22

The elevator stopped and the doors opened. A large room with industrial gray walls spread out before us. There were neat rows of equipment on display, arranged by size. On one side of the room were smaller inventions like militarized exo-suits and weapons. On the other side were armored clockwork vehicles and what I could only describe as crab tanks. The armored hulls were shaped like crabs with giant pincers, eight legs, forward facing gun barrels on the front, and a cannon turret on the top.

Layla snorted. "These people have a thing for crabs, don't they?"

I pointed toward a pedestal holding a set of chrome clockwork wings. "There's our grand prize."

Layla pouted. "I want a crab tank."

"We'll get you one another time." I jogged over to the clockwork wings and took note of the number on its pedestal. "This must be the storage location."

"Hmm, chrome." Layla shook her head. "They're certainly not subtle."

A red emergency light began flashing on the wall. "This is a test of emergency protocols. All customers must begin making their way out of the retail store. Thank you."

"Not only are they looking for us, but they're desperate." Layla practically giggled. "Gods, I love being invisible."

I hurried into the warehouse beyond the display room and located the shelves with the corresponding numbers from the wings display. Several narrow wooden box crates were stacked in the section. I pulled one off the shelf and unlatched the lid. Inside was a pair of folded clockwork wings. These were painted in gray and white urban camouflage colors.

"Thank the gods they're not chrome." Layla pulled them out. "How do you unfold them?"

"Let's worry about that later. You're going to take the wings back to Sanctuary with Panoptes."

Layla grimaced. "I don't think that's a good idea. It nearly drove me insane last time."

"Well, it's either that, or we're lugging them out of here." I pointed to the clearly visible wings she held. "They're too big for the cloak to hide, so we can't just sneak out of the front door."

Layla huffed. "Okay, fine. I'll risk my sanity. Then you can just sneak out of here by yourself?"

I nodded. "It's not ideal, but this place is on lockdown, and I don't think we can make a run for it."

She pointed up. "What if we took the elevator to the helipad and flew out of here?"

"I've never used clockwork wings, and I don't want this to be the first time."

"Point taken." She opened two more crates and took out the wings, bringing us to a total of six sets. "Might as well get some spares in case we wreck a pair." In their collapsed forms, the wings weren't much larger than a folded deck umbrella.

I considered asking her to set an eye of Panoptes to watch this place so we could come back, but the risk to her sanity might be too great. I closed the crates and set them back on the shelf so no one would realize we'd liberated a few pairs for ourselves. I counted at least thirty more crates stacked on the shelf, meaning the Futurists were manufacturing an awful lot of restricted gadgets. The military camouflage only reinforced the suspicion that they were preparing for something big.

Whatever it was, I had the feeling it went hand-in-hand with the fae and the provisional government. I also had little doubt that Cain Alpha and I were primary targets.

Layla took a deep breath. "I'm ready." She wrapped an arm around the six sets of wings. "See you soon...I hope."

"Yeah." I waved goodbye.

The instant she slipped on the ring, her eyes squeezed shut and her mouth opened in a silent scream.

"Layla, what the—"

She vanished.

"That can't be good." My stomach knotted. "Fuck." I had to get out of the building and back to Sanctuary ASAP to make sure Layla was okay.

I went to the elevator door, but it didn't respond to the insignia, thanks to the lockdown. I looked for another door, a stairwell, anything to get me out of the building. I took out my staff and used the scope to search for hidden exits. The infrared picked up a heat signature emanating weakly from behind the concrete wall near the crab tanks.

Barely discernible seams in the concrete outlined a large door for moving the big equipment out of the sublevel. This room was far underground, so there was probably a cargo elevator on the other side. A diamond shape was faintly shaded onto the wall on the right side—probably to indicate where to stand when opening the door with the insignia.

I doubted it would work but stepped in front of it and waited. A small section of the wall slid up to reveal a panel with a button and a speaker. I pressed the button. The speaker buzzed and the button flashed red, refusing to open the cargo door.

This cargo bay had become my prison.

"This is starting to irritate me," I muttered. If I could just get into the elevator shaft, I could probably climb a ladder to the top. That was assuming they had ladders built into the shafts for maintenance.

It was never safe to assume anything when it came to mechanists. For all I knew, they utilized a complex series of clockwork rungs for access.

I followed the faint seam in the concrete, looking for another seam in the middle that might indicate where the doors opened. There was no seam in the middle, so that meant the door probably slid up from the bottom like most cargo elevator doors I'd seen. Again, these were the mechanists I was dealing with, so there was no telling without a little experimentation.

I summoned my staff and ignited my brightblade, then pressed it against the seam at the bottom where I imagined a latch might be. The blade sparked against the concrete as I tried to work it into the seam, but progress was painfully slow. It was too dense and difficult, so I gave up.

The button panel, however, might be an alternative. I carved around the edges of the panel then used a shield spell to pry out the metal. I left it hanging by two wires that ran into a conduit beneath. There was also a clockwork cog about the size of the palm of my hand. A small latch locked the cog from turning.

I pressed the button on the hanging panel and the latch lifted. The cog turned a notch before the latch stopped it. The button flashed red, and the speaker buzzed. Using a shield, I lifted the latch. The cog didn't move. I tried turning it by hand, but it didn't budge. There was probably more machinery above that prevented it from moving unless the button was pressed.

I had no idea how to troubleshoot or bypass a mechanism like this. Only the mechanists would utilize something so idiotic instead of simply controlling it electronically. My fists clenched in frustration. I had the skills and tools to bypass just about anything the nub or magical world threw at me, but the mechanists were something entirely different. There was no rhyme or reason to their mechanisms. No way for me to use logic to get the damned things to work.

I ignited my brightblade again and pressed it into the cog, turning it to slag. Removing the cog didn't elicit so much as a creak or groan from the rest of the machinery hidden behind the wall. I was just about ready to cut everything out of the wall when I remembered something so painfully obvious, that I slapped my face.

Turning around, I faced several possible answers to my current dilemma—the crab tanks and numerous other war machines lined up in neat rows.

I jogged to the nearest crab tank since it seemed the most likely agent for my freedom. The vehicle mimicked crabs almost precisely, complete with claws, eyes, and legs. All things considered, there were worse animals to base a weaponized vehicle on.

The legs were bent all the way down so the body sat on the floor. I used the crab claws as a ladder and climbed onto the top. There was no hatch in the turret or anywhere else on the top of the shell. I slid off the shell to the ground and walked around to the back to find a door there.

I pulled on the handle and the door swung open to reveal a small cockpit with enough room for a driver and a gunner. The driver sat at the front. There was no windshield, but a pair of goggles hung from the ceiling. I climbed inside and pulled the goggles down to my eyes. It was like looking through a submarine scope, but with excellent peripheral vision.

The goggles connected to the crab eyes and combined the two different views in a way that was only mildly disorienting. Then again, after using Panoptes, binocular split vision wasn't all that bad. Pulling on a lever raised the eyes up on stalk. If I strapped the goggles to my head, I could simply turn my head to rotate the view.

The controls were similar to that of the mechanist submarines, but with a few additions. One lever controlled forward and reverse speed. Foot pedals probably controlled the direction. A pair of long, sleeved gloves hung on either side. Wires ran from the gloves and into the sides of the tank. I suspected they had something to do with controlling the claws.

I rotated the ignitor handle. There was a faint sparking sound and the crab tank hummed to life. The analog gauges and indicators lit up and the needles pointed to the current values. A light blinked next to the fuel gauge. The liquid mana tank was almost completely empty.

They'd probably only put just enough into the vehicle to test it and pilot it into this storage space.

A quick check of the gunner's chair told me what I'd already expected—no ammo of any kind was loaded. This thing was apparently equipped with dual gun barrels on the front, the turret on the top, and flamethrowers on all sides of the shell in case infantry tried to approach it. It was impressive and way over the top all at the same time.

Who in the hell did the mechanists expect to fight with these things? What fresh world dominating aspirations did the Futurists have for Alpha? It was a mystery I'd have to revisit once I solved my current dilemma.

First, I needed to find some ammunition for the crab. A few explosive rounds from the turret would be sufficient to blow open the cargo elevator door. Then I could hopefully find a ladder inside because those explosions would likely trigger an alarm and bring an army of mechanists and bots down here.

But searching the shelves and the rest of the storage facility proved fruitless. There was no ammunition down here. The mechanists probably used a separate, hardened facility to store explosives, because it would be stupid to keep a literal bomb below the place where they lived and worked. It was likely their munitions warehouse and production was somewhere not in the middle of a busy city that was currently being rebuilt.

At least I understood their reasoning for that even if nothing else they did made sense. But it didn't help my predicament. I went back to the crab tank and realized that maybe I didn't need explosives at all.

I turned the ignition handle and slid into the driver's seat. I fastened the harness and slipped my arms into the sleeves and gloves on the sides of the chair. I moved my left arm and the crab moved. I assumed it moved left, but since I didn't have the goggles on, I couldn't see outside. I had to pull my arms out of the sleeves so I could pull the goggles to my face.

When I put on the goggles, I could see everything outside, but nothing in the cockpit. I didn't understand how the driver was supposed to keep things under control if he couldn't also see inside the cockpit when necessary. The analog gauges were probably important to keep track of while driving.

I noticed a small tube extending from the side of the goggles. At first, I'd thought it was a microphone for radio communications, but it was actually flexible tubing. I squeezed it between my fingers and the front of the goggles flipped up like a visor allowing me to see straight through and into the cockpit. Pressing it again closed them.

I put on the goggles and pulled the tube down. The very end of it went into my mouth. By gently biting or pressing with my lips, the visor went up and down, allowing me to control my view without constantly pulling a hand in and out of the control sleeves and gloves. With that issue solved, I put my hands back into the control sleeves and bit the tube to close the visor so I could see outside.

Then I proceeded to test the control sleeves.

Lifting my arms raised the crab claws. Opening and closing my hands controlled the pincer action. I moved my arms around, testing the motion and range. The crab claws mimicked my motions almost as fast as I could make them. There were buttons on the index fingers. I pressed them and heard a faint clicking. They probably fired the guns on the claws, but there was no ammunition.

With that part of the crab under control, I tested the foot pedals next, but when I pressed down on them, they didn't budge. I pulled my hands out of the claw control sleeves and examined the pedals more closely. There were straps I hadn't noticed before, so I reached down and strapped them onto my feet. The pedals still didn't move, so I sat back and looked the other controls around the seat.

The only other control I hadn't touched was what I'd assumed was the acceleration lever on my right. I pushed it forward gently. It locked into position with a click. The pedals suddenly moved under my feet and the crab began to move with them. The pedals didn't simply go up and down, they moved left and right and tilted forward and back.

I bit down on the visor tube so I could see outside.

Tilting the pedals forward, backward, or sideways caused the crab legs to tilt the angle of the body to match. Pushing the pedals left or right caused the vehicle to crabwalk sideways. Moving one pedal forward caused that side of the crab to rotate in the same direction. By moving one foot forward and the other back, the crab rotated even faster. Pushing both feet forward accelerated and pulling them back slowed the crab and put it into reverse.

I gently pushed both feet forward and the crab began to walk, the metal legs pinging on the concrete outside. I rotated left, then accelerated. The crab walked faster and faster until it was at a full run. I pulled my arms back to slow down before I rammed into the wall. This thing was surprisingly fast, and I was having way too much fun for someone who was trapped in a mechanist base.

I was also really starting to want a crab tank of my own. This thing would be a blast to take for a drive around Sanctuary.

First things first. I cleared my throat and got back to business.

I might not have explosives to blow open the cargo elevator door, but now I had giant crab claws to work with. I just hoped they were powerful enough to do the job, or I'd be well and truly stuck until the Futurists cornered me.

23

I drove the crab to the approximate center of the elevator door. I jabbed the claws forward. They pounded against the concrete, leaving tiny divots. The concrete might not be the same as the super strong material they used for the walls in the upper levels, but it was still concrete. I rammed the claws into the concrete again and again until it began to crack.

Metal became visible beneath the thick slab of concrete.

The claws finally made holes large enough for them to grip the wall. I pushed them inside and lifted. Metal creaked and groaned. I wasn't sure if it was the crab or the elevator door making the noise. The wall shuddered and lifted a fraction. Metal snapped and shrieked, and the door ripped out of the wall. I pulled my feet back and the crab reversed.

But the claws didn't have much of a grip, and the slab of concrete and metal toppled, falling onto the crab. Clockwork ticked furiously to counter the weight, but it was too much. Gears clanked and ground together. I yanked my arms out of the claw control sleeves, unstrapped myself from the foot pedals, and seat, then tore off the goggles.

I unlatched the back door and dove outside just as the crab

collapsed beneath the weight of the massive door. The shell groaned but held up despite the slab of concrete and metal leaning on it.

Beyond the door was a dark shaft. A klaxon blared from somewhere inside the storage facility. It seemed that breaking the door had set off another alarm. Within minutes, this place was going to be swarming with bad guys.

I ran around the fallen crab tank and went to the elevator shaft. I sent several light balls up and inside for a better look. The shaft didn't run vertically, but diagonally up and away from the door. There also wasn't an enclosed elevator car inside, but a metal platform with railing. A massive chain on the back wall apparently pulled the platform up along the shaft and to the top, wherever that was. My light balls hadn't risen high enough to reveal the ceiling.

There were, in fact, ladders bolted to the rear angled wall, one on either side of the giant chain. I cast larger light balls and sent them soaring into the shaft. They kept rising until they hit a ceiling far above. It appeared that the shaft went from diagonal to horizontal beyond that point, meaning I'd have to climb up there to see the door.

But what if that door was also locked down? Was there any way for me to open it from the inside, or was the shaft just another place to be stuck in? I didn't have much time to find out. I ran onto the platform and found the lift control panel bolted onto the railing. I pressed the up-arrow button, and the chain began clinking. The lift began to move.

I released the button and quickly considered my options. If I went up this lift, I'd be cornering myself if the door at the top didn't open. And what if the door opened somewhere I didn't want it to?

There was only one way to do this, and it required six legs and a pair of metal claws. I ran to another crab tank, jumped in, and started it up. Like the other one, it didn't have much fuel in the tank. That was fine. My plan didn't require much. I strapped in my feet, pulled down the goggles, and ran the crab onto the lift. There was enough room for four more crabs to fit, but just one would do nicely.

I put my arm in a claw control sleeve, then reached out and gently pressed the up button. The chain clanked and began raising the lift. I got out of the crab and activated my oblivion cloak. The cargo lift was made for moving heavy objects, and certainly not for speed. It was going to take this thing several minutes to get where it was going.

That was fine by me.

I moved into position and waited. Barely two minutes passed before a large section of wall popped out and slid up right next to where the small personal elevator was. Dozens of bots marched out of the large personnel elevator followed by a squad of constables. Four people in oblivion cloaks emerged after them, staffs in hand. Sato strode alongside them, his white uniform standing out in stark contrast to the others.

"He's in the cargo elevator!" a constable shouted.

The formation of bots abruptly changed direction and marched toward the moving cargo lift. Constables with their shiny chrome clockwork rifles raced ahead. They poked the gun rifles up into the shaft and peered up.

"It's about halfway up," one of them said.

Sato approached with the guardians. "Climb the ladder after it. The door is locked down, so it won't open when he reaches it."

The constable looked at the fallen cargo door. "Sir, I think he has a crab tank!"

"It has no ammunition," Sato replied. "He can't go anywhere."

"Yeah, but those claws will tear us apart."

Sato glared at him. "Follow my orders, lieutenant!"

The man nodded. "You heard him. Start climbing!"

Constables strapped their rifles onto their backs and began climbing the ladders.

I had a nice view of the proceedings because I was cloaked and standing behind a shelf not far from the lift they'd used to come down here. I made my way into the personnel elevator and examined the buttons. The door remained open instead of closing automatically. With everyone preoccupied by the cargo lift, I hopefully still had a good chance of going unnoticed.

This elevator seemed to use the same shafts as the private one because the button layout looked the same. I pressed a button that looked like it would take me to the lobby. Despite being a slab of concrete and metal, the door lowered and shut with only the faint ticking of clockwork, and the lift began its journey. I just hoped it would complete said journey before everyone in the cargo bay realized what was happening.

The seconds ticked past like minutes as I braced myself and waited for the elevator to make an unexpected stop. I might have an oblivion cloak, but even they weren't perfect. If they barricaded me into a hallway, I'd have to fight my way through, invisible or not.

The lift suddenly stopped, and it wasn't at the lobby.

A squad of constables stood outside.

FUCK ME.

It looked like I was going to have to commit a small massacre to make it out of here.

"Everyone in!" someone shouted.

There was no way to slip past the crowd, so I backed myself into a corner and made myself as small as possible. The squad piled inside, but there weren't more than twenty of them, so they fit inside the lift without coming near my position.

The commander stepped inside and pressed a button. I couldn't see which one thanks to the bodies between me and the panel, but I had a feeling I knew where they were going.

One of the constables took a deep breath and asked a question. "Sir, does he really have a crab tank?"

"Yes."

Murmurs rose from the others.

"How the hell are we supposed to fight a god damned crab tank?" an older constable said. "Our incendiary rounds won't do shit to it."

"The crab is unarmed."

Someone laughed. "Because crabs have ten legs and no arms."

"Crabs have arms, you idiot." The older constable popped him on the back of the head. "And those claws can tear us to ribbons."

"The cargo lift doors are locked down," the commander said. "We're just going there to ensure they remain that way."

"Good." The older constable shook his head. "I'm only a week from retirement. I'm sick of this crap."

"You're also too old for it," the young guy said with a snicker.

The old constable looked like he wanted to smack him again.

The lift stopped and the door opened to the outside. The constables piled out and started jogging. I got out of the lift and watched as they ran around the perimeter toward a large loading dock. I was somewhere on the eastern side of the building. The loading dock was concealed from the outside by a large wall.

The wall ran a hundred yards in either direction of the loading dock then curved in to meet the building. A road ran from the loading dock to the eastern part of the wall. I didn't see any gates, but they were probably just concealed like everything else around this place. There was probably an exit at the end of that road unless everything was airlifted out of here.

I followed the constables hoping someone might mention the exit, but they were too busy speculating about the crab tank. I didn't blame them. If the cargo lift door hadn't completely crushed the first one, I doubted their small arms fire would even scratch the armor of the second.

I stood near the commander, enjoying my invisibility perhaps a little too much. It was damned nice to have this bit of fae magic at my disposal. At this point it probably didn't have much of a charge left, though, so I'd have to be careful.

The radio on the commander's belt crackled. "Lift has stopped. Units are approaching down the horizontal shaft. The crab is not moving."

Sato spoke. "Say again, lieutenant?"

"The crab is stationary," he replied.

"Hold position and observe," Sato commanded.

"Holding position."

A minute passed and Sato spoke again. "Any movement?"

"No, sir."

"Cain isn't on the lift," Sato said. "He doubled back on us!"

Audible sighs of relief rose from the constables around me.

"Thank god." The old constable wiped sweat from his forehead. "Last thing I ever want to do is fight Cain, much less Cain in a god damned crab tank."

"Amen to that," another constable said.

The commander spoke into the radio. "What are our orders, sir?"

A few beats passed before Sato answered. "Hold position. Send a unit to patrol the eastern side just in case."

"Yes, sir." The commander lowered his radio. "McGillicuddy, you and Francis take the patrol. Should be plenty safe so you can survive to retire."

The old constable nodded. "Thanks, sir."

The young guy he'd hit on the head smirked. "I'll make sure he doesn't fall in a hole."

The pair headed past the loading dock and toward the road. I followed right behind them. They stopped at the end of the road. McGillicuddy stopped at the wall and spoke on his radio. "Requesting an override on eastern door P Alpha."

"Request granted," Sato said.

"Acknowledged," another voice said.

The wall slid open to the outside. I followed the pair out of the door and resisted breathing a sigh of relief. The city and surrounding area were visible again. All I had to do was get out of the safe zone protecting this place and I could use the Tetron to go home.

My oblivion cloak flickered.

The constables stopped dead in their tracks, staring at me. I deactivated the cloak and smiled. "Howdy, fellows."

They froze in place, neither reaching for a weapon.

"Please, Mr. Cain, sir, I'm about to retire. I don't want to die."

I sighed. "Well, maybe you should have thought about that before, McGillicuddy."

Sweat poured down his forehead. "Please!"

"You have a wife and kids?"

He looked confused. "No, but I want to go fishing!"

I nodded. "Hey, whatever makes you happy."

Francis moved his hand slowly toward his waist.

I waggled a finger at him. "Let's not ruin this moment with blood-shed, Francis."

The other man's mouth dropped open. "Jesus Christ, it's just like all the stories. The man knows everything."

"Yep. And Santa isn't going to be pleased this year." I snatched the radios from their belts and tossed them. "I want you two to stay in place until I've left the campus, okay? Or I can just kill you right now."

McGillicuddy gulped. "I'm fine standing here."

I nodded. "Good. Probably better you don't tell anyone you saw me, or Sato might not let either of you survive to retirement."

Francis added his own gulp. "You're probably right."

I turned and started walking, glancing back to make sure neither of them decided to get brave. They followed instructions, not moving even after I'd crossed the street and walked into a building under construction.

Hiding behind a concrete column, I took out the Tetron and took myself into the interdimensional array. The same geographical spot in Prime was in a dog park. I willed myself back to Gaia Prime and hurtled to the ground. I landed on the ground just as a pair of dogs raced past. Their owners shouted in alarm.

"What the hell?" A man rubbed his eyes. "Did he just—"

A woman nodded. "He just appeared out of thin air!"

I bowed and walked over to them. "For my next trick, I'll pull a dead rabbit from my hat."

"But you're not wearing a hat," the man said.

"True." I pointed toward the trees. "My friends and I are filming prank videos. Is it okay if we put you on the internet?"

The woman laughed. "I should've known. You can put me on YouTube but tell me how you did that trick."

"I could tell you my secret, but then I'd have to kill you."

They laughed heartily.

I walked past them and out of the dog park. "Keep an eye on the internet for the video."

The man looked confused. "Which site?"

"You know, the boob tube one." I walked down the sidewalk, leaving them with confused expressions. It was damned nice to be home.

It took about fifteen minutes to walk to Dolores, during which time I texted Layla. She didn't answer right away which was typical. I messaged Hannah to check up on their progress and again received no reply.

There was a slip of paper under the windshield wiper which at first, I thought was a parking ticket. I slid it out and read it.

Choose the second.

I frowned and looked at nearby cars. None of them had anything under their windshield wipers, so this thing wasn't a flyer someone had distributed to everyone. Was this targeted at me, or completely random? Dolores was disguised by camouflage so there was no way for anyone to know it was my car.

I examined the paper through my scope. There was a faint glow of residual magic about it, but the paper itself wasn't enchanted. It looked as if it had been torn from a regular notepad. I checked it for fingerprints and found none. Then I noticed a slight glow coming from something beneath the windshield wiper. I lowered the scope and the glow vanished.

Using the scope, I found a slender piece of thread stuck there. Whoever left the message must have had a thread dangling from their enchanted clothing. Who in the hell would have known this was my car and left such an enigmatic message?

I checked Dolores from top to bottom and found no magical or nub trackers. She was clean, but I felt dirty. Someone had violated her, and I intended to find out who. The paper and thread looked harmless, but I didn't dare take them to Sanctuary. I folded the paper around the thread and put them under a rock in a nearby alley.

Then I returned to Dolores and stared dolefully at her. She was definitely clean of trackers and anything else, so it would be fine driving her home. I seethed with anger that someone had found her somehow and left that stupid message under her windshield wiper.

I got inside her, started the engine, and pulled into traffic. I followed an even more circuitous route home to ensure I wasn't being followed despite wanting to reach Sanctuary as soon as possible. I arrived nearly an hour later and went inside, still thinking about the paper and thread.

The house was empty, and that was concerning.

"Layla?" I went into my room where I'd set an eye of Panoptes to watch so I could use it as a quick travel point.

I'd expected a pile of clockwork wings on the floor and Layla to be sprawled out on the bed taking a nap, or even in the kitchen drinking my good alcohol, but she wasn't anywhere on the main floor. I went to the basement, but she wasn't there either.

My phone buzzed with a new text from Hannah.

We're in jail.

I stared in disbelief then replied. *For what? Where?*

Illegally flying a drone and going to the roof of a building. She sent an address that was just down the road from the Sovereign Building.

I'll be there shortly. I couldn't believe they'd allowed themselves to be taken to jail in the first place. I called Layla. An error message told me her mobile device wasn't available. That usually meant she was out of range of a cell tower. It meant she hadn't come back to Sanctuary with Panoptes.

The corruption had overwhelmed her, meaning Layla could be anywhere in three dimensions and three different worlds, Gaia, Feary, or Oblivion.

And I had no way to find her.

24

Layla might have been so overwhelmed by the corruption in Panoptes that she'd ended up in the warehouse where I'd formerly stored the apocalypse weapons before they were stolen. Or, she might have traveled to the summer or winter courts in Feary. I'd set eyes to watch places in Oblivion and elsewhere as well.

In short, she could have ended up anywhere, and I had no way to reach her.

To make matters worse, Hannah and Aura were in jail. There was nothing I could do to find Layla, so I opted to drive to Buckhead and spring the others from jail.

"Fred?" I went to his pool and splashed a hand in the water. "Fred?"

No answer.

I'd hoped he could keep an eye out in case Layla returned, but it seemed Fred was too busy having adventures of his own to help little old me. I took a quick shower, put on fresh clothes, and took the oblivion cloak with me to the car.

Traffic was awful so it took me thirty minutes to reach the police station. It was located in an old strip mall near the back which seemed a strange place to put a police precinct. I put on the oblivion cloak, activated the glamour, and walked inside.

The front clerk looked up with confusion as the door seemingly opened by itself but shook it off and went back to typing on his computer. The people sitting in the front lobby noticed, though.

"What the hell?" An old woman in one of the waiting chairs glared at the door. "Did someone come in or go out?"

"You on drugs, girl?" Another woman looked her up and down. "Ain't nobody come in or out."

The clerk sat in a room facing the lobby, a pane of glass his first line of defense from having to breathe the same air as the people in the lobby. A secure doorway on the left of the room probably led to the holding cells.

The door to his room was locked, so I couldn't get inside to see if there was a button to release the magnetic lock. There was a gray pad next to the door that allowed people to swipe a card to unlock it.

A police officer came to the front and looked at a sheet of paper. "Larry Jones?"

A man in stained sweatpants and a football jersey stood up. He looked like a young person with the skin of an old man. "Yeah."

The officer waved him to follow. "Come back with me."

They entered another hallway.

I considered slashing open the clerk's door, knocking him out, and looking for a button to open the door, but that would cause way too much commotion among the lobby patrons. Instead, I went down the hallway where the officer had taken Larry. It led to a room with rows of desks occupied by uniformed officers in the front section.

Detectives and other personnel in street clothes were in another section further back. Nearly everyone had at least one civilian sitting in a chair on the other side of their desk. There were people in business suits, women in platform shoes and fishnet stockings, men in oversized sport regalia, and even one man in nothing but underwear.

Every walk of life was represented in here, and unbeknownst to them, even an elf and a demigoddess. I spotted members of that demographic sitting in front of a detective's desk near the back. His brow was furrowed in a sharp V, and his face displayed a mix of anger and confusion.

I walked back, careful not to bump into anyone so I could eavesdrop on the conversation.

"I'm sorry, I don't know what else to say." Hannah sighed. "I thought it was okay to go to the roof and fly my drone."

"That's not what the concierge said." The detective held up a sheet of paper with writing on it. "Her statement says you barged past her and somehow entered the secure stairwell without authorization. I've got you for criminal trespass and illegally flying a drone above four hundred feet without a license."

Hannah blew out a breath and turned to Aura. "Remind me why we're doing this again?"

"Because if we raised a huge scene, it might draw unwanted attention."

"Yeah, and now we're in jail." Hannah rolled her eyes.

The detective narrowed his gaze. "Unwanted attention? From whom? Are you corporate spies? Is that why you didn't have any form of identification on you?"

I unsheathed a dueling wand and gave the detective a jolt in the neck. He slumped, but I caught him and leaned him back in his chair, so it looked as if he were just resting his eyes.

Hannah flinched and looked around. "Cain?"

"Yep." I took the handcuff key from the detective's desk and unlocked Hannah's and Aura's restraints. "Walk out of here like you know what you're doing."

"Don't have to tell me twice." Hannah stood and walked away.

Aura frowned in my general direction. "That's some amazing camouflage you're using."

"Shut up and go." I prodded her back and she followed Hannah.

A few people glanced at them, but nobody stopped or questioned them. The front desk clerk glanced up from his computer as they walked toward the door. "Hey, I haven't processed your paperwork."

"Detective Craig said he'd take care of it." Hannah opened the door to leave.

"That's not how it works." The detective picked up his phone. "Wait there."

"No, thanks." Hannah exited and Aura followed after her.

"Hell yea, girl!" A woman in a short skirt that left nothing to the imagination pumped a fist.

"Nuh-uh." A man shook his head. "That girl going to jail."

"Mother fucker!" The officer jumped up and opened his door, then ran after them. I grabbed his shoulder and gave him a nice jolt from my dueling wand. He went limp.

The other people in the lobby shouted in alarm as the officer seemingly levitated into a seat next to them, snoring gently.

"I told you this place is haunted!" the woman from earlier said.

"That old boy shit his pants!" A man sitting nearby pinched his nose. "Look, he got crap running out his britches!"

I'd probably jolted him a little too hard. As I walked toward the door, I shouted, "Behave, sinners, or verily wilt thou also shit thy pants!"

People jumped up from their chairs, tripping over one another to get away from my voice. I opened the door and left.

Hannah and Aura were jogging down the sidewalk. I caught up to them. The cloak was running out of charge and starting to flicker, so I dispelled the glamour.

Hannah didn't even blink. "Where'd you park, Cain?"

"Down the street." We hurried down the sidewalk and climbed inside Dolores who was disguised as a light blue minivan.

"Where'd you get the oblivion cloak, Cain?" Aura met my gaze in the rearview mirror. "Did you run into more than you were expecting on Alpha?"

"Of course." I pulled onto the street and started driving. "I assume the cops have no idea who you are?"

"We didn't have an IDs." Aura shrugged. "They ran our prints and got nothing."

Hannah turned to me. "Did you get the clockwork wings, Cain?"

"Sort of." I told them about mine and Layla's adventure. "I assume Layla took them somewhere, but I don't know where."

"Oh, shit." Hannah grimaced. "Did Panoptes drive Layla insane?"

"You mean more insane?" Aura muttered.

"I don't know." I blew out a breath. "I have no way to reach her either."

"Just great!" Hannah threw up her hands. "Well, we scoped out the top of the Sovereign and it wasn't easy. The wind kept blowing the drone all over the place."

"That, and we also pissed off the concierge in the neighboring building, so she called the cops on us." Aura leaned back and stared out of the window. "There is a balcony on the northeastern side of the penthouse. It might have wards or other security, but at least we know it exists."

"It's hidden from the ground by illusion," Hannah said. "I guess it's just to keep people on the street from looking up and seeing it."

"Did you record video?" I asked.

Hannah nodded. "It's saved on my cell phone."

"How did you manage to hold onto your phones after they arrested you?"

"There was a line waiting on the clerk when we got there, so the cops just took us straight back to the detective." Aura frowned. "I don't even know why they decided it was worth taking us to a detective."

"Criminal trespass and illegal drone flying aren't like speeding tickets." I navigated through the heavy traffic, wishing I could blast the slowpokes out of the far-left lane. "Don't these idiots know this is the passing lane?"

"No, Cain, they don't." Hannah made finger guns and mimicked firing sounds. "I just want to blow them all to hell."

"You and me both." I sighed and leaned my elbow on the arm rest. "Show me the video."

"While you're driving?"

"Yep."

She took out her phone and played aerial footage. The balcony was nice and big, but the awning hanging over it made it extremely difficult to land on, especially for unseasoned fliers like us. The roof seemed to have plenty of space for landing, but it might be covered in wards. I'd have to scope it out while flying over. Without the clock-work wings, there was only one way to do that.

I checked the time. It was too late in the day to do anything right now, but we could schedule something for tomorrow. "Hannah, look up helicopter tours for the area. I need to book us a flight."

Her forehead pinched. "Are we parachuting in from a tour chopper?"

I gave her a sideways look. "No. I need a better look at the rooftop."

"Why didn't you let us rent a helicopter in the first place?"

I rubbed my thumb and two fingers together. "Money. Now that I know the general layout, I need to scope out any wards with my staff."

"Ah." Hannah seemed mollified. "I want to go on the helicopter."

"Fine by me." I glanced in the rearview mirror.

Aura shook her head. "No, thanks."

Layla still hadn't shown up by the time we finally got back to Sanctuary. I was worried about her, but there was absolutely nothing I could do to help her except hope for the best and expect the worst.

I booked a touring helicopter the next morning. It was much cheaper than I thought it would be, though it took a little extra cash to ensure that the pilot would take us exactly where we needed to go. All things considered, it would've been better to put Hannah and Aura on a chopper instead of having them use a drone. I might have lived in the nub world for years, but I still overlooked the simple things sometimes.

Hannah and I arrived at PDK airport and walked inside where I paid in cash for the tour.

Hannah narrowed her eyes at me. "I went to jail because you couldn't give me three hundred dollars for a tour?"

The man taking the money looked back and forth between us but went back to minding his own business when I gave him a sharp look.

"I didn't realize it was this inexpensive." I shrugged. "Sorry."

Hannah huffed. "Keeping a drone from smashing into a window or being blown away is a lot harder than you think. This is going to be a lot more fun...I hope."

I went into the bathroom and summoned my staff since it would be awkward doing so while in the helicopter, then went outside to the tarmac. The rotor spun on a small helicopter a few hundred feet away.

The pilot approached me, a hint of confusion on her face. "Mr. Smith, you said you wanted a tour specifically over the Sovereign Building and nearby?"

"It's one of my favorite buildings in Atlanta, and I've always wanted an aerial view." I shrugged. "Hopefully it's not a problem?"

She grimaced. "There's actually a no-fly zone for several blocks around it."

"Say what?" Hannah raised an eyebrow. "How does a private building have a no-fly zone?"

"The city of Atlanta put it in place shortly after it was built." She pressed her lips together. "I can get us fairly close, but not too close."

I nodded. "I just need to see the roof and top level. Can you get us high enough?"

"Yeah, but we'll be pretty far away."

"That's ok. I brought a scope." I tapped my staff.

She glanced down at it, a slight frown forming. "Sounds good to me. Ready to go?"

"Yep." We went to the helicopter. Hannah got into the front seat, and I took the back, so I'd have more room to use my scope. I really wished I could detach the scope from the staff, so it wasn't so awkward to use in tight spaces, but that wasn't possible.

The pilot took off and guided us toward Buckhead, pointing out buildings and landmarks as we went. It didn't take long for us to reach the place I was interested in. She made a wide circle around the Sovereign, and I used my scope in aura mode to look over the entire top level and rooftop.

The place was covered with one-way illusions designed to disguise certain aspects of the building from people at street level.

There wasn't anything to hide the true design from this view, but most nubs wouldn't even realize the subtle differences. Glass panels rose above the roof, forming an oval wall around it. There were gaps in the sides, presumably to let wind in for the air conditioning units.

The penthouse jutted out from the side of the building on either side, with a wide balcony running halfway around the building. The awning I'd seen in the drone footage made it far too difficult to attempt a landing on the balcony itself, but the roof looked easy enough even for noobs.

I was relieved to see a gray sigil slate next to the balcony door. Now the only thing to do was see if the sigil card from Torvin's pocket dimension bathroom worked on it.

I flicked through several modes on the scope but didn't see any wards on the roof. That wasn't too surprising since nub maintenance needed to go up there from time to time, and window washers probably went up there to clean the glass panels as well.

The balcony and windows around it also didn't have any wards on them. The God Hand probably thought they could handle anyone who made it into the penthouse, and with the no-fly zone, an aerial attack seemed inconceivable.

But now there was a problem with our aerial infiltration—a major one. Layla and I had specifically requested clockwork wings from the Futurists only to find out they were in league with the fae and the God Hand. Sato would likely report our request to his coconspirators, and they'd wonder why we'd wanted wings.

I just had to hope they didn't figure out the truth or this plan was dead in the water.

25

A fter the tour, I told Hannah what I'd seen during the drive back home.

"No wards?" Hannah scratched her chin. "That seems odd for a place run by rogue guardians."

"I don't think they expect anyone to have the balls to do what we're planning." I glanced into the rearview mirror and scanned nearby traffic as I habitually did. "I'm just concerned about who might be living there. It could be empty, or all the rogue guardians might be bunking there."

"Yeah, that would be bad." She chewed the inside of her lip. "What happens if Layla never returns with the wings?"

"Then it's back to using parachutes." I pulled into the parking lot of a restaurant because I was hungry, and I needed a place to think. "Let's eat."

Hannah's eyes brightened. "Tacos, yum!"

We went inside and got a table. I ordered a margarita because the mangoritas at most nub restaurants were syrupy and too sweet. I took out my phone and started searching for skydiving places. There were only a few and those were located far outside of town. Most offered training and certification.

I placed a call to someone I hadn't spoken to in a while—not since using him to help me find Hannah's mother.

"Cain?" the man on the phone sounded uncertain. "It's been quite some time."

"Yep." I paused a beat. "Do you know anyone qualified to help me with an aerial insertion?"

It was his turn to pause. "I'm sorry—like HALO jumping?"

I knew the term from the Human-Fae War. "Something like that, but the landing zone is on a skyscraper."

"This is far outside your usual request."

"I'm aware of that, Agent Brines. I just need someone with expertise."

"I don't know of anyone, but I know a guy who knows a guy." He blew out a breath. "I assume you want someone in the Atlanta area?"

"Yep."

He grunted. "I'll ask him."

"Thanks. I'll wire over your finder's fee once I have some names."

"One thousand sound fair?"

I considered it. "Five hundred for the info, and another five hundred if it turns out to be good. Otherwise, I'll need you to find me someone else."

"Fair enough." He ended the call.

"Well, now I see why things get so expensive so fast." Hannah looked enviously at my margarita. "That, and your drinking habits."

"Even if Layla shows up with the clockwork wings, we'll probably need to jump out of a plane." I waved down the server so I could order some tacos. "Cain Alpha told me clockwork wings are notoriously bad at taking off from the ground, but once they're airborne, you can use them like gliders."

"Maybe the ones the Futurists made are better."

I shrugged. "Maybe."

A text from Agent Brines arrived shortly after our tacos did. *Here's the list.* He sent ten names, locations, and place of employment. Four were north of Atlanta all the way up near Chattanooga, Tennessee. The other six were located around the metro area and worked for various security firms, which made sense. People who'd been in the military often ended up in such jobs.

Brines sent a file with more information a few moments later. This one detailed job experience for each candidate. All of them had been in the special forces, and three of them seemed particularly qualified to teach precision parachuting, or whatever the nubs called it.

One guy had almost no information next to his name, not even the military branch he'd been in. His only qualification seemed to be that he ran a skydiving school in north Georgia. Another candidate had served long tours in Afghanistan and Iraq but didn't seem to have much in the way of skydiving experience. I worked down the list, ranking them from worst to first.

Hannah peered over at the file. "How does it look?"

"Promising." I finished eating and called the one I'd ranked first.

A gruff voice answered. "How'd you get this number?"

"A mutual acquaintance. I'm looking for someone who can assist me with a precision airborne insertion."

"Well, now I know how you got this number." He chuckled. "Our paramilitary services are excellent, and we offer package deals. I'm about to board a plane and leave the country for two days, but I'll be available to talk later this evening. I'll have my assistant send you an off-menu list."

"Thanks." I ended the call and received the package moments later. The packages consisted of hiring soldiers with different levels of training for various jobs but there was nothing about skydiving or training.

I continued calling those located closer to Atlanta. Two of them offered similar paramilitary services. Another was working as a security guard and had injuries preventing him from training anyone. The next one was a woman who had thousands of hours of airborne experience, including HALO jumping, skydiving, and precision landings. She sounded perfect for the job, but her availability was limited.

"I think she's the one," I told Hannah when I hung up. "But she's not available until three days from now."

Hannah paused biting into her taco. "Three days is a long time."

"Yeah, but we're about out of options." The last three on the list didn't seem worth calling due to their locations and sparse information. I called the woman who'd served several long tours, but her phone went to voicemail.

"Ugh." Hannah stared at the list. "What about this guy who has a skydiving school?"

"He doesn't have any qualifications." I pointed to the mostly empty notes. "Just says he was in special operations."

"Brines listed him second, so maybe that's a good thing?"

"They're not listed in order of recommendation." I opened my mouth to say something else and thought of the slip of paper. *Choose the second.*

"Cain, are you having a stroke?"

I worked my jaw back and forth a few times. Was it remotely possible that paper was referring to this? And if so, how? I dialed the number.

"Elton speaking." He spoke with a slight accent I couldn't place.

"I'm Cain."

"You might not believe this, but I was expecting your call."

"Brines told you I was calling?"

"Who is Brines?" He cleared his throat. "No, I had a slip of paper on my doorstep that said if my phone rang today, I should answer it."

"You run a skydiving school. Doesn't your phone ring a lot?"

He chuckled. "Not this phone. This is my private number."

"Just so happens I had a slip of paper telling me to choose you for a job." I met Hannah's questioning gaze because I'd not mentioned the mysterious message left on Dolores. I also had a distinct feeling I knew exactly who had left it. "You might call it a strange twist of Fate."

"Fate is a bitch." He paused. "How can I help you, Cain?"

"Skydive training and aerial insertion onto a target."

"I can handle both. What's your budget?"

"What's your pricing?"

Elton chuckled. "Let's meet in person and haggle it out, okay?"

"I have a general location, but no address."

"It's an hour and a half drive from downtown Atlanta."

I shrugged. "I'm free the rest of the day."

"Me too," He said. "Three-thirty sound good? I'll text you the address."

"See you then." I ended the call. The address arrived as promised a moment later.

"Someone forgot to tell me about a mysterious message." Hannah glared at me accusingly.

"With everything else going on, I forgot to mention it." I told her about the paper and the thread.

She gasped. "That's why you mentioned Fate. The thread was her calling card."

"Glad one of us can connect the dots." I pursed my lips. "After all those lectures about interfering in the timeline, I can't figure out why she'd do this. Isn't this interfering?"

"Maybe it's just a nudge?" Hannah finished her third taco and grabbed a chip from the bowl. "I mean, it's obviously important that we use this exact guy."

"Wish I knew why."

"Because he's available and no one else is?" Hannah dipped the chip in guacamole and bit into it with a satisfying crunch. "The odds are always stacked against us, so I'll take a little help from our friendly neighborhood deity."

"Unless it's not from her and it's from a god of chaos or one of their minions." I sipped on my margarita. "This could be sending us in the wrong direction. The guy doesn't seem qualified to help."

"Well, let's figure that out when we meet him, okay?"

I nodded. "Yeah, let's."

"Skydiving lessons!" Hannah rubbed her hands together. "I'm excited!"

"Yeah. It'll be hours of family fun." I paid the bill and we left. The address was a little more than an hour north of us and we had three hours to kill. I swung by Sanctuary and picked up a bag of money in case we needed a down payment.

Aura entered the front door a moment later, a concerned look on her face. "I hope you don't mind, but I used the ankh you gave me to run an errand."

"I hope you followed protocol to come back." I gave her a severe look. "We can't just go gallivanting around running errands."

"I needed to go to one of my secure locations to retrieve some equipment." She held my gaze. "I had another laptop I stole from Eclipse so I could still have access to their database, but I haven't used it in a long time."

I continued staring at her. "Why didn't you mention this before?"

"Because I wasn't sure it would still work." She sighed. "My cyber-mancer secured each of these sites with only hardline network connections, redundant firewalls, and a VPN relay system to keep it from being traced. I thought I could use the laptop without a prob-lem, but I was wrong."

"Oh, boy." Hannah groaned. "What happened?"

"I turned on the laptop and tried connecting. It takes a while to do that through all the relays." She pressed her lips together and looked down. "Elektrode must have been waiting for that laptop to come back online, because the trace alarms went off immediately." She took out her phone and opened a video. "I was recording the screen so I could copy the information securely and bring it here, but this is what happened."

In the video, her laptop screen blinked with a message: *Secure connection established.*

An alarm started blaring in the background and the video turned toward a bank of monitors above a desk. *Trace detected. Deactivate Network?*

"Oh, fuck," Aura said in the recording.

"Hey there, Janice, you little minx." The video rotated to the laptop. A pale, thin face leered at us from the screen. The man was in his thirties, wearing a black hoodie and a pair of large headphones with a microphone attached. "I was hoping you'd open this laptop soon, because I've been tracking you and your little friends for some time."

"Hello, Elektrode." Aura's voice was calm. "I'm afraid this laptop won't help you much."

He laughed. "Oh, Janice—or should I say, Aura?" He laughed again, this time more maniacally. "That's right. I know your real name."

"I'm proud of you, Horace."

Elektrode's laugh disappeared behind a mask of shock. "How did you—"

"Oh, Horace, did you really think you could hide that awful name behind a computer screen?" She tutted. "You leave me and my little friends alone and I won't kill you in your sleep, okay?"

Hannah's eyebrows rose and she looked at Aura. "Dude, you're twisted, and I like it."

Aura managed a small smile. "It was just meaningless talk since I'm sure he lives at the secret headquarters."

Elektrode scowled. "Southeast Atlanta inside the perimeter isn't a large place, Aura. I think you'll find my friends are much better at their job than you are." His scowl reversed into a mad grin. "Oops, someone talked too long." He quickly pressed down on a key.

The video jolted backward and spun around. There was a loud explosion and sparks flew. The image rotated back to show a smoking laptop. The other monitors in the room were smoking and sparking. The video ended.

"Needless to say, that secure location is burned." Aura blew out a breath and tucked away her phone.

"How did he make the laptop and the monitors explode?" Hannah looked confused. "That's not how they work."

"Cybermancers can do it with their form of magic." Aura shrugged.

"Fuck me." I clenched my fists. "That little bastard is too close for comfort if he knows Sanctuary is in the southeast quadrant of the perimeter."

"That's still a lot of ground to cover." Hannah gripped my arm. "He's not that close."

"Oh, he's really damned close. We need to do everything within a week." I gritted my teeth. "We can't take any more chances." Dark worms crawled at the periphery of my vision as anger clouded my mind. I needed another visit with Fred's malgorth.

"I'm in," Aura said. "Just tell me what to do."

I put a finger in her face. "First of all, no more side quests without telling me, okay? I'll break your neck myself if you lead that pencil-necked geek to Sanctuary."

Aura's gaze hardened. "Don't worry, Cain. I'll be a good girl."

"Dude, don't fuck with Aura." Hannah grinned. "She's been hiding her metal side all this time."

I nodded. "Yeah." I lowered my finger. "She's good at hiding her true nature."

Aura cleared her throat. "Okay, so now what?"

"Now we work out the logistics." I went to Fred's pool and splashed the surface. "Have you seen Fred?"

She shook her head. "All silent on the home front."

"Damn it." I went to the basement and looked around then checked my bedroom in case Layla had miraculously appeared. "This isn't good."

Hannah snorted. "What, that you drove Layla insane and now she's probably curled up in a puddle of her own vomit and shit in the warehouse?"

"Yep." I turned to Aura. "We're going to talk to someone about parachuting."

She nodded. "I'll get dressed."

I shook my head. "Just us for now. I need you to text me if Fred or Layla shows up."

"Why Fred?" Hannah said.

"Since Layla was infected by the ring, maybe Fred can use me to track her location."

Aura frowned. "I don't follow."

"We share the same mind poisoning." I shrugged. "It's worth a try."

Aura sighed. "Will do."

Hannah and I drove up to Dawsonville to meet Elton at Atlanta Motorsports Park.

"He's at a racetrack?" Hannah went to the railing and gawked at the cars parked there. "Dude, that's a Lamborghini, a Ferrari, and a Dodge Challenger!"

"Back up a sec. Did you just include a Dodge Challenger in the same sentence as a Lambo and a Ferrari?"

She grinned sheepishly. "I mean, they're all cool cars."

"Yeah, some cooler than others." There was a white tent where people were registering to drive the cars. A large sign read *Xtreme Xperience.* "Interesting."

"Can we drive a Lambo, Cain?"

"That's not what we're here for." I went over to someone with an Xtreme logo on their shirt. "I'm looking for Elton."

"He's on the track." The woman pointed to an area where several people in helmets waited their turn to drive. "He's one of the instructors. Are you scheduled to drive today?"

"No. I just needed to talk to him for a moment."

She checked a tablet computer. "He's taking a break in ten minutes."

"Thanks." I glanced at Hannah who was watching the cars zip past on the track. "How much for her to drive a Lambo?"

"Let me see if we have a slot open." She checked her tablet. "I do have an opening in twenty minutes. She'll need a license and proof of insurance."

"Thanks." I joined Hannah at the railing. "You can drive."

Her eyes grew large. "Really?"

I nodded. "Provided you can get that woman the information she wants."

"Yeah, I totally can!" Hannah ran over to the woman and spoke with her.

I watched the cars and waited. A bright green Lamborghini stopped. The driver and passenger got out, spoke a moment, and then the passenger climbed over the railing and looked around. I already knew who it was from the name patch and approached him.

He was young, maybe in his early thirties, medium build and

about five feet eleven. His gaze scanned the general area and caught on me for an instant before moving on.

He was obviously trained in situational awareness and someone who didn't let down his guard even when working a job like this. I just hoped he had what it took to help us.

"Elton."

He nodded. "Cain." His voice sounded as young as he did, belying the experience hiding behind his eyes.

I nodded. "Got a moment?"

"Yeah." Elton motioned toward a food truck. "Mind if I get something to eat?"

"Go for it."

Hannah ran over. "I emailed her my information. I just need to pay for it."

I gave her cash. "Have fun, kiddo."

She hugged me. "You're the best! And the worst!"

"Um, thanks?" I watched her run off to get a helmet and couldn't help but grin. "Ah, the excitement of youth."

Elton returned with a burger and fries and led me to a table around the back of the office building. Once he was settled, he took a sip of his soda and looked at me expectantly. "I assume you're doing something that's not entirely legal?"

"I mean, if you consider something like cliff jumping illegal." I shrugged. "We want to parachute and land on a building in the city. To do that, we need a ride and some training."

"That's insane, actually." He shook his head. "Do you realize how much training it takes to nail a landing like that?"

"A lot, I'd imagine." I leaned my elbows on the table. "So, can you help us?"

"I can." He took a bite of his burger. "There are plenty of retail skydiving outlets that might be cheaper, but those are just for adrenalin junkies and enthusiasts. I'm certain that what you're doing has nothing to do with adrenalin or fun."

I raised an eyebrow. "What makes you think that?"

"Because you're not that kind of person, Cain." Elton leaned back in his seat. "You're a professional of some kind, probably former special forces. There's something different about you from other people in that trade, but your demeanor checks all the other boxes."

"I could say the same things about you." I crossed my arms. "Special forces?"

He nodded. "You could say that. I was assigned to something a little more special than that."

"Sorry, I don't know much about military branches." I assumed he was in black ops of some kind, but what little I knew of that came from movies.

"You don't have to. All you need to know is that I can help you."

"Then let's talk pricing."

He grinned. "Yes, let's."

We haggled for ten minutes over a variety of options. In the end, it was going to cost me an even fifty grand, but I had a feeling it'd be worth it. I didn't know why Fate wanted me to meet this guy so much. He seemed capable, but nothing stood out.

Elton was confident but not a braggart. His demeanor told me he'd seen some serious shit and knew how to keep a cool head under pressure. I also had a feeling there was a lot he wasn't telling me. When he finished eating and walked back to resume his job at the track, I examined him with my true sight scope. Nothing stood out about him. His aura burned a tad brighter than the other nubs, but that wasn't uncommon.

He was just a human. A nub.

Hannah climbed out of the Lamborghini she'd been driving and was all smiles and giggles when she took off the helmet. She hugged the track instructor then skipped over to me. "Oh my god, that was fun!"

"Glad you enjoyed it."

"Can we get a Lambo, Cain? Let's go rob another bank."

A woman standing nearby smiled when she overheard Hannah, not even suspecting that she was dead serious.

"Maybe another time." I started walking back toward Dolores. "We're meeting Elton for some instructions later today."

Her brow furrowed. "Are we gonna jump out of an airplane today?"

I shook my head. "No. That'll come tomorrow."

She looked around. "What now?"

"Now we kill some time." We had a couple of hours until Elton was done with work, so I drove us to a nearby farm with its own marketplace. I'd been up here years earlier and discovered their barbeque and homemade ice cream. It was a little early to eat, but I figured Hannah might enjoy the farm tour they offered.

"Cain, this is the most father-daughter kind of stuff you've ever done with me." Hannah looked puzzled as I paid for the tour. "Usually, you take me travelling to kill necromancers, not to pick apples."

I shrugged. "Time for a change of pace."

She laughed. "This seems pretty dull compared to fighting eldritch abominations and climbing collapsing skyscrapers."

"Yep. Enjoy the slow pace because things are about to heat up again." I headed toward the start of the tour. "Do you like farms?"

Hannah looked uncertainly at the families with young children waiting for the tour. "I've never been to one like this."

The tour started with a walk through the horse stables. Hannah's eyes lit up and she made it a point to pet every horse within reach. The next stop was the pigpen where the youngsters got to dump buckets of slop into the troughs and watch the hogs pig out. The dairy cows, however, seemed to be the biggest hit. Hannah giggled like crazy as she tried to coax milk from the udders of a heifer.

The girl in charge of the dairy cow part of the tour helped Hannah finally squeeze a few drops into the pail. "That's it! You've got it!"

Hannah looked up at me, eyes shining. "Okay, this has been way more fun than I ever thought it could be."

I smiled back. "See? Life isn't always about fighting assassins and eldritch monsters."

The tour girl giggled. "Fighting monsters sounds more fun than milking a cow."

"Both are fun, but for different reasons." Hannah squeezed more milk into the pail. "But this is amazeballs."

After the tour was over, we had BBQ and ice cream, then drove out to the address Elton had given me. Hannah couldn't stop talking about the cows, and every time we passed a pasture with bovines, she'd point out the window. "Look! More cows!"

"Yep." I couldn't help but grin. "Maybe I need a few for Sanctuary."

Her eyes widened. "Oh, that would be so cool! Maybe some goats too?"

It wasn't a bad idea. I'd considered keeping the farm going after Old Joe had passed, but it was too much responsibility for someone who was constantly travelling for work. Maybe it was okay to slow down a bit once this nasty mess was sorted and start a farm.

The idea sounded absurd in my head. Me starting a farm? Layla would have a field day with that one.

Thinking of Layla sobered me instantly. I had a sinking feeling that I'd doomed her to a terrible fate by asking her to use Panoptes. We should have taken a chance and tried to escape with the wings. It would've been extremely difficult, but we'd survived worse.

"Cain, you look upset." Hannah touched my hand. "By that, I mean your right eye twitched just a little bit."

I nodded. "I'm worried about Layla."

"Me too." She sighed. "It was the best play, though. You couldn't use Panoptes, but she could."

"Yeah, and now she's probably insane and trapped forever in the warehouse."

"Or maybe she ended up in Feary and froze to death in the winter court or is getting horribly sunburned on the beach at the summer court."

"Maybe I should drop all this skydiving business and go looking for her." I gripped the steering wheel a little tighter. "The only place I can't go is the warehouse."

"Cain, you can't go to the summer and winter courts. Last time Lord Aeolus tried to kill you."

"He pretended to. They can't act directly against me."

Hannah made a raspberry. "Dude, they have the workaround for that. If you go to Feary right now, they'll have the homefield advantage with Oblivion Guard from the other dimensions."

I turned onto a winding gravel road. "Yeah, but Layla would come looking for me."

"I doubt it." Hannah looked out at the forest. "Maybe I can go looking for her. Or Aura."

"We'll talk about it later." I followed the winding road until it ended at a white farmhouse. A large, corrugated steel hangar sat behind the house near a flat, grassy field. It looked like a pasture, but it was also the perfect runway for light aircraft.

I took another look at Elton with my true sight scope just to be sure. He looked normal, but a glowing sigil on his front porch lit up like a beacon. It was the kind used to ward off vampires and werewolves. No nub should know anything about sigils, but it was there plain as day.

Elton, it seemed, knew about the supernatural.

26

I decided not to mention the sigil on his front porch. There were no other sigils visible, so some other factor might be in play. It was best to let this one play out and see where it led. Maybe Fate had a reason for leading me here after all.

Elton sat on the front porch of the house, a beer in his hand. He stood and walked over to meet us. "You have the down payment?"

I gave him a bag with twenty-five percent of the total in it. "Yep."

"Good. Let's get started."

"If you're into shady business like this, why do you work at a race-track?" Hannah said.

Elton took the bag and smiled. "Because this kind of work doesn't come along all that often. I need something regular to pay the bills."

"And yet you've got solar panels on your hangar, a well head on the side of the house along with a septic tank, and a private cell tower in your back yard." I shrugged. "Looks like you don't have many bills to pay."

"Oh, I got bills to pay." He opened his front door and put the money bag inside. "Want a beer?"

"Sure," Hannah said.

I nodded.

Elton went inside and returned with beers for all of us.

Hannah grinned. "Wow, I wasn't expecting one."

He shrugged. "You're with someone like Cain, so I imagine you're emotionally old enough to drink."

She laughed. "You can say that again."

Elton headed toward the aircraft hangar and slid open the tall metal doors. He flicked a switch and the overhead lights clicked on in sequence. I'd suspected what might be inside but was still surprised to see no less than four aircraft inside. I only vaguely knew the kinds of planes these were. One was a single propeller Cessna, another a two-prop small cargo hauler. The third was a small helicopter, and the fourth was a corporate jet.

"How in the world did you fit all this in here?" Hannah's mouth dropped open. "And how much money did all this cost?"

"Minimal cost. My former line of work allowed me to acquire some very expensive hardware."

"Impressive." I walked around the jet. "Well, you certainly have the equipment needed to help me get the job done."

"Yep." Elton leaned against one of the metal doors. "The fuel costs are what kill me. Thankfully, we can practice with the dual prop hauler. The Eclipse jet will be the one for the actual job."

Hannah blinked. "Did you say Eclipse jet?"

He nodded toward the jet at the back of the hangar. "Yep. Eclipse Five-Fifty. It's small, but it gets the job done. And it's much less noticeable to fly a jet over the city. People tend to look up when they hear a prop-driven plane overhead."

Hannah grinned and turned to me. "An Eclipse for Eclipse. This feels right." She sipped her beer and grimaced. "Ugh, this tastes awful."

Elton laughed. "It's an acquired taste."

I walked around the cargo hauler. It looked plenty spacious for what we needed to do. "I'm ready to get started."

"Great." Elton grabbed one of several backpacks hanging from a rack. "There's a lot to learn about parachutes—how to deploy, how to repack them, how to care for them, and so forth. I'm going to keep this part brief since your primary goal seems to be landing on a building and nothing else. I'll give you some basics about the parachutes and then the real work begins bright and early tomorrow morning."

"Sounds good."

We spent the next hour learning how parachutes worked, what to do in case of emergency, and then practiced jumping out of the door of the cargo hauler while wearing a parachute. It was on the ground without wind and turbulence, but it was still a good way to get acquainted with the feel.

He was explaining how to properly jump from the plane during extreme turbulence when my phone buzzed with a text from Aura.

Layla is here!

I stared at the phone for a moment, then texted back. *How is she?*

Aura replied a moment later. *She looked fine, but she went straight to bed. She was dirty and smelled bad, so the sheets are going to be filthy.*

Glad you have your priorities in order.

"Something wrong, Cain?"

I looked up at Elton. "A missing friend just turned up."

"What?" Hannah's eyes widened. "Are they okay?"

I was proud of her for not blurting out a name or gender in front of a practical stranger. "They seem to be." I pocketed my phone. "We need to get back. We can pick this up tomorrow."

Elton nodded. "Hey, be careful on the drive out. There are some folks around here who like to take midnight walks in the middle of the road."

"Folks?" I thought of the sigil on his house. "Do they play dead and try to get strangers to stop their cars?"

"Ah, you know what's up." Elton grinned. "Just don't stop for anyone, okay?"

"Yeah, I'll watch out for vampires." I said it jokingly, but his eyes flared slightly.

His grin faded. "Yeah, vampires."

There was definitely something going on with this guy. He might have been exposed to the supernatural before and knew a little about the hidden world of supers. I considered asking him outright, but there was no time for idle chitchat. "See you tomorrow."

Hannah and I went back to Dolores and got inside.

Hannah spoke the instant the doors closed. "Layla's back and she's okay?"

"According to Aura."

She took out her phone and dialed. The phone rang and went to voicemail, but it dinged with a text a moment later. Hannah read it aloud. "There's nothing to talk about. Layla is asleep."

"Guess Aura doesn't feel like talking."

Hannah snorted. "She's probably still pissed for how you yelled at her earlier."

"What she did was stupid." I blew out a breath. "But at least we know how close Elektrode is to finding Sanctuary."

"Well, that's an awfully slender silver lining." She leaned her head against the window and looked outside. "I think Elton has secrets."

"He was special forces, so I'm sure he does."

"No, I mean, he's had experience with the supernatural."

I nodded. "Of that, I'm sure."

Despite Elton's warning, we made it out of the mountains without running into any strangers on the roads and arrived home without incident.

Aura was curled up on the couch watching a reality show. "I'm sleeping out here. Layla smells bad enough when she's showered." She pointed to the kitchen counter. "Panoptes is over there."

"Yeah, well your elf farts aren't great either." Hannah looked at the television with a frown. "This reality stuff rots your brain."

"I'm not taking advice about how to live my life from a kid."

"Well, maybe you should." Hannah picked up the remote and switched to another show. "Watch some sci-fi for a change."

Aura huffed. "Rude."

"You'll thank me later."

"Doubtful." Aura pushed off the couch. "I put the clockwork wings in the corner."

I picked up Panoptes and slid it into my utility pouch, then walked around the basement stairwell entrance and found the still folded wings stacked on the other side. "Thanks." I picked up a pair and examined them. The wings were tightly furled like a burrito with a harness hanging from the front.

I pressed a button on the harness and clockwork mechanisms ticked to life. The wings slowly spread out until they were about twelve feet wide from one wingtip to the other. Even then, the wings weren't fully expanded. The apparatus rested on the bottom wingtips, balanced by an internal gyro.

The harness was made of synthetic material like nylon instead of leather which the mechanists typically favored. A skeletal frame was covered in thin metallic feathers that were slick to the touch. I bent a feather. It flexed slightly but didn't warp or break. The Futurists had certainly improved the design.

Hannah stood over my shoulder. "Wow, so cool. Can we go flying?"

I cast a look at her. "You want to take your virgin flight in the dark?"

Her forehead pinched. "Kind of."

Aura laughed derisively. "And I'm supposed to take health advice from her?"

I lifted the wings by the harness. They were deceptively light. I took them into the front yard and strapped on the harness.

Hannah's mouth dropped open. "Are you really about to use them after what you just said?"

"I'm testing the controls." I had limited experience with Icarus wings and other magical flight devices. They were all extremely dangerous to the uninitiated, and even to those who were skilled with them.

There were only a couple of buttons and a dial on the harness. One folded and unfolded the wings. Another controlled the wing flare. The dial controlled the flapping. There were no propulsion controls. Like Icarus wings, these required the pilot to fly like a bird.

Despite my warning to Hannah, I was eager to try them out. On the other hand, I was also smart enough to heed my own advice. I turned on the flapping and let the wings carry me about a foot above the ground. The more I turned the dial, the faster the wings flapped and the higher I rose.

"Can I try, Cain?" Hannah clasped her hands. "Please?"

"Tomorrow." I turned the dial to off and dropped to the ground.

Hannah ran her hand along the wings. "So, do we still need Elton?"

I nodded. "It'll be safer using the wings. We can jump out of the plane and glide to the roof. Then when we escape, we'll use the wings again."

"Ah, yeah. Can't use a parachute twice."

Aura watched from the front porch. "I'm kind of excited to try these things out."

"Me too!" Hannah rubbed her hands together eagerly then abruptly frowned. "How are we going to explain these things to Elton?"

"I'll just tell him I bought them from an inventor." I slid out of the harness and pressed a button. The wings furled into a tight cylinder. "Rest up. Tomorrow is going to be a busy day."

I went to my room. There was a dark spot of grunge on the floor and a slight odor. This was where an eye of Panoptes watched Sanctuary. It was where Layla had arrived. I sprayed some cleaner on the floor and wiped it up. I wasn't looking forward to seeing what the guest bedroom looked like.

I woke up early the next morning and made a simple breakfast of sausage and eggs. Aura got off the couch and went to take a shower. Hannah emerged from her room a little later dressed in a t-shirt and cargo pants.

She plucked a sausage from the plate and bit into it. "Should I try to wake up Layla?"

"I got it." I went to the guest bedroom door and opened it. Layla was on her back in the middle of the bed snoring gently. The room reeked of stale sweat and other aromatic body odors. She was coated in dirt and unidentifiable grunge. Even for a seasoned vet like me, the odor was a bit overwhelming.

Layla's reflexes were lightning fast and dangerous, so I gently prodded her and stepped back. She grunted and swatted her arm but didn't wake up. I tried again. She snarled and rolled around, but never opened her eyes. I had a terrible feeling about what the corrupted Panoptes might have done to her mind.

The question was, did I leave her here to sleep, or try to rouse her and make her take a shower? This entire room was going to need a deep cleaning at this point. I also didn't know if it was safe leaving her unsupervised. What if she woke up, insanity still clouding her mind, and started throwing her own shit on the walls?

I hated to touch her with more than a finger, but I reached over and slapped her face. Layla lunged up from the bed with a roar, landing on her feet at the edge of the bed. She crouched slightly, arms in a defensive fighting stance. She blinked several times and squinted as if trying to clear her eyes.

"Cain?" Her voice was ragged, tired.

I nodded. "You look and smell like shit."

Layla slowly held out her filthy hands. "What the fuck happened to me?"

"I was going to ask you the same thing." I motioned toward the shower. "But first, can you clean up? I think you crapped your pants."

She looked down at her dirty yoga pants and gagged. "Oh, gods. I'm going to be sick." She ran into the bathroom and started throwing up.

I stripped the sheets, blankets, everything from the bed. The mattress protector had thankfully done its job, but everything else smelled so bad I didn't even want to clean it. I put on some rubber gloves, got a large plastic trash bag, and stuffed the pillows, sheets, and comforter inside.

Hannah wrinkled her nose as I walked toward the front door. "What's that odor?"

"I don't want to know." I went outside and tossed the bag into my incinerator. Then I went back inside to check on Layla. The shower was running, so that was a good sign. I picked up her clothing where she'd left it outside the bathroom door and took it outside to the incinerator. She had plenty of extra clothing here, so that wouldn't be a problem.

I sprayed cleaner on the tile flooring and mopped up the dirt and other filth. By the time I was done, I'd managed to purge the unholy stench.

Aura watched with an amused expression. "It's always so strange when I see you doing household chores."

I took the mop into the utility room to clean it and empty the bucket. "It's not like I can just wave a magic wand."

"I mean, you probably could, but you'd have to know the proper spells."

I took off the rubber gloves and washed my hands. "It's just something that needs to be done."

Layla emerged from the guest bedroom with fresh clothes. Her wet hair hung down past her shoulders. She looked tired and miserable.

"Want some food?" I asked.

She shuddered. "I don't think I can eat right now."

"Can you go on a car ride, or do you want to stay here?"

She rubbed her eyes. "Where are we going?"

"Skydiving." I touched her shoulder. "Look, I'm sorry about Panoptes. I think it really messed you up."

"Did it?" She rubbed her eyes again. "I don't remember much except being really sick and crawling around in a pit of worms or snakes." Layla shivered violently. "It was all so fuzzy. Then I had a moment of clarity and grabbed the wings and wished myself home."

"You did good."

She wiped tears from her cheeks. "Shut up, Cain."

I checked the time. We were going to be late to meet Elton, so I texted him to let him know. Then I went to Fred's pool and splashed the water. I already knew he wasn't back, because he was typically the first to rush to the kitchen when I cooked sausages, one of his favorite meals.

"You want Fred's pet to help me?" Layla said.

"Yeah." I stood and sighed. "But that'll have to wait. Let's get going." I packed the rest of the sausages and other snacks in a cooler and put that and the wings in Dolores's trunk. Then everyone piled inside, and we headed north.

Today was going to be a long day. I just hoped Layla could hold it together.

27

It was already nine in the morning by the time we reached Elton's place, but he didn't seem too concerned about us being late. He was, however, surprised to see two more of us.

"I thought it was just the two of you." Elton walked off his front porch, steam rising from the top of his coffee mug. "That wasn't factored into your price, Cain."

I'd expected this, so I held up another duffel bag. "How much?"

"I'll have to factor in the fuel and equipment costs." He looked Layla up and down. "You look even more dangerous than Cain."

"I am." Layla's voice still sounded weak, but the confidence was there.

His eyebrow rose when he looked at Aura. "Interesting."

Aura frowned. "What, I don't look dangerous?"

Elton's hand blurred and a pistol appeared in his grip. "Okay, what kind of trick is this? I thought we had an agreement."

I frowned and glanced at the others. "An agreement with whom?"

He scowled. "No games. What, did you think I wouldn't notice her ears under that hair?"

"Mine?" Aura touched her pointy ears. "That's a birth defect."

Elton's eyes narrowed and the gun vanished. "My bad. You're an elf, not a fairy."

"I knew it!" Hannah said. "He does know about supers."

"Fae, not fairies." I took a sip of coffee from my travel mug. "I take it you struck a bargain with the fae before?"

"This is just plain disrespectful." Elton pursed his lips. "How about an honest explanation about who you are and what you want? Otherwise, I'll give you your money back except for a small fee for my time and we go our separate ways."

"Sure." I shrugged. "Will you return the same courtesy?"

"I'll tell you what I can." He looked us over again. "No vampires, though. Those cold-blooded sons of bitches are the worst."

"Yeah, they are." I went to the back of the car and pulled out the clockwork wings. "Are you familiar with the mechanists?"

His forehead pinched when he saw the folded contraptions. "No. I suppose you're going to tell me what they are?"

"I'm going to summarize so we can get back to the business at hand. I have an idea what you're about though." I set the furled wings on the ground and picked up one. "You were in special forces, but not the kind that deals with ordinary humans. Yours dealt with supernatural threats."

Elton didn't look surprised. "That sums it up. I somehow ended up going against the powers that be—the fae—and they called a truce. My commanders made a deal that we leave each other alone, but the human supers were still fair game."

"You killed supers just because they were different?" Hannah winced. "That's not right."

"First of all, I never said a word about killing. Second of all, I said supernatural threats." He shrugged. "We know quite a bit about the secret society of supers hiding right beneath our noses. Our job was just to respond to the ones who got out of hand—mainly vampires."

"Oh." Hannah sighed in relief. "I thought you were wholesale murdering supers or something."

"We weren't." Elton watched me intently. "What's this thing you've got?"

I pressed a button and the wings unfurled.

His eyes widened and he whistled appreciatively. "Wow, now those are something." He walked closer and prodded them. The wings wobbled but remained upright due to the internal gyro. "They weeble and they wobble but they don't fall down."

"These are clockwork wings made by a faction of the supernatural underworld called mechanists." I strapped on the harness. "They claim to hate magic, but they use some aspects of it to create their inventions."

"I'm officially intrigued." Elton's eyes lit up like a little kid's. "Those things look crazy."

"They are." I turned the dial. Clockwork gears ticked rapidly. The wings flapped, lifting me slightly off the ground. "We plan to use these instead of parachutes but jumping from a plane is still the best way to glide into our target."

"You can't just fly up there?"

I shrugged. "Maybe, but we don't have a lot of time to learn how to operate these things. If we can just glide to the target, get what we want, and then use the wings to glide down to ground level, I think that'll be good enough."

Elton picked up a pair of furled wings. "Mind if I give them a try?"

"Sure." I turned the dial on mine slowly down and the flapping slowed until I landed. I unstrapped the harness. "Just use mine."

He put down the other wings and strapped into mine. "The dial makes the wings flap?"

"Yeah. That's about all I know."

He rotated the dial and the wings flapped faster and faster until he levitated about ten feet up. He shifted to the right and drifted slowly that way. He leaned to the other side and suddenly flipped out of control, crashing to the ground on his back. The wings continued flapping, jolting him off the ground with every thrust.

Elton quickly turned the dial down and slid out of the harness. "Ouch." He flexed his neck and stood slowly. "I thought I had it, but apparently not."

"We kind of stole them so we have no idea how they work." Layla shrugged. "Maybe we should use parachutes instead."

Elton laughed. "Hell no. I love these things." He lifted the wings from the ground and inspected them. "They're not even damaged." He balanced them on their tips and took a step back. "Give me a minute to look them over."

I sipped on my coffee and looked them over myself. There didn't seem to be much to them except for the dial on the front and the two buttons on the harness's chest panel.

Elton grunted and worked his fingers on the side of the chest panel. A slender ring popped out of the surface and hung by a slender wire. He pushed in on the chest panel on the other side and another ring popped free. He pulled them both out until they went taut.

"Okay, I didn't see those at all." I walked to the side for a better look. "What do they do?"

Elton slid into the harness and slid his index fingers into the rings. He pulled down and the wings folded back behind him. He held his hands extended to the sides and the wings flared. Pushing his hands away from him caused the wings to tilt slightly.

Hannah watched closely. "Ooh, that's what bird wings do. They fold back for diving, or they widen for gliding. I guess the tilt is for steering?"

"You got it, little lady." Elton turned the dial and rose from the ground. He pulled on the wires and drifted left and right. He pushed the other button on the chest panel and immediately began to wobble madly. Another press of the button steadied the wings. He turned the dial down and landed.

"Does that button turn off the gyro?" Hannah said.

"The gyro keeps them steady for takeoff, but once you're airborne, I think you'll want to turn it off." He grinned. "Cain, if you let me have a pair of these, I won't charge you another red cent for training."

"Deal." I held out my hand and we shook.

Elton walked around, the wings still on his back, wobbling uncertainly. He pressed the gyro toggle, and his gait became easier. "Turn off the gyro when you walk in them." He put his hands over his head, pulling the wires in the one direction he hadn't tried. The wings folded even tighter than when he pulled down. "This must be for a faster dive."

I put on another pair of wings and practiced with the wires. The others did the same. We looked like a bunch of fools prancing around with our camouflaged wings in Elton's front yard for the next twenty minutes, then followed him to his aircraft hangar.

Elton vanished inside and came out with a small backpack. "I'm going to conduct some dangerous experiments."

I put out a hand. "Hold up, if you die, who's going to pilot the jet?"

"That's why I'm taking a parachute along." He patted the pack.

"You know a chute won't deploy unless you're high enough." I shook my head. "There's got to be a safer way to test these things."

He blew out a breath. "If you want to glide in on these things, then we need to understand how they operate."

"I'll do it." Aura stepped away from the group. "If something happens, I'll see you at midnight."

Elton blinked. "I'm sorry, but what?"

"If she dies, she resurrects at midnight." Hannah shrugged. "It's her thing."

He stared uncertainly at her. "Elves can do that?"

"Only this elf." Layla chuckled mirthlessly. "It was part of this curse Athena put on her bloodline ages ago."

"The goddess, Athena?" Elton held up a hand. "You're telling me she exists?"

"Ah, the fae didn't tell you everything, did they?" Hannah rolled her eyes. "So typical. Yeah, gods of all kinds exist. But they're not very nice."

"A-fucking-men." Layla scowled. "Mars killed me once."

"And Cain had to become Death so he could find a way to resurrect her."

"I'm flying!" Aura said.

We glanced up and saw her rising slowly but steadily, the wings flapping vigorously.

She twisted the dial, but it was apparently already maxed out. "Gods, these things are slow for gaining altitude."

We watched as the wings labored to climb higher. Moments later, she was about a hundred feet up.

"I think that answers a question," I said. "These wings don't have enough lift. It'd take us an hour to reach the top of the Sovereign building."

Elton took notice of the building name but didn't comment.

Aura continued climbing until she was about three hundred feet up, then pushed her hands down to her sides. The wings folded and she dove a few feet. She spread her arms and the wings flared, allowing her to glide. She spiraled downward one way, then adjusted the wires to turn the other way, wobbling unsteadily with every move.

"I can't watch." Hannah covered her eyes, then peeked through her fingers. "Never mind, I've seen her die in worse ways before."

Elton watched, jaw tight with suspense. "She's coming in pretty fast."

"Yeah, she is." Layla cupped her hands over her mouth. "Go faster, elf! I want to see you crash really hard."

"Shut up, Layla!" Aura nearly spun out of control but flared the wings at the last minute as she neared the ground. Panicking, she thrust her hands straight out and the wings cupped down, slowing her and rotating her upright. Her feet touched the ground, spinning furiously like a cartoon character in a vain attempt to remain upright, but she had too much speed.

Aura flopped on her belly, leaving a small furrow in the grassy field. I took off my wings and ran to her. She rose to her knees, spitting out dirt and grass.

"You okay?"

She wiped off her mouth, but her face was stained green from the grass. "I don't think I broke anything."

I helped her up. She brushed off her clothes and spit out a few remaining bits of grass.

Layla clapped enthusiastically. "Loved it. Ten out of ten."

Hannah pretended to hold up a sign. "I give that landing a solid ten."

Elton shook his head. "You people aren't right."

"That's for damned sure," Aura said. "Just because I resurrect doesn't mean it feels good plowing into the ground."

I pulled some grass from between the metal feathers on her wings. "Actually, you showed us exactly what to do, and I appreciate it."

"Thanks, Cain." She smiled and wiped a tear from her eye. "See, I can take one for the team."

I snorted. "Yeah, you've taken a few."

"Deserved some of them," Hannah added.

Elton dropped his backpack and fiddled with his wings, testing the control wires again. "I'm gonna give this a try."

"Maybe you don't remember the part where we need you alive?" Layla said. "I sure as hell can't fly a nub plane."

"Nub." Elton snorted. "I haven't heard that word in a while. It's what you supers call us normal people, right?"

"Yeah, no offense." Layla shrugged. "It's just slang."

He turned the dial on his wings and lifted off, climbing about a hundred feet, then he leaned forward and flared the wings, gliding gently. He turned side to side, circled downward, then straightened out, legs dangling beneath him. At the last moment before his feet touched down, he pushed out with his hands. The wings cupped, braking hard, and rotating him completely upright.

Elton jogged to a stop and grinned. "Now that was fun."

"How'd you make it look so easy?" Hannah asked.

"I did a lot of flyboarding and water jetpacking." He held out his hands and mimicked steadying himself. "You have to get really good at keeping your balance."

"Then this should be a cinch for us." Layla cleared her throat. "Um, I guess I'll try it."

I put a hand on her arm. "Are you sure you're up to it?"

"I've been through worse, Cain." She walked to a spot away from us. "You're the dumbass who looked Cthulhu in the eyes and did this to me."

Elton flinched. "Cthulhu? The Lovecraft dude?"

Hannah laughed. "Yeah, the tentacle mouth dude."

He stared uncertainly at her for a long moment, then shook it off.

Layla rose to about a hundred feet and began gliding down. Her landing was much rougher than Elton's, but her muscular legs prevented her from faceplanting like Aura. We each took a turn gliding and landing. Hannah flopped on her belly. I braked the wings so hard that I nearly toppled over backwards when I landed.

All in all, we were off to a decent start. But we were going to have to get a lot better to survive jumping from a jet and landing on something as small as a rooftop.

Elton marked off an area about as large as the landing zone on the roof. The space was a lot tighter once all the obstructions were accounted for, leaving only about twenty feet of space. To make it even trickier, there were large air conditioning units and the decorative glass panels we'd have to navigate past before landing.

He marked off the obstacles with tall stakes, measuring everything by looking at the pictures I'd taken and then guesstimating the distance between. Once he was done, we started practicing the landing. No one, not even Elton, came close to planting the landing. As the sun passed its zenith, everyone looked discouraged.

"Maybe parachutes are better," Hannah said as we took a break for lunch.

Elton shook his head. "I could probably land on that rooftop without snagging my chute, but there's no way any of you can do it without hundreds of jumps. I'm starting to think you need to give up on this plan unless you want to keep practicing for weeks."

My brilliant plan, it seemed, was a dud.

28

"If you let me keep my wings, I'll refund your money." Elton looked at his furled wings and sighed. "I just don't think this plan of yours is going to work."

"We've only been at this for a few hours." Hannah shook her head vehemently. "I'm not giving up!"

Elton zoomed in on the rooftop picture on his tablet and pointed out the decorative glass structure on the south side of the roof. "Yeah, but the last few times, you would have hit this structure or smacked into the air conditioning units. You haven't even come close to making a safe landing."

Hannah huffed. "Because it's so freaking hard keeping straight!"

Elton pointed up. "It's going to be much windier at rooftop level. If you can't adjust for the gentle breeze at ground level, I don't know how you expect to counter high winds."

"We just have to keep at it." I finished off my sandwich. "Everyone can land without falling on their face, so that's an improvement."

"Not falling on your face and nailing a perfect landing are two different things." Elton shrugged. "But I'm willing to keep going if you are."

Layla raised an eyebrow. "Why are you practicing with us, anyway? You won't be jumping. You'll be flying the jet."

He bit into an apple and chewed for a moment before answering. "Because it's fun. It reminds me of the squirrel suits my friends and I used when base jumping." He stopped chewing and his gaze went distant. "Maybe we're approaching this the wrong way."

Everyone looked at him expectantly as he went silent.

"Well, spit it out," Layla said.

"We're trying to use these wingsuits like parachutes." He dropped the apple, put on his wings, and went back to the field. The rest of us followed. He rose a hundred feet up and glided in a wide circle before making his approach to the mock rooftop. He was still about forty feet up when he cupped the wings to come to a hard stop, then he turned the dial, activating the wing flapping again.

The wind picked up, causing him to drift. Elton turned into the wind and increased the wing flapping so he could drift back over the target. Once he was over the mock roof, lowering the wing speed allowed him to slowly drop to the ground. He landed right where one of the air conditioning units would be and pumped his fists. "Perfect landing!"

Hannah frowned. "Is it though? You're on one of the air conditioning boxes."

"Doesn't matter." He pointed to his feet. "I landed lightly on top of it instead of smashing into it at high speed."

"They can easily support our weight." I clapped my hands. "If we land like this, we can land just about anywhere on the roof."

"Exactly." Elton walked over to us. "The biggest challenge will be adjusting for the wind."

I rubbed my hands together. "All right, let's get back to it."

I went first, gliding over the target, braking hard, and then activating the wing flapping. The wind was blowing harder, so it took me longer to fight against it to stay over the target. I dropped lower and lower, but every time I flapped the wings slower, the wind would carry me away from the target.

The wind died down. With the wings still flapping hard, I over-shot the roof.

Elton cupped his hands and shouted, "You just hit the decorative windows, Cain."

"Wonderful." I flew back over the roof and managed to lower myself to the ground more easily without the wind interfering.

We continued practicing until dusk set in. Everyone was tired, cranky, and ready to go home, but I felt like we'd made some progress.

"I still haven't landed on the roof!" Hannah shook her head. "I should be better at this!"

"Don't lose hope." Elton patted her on the back. "I feel like you really have a shot at it now."

"Maybe we can shoot grappling hooks at the AC units and pull ourselves down." Layla shrugged. "That way the wind can't mess with us."

I had to admit I was feeling better about it too.

Elton turned to me. "You still owe me some bios on you and your crew. You know about me, so I'd like to know how an odd bunch like you fit together."

"It's complicated." I climbed into my car. "We'll talk about it tomorrow." Dark worms threatened at the edges of my vision. The stress of the day was taking a toll, and I needed to give my mind a chance to rest.

WE RETURNED bright and early the next day. Elton stood on his front porch, coffee in hand. He set it down and came out to meet us, an eager look on his face.

I unloaded the wings from the back. "Why do you look so excited?"

"Because I kept practicing after you left yesterday." He motioned toward the field. "I figured out an easier way to fight the wind."

"I'm listening."

He dampened his index finger with his tongue and held it up. "Wind isn't too strong right now, but I can still show you."

We went to the field and Elton put on his wings. He lifted a few feet off the ground. "When the wind is blowing straight at you, you need to rotate." He pulled on a control wire and one wing tilted slightly, causing him to rotate as he hovered. "With your profile to the wind, it won't move you as much, and you can just drop down to the target."

"Simple but effective." Layla ran a hand down her face. "Why didn't we think of that yesterday?"

"Because we're not birds," Aura said. "I hardly gave a thought about how to fly before getting these wings."

Elton checked his phone. "We might have a storm rolling in late this morning, so the wind is bound to pick up."

"I can hardly wait," Layla said dryly.

While the others practiced, I gave Elton a summarized breakdown of who we were and our mission but without giving too much away.

"So, you're a wizard assassin and the other wizard assassins are trying to kill you." Elton nodded. "Not the first time I've heard that."

My eyebrows rose. "It isn't?"

"Nah." He sipped his coffee. "I've dealt with vampire assassins, werewolf soldiers, and more. Other countries have tried to militarize their supernatural population, but the results are never pretty."

"The fae don't like it when nubs know too much about supers, so they'd send in the Oblivion Guard to put a stop to it whenever things got out of control." I watched Hannah make an almost perfect landing and clapped my hands. "Good job!"

She grinned. "I did it!"

I turned back to Elton. "North Korea had a program where they were intentionally turning people into vampires so they could use them as assassins. We paid them a visit, killed most of the officers in charge, and told them if they continued, we'd wipe their slate clean."

Elton whistled. "You would've done the world a favor by killing all their leadership."

I shook my head. "That's not what the Oblivion Guard does. We just make sure the nubs don't know too much, and if they do, we prevent them from abusing it." I almost brought up how wildly things had changed on Gaia Alpha since that wall separating the normal from the supers had come down but didn't feel like opening the can of worms about multiple dimensions.

It seemed Fate had directed me toward Elton for a very good reason. He was the perfect person to help us with our heist since he already knew about the supernatural community. I didn't understand how she could do such a thing without breaking the loom—something she bitched about constantly when I was Death. Seeing as I hadn't heard so much as a peep from that crowd in a while, it looked like I'd have to threaten Alistair the necromancer again just to get an audience.

Right after lunch, a storm front rolled in, creating higher winds and harder practice conditions. But that was just what we needed. One at a time we flew up into the winds and practiced the maneuvers Elton had taught us. Putting our profile to the wind significantly decreased the drift while landing. Unfortunately, we had to cut the day short once lightning lit up the sky.

WE CAME BACK the next day and the next. By the end of the week, we were ready for our first high altitude attempts. When we arrived, Elton was on his porch, but this time there was a tall, thin guy sitting in a chair next to him.

"Wait in the car," I told the others. I got out and approached the pair. "Who's this?"

"A pilot friend." Elton stood. "Jim, this is Cain."

"Pleasure." Jim tipped his ball cap revealing wispy hair on a balding head that belied his young age. His grin was lopsided, and his eyes looked slightly crazed.

"I thought you were a pilot." I looked Jim up and down. "You should have consulted me before bringing someone else into my business."

Elton held up his hands. "I know but hear me out. I think it's safer if I do the practice jumps with you. I can monitor the situation and rescue anyone with a parachute if something goes wrong."

I narrowed my eyes and held my gaze on him for a moment. "Can he be trusted to keep quiet?"

"He was in my unit, so absolutely."

"Sir, I continue to make a living by keeping my mouth shut." Jim's mouth stretched into a lopsided grin. "I'm pleased to be at your service." The man's voice was slightly goofy and endearing, but his eyes were deadly serious.

I sighed. "Fine. But don't bring in anyone else without telling me."

"I don't plan on it." Elton patted Jim on the back. "Go get the Gander warmed up. We'll be along in a minute."

"Yes, sir." Jim saluted and headed toward the hangar.

Elton turned to me. "It'll be safer this way, believe me."

I didn't see a reason to belabor the point. What was done was done. Besides, he was probably right.

The others were already out of the car, furled wings in hand because of course they hadn't stayed in the car like I'd asked. Propellers buzzed to life and a moment later, the Gander taxied onto the grass runway.

We joined Elton inside the hangar. He rolled out a clothes rack with black flight suits and matching full-faced helmets with built-in headsets. "I picked these up yesterday."

Layla frowned. "Why do we need these?" She patted her yoga pants. "These are fine."

"The flight suits cut wind drag and are more comfortable. The helmets will keep you from getting knocked out if you collide with each other." He slid on a suit and grabbed parachute packs from a rack. "If anything goes wrong, I'll have a couple of chutes with me."

Hannah put on her flight suit. It fit snugly but left some wiggle room. "Oh, this makes me feel like a professional spy."

"These are what we wore for HALO missions." Elton zipped up his suit. "The only thing we won't be using is an oxygen mask."

Hannah put on her helmet. "What's HALO?"

"High altitude, low opening." Elton mimicked falling with his hand. "You wait until the last minute, then open your chute so you can land undetected in enemy territory."

"Sounds exciting." Layla's eyes brightened. "How low?"

"Eight hundred feet or less." Elton adjusted the strap on his helmet until it fit snugly. "But one of our guys did it at three hundred because he was an idiot."

Aura finished suiting up. "Sounds terrifying but I'd give it a try."

Hannah grinned. "Me too."

"Maybe we should concentrate on sticking this landing first." I went outside to the waiting aircraft.

We boarded the Gander and Elton slid the door shut. I unfolded a seat from the side and buckled in. The others did the same.

Elton flipped up the visor on his helmet and tapped a button on the side. "Turn on the headsets right here."

The helmets muffled the sound of the propellers only a little bit. When I pressed the button to turn on the headsets, the engine noise went almost completely silent.

Hannah oohed. "Noise canceling headsets. Nice!"

Elton spoke. "Jim we are ready for takeoff."

"Roger that. Taxiing down the runway."

The plane began moving to the far end of the field, turned, and then accelerated. The scenery rushed past and the trees at the end of the runway got closer and closer. Just when I thought he planned to crash us, the plane lifted from the ground. We couldn't have missed the treetops by more than a few feet.

"Did he really need that much runway?" I asked.

Elton shrugged. "He knows what he's doing."

"She's a bit heavy with a full load," Jim said. "Needed more speed."

Layla lifted her visor and rolled her eyes at me. "After everything we've been through, this is what scares you, Cain?"

I leaned back in my seat. It wasn't even remotely comfortable, but it wasn't meant to be. "It'd be awfully anticlimactic to die on a practice run, wouldn't it?"

Layla snorted. "Or ironic."

"I don't see the irony in it," Hannah said. "Maybe you don't know what that word means."

I tuned out the inevitable argument and closed my eyes while the plane gained altitude.

"Sir, we're at one thousand feet," Jim said sometime later.

"Distance to target?" Elton replied.

"Three clicks and counting down."

Elton stood and slid open the door. "Put on your wings. We jump at one click."

We put on the harnesses, keeping the wings in their compact position since there wasn't enough space to open them in the cabin.

Jim began counting down. "One point five clicks. One point four."

When he reached one click, Elton motioned us out. "Go, go, go."

We jumped out one at a time, Elton coming last, two parachute packs in hand.

I looked down and realized we weren't falling toward the field, but toward the top of the mountain near the end of the runway.

Elton spoke. "Sound off, team."

"Hannah here."

"Layla reporting for duty, sir."

"Aura checking in."

"Cain."

Hannah laughed. "Always so serious."

Layla snorted. "Unless we're in a life-or-death situation, and then he has jokes."

I sighed. "Cut the chatter."

"The target building is six hundred and thirty-five feet tall." Elton pointed toward the mountain. "That means we can fall about two hundred feet before deploying our wings. As you may have noticed, we're falling toward a mountain top that is approximately five hundred feet above sea level. The wind will be about as strong up there as it will be at roof level for the target building. When I give the order, deploy your wings, but we'll be traveling too fast for you to open them all the way at once, so flare them slowly."

Hannah did a barrel roll. "Roger, dodger!"

Elton gave the order a short time later. We hit the button to open our wings. The wind caught them, slowing me slightly, but they were still folded back in dive position. I pulled the wires, gradually flaring them wider until I began to glide.

"Oh, shit!" Hannah turned sideways and narrowly avoided colliding with Aura.

Layla had drifted away from us, probably to avoid the same thing.

Elton managed the smoothest transition. He kept an eagle eye on us, chutes at the ready. "Okay, the next part is what we've done a hundred times already. The only difference is that we're doing this as a team. Hannah, you land first and get out of the way. Then Layla, Aura, and Cain."

"I'm on it." Hannah saluted and went into a steep dive.

I grimaced. "Hey, be careful."

Hannah giggled. "You too, Dad."

I flinched at the last word. It hit me in a strange way that wasn't entirely unpleasant. Then again, she'd been calling me her big brother not all that long ago either, so maybe it was just weird.

Layla dove after her at a slower rate, and Aura lined up behind her. I continued spiraling down behind them. Hannah thrust out her hands and the wings cupped, braking her suddenly. The wings flapped and she began lowering herself. The wind was strong at this altitude, but she turned sideways and mitigated the interference.

She landed at the outer edge of the peak and raised her hands triumphantly. Layla followed, landing even more smoothly. Aura came in slowly and took three times longer than the others to land. I came in faster, braked about twenty feet up, turned sideways to the wind, then flapped to a smooth landing.

Elton glided overhead. "Amazing job. Fly back to the airfield for another practice run." He continued over the mountain and flew down toward the far end of the airfield.

Hannah held up a hand. "Awesome job, team!"

I gave her a high five.

Layla hesitated, then high-fived her as well. "Yeah, not bad, but the elf was too slow."

"Sorry, I'll do better." Aura blew out a breath. "It took us fifteen minutes to land. That's mostly my fault, but we need to cut it down to five minutes to avoid chances of being spotted."

"Agreed," I said. "Let's keep at it." I turned up the dial. The wings flapped and I gained altitude. Then I turned toward the airfield and began gliding down.

I was starting to feel hopeful. This crazy idea might work. But landing on a mountain was a lot different than landing on a crowded rooftop. Since there was no way to practice such a landing, we'd have to do it perfectly on our first time.

29

W e did eight more practice runs and reduced our time to ten minutes. Cutting it down to five looked impossible, but we had to keep trying.

"I'm so tired," Hannah said as she loaded her wings into Dolores. "But that was a lot of fun."

"Yeah, it was." Layla grinned. "And Elton's kind of hot for a nub."

"Oh, great." Aura shook her head. "Layla's already sexualizing our instructor."

"Hey, I've caught him looking at my ass a few times."

Aura snorted. "It's kind of hard to miss."

"Yeah." Layla's grin widened. "Glorious, isn't it?"

We'd packed clothes so we could stay at a nearby hotel and save the long drive home. We woke up early the next morning, had a quick breakfast and went back to Elton's where we had another long day of practice. After four jumps, we lowered our time to seven minutes.

On the fifth jump, we tried landing in formation to further reduce time. Despite all our practice runs, we still weren't ready for something like that. Hannah's wing tip hit Layla's and sent the two of them spiraling out of control. Layla managed to get hers under control, but

Elton had to strap a parachute onto Hannah so she could land safely on the airfield.

I flew straight to Hannah instead of the mountain. "What happened?"

She took off the wings and let them balance on the tips. "I don't know. I couldn't get them to flare after the collision."

I examined the wings and found three of the metallic feathers jammed into each other. The material was flexible, so there was no permanent damage, but it had prevented the controls on that side from working properly. I worked out the kinks and the wing controls functioned again.

"Safe to say we won't be trying to land in formation again." I put on her wings and levitated a few feet to make sure they worked properly.

"Cain, we suck." Hannah threw up her hands. "We should be nailing the landings by now."

"We've barely been at this for three days." I folded up the parachute and stuffed it back into its pack. "This isn't something you can expect to master immediately. It takes hundreds of hours of practice."

She looked up the mountain where Aura and Layla stood, sunlight beaming through their wings as if they were goddesses looking down on their creations. "I just thought that our training and supernatural abilities might help us learn faster."

"Well, flying is a lot different." I shrugged. "Let's get back to the aircraft hangar."

We donned our wings, picked up the parachute pack, and walked down the airfield. Jim was already taxiing the aircraft for another run.

By the end of the day, we'd achieved three six-minute landings in a row, and it seemed like that was the best we were going to do. It took each of us a little more than a minute to land from the moment where we deployed our wings. That was sixty seconds of hanging in the air like a sitting duck.

If someone inside the penthouse saw us coming, they'd have plenty of time to get to the roof and blast us. A couple of well-placed longshots from guardians would put an end to our adventure real fast. If we executed everything perfectly, then we'd remain directly over the building and out of line of sight of the windows, but I wasn't counting on us pulling this off perfectly.

After the final run, we gathered in the aircraft hangar to plan next steps.

"Not a bad day, all things considered." Elton popped open a beer. "I've got steaks. How about we have a cookout and talk about what comes next?"

"A cookout?" Hannah's eyes widened. "Do we get to sit around a campfire and tell stories?"

"Well, I was going to use my grill." Elton shrugged. "Stories are optional."

"I'm starving." Layla folded her wings and set them next to everyone else's. "Let's get this party started."

Elton wheeled out a charcoal grill and heated it up. He brought a plate of steaks outside and set them on a long wooden picnic table for seasoning.

Hannah glanced at his house. "Can I use your bathroom?"

"There's one in the hangar." Elton nodded toward the airstrip.

"You really don't like people going in your house," Layla said. "Do you have a pile of dead bodies in there?"

Jim chuckled. "Elton ain't much for letting people into his house." He scratched his head. "Hell, I've never been further than the porch myself."

"That's pretty sus." Hannah narrowed her eyes. "Maybe we should investigate."

Elton sprinkled pepper on the steaks. "Don't take offense just because I don't like anyone going in my house."

"None taken." I completely understood the sentiment. I'd had very few people in Sanctuary until the fiasco with Hannah. Then I'd gone off the deep end.

"Of course, Cain agrees with him." Hannah rolled her eyes. "He didn't trust anyone until we wormed our way into his cold heart."

"That's an accurate description." I took a plate of seasoned steaks and put them on the grill. I usually had my fae glamping tent when we went on our expeditions, so cooking over an open campfire or on a grill wasn't something I'd done in a long while. "The worming into my life part."

Layla snorted. "Cain still doesn't know where I live, so while I want to know what secrets Elton is hiding, I also understand why he doesn't want to share."

"Wow, really?" Hannah laughed. "Cain, how have you not been to Layla's place yet?"

"Because he doesn't care enough to find out." Layla smirked. "And that's what I love about him."

Aura looked up from a book she was reading. "That's so fucked up."

Hannah raised an eyebrow. "Don't even get me started on you."

"Yeah, please let's not." I blew out a breath. "I'd like to enjoy a meal without bickering for once."

"Y'all are like a real family." Jim gulped down a beer. "That's real nice. My parents disowned me because of my mental health issues, and my siblings ran away after high school. What I wouldn't give for a good old family argument."

"Mental health issues?" Layla frowned. "Explain."

"Oh, I got a couple of different personalities wandering around in my noggin." He tapped his temple. "They ain't nothing to worry about, though. I managed to get into the military when I was sixteen and was flying jets by the time I was eighteen before they found out and booted me."

"Sixteen?" Hannah's mouth dropped open. "Don't you have to be eighteen? And how did you get to fly jets so young?"

"Jim's got the art of trickery and persuasion down to a science." Elton put on a couple more steaks. "He wasn't booted out of the military, so much as he was drafted into the black ops side of things."

"Technically, Margaret is the one who's good at persuading people." Jim grinned. "She could sell a bridge to a used car salesman."

Layla pursed her lips. "You people are a lot more interesting than I gave you credit for."

I felt a chill on the back of my neck. At first, I thought it was my body sigils warning me, but the sensation was different. I glanced back at the house. The curtains in a window shifted as if someone had been peeking through and stepped back. I stepped back from the grill. "I'll be right back."

"Are you going number one or number two?" Hannah said.

"I'll let you know in a minute." I stepped into the woods then took out my staff and switched to aura mode. Sigils glowed on the side and back of the house, but I already knew they were there. A ghostly blue aura shimmered just behind the curtain I'd seen move. The shape was humanoid, but the aura wasn't like anything I'd seen before.

I switched to infrared and the figure vanished. I switched through other modes, but only aura mode picked it up at all. The figure went back to the curtain and pulled it to the side. I banished my staff and went back to the others.

"Must've been a number two." Layla sniffed the air. "Yep, definitely."

Hannah grimaced. "Ew, what did you wipe with? Pine straw?"

"I didn't wipe."

Hannah giggled. "Nasty!"

I went to the grill and watched Elton for a moment, pondering whether I should ask him about the presence in his home. I was curious, but it was none of my business, so I opened another beer and started drinking.

Elton gave me a discerning look. He seemed to know that I knew something, but instead, just asked, "How do you like your steak, Cain?"

"Medium rare, please."

"Rare for me," Layla said.

Hannah quirked her lips. "Um, medium well. I don't like the blood."

"That ain't blood," Jim said. "It's myoglobin. It's what supplies the muscles with oxygen. All the blood is drained when the cow is slaughtered."

"Ah, okay." Hannah tilted her head. "I guess that's useful information, Jim."

Elton chuckled. "Oh, that's not Jim, that's Murdock. He's a know-it-all."

"Happy to make your acquaintance." Jim tipped his cap.

Hannah stared at him with a deadpan expression. "I'm not learning the names of all your personalities." She looked at Elton. "Is this for real or are you messing with us?"

"Oh, it's real, all right." Elton put a steak on a plate and gave it to Layla. "Rare, just like you asked."

"You know how I want it," Jim said. "Just skin the cow, cut off the horns, and drop it on a plate."

"Hell no!" Jim scowled. "Murdock, you shut your mouth. You know I like my steak medium rare."

"Raw or nothing!" Jim shouted.

Hannah blinked and turned to me. "Cain, this is a joke, right?"

"One way to find out." I summoned my staff and used aura mode on Jim. His aura was slightly yellow like most nubs, but it flickered strangely. People with mental issues usually had a fuzzy tinge to their aura, but that was about all I knew. Jim's wasn't like that. I zoomed in and realized why. There wasn't just one aura in his body—there were several. I couldn't discern one from the other, but it looked like he had at least three or four.

Elton put a steak on a plate. "Cain, is that an oblivion staff?"

I nodded. "And it's telling me that Jim has at least three distinct spirits or souls inside him." I banished the staff. "He doesn't have mental issues—he's possessed."

Aura looked up from her book again. "Are you telling me he's got demons?"

I shrugged. "I don't know what they are. Fitz could probably tell us."

Jim slapped his face. "Give it back!"

"This is the guy that's flying us on a top-secret mission?" Aura closed her book. "I'm a little concerned."

"Jim is solid. His other personalities don't mess with him during missions unless he asks for help." Elton dished out the rest of the steaks. "I would be very interested to know exactly what ails Jim."

"Yeah." I glanced at the house. "Lots of interesting mysteries around here."

A look of understanding passed between me and Elton, but he didn't offer any information.

Hannah sat down at the table next to Jim. "Tell me about your childhood."

He grinned. "Ain't nothing special, but I'm happy to talk about it, little darling."

I sat at the end of the table and started eating while I pondered the challenges ahead. Elton went inside his house and returned a moment later with another cooler full of beers. He set it on the ground and took a seat near me. He produced a small gray device and set it on the table, then pressed a button on the side.

"Seems you saw my guest."

"Guest?" I shrugged. "The phantom at your window?"

"Wanda." He cut into his steak and took a bite. "Recovered her on a mission. They would've stuck her in a warehouse or found a way to kill her if I'd turned her in."

"You know you don't have to tell me this, right?" I glanced down the table. "Plus, the others have super hearing."

"Not with this on." He tapped the device.

"Interesting gadget." I picked it up and rolled it in my fingers, then set it down. "So, why are you telling me this?"

"I'm hoping you can help me." Elton took a long swig of beer. "We had a mission to a portal world, and—"

I frowned. "Portal world?"

"That's what mission control called them." His eyes focused on the table. "Sometimes our world would get invaded by creatures from another world. They come through portals that look like snake mouths or worms." He shuddered. "And the monsters are some of the nastiest creatures you'll ever see."

I took out my phone and displayed a picture of a shoggoth. "Like this?"

He nodded. "Yeah, exactly. I don't know if you're familiar with H.P. Lovecraft, but—"

"I'm intimately familiar with his works." I put down my knife and fork. "You're telling me that the nub military is actively fighting eldritch invaders?"

"Eldritch, yeah, that's the term HQ used for them." Elton stared at me for a moment. "I thought we stopped all the major invasions, but I guess you've run into some yourself?"

"There's an alternate dimension where Gaia is completely overrun with them."

His eyes flared. "Alternate dimension? Holy shit, my commander really wasn't blowing smoke up our asses about that."

I cut another piece of steak. "Tell me more about Wanda."

Elton glanced at the window then turned to me. "We invaded a portal world and ended up in a temple on the other side. Now, what those things consider a building is nothing like what we have. All sorts of odd angles, spikes in the walls—" He shuddered. "We have to wear special gear just to keep it from fucking with our heads. There were these starfish looking monsters gathered around a spiky crystal. They were chanting in a language that would turn your brains inside out if not for our ear protection. We'd seen these crystals in other raids, but we never messed with them. HQ just said to plant explosives and exfil out of the portal before they blew."

"And that would close the portal?"

He nodded. "But this time we ended up in a fight with the starfish and walking brain monsters. A grenade exploded near the crystal and shattered it. We lost a lot of people, but we managed to get the explosives down and got out of the portal. What I didn't know was that a piece of the crystal lodged in my gear. When I got home, a ghost came out of it." Elton bit his lower lip. "I about freaked, because I thought I'd brought home one of the monsters."

"Is Wanda humanoid?"

Elton nodded. "It took some time before we could communicate. She speaks a language that doesn't even exist on Earth."

I frowned. "She's humanoid but eldritch?"

"No, she's not eldritch, or even human." He blew out a breath. "I've seen a lot of strange stuff in my life, but it still freaks me out to hear her story. She was alive before our universe existed. Her world was full of people that look just like humans, but then their entire universe ended, and they all died." Elton looked up at the stars. "Cain, there was a whole other universe before ours. It collapsed and blew up again, making the one we live in now. Thousands of beings from that world who died when their world collapsed had their souls trapped in crystals like hers, and the eldritch are using them like batteries to open portals and invade Earth."

My mouth went dry. "Did Wanda have a name for her people?"

He nodded. "They called themselves Ekhsis."

30

Now there was no question in my mind why Fate wanted me to meet Elton. "May I meet Wanda?"

Elton leaned his elbows on the table. "Do you think you can help me?"

I shrugged. "I'm not sure, but I can tell you that not all Ekhsis died when their planet was destroyed."

His mouth dropped open. "You know about Ekhsis?"

"Yeah." I gulped my beer, but it didn't help my dry mouth. "I'm a descendant of survivors."

He whistled. "Holy shit. So, this is why we were supposed to meet."

"Strange twist of Fate, indeed."

Layla and the others were looking at us, probably because they realized they couldn't eavesdrop on our conversation. I cut a piece of steak and put it in my mouth. "What problem are you having with Wanda?"

"She says the eldritch have thousands of Ekhsis shards. The only reason they haven't launched a massive invasion is because they aren't coordinated."

I nodded. "They thrive on chaos. It's every god for itself over there.

But what they lack in coordination, they more than make up for in infestation. Once they get their hooks into a place, it's hard to stop the cancer."

"Cancer is right." He scowled. "One world had these face huggers that impregnated thirty soldiers during a major engagement. We had to abandon them, or they would've spread the infection."

"I've encountered face huggers before." I regarded him for a long moment. "Sounds like we've had some similar experiences."

"Yeah, Dyanna wanted to go back to that world with flamethrowers."

I understood the sentiment. "Dyanna is another of your squad members?"

"Yeah." He glanced at the house again. "Maybe you ought to have a word with Wanda."

I nodded. "I'd like that."

Elton fetched another beer, then we walked toward the house.

"Hey, where are you going?" Hannah called out.

I held up a hand to stop her from rising. "Wait here. I'll be right back."

Elton traced a pattern on the door frame and the front door clicked open.

"Sigil lock?" I asked.

"Something like that." He stepped inside.

I followed and went into a very plain-looking foyer. There was a mud bench to the right with a pair of dirty work boots and a rugged jacket hanging from a hook. There was some dried mud on the tile floor, but nothing else of note. What was strange was that the room beyond the foyer was dark and fuzzy, almost as if it were out of focus. Try as I might, I couldn't make out any details beyond the doorframe.

Elton traced another pattern on the wall and the air shimmered. The room beyond became brighter and resolved into focus. He shrugged. "Can never be too careful."

"You're starting to remind me of myself." I motioned him on. "Please, lead the way." I couldn't be sure, but it seemed he'd dispelled an illusion and possibly a protective barrier.

He stepped into the room beyond. "I take it you can spot invisible things with your staff?"

"Maybe."

Elton chuckled. "We're a pair of trusting souls, aren't we?"

"Very." I grinned. "I have a feeling that mutual trust would be very beneficial to us."

"Agreed." He stopped in the den. Like the foyer, there wasn't anything decorative in this room. Just a desk with a bank of computer monitors, a sofa, and some bookshelves that were full to bursting with texts. Some of them bore symbols and bizarre designs that identified them as R'lyehian. "Hey, Wanda, you can come out."

A shimmering blue form emerged slowly from another room. The shape was humanoid, but fuzzy around the edges, like mist trying to hold itself together. It flickered like a television station with a bad signal and was two-dimensional with a flat edge. "Why did you bring the stranger inside?" Like her form, the voice was audible, but diffuse. It crackled slightly in time with the flickering of her form.

"This man is Ekhsis."

Her form solidified into three dimensions, filling out all the soft edges with high resolution clarity. She was certainly humanoid, but the rest of her features were something else entirely. Her head and face were feline, with long pointed cat ears and a wide nose. Her skin was covered in velvety looking blue fur, and a long tail twitched behind her.

I stared at her in surprise for a moment. "Um, does she usually look like this?"

Elton nodded. "When she's in true form. But it takes a lot of effort for her to maintain this."

"You are Ekhsis?" Wanda stepped forward, hands outstretched.

I almost dodged back but held firm and let her touch me. Her skin was warm, her fur soft to the touch. "I thought you were a spirit or a ghost."

"I am but a shadow of my real self." She put a hand on my cheek, and it took everything I had to go against my reflexive urge to jerk back. "I feel the spirit of my people within you. The echoes of our dead world and our unrivaled potential for expansion." She gasped softly. "You have already discovered new parts of yourself and expanded beyond the realm of the physical."

I assumed she was talking about my newfound abilities to sporadically interact with the world telekinetically, but I still needed convincing. "What do you mean by that?"

"You can reach out with your mind, extend your physical self, and affect the world around you." Wanda nodded. "It is a very early step of development, but it is easily the most important step in your long journey ahead."

"Just because you know things doesn't mean you're Ekhsis." I shrugged. "You might be a djinn or some other entity I'm not familiar with."

"A djinn is of this world." She walked around me, trailing her fingers along my back. "There are few beings of this world who know of Ekhsis and the fae tightly guard the secret. That is all the proof I can offer."

"Then why do you look like a human cat?"

She stopped in front of me, her head tilting curiously. "Because it was a form that pleased me. I was one of the Enlightened. There were many of us across the world, those who had achieved a heightened state of being, able to impose our will on not only our physical form, but on our mental state of being. Even so, we were well short of the true dream—achieving godhood."

It was as if the air suddenly rushed out of me. Not only did I believe her, but for the first time, I truly believed in the potential of Ekhsis. Then the logical side of my brain quickly snapped me back to reality.

"What are you now? A ghost or a physical being?"

"Somewhere in between." She sighed, purring slightly. "Ord and Cha did their best to protect Ekhsis from destruction during the next universal expansion. When they saw their deaths were imminent, they entombed many of the Enlightened in crystalline wombs and slid them into a pocket dimension to protect them from the blast. We were to sleep for billions of years, our minds free to develop so we might be advanced enough to take on the next stage of creation ourselves."

"That obviously didn't happen," I said.

"No, but new gods were created practically overnight when the soul shards of Ord and Cha rained down on the populace. The Elder Things and the Elder Gods soon came into being. They protected the remnants of our people, but me and the other Enlightened were hidden away in the pocket dimension, sleeping in our crystal wombs."

Her gaze went distant. "I imagine that the pocket dimension collapsed sometime after the energy from the new expansion killed Cha and Ord, but I can only guess. By then, the Elder Gods and Elder Things had fought a war and gone their separate ways. I regained consciousness in the vastness of space, drifting alongside other crystal wombs. Our physical bodies were gone, replaced by whatever form this is."

Wanda laughed mirthlessly. "I believe it was the only way Cha and Ord could preserve us, but it also chained us to the wombs they created. When mine was shattered, I was able to tether myself to the crystal shards that landed in Elton's clothing. Now I am trapped in this odd simulation of life."

"Elton tells me that the Elder Things are using others like you to power their wormholes." I hesitantly touched her fur. "How did they find you?"

"I'm not certain. I believe we fell into the gravity well of a black hole. Time outside passed quickly. What was for us perhaps a thousand years was billions in real space. I spent most of the time trying to expand my consciousness, trying to achieve a higher level of being that I might escape my prison, but I lacked the energy to do so and ended up slumbering for I do not know how long. At some point I awakened in a vast void, swallowed by an entity that fed on dark matter."

Wanda touched her face as if to assure herself that she existed. "The crystal wombs were ejected into real space and some hundreds of years later we crashed onto a planet controlled by Elder Things.

The world was torn apart by constantly warring factions. I later learned that a priest named Cthulhu had rebelled against Shub-Nuggurath and other beings greater than himself. The war had drawn in many elder beings, Nyarlathotep among them."

She shivered. "Thousands of our wombs were scattered across that world. That was when the various factions claimed us for themselves. The Thegmil, a race that Elton says resemble earthly starfish, took me. Their mother goddess, J'lemgowuil, was fascinated with me and kept me in her birthing cave."

"Like a toy." Elton looked disgusted. "Can you believe that thing pumped out a hundred babies a day? And then threw them like cannon fodder at the enemy."

"That was one of the early eldritch worlds," Wanda said. "Shub-Nuggurath's newest creations, the dark young, as Elton calls them, were easily defeating the Thegmil, so J'lemgowuil shoved me into a birthing pouch and launched herself into the void of space with only a few thousand Thegmil attached to her sides. Hundreds of years later, we reached a desolate world that barely supported life, but was close enough to a white dwarf star for J'lemgowuil's purposes."

"I've never heard of that goddess." I was still processing how old Wanda had to be to have seen the eldritch all on one world. "How many Elder Things were on that first world?"

"Thousands." Her hackles rose. "They had once been mostly united against the Elder Gods and fled to the same world, but that small drop of order quickly descended into never-ending war."

"Gods be damned, that's quite a story." I wanted to hear more but imagined it would take a long time for her to tell me everything. "Cthulhu was exiled to Gaia."

"As punishment for his rebellion, he was to lead one of the first invasion waves against the human realm." Wanda shrugged. "He was supposed to die, and the energy from his death would have created a way for the Elder Things to latch onto Gaia with dozens of worm-holes. That is why the Elder Gods put him to sleep, keeping him between life and death."

"That's new information to me." I took her hand. "Wanda, you could help us end the eldritch threat once and for all with your information."

"What I know is but a smattering of all there is, I'm afraid." She patted my hand. "What we need is to collect more of my kin. Then we can protect this fragile world."

"Hashtag life goals." I considered her proposal, if that's what it was. "You can speak their language?"

"Indeed. I can speak the core R'lyehian language. Many variations and dialects have arisen over the millennia, of course." Her feline nose wrinkled. "Only my enlightened state allowed my mind to withstand the convoluted madness they consider language."

I was excited but wary. Fate had certainly arranged this meeting for a reason. Did she want me gallivanting off to these eldritch worlds so I could rescue more Enlightened? Or was there another reason?

"I'm familiar with wormholes to a certain extent. I saw a giant one open on Feary after I drove Shub-Nuggurath's minions out of that world."

Wanda's eyes flared. "You vanquished Shub-Nuggurath's creatures?"

"I had help." I paced a few steps. "How often are the eldritch opening portals to Gaia? What are their goals?"

"They seem to be somewhat united in their thirst to take over the human realms." Elton folded his arms over his chest. "Thankfully, it takes years for them to recharge their portals even with the help of the Enlightened."

"I was able to control the rate of recharge to an extent," Wanda said. "I made them wait a full century between each attempt. It seems other Enlightened are doing the same since Gaia is not overrun with portals."

"Let's get back to the original matter at hand." I turned to Wanda. "Elton said maybe I could help. Help with what? You're far more advanced than I am."

"There are other Enlightened held captive by the eldritch. Elton tried to make a case to his superiors that they should attempt to rescue them during portal world operations, but his commanders are intent only on destroying the portals as they appear." Wanda took my hands. "I will teach you all you wish to know if you can help Elton achieve this purpose."

I patted the top of her hand, marveling at the soft, ethereal fur. "That's a very tempting offer, but I have major problems of my own right now. That's why I'm here in the first place."

"I know it is a great deal to ask of you, but it is also in your best interests." Wanda patted my hand in return. "You will make the decision when the time is right."

I raised an eyebrow. "You're not going to argue the point?"

She smiled softly. "Fate has put us together for a reason. I have planted a seed. It will grow or it will decay. You are not one to make hasty decisions, nor are you overly concerned with things you perceive beyond your control. But I think you will come to the realization that while the gods are doing all they can to maintain the balance, there are others lurking behind the scenes that seek to tip that delicate balance. Sometimes, even the lightest of feathers can tip the scales in one direction or the other."

I grunted. "Well, I'm a pretty light feather compared to the heavy hitters out there."

"Perhaps."

I pursed my lips. "By fate, do you mean Fate the entity, or just some vague notion of luck?"

"The entity. I am not in tune with this world, but I have studied it a great deal." She motioned at the bookshelves. "I have memorized all of this and more. I am a fly caught in the web of fate the same as you. But I sense that our meeting was ordained by her. It seems Fate is trying to maintain a balance made precarious by the meddling of gods."

"The gods of chaos, certainly." I shook my head. "Fighting against them is some long odds."

"Indeed." Her outline began to fray. "Think about it, Cain."

"Hold on." I tried to grip her hand, but it had become ghostly. "Can you help me with my problem? If you're enlightened, surely you can take out a few rogue guardians."

"I fear my powers are limited while I'm trapped in this state of semi-existence." She shook her head sadly. "Knowledge is my only helpful power."

"Okay, then hit me with some knowledge." I stepped back. "Tell me who's responsible for the current plot against me. Tell me who Hannah's father is. Tell me something, anything that's useful."

"I don't possess real time information like that," Wanda said. "And I don't know who Hannah is. I can touch her and read her if you'd like, but it's unlikely I'll be able to reveal her parentage."

I blew out a breath. "So, that makes you mostly useless to me." I turned toward the door. "I'll think about your proposal. Just pray that I survive my current ordeal."

"I have faith in you, Cain." Wanda's form dissipated and vanished.

I looked at Elton. "Is her real name Wanda?"

He shook his head. "It's Wandaightar Kior Do. Wanda is just easier."

"That's for damned sure." Ekhsis names were strange. I hesitated but asked my next question anyway. "What's your relationship with her?"

He didn't flinch. "It's complicated."

"Okay." I was extremely curious about their sex life but didn't ask.

Elton seemed to read my mind. He grinned. "Yeah, it's interesting."

"I'll bet." I turned for the door. "We should get going. We've got a long day tomorrow."

"Actually, I had another idea." He walked to the door. "I think we should practice a night drop."

I raised an eyebrow. "On the mountain?"

He shook his head. "On a building in the city. It's time for you to get your feet wet."

31

A night drop on the mountain was one thing but doing it on an actual building in the city sounded crazy. "We're not ready yet."

"I think it's time to level up." Elton shrugged. "Landing on the mountain still isn't anywhere close to landing on a skyscraper's rooftop."

"True, but we haven't perfected the mountain landing."

"You've gotten about as perfect as you're going to get without hundreds of more jumps." He took out his smartphone and displayed two buildings. "The King and Queen buildings are perfect for practice. If you and your team can land on one of these, then the Sovereign won't be a problem. It's a perfect test location."

"And if something goes wrong?" I stared at the picture. "Will you be there with an emergency chute?"

"I can do one better. I retrofitted the straps on one of my parachute packs after Hannah's close call. It fastens onto the grooves in the center piece between the wings without getting in the way." He switched to another image of the retrofitted pack attached to clockwork wings. "The ripcord comes up and over the shoulder. The only caveat is that it has to be pulled up and out."

I zoomed in and examined the setup. "So, we can all have a backup in case of wing malfunction or pilot error?"

He grinned. "Exactly. It does add some extra weight, but I don't think that will be an issue."

I pursed my lips and gave it some thought. "Let's run it by the others. Maybe it's time to take off the training wheels."

Elton nodded. "I think it's your best bet if you want to be ready to do the real drop."

We went back to the table. The others greeted us with raised eyebrows.

Layla smirked. "You boys rub one out together?"

I got straight to the point. "Who wants to do a practice run on a building in the city?"

Layla jolted to her feet. "I am so in."

"Me too!" Hannah clapped her hands. "When do we leave?"

Aura's forehead pinched. "Wait, what? We're not ready for that."

"I think we're plenty ready for it." Layla took a swig of beer and slammed down the bottle. "Are we taking the jet or the cargo hauler?"

"I can fuel up the jet." Jim grinned. "I've been dying to fly it."

Aura flicked her gaze to him. "Have you flown this jet before?"

He shook his head. "Nah, but I've flown plenty like her."

She grimaced. "This is a bad idea."

"Then don't come." Layla walked over to Jim. "Go fuel the jet. I don't want to wait around all night."

Jim glanced at Elton. "Are we on?"

Elton gave him a thumbs up. "We're on."

The Eclipse 500 was a small jet with a smaller cabin than the cargo hauler. Elton had removed the seats and replaced them with small foldouts on the bulkhead. He'd also bolted straps to the floor to secure the wings during takeoff.

Layla looked dubiously at the cabin door. "I'm no expert at jumping out of planes, but how are we supposed to jump out without smashing into the engines or the tail?"

Like most jets, the cabin door was right in front of the wing. The jet engines were mounted on the fuselage right behind the wing.

Jumping out at high speeds would almost certainly result in our bodies smashing against the jet engine. By comparison, the cargo hauler door was behind the wing and the propellers.

Elton crouched and patted the belly of the jet. "I had a hatch built into the fuselage to make it easier to do cargo drops and skydiving. It opens from inside the cabin."

Layla looked up at it. "I can hardly tell it's there."

"That's the point." He stood. "The jet can't handle larger payloads like the cargo hauler, but sometimes you need speed."

Jim coiled the large fuel hose around a spool at the base of a large metal tank. "Fueled up and ready to go."

Hannah shivered. "I'm stoked and nervous at the same time."

Aura sighed. "Well, I hope we're not jumping the gun. I'll resurrect but the rest of you won't if anything goes wrong."

Elton brought his wings with a modified parachute latched to the back. "This will give us some extra insurance." He put on the wings and demonstrated how to work the ripcord. "Make sure you thread the ripcord under the wing harness, so it doesn't flap around behind you."

Hannah latched a pack onto her wings and tested it. "It's a little heavy. You sure this won't mess up our landing?"

"Once you're gliding, you won't even notice it."

Hannah activated her wings, levitating a hundred feet up before gliding down. She landed lightly a moment later. "It's nice and balanced."

"Did you test deploy the chute?" Aura asked.

Elton nodded. "Yeah, several times. The landing is harder than usual because of the added weight of the wings, but it's a lot better than landing at terminal velocity."

Layla laughed. "That's for damned sure."

He took out his phone and showed us another picture, this one of a small cylinder attached between the wings instead of the parachute. "I also looked at adding a micro-jet engine to the wings but decided that a parachute was a safer option."

"Dude, that's sweet!" Hannah stared open-mouthed at the modification. "Can we get jet engines on our wings for the heist?"

"I think you're better off with parachutes for the time being." Elton tucked his phone away.

With that settled, we climbed into the jet and buckled into the bulkhead seats. Jim fired up the engines and Elton slid into the copilot's seat.

Elton turned around in his chair. "I'm making the jump with you, by the way."

Layla raised an eyebrow. "Just for fun?"

He grinned. "Of course. It's been a while since I've made a jump like this."

"But this time you have wings." Hannah mimicked a flapping motion with her hands.

"That I do." He turned back around and buckled in.

Jim taxied to the end of the runway. "Hold on, folks. It's gonna be a tight takeoff with this load."

Hannah gulped. "Why did you have to tell us that?"

Jim thrust a lever forward and the whine of the engines turned to a scream. The jet accelerated slowly. It was too dark to see the end of the runway through the front window, so I just leaned back and tried not to think about it.

Gravity pulled down on my insides and we climbed at a steep angle.

Elton whistled. "Cutting it real close, Jim."

Jim chuckled. "Aw, that's nothing compared to some of the takeoffs we've done."

"True."

Hannah opened her eyes and looked at me. "I almost peed my pants, and this doesn't even rank close to the scariest thing we've done."

I shrugged. "Almost dying is almost dying no matter how mundane the cause."

She managed a weak grin. "There's something about flying that makes it scarier."

"It's because your life is totally in the hands of someone else." I nodded at Jim. "In this case, someone who's possessed by multiple beings."

"I can hear you," Jim said.

"I'm well aware," I replied.

The jet leveled out and circled around to the southeast. Jim pulled out a small black box and pressed a button. "Jammer activated."

Layla frowned. "Jammer?"

"Keeps us off the radar." Jim flashed a grin. "We have a few toys from our days with the Monster Squad."

That got my attention. "What kind of toys?"

"After our first encounter with the eldritch, we realized that bullets weren't enough when you've got a mob of monsters running at you." Elton looked back at us. "The boys in research came up with some goodies that deliver area of effect explosions, electrical discharges, and more. Unfortunately, we lost access to most of the heavy weaponry, but we were able to smuggle out this jammer and a few other things in case we ever needed them."

Hannah leaned against her seatbelt. "I'm super interested in hearing more about this monster squad."

"The Monster Squad," Jim said. "Honey, we were legends back in the day even though nobody expected us to survive a single encounter."

"That's why they recruit troublemakers and people unfit for regular duty." Elton sighed. "They were the good old days until some of our leaders got greedy. They wanted access to the biotech weapons the eldritch used. I don't think they understood that shoggoths and some of the others were bioengineered by literal gods."

Jim guffawed. "Yeah, if we hadn't cleaned up the mess, you'd be bowing down to an Elder Thing by now."

Layla smirked. "And here I thought we were the only ones keeping humanity safe."

Aura shook her head. "This is a bit much to take in. You're telling me that the nubs have special units constantly fighting off eldritch invasions?"

"Not constantly," Elton said. "The power source for their worm-holes takes years to recharge. They have satellites that detect the energy signatures when a new portal opens, so they can send in a unit before the invaders come through."

Layla sighed in relief. "Thank the gods. For a minute there I thought we were totally fucked."

"Entering Atlanta airspace." Jim flicked some switches. "Running lights off. Target is four clicks out."

Elton unbuckled and slid out of his seat. He had to crouch-walk since the cabin wasn't very tall. He dropped to his knees and pulled up a section of carpet between us. Beneath it was a recessed handle, presumably for opening the hatch.

He unbuckled the straps holding down the wings at the far back of the cabin. "Put on your wings and jump out one at a time. There's not enough room for everyone to put on their wings inside the cabin."

"Two clicks out," Jim said. "Optimal jump point is coming up soon."

Elton handed out our helmets. We put them on and activated the headsets inside.

"Sound off," Elton said.

We checked in, ensuring the headsets were working.

Elton nodded. "Okay, let's get our first contestant."

"I'll go first." Aura unbuckled and identified her wings by mark-ings we'd put on the straps. She had to get on her hands and knees to strap on the furled wings because of their length. "Guess I'm jumping out headfirst?"

Elton nodded. "Once you're out, open the wings and glide toward the target just like we've been practicing." He twisted the recessed handles in the hatch and pulled it open. Wind whistled in the cabin, though it was muted somewhat by the helmets and headsets. Hannah had to move her legs sideways to give the hatch enough room to fully open.

"We're over the target," Jim said. "I'm entering a holding pattern so everyone isn't separated by a mile by the time they get out."

Aura dove through the hatch. I went next, awkwardly following the same procedure to put on the wings. It took a full minute from start to the finish, which was nowhere near ideal. I opened the wings and began gliding in a circle. Aura circled a short distance away, wings flapping to maintain the same altitude.

The King and Queen buildings were clearly visible far below us, each one identifiable by the crown structure on their roofs. The landing zone was even more obstructed than the one on the Sovereign, so if we were able to nail our landings here, then we could probably land on the real target when the time came.

Another silhouette appeared in the starry sky above. "I'm out," Hannah said.

The next figure dropped a moment later. "Layla is in the hizzouse."

Elton made his appearance a few seconds later. "Jim, we are airborne. Batten down the hatch and head to PDK."

"Affirmative." The jet angled east and headed toward Dekalb-Peachtree Airport for a landing.

I spoke into the headset. "Let's aim for the King Building."

"Roger," Elton said. "Starting descent."

I folded the wings and entered a dive. Wind whistled madly through the helmet. I aimed for the outer corner of the roof since the crown structure made landing dead center next to impossible from a direct angle. I hit the brakes and the wings cupped, slowing me abruptly. I eased up on the cords and the wings flared.

The fit between the beams of the crown was tighter than I'd imagined, but I still had plenty of room. I flared the wings and glided between the girders, angled low, and braked hard. My feet touched the roof. I stumbled on a small pipe connected to an air conditioning unit but managed to keep my balance despite the extra weight of the parachute.

The others followed close behind, maintaining the same distance we'd practiced on the mountain in order to avoid another collision. Aura glided between the prongs of the crown. I pointed toward the pipes I'd tripped on and motioned her to angle slightly to the right. She did so and landed, then quickly furled her wings and got out of the way.

Hannah landed a moment later and joined us. Layla and Elton followed suit and within moments, we were all standing atop the building and looking out at the city skyline.

Hannah high-fived Elton. "We did it! That was awesome!"

Layla grinned. "Yeah, it was fun." She turned to me. "You're starting to remind me why I enjoy risking my life to hang out with you, Cain."

"Just keeping life interesting." I walked over to the edge and summoned my staff. Thankfully, the wings didn't impede my ability to call it from its pocket dimension. I used the scope and zoomed in on the Sovereign building. From this height it didn't look all that far away. Atlanta was a big city, but it had nowhere near the crowded feeling of New York or other cities clogged with skyscrapers.

Layla rubbed her hands together. "Okay, so now what?"

I pointed toward the flashing lights on the air traffic control tower at PDK. "We're flying over there."

"Last one there's a rotten egg." Layla jumped off the roof. Her wings flared and she glided eastward.

Hannah ran and jumped off after her. I waited until the others had followed, and then brought up the rear. It was about four miles distant as the crow flies, so I kept the wings flapping to maintain altitude. Even at full speed, the clockwork wings weren't very fast, especially not compared to the ones Esteri and the demis had used on Gaia Alpha.

It was possible we didn't know how to operate the wings properly. There might be a way to increase the speed. It was also likely that the Traditionalists had made better wings than their Futurist counterparts. Either way, it seemed unlikely that this version of clockworks wings could be easily militarized as the Futurists seemed to intend.

On the upside, it did give me plenty of time to think. Our practice had paid off. We weren't amazing with the clockwork wings, but we were good enough. I didn't see any reason to delay any longer. We were ready for the real thing.

It was time to infiltrate the Sovereign.

32

I landed at the airport shortly after the others. We strapped our wings inside the cabin and got situated inside. Once we were all buckled in, Jim took off and we headed back to Elton's airstrip.

Hannah glowed with happiness. "We did great, didn't we, Cain?"

I nodded. "It went better than expected."

Aura yawned. "I am so ready for bed right now."

I stifled a yawn of my own and let them know what I was thinking. "We're ready for the Sovereign."

Layla snapped her fingers. "I'm ready, baby."

"Me too," Hannah said.

Aura nodded as she yawned. "I agree. How much gear are we bringing?"

"Not much. A few weapons and the sigil keycard." I looked at the list on my phone. "If all goes well, we won't need much. If all goes to shit, then we'll have to play it by ear."

"If it goes to plan, I'll be surprised." Layla sighed. "Then again, I wouldn't mind killing the assholes responsible for disrupting my routine."

. . .

WE STAYED at the hotel that night, then went back to Sanctuary early the next morning to get everything in order.

I walked inside and found Fred on the couch watching a movie. Popcorn was scattered all over the cushions and nearby floor.

"Cain!" he got up and waddled over.

"Where the hell have you been?" I looked at the mess he'd made. "And you'd better clean that up."

"I have been searching for others." He tilted his head. "You were not here last night."

Hannah patted him on the head. "Yeah, we've been practicing our flying."

I walked to the kitchen. "Layla and I need sessions with your malgorth."

"Layla?" He looked up at her. "What happened to Layla?"

"Cain happened to me." She glared at me. "I used Panoptes after he corrupted it and now, I can't sleep without some of the worst nightmares I've ever had."

"I am sorry." Fred patted her leg. "My friend will help."

I poured myself a glass of water. "Right now would be ideal."

"Okay." Fred reached for Layla's hand. "Ready now?"

She puffed out her cheeks and blew out the air. "Sure. Just don't lobotomize me."

I took my glass of water into my bedroom and locked the door. I needed some alone time and I also wanted to think over our plans and make sure I wasn't missing anything. There was an awful lot I couldn't account for.

My primary concern was getting inside from the balcony. The sigil keycard we'd found in Torvin's secret toilet in Beta might not work on the sigil slate in Prime. Until I reached the target and tried it, I wouldn't know for sure. There was no backup plan if the keycard didn't work. We couldn't blast our way through the enchanted glass or the mithril door in the stairwell.

The keycard had existed before the split in the timelines, meaning it was a duplicate of the original in Prime. It seemed unlikely anything had changed in the way it operated, so I had high hopes that it cycled through the same exact codes as its counterpart here.

I sat down and studied the diagram of the building, trying to account for other possibilities that might occur once we were inside. The best-case scenario was that someone had claimed Torvin's throne and was living in the penthouse. If that was true, then we'd only have one person to worry about. The worst-case scenario was that Eclipse had removed everything related to its operations, or that a small army of guardians were stationed there.

There was no way to know what waited inside until we reached that point. My plans hinged on a lot of unknown factors. We might be walking into a deathtrap or a cakewalk. All I knew for certain was that we were meeting Jim and Elton at PDK tonight at eleven and skydiving to the Sovereign rooftop with our clockwork wings.

The road beyond that was full of forks, curves and branches—unexplored territory on the map of our futures. I just hoped we didn't reach a dead end.

"Want to throw some more help my way, Fate?" I wasn't expecting an answer since not even she could simply waltz inside the safe zone around Sanctuary.

I emerged from my room about the same time Layla emerged from Fred's pool.

"I feel so much better." She sighed in relief. "I'm going to take a nap."

I slid into Fred's pool. His tentacle wrapped around my wrist. *Ready?*

I nodded. "Let's go."

THE DAY WAS ALMOST GONE by the time I crawled out of the pool, shaking and weak from the malgorth's madness purging. I rolled over and lay on my back, the cool stone tiles soaking the dripping water from my body.

"Are you okay?" Layla looked down at me. "You're shaking like a sick dog."

"I'm fine." I pushed to my knees and slowly climbed to my feet. "I need a nap."

She touched my arm. "Maybe we should postpone the mission until tomorrow night."

"I'll be good after a nap."

She pursed her lips. Nodded. "Fine."

I didn't know why the second session had hit me so much harder than the first one, but it was probably because the malgorth had to dig deeper into my mind to uproot the poison. I crawled into bed and closed my eyes. The worms were faded shadows against my vision, much weaker than before.

Cthulhu's eyes glowed on the horizon, orange suns flickering dimly. His voice echoed on the wind, but I couldn't hear what he was saying, nor did I feel the creeping madness that usually accompanied it.

I belatedly realized I hadn't been taking Fitz's pills. Thanks to Fred's malgorth buddy, I probably didn't need them.

It was nearly ten at night when I woke up, feeling more refreshed than I had in a while. I dressed, put on my utility belt and the oblivion cloak, then went into the den. Hannah was lounging on the couch reading her phone. Aura was watching a nature documentary on television.

They looked up at me.

"I wasn't sure if you were going to wake up." Hannah sat up. "We'd better get going."

Layla emerged from the guest bedroom. "Sleeping Beauty is finally awake?"

"Yep." I stretched my back. "Is everyone ready to go?"

"I need to pee first." Layla went into the bedroom.

Hannah jumped up from the couch and went to the door. "I'm excited!"

I checked my utility belt to ensure the sigil keycard was still there along with any other useful items I might need. Layla emerged from the bedroom a moment later, oblivion cloak on and a belt of daggers around her waist. I assumed those were in addition to the ones she kept hidden, meaning she was ready for the worst-case scenario.

We got into Dolores and headed to PDK. Elton and Jim were waiting in the jet when we arrived.

Elton dropped down to the tarmac when he saw us coming. "Ready for your big night?"

"I am!" Hannah climbed up into the jet.

"I'm always ready for a good time," Layla said.

Aura looked up at the night sky in grim determination. "I'm ready as I'll ever be."

I climbed into the jet last and buckled into my seat. The wings were already strapped into the back.

Elton opened a black case to reveal four handguns in holsters. "I brought some of our special toys in case you want a little extra firepower."

"Pistols?" Layla frowned. "I don't think they'll do us much good against Oblivion Guard."

"These fire lightning rounds." Elton slid out the magazine to show a bullet with a blue tip. "They explode near the target for an AOE effect that will shock anything in range."

"Oh, neat." Hannah took one of the weapons and clipped the holster onto her utility belt.

"Reminds me of the clockwork rifle bullets." Layla shook her head. "I brought my enchanted daggers, so I don't need a gun."

I found a free space on my utility belt and clipped on a holster. Aura did the same.

Jim looked over his shoulder at us. "Ready for takeoff?"

"Ready," I said.

Elton closed the cabin door and the plane taxied down the runway. Moments later, we were airborne. When Jim reached the preferred altitude, he circled around toward Buckhead. There wasn't much to see out of the forward windows since the city was far below us.

"Two clicks out," Jim said. "Get ready for drop."

We put on our helmets.

I turned on the headset. "Check, check."

"Ready," Layla said.

Hannah gave a thumbs up. "Ready."

Aura nodded. "Good to go."

Elton raised a thumb. "Good luck."

Jim held up a fist. "Entering a holding pattern over the target."

I opened the floor hatch. Hannah got on her hands and knees and strapped on her wings, then dove out. Layla went next, then Aura, and I followed last. Wind whistled outside the helmet. I spotted the others circling like vultures over the Sovereign. The wind gusted at this altitude, but it wasn't windy enough to push us off course.

I dove past them, aiming for the spot on the roof we'd practiced virtually for the past week. It was different approaching the real thing, but after landing on the King Building last night, it didn't seem quite so difficult. I hit the brakes, lifted my feet to avoid an air-conditioning unit, and landed with hardly a stumble. I quickly furled the wings and got out of the way. Hannah came in next. Her foot clipped the same air conditioning unit and she spun to the right.

She pulled on the cords and managed to wrest control back before she smacked into another AC unit and landed unsteadily on her feet. Following too close behind, Layla swerved to avoid hitting Hannah, braked hard, and dropped five feet with a thud. Aura flared her wings to stop sooner since Layla wasn't out of the way. Her foot caught on the same AC unit.

Aura tumbled forward and thudded face down on the other side. She lay still, groaning. I removed my wings and set them on the roof, then went over and helped her up.

"You okay?"

She brushed off her clothes. "That hurt."

Hannah giggled. "That was a classic face-plant."

"Thanks to you." Aura took off her wings and set them down. "What now?"

"The moment of truth." I held up the sigil keycard. "Let me test this out before we do anything else." I went to the edge of the building and peered over. There was about a one-story drop to the glass roof of the balcony. I pulled climbing rope from my pack and clipped it onto a sturdy pipe.

I could have dropped over the edge, but using the rope enabled me to be as quiet as possible. I took off my helmet and detached the small headset from the inside. It fit neatly into my ear.

"Can you still hear me?" I said into the mic.

The others nodded.

I activated the oblivion cloak.

"Freaky." Hannah reached out and touched me. "I want one."

"I think I can make that happen." I went to the edge of the roof and prepared myself for the descent.

Since I had no rappelling harness, I gripped the rope in my gloved hands and slowly slid down it to the balcony roof. Lying on my stomach, I slid to the edge of the roof and peered over. The height was dizzying but I'd take being a little dizzy any day instead of a giant dhole worm shaking the building apart around me.

The ledge was too wide to peek over, so I wrapped the rope around a leg to create friction, then lowered myself over the side until I could see the balcony proper. Several cushioned deck chairs sat around a table littered with empty bottles and beer cans. It was the last thing I expected to see in a place presumably used by guardians.

I slowly lowered myself, trying not to think about the long drop below should the rope fail. I gripped the balcony railing and pulled myself over, then unwound the rope and crouch-walked to the far end. Whereas most ordinary balconies would have a sliding glass door, this one had only a long pane of seamless glass with a sigil slate on the right. The glass was darkly tinted, prevented me from seeing inside.

This was the moment of truth. I took out the sigil keycard and held it close to the slate. A series of sigils lined up lengthwise along the card. I touched the keycard to the slate, hoping it might automatically accept the combination, but nothing happened.

Using a finger, I traced the symbols one at a time on the slate. The window slid silently to the side, revealing the inside of the penthouse. Four individuals sat at a table inside, one of them pouring a thick yellow liquid into his glass.

Three of them were Oblivion Guard. The fourth was a bridge troll. The penthouse layout was vastly different from the one on Beta. Gone was the open floor layout. The kitchen was walled in, sharing a space with the den. A hallway to the side of the kitchen led presumably to the bedrooms.

That was all I had the time to notice, because the guardians jumped up from the table an instant after the glass slid open, eyes alert as if they hadn't had a single drop of alcohol.

"Cloaked!" one of them shouted. "Hit the dispel!"

His comrade ran to the wall and traced a sigil on a gray slate.

Magic crackled and a bubble of blue energy swelled from the slate, flashing across me before I had a chance to react. The cloak fizzled and flickered off. I was exposed. A dispel powerful enough to take out the enchantments on my oblivion cloak had to be fae-level magic.

Layla poked her head over the side of the balcony roof. "Cain, what the hell was that?"

"A massive dispel charge." I summoned my staff. "Get down here now."

"Coming!" Hannah said.

Fighting on the balcony was a bad idea. It wasn't a great chokepoint, and I didn't want my back to a steep fall. I stepped inside and circled to the left. The only visible exit besides the balcony was the hallway and the same mithril door I'd seen in the penthouse on Beta.

"Cain Sthyldor?" One of the drow stared at me in confusion. "Is this a gift?"

The other drow drained a shot glass of the yellow liquid and grinned. "We've been hunting for you."

The bridge troll stood and clacked his thick tusks together. "This the little man we seek?"

"Yes, it is, Thog." The first drow summoned his staff. His fingers flicked in guardian sign language and the other two guardians spread out to either side of him. "We will take care of this."

Thog growled. "But Liem, I like to smash."

The first drow rolled his eyes. "Yes, but this is none of your concern."

Thog huffed but backed away. Like most bridge trolls, he was about eight feet tall, wide and muscular, and almost too large to be inside a building sized for nubs. The high ceiling helped, but his bulky figure would get in the way of his guardian comrades.

I tried to buy some time so the others could get inside. "Sorry to interrupt your evening. Were you playing Uno?"

"There's no reason to talk, Cain." Liem's brightblade hummed to life. "Surrender or die."

"I don't like those choices." I pursed my lips. "How about we sit down, talk, and finish off that bottle of troll piss? I'd like to use a few Draw Four cards on you."

Thog picked up the bottle of yellow liquor. "This mine!"

Liem lunged. I blocked his attack with my staff then jumped back and deflected an attack from his drow friend who'd circled to my right. Fighting in such close quarters was going to be a major pain in the ass, especially with them poking at me from three sides, so I waited for the next attack. Liem's right foot came forward as it had the last time just before he'd lunged. I waited patiently to see if he repeated the move. I'd never met him or seen him in combat, so this might be a tell or it might be a fake-out to lure me into anticipating a move that never came.

The Oblivion Guard was an elite, selective organization, but that didn't mean everyone was a master of the sword. There were different branches with different specialties and judging from the insignias on the cloak of the low fae guardian, it appeared she was a magic caster. She had her brightblade at the ready, but if she started slinging spells at me while the others corralled me with their weapons, that would be bad.

Layla appeared at the open balcony window.

Thog's gaze flicked toward her. "Intruders!" He charged.

"Fuck sticks!" Layla rolled inside to the right, away from the guardians around me.

Thog barreled through the kitchen table, reducing it to splinters, his meaty fists upraised.

Liem lunged.

This plan was going off without a hitch.

33

I sidestepped Liem's thrust, activated my brightblade, and parried two lightning-fast jabs. He feinted, sidestepped, and jabbed again. Even with my body sigils powered, my human reflexes could barely keep up with him. Drow were deadly and efficient fighters. He wasn't trying to kill me outright, Instead, he was driving me back toward his other companion.

I couldn't let that happen. I might not be as fast as him, but I had an advantage he didn't. I let him push me toward the other drow, waiting for them to thrust their brightblade into my back. My sigils tingled in warning. I ghostwalked behind Liem just as he lunged for me. His companion put everything he had into stabbing me in the back.

He'd expected his brightblade to meet my flesh. Instead, he found thin air and overextended. His blade pierced Liem's shoulder. It wasn't a fatal wound, but I'd ghostwalked right behind Liem. A quick slash took off his head before he could figure out what went wrong.

The other drow shouted in alarm. "Liem!"

I drew a dueling wand and flung an orb of energy at him. He deflected the spell at the last instant. I ran toward him. He narrowed his eyes and planted his feet in a defensive stance.

I threw another spell from my wand and ghostwalked. He anticipated my move and spun around to guard his back, but I appeared to his left instead. I slashed off his arm, kicked him in the side to send him tumbling, then stabbed down into his chest.

Flesh sizzled. He roared in pain, but only for an instant before the life fled from him. I turned to the magic user. "Do you want to live or die?"

She bared her teeth. "I'll never surrender to a dog like you, Sthyldor."

Thog roared in pain. I flicked my gaze to the side for a quick update on that battle. Layla daggers protruded from his chest, arms, and legs. Blood poured from the leg wounds.

I took a chance with the troll. "Thog, do you want to live?"

"Yes!" he shouted. "Please! Thog not smash!"

Layla frowned. "Hey, all the guys want to smash me."

I turned back to the low fae. "Looks like you're off the hook. Tell your friends hello when you get to the other side."

Her eyes flared. "Wait!"

I stepped closer, brightblade extended. "Change of mind?"

She dropped her staff. "Yes."

Her eyes darted to the right ever so slightly and that was when I knew someone else was here. I spun as another guardian sprinted from the hallway, staff glowing with magic. It was another caster.

Gunfire rang out. Hannah dropped to a knee and unloaded her weapon on the newcomer. Electricity crackled and the guardian shouted, dancing like a puppet on a string as the energy burned through him.

The low fae dropped to a knee to retrieve her staff while I was distracted. I flung a spell from my wand and knocked the staff out of reach. She rolled to the side then sprang toward me, hands outstretched. I could have cut her in half, but I wanted someone besides a bridge troll to question, so I spun and kicked her in the chest.

A grunt exploded from her mouth. I banished my staff and dashed forward, leaping and landing on her with a knee. The rest of the air in her lungs wheezed out. I rolled her onto her stomach, produced some restraints from my utility belt, and fastened them to her wrists.

She was still gasping for air as I jerked her to her feet. Thog was on his knees in front of Layla begging for mercy.

Hannah walked over to the guardian she'd hit with the lightning rounds and shook her head. "Uh, I think I killed him."

Aura pshawed. "Because you emptied your magazine on him."

I held up a hand. "Stop talking. Go clear the rest of the penthouse."

"No one else here," Thog said.

Hannah and Aura vanished down the hallway. I dragged the wheezing guardian to one of the chairs that had survived Thog and Layla's battle and secured her arms and legs to it. "What's this one's name?" I asked Thog.

He pulled one of Layla's daggers from his arm. "Myrna."

Hannah returned. "All clear."

Aura appeared a second later. "Clear."

I posed another question. "Why are you here, Thog?"

"I just a guard for this place." He motioned a bloody hand at the penthouse. "I here all the time."

Aura stepped in front of him. "Where is the headquarters for the God Hand?"

His forehead pinched. "I not know. They tell me guard here, so I guard. They tell me nothing else."

"Are there computers here?" Aura said.

"Computers?" He scratched his head. "What is computer?"

"This guy's useless." Layla scowled. "Can I kill him now?"

"Wait!" Thog threw up his hands. "I have wife and kids."

She barked a laugh. "Do you know how many times I've heard that one before?"

Aura frowned. "I found two bedrooms with bathrooms. The arch for the pocket dimension bathroom isn't here."

"Arch!" Thog nodded eagerly. "They took arch away long time ago. They not like it."

"Again, not helpful." Layla narrowed her eyes. "Tell me one useful thing, or I'll let your wife cash in on your life insurance."

He blinked. "What is—"

Layla held up a dagger. "Say something useful."

Thog squinted as if desperately trying to think of something. He gasped. "Sometimes Liem vanish when he here. I look for him, but he not here even though I know he not leave."

Aura tapped a finger on her chin. "They must have a secret room here."

I lightly slapped Myrna on the cheek. "Hey, where's the secret room?"

She spat at me. "Die, dog."

I put my wand to her temple. "Maybe a few thousand volts of magical electricity will jolt your memory."

Her lips peeled back from her face. "Burn my mind to ash. I will die before I betray—" She abruptly stopped talking.

"Betray whom? The queens of summer and winter?" The slight tick in her eyes told me I'd hit home. Unfortunately, we didn't have all night to question her.

Thog's gaze kept darting toward the sigil pad on the wall—the one that had delivered the dispelling blast. I'd used dispel bombs before but had never seen anything this powerful. The ones we'd used during the war couldn't take out fae enchantments.

"Why are you looking at that slate, Thog?"

He gulped. "They put here four days ago. They say you have cloak now. Say this can destroy enchantments."

I checked Myrna's cloak with my scope. The sigils weren't glowing anymore. The dispel had effectively ruined every oblivion cloak within range. The fact that the fae had given them such a powerful dispel demonstrated just how much they feared me with a cloak at my disposal. I tugged off my cloak and tossed it on the floor.

When Liem had activated the blast, he'd fried all their cloaks. It also meant he'd fried any illusions that might be hiding secret doors in this place. But it had already been used, so why was Thog still looking at it? Then I saw the small red button just to the side of it.

"Thog did that alert other guardians that this place has been breached?"

He grimaced. "Yes."

"You idiot," Myrna hissed.

Thog looked down. "Thog is not good at secrets."

"Fucking knew it." Layla clenched a dagger. "He's stalling for time."

"Split up and look through the rooms. This place isn't very large, and the dispel bomb they used would have destroyed any illusions hiding a secret room."

"It's probably hidden behind a real wall." Aura pressed her lips together. "I'll find it."

I secured Myrna's legs and arms to the chair. "Layla, keep an eye on our guests, please."

She bared her teeth. "Gladly."

I ran to the end of the hallway and took a quick look in the two bedrooms. Each one had its own bathroom and closet and a striking view of the city since one wall was nothing but windows. Aura was already in the first bedroom, so I went into the second and began throwing the clothing out of the walk-in closet. The guardians who lived here had quite the collection of civilian garb.

Once the hangars were empty, I rapped my knuckles on the wood, listening for a hollow thump that told me something was behind the wall. I made a quick circuit through the closet, the bathroom, and then the bedroom but didn't notice anything off about the walls. Aura emerged from the other bedroom looking frustrated.

"I don't understand." She pursed her lips. "Unless Thog just said that to keep us here a little longer."

"Maybe." I looked back down the hall toward the kitchen. "I don't know where else they'd hide anything." I considered the layout and compared it to what I'd seen in Beta. Even with the bedrooms, bathrooms, and closets, this layout didn't cover enough space to match the size of the penthouse I'd seen on Beta.

I rapped my knuckles on the wall at the end of the hallway. It echoed hollowly. I took out my mister and sprayed it along the wall along the right side. It reacted with finger oil near the corner. I put my fingers against the fingerprints of whoever had used it before, and pressed in.

There was a slight click as a magnetic latch released and a small panel swung open to reveal a sigil pad. I took out the sigil keycard and tapped it against it. The keycard fizzled. The dispelling blast had killed it.

I walked to the center of the wall, leaned on my back foot, and slammed it with my other foot. The wall rattled, revealing faint seams in the wood. I drew my brightblade and rammed it into the wall along the seam on the left. It burned into the wood and met with something more substantial underneath. At first, I feared it was mithril, but the brightblade finally pushed through it.

The blade cut through a latch and the door slid to the side. I pulled out the blade and banished it, then used my foot to push the door open further. Beyond the door was a large, windowless room with banks of monitors and a rack of computers to the side.

"Jackpot," Aura murmured.

Some monitors displayed views all around and inside the building. Another showed the entrance to Voltaire's. The other monitors showed interior and exterior views of various supernatural supply shops. The God Hand had its eye on a lot of places, presumably keeping a sharp eye out for me.

Aura frowned. "How did this survive the dispel blast?"

"Because it was a magical dispel, not an electromagnetic pulse that destroys computers." I stepped closer to the banks of monitors and examined what was happening in the hundreds of live feeds arranged in neat split screens.

Whenever a person stepped into view of a camera, little boxes formed around their face as facial recognition software took note of who they were. Judging from the log files running alongside the images, some faces triggered alerts. I imagined my face would trigger flashing red lights and a klaxon.

I wasn't surprised to find Eclipse tracked the major hubs of supernatural activity. Most of their targets were supers, though I'd also been tasked with tracking down nubs as well. Just about anyone in

the community would go to Voltaire's or magical supply shops at
some point. There were hundreds of split images spread across the
various monitors. It was likely they had eyes all over the world.

"Gods be damned. Is there any place they aren't watching?" I
leaned closer and saw the names of each location in the upper left of
the live feed. They were grouped geographically, so it didn't take me
long to find the places being monitored in Atlanta. Even the few
secret shops I knew about were being watched.

One screen showed a live map of Atlanta. There were dots all over
the map in various colors. Aura clicked a dropdown box and revealed
a long list of names. One of them was mine and it had a red dash next
to it. She clicked my name and all the dots except the red ones
vanished. The vast majority of them were near Voltaire's.

"These are all your known locations." She clicked another
checkbox on the screen and lines began to connect the dots, forming
an ever-shrinking pattern of triangles until a portion of the southwest
part of the map was contained in one. They'd narrowed down the location of Sanctuary to about fifty square miles—far too close for comfort.

She opened the dropdown and clicked more names—Aura, Layla,
and Hannah. With those dots on the screen, the triangulation
narrowed to forty miles. Another set of triangles formed around
Voltaire's and more appeared in downtown Atlanta.

"Well, at least we know Layla's general home coordinates." Aura
shook her head. "Elektrode might have even more data on the mainframe at their secret headquarters. He might be closer to a location
than this indicates."

"Wonderful."

"I knew Eclipse had eyes everywhere, but this is ridiculous." Aura
sat at the main console and switched the map screen with a long list.
"They've been apprehending a lot of people." She scrolled through a
list. "There's tons of data on here—too much for me to download. I'm
going to need a minute to find what we're looking for."

"Can you trace the location of the secret headquarters from here?"

She shook her head. "I have a geotracker program, but even if I use it from here, Elektrode will know something's up. We also don't have time to do it now if reinforcements are coming."

"Get the info you need and let's get out then."

"Cain!" Hannah ran into the room. "Holy crap, you found it?"

"Yeah." I looked back at her. "Everything under control?"

She shook her head. "The elevator is on the way up."

"Great." I put a hand on Aura's shoulder. "Get what we need. I'll guard our back."

Aura blew out a breath. "I'll see what I can find."

"If worse comes to worst, wreck their servers."

She patted the gun at her waist. "I think lightning rounds will make short work of them."

I stepped out of the room and slid the door shut. It wouldn't latch anymore, but it would give her some protection if anyone came this way.

Hannah and I ran back down the hallway to the kitchen. The elevator door was next to the emergency stairwell exit. Thanks to the renovations, a wall formed a short bottleneck from the elevator to the kitchen.

Thog lay face down on the floor, but he was still breathing.

I raised an eyebrow in Layla's direction. "You didn't kill him?"

"I gave him a jab with a sleeping dart." She shrugged. "I guess I'm going soft, Cain."

Myrna struggled against her restraints, glaring daggers at us. "The others are coming for you, Cain."

"A party just for little old me?" I fanned my face with a hand. "Heavens to Betsy, I'm blushing."

Hannah stared at me uncertainly. "See what I mean? He's so serious until the shit hits the fan and then he's got plenty of jokes."

"It's how he deals with pressure." Layla flashed a grin. "We all have our methods."

Hannah snorted. "You cope by making fart and sex jokes."

"Wouldn't have it any other way." Layla twirled daggers in her hands. "How slow is this elevator?"

I summoned my staff and switched to longshot mode. "Ten seconds."

Hannah ejected the empty magazine from her pistol and reloaded it. "Five, four, three, two, one."

The elevator dinged and the doors slid open to reveal nothing and no one. Three of Layla's daggers flashed into the doors an instant after they opened. Someone cried out in pain. Something invisible deflected the other two daggers.

I fired a longshot and watched as it was deflected into the wall by something unseen. "They're cloaked!"

Hannah unleashed a hail of gunfire. Sparks flew and electricity crackled as the bullets were deflected.

Layla threw two marble-sized orbs. The cloaked guardians tried to deflect them, but they puffed into green mist on impact. Our uninvited guests began coughing.

"That won't hold them for long," Layla said.

Hannah ran out of bullets and holstered her pistol. "How are we supposed to fight these invisible assholes?"

That was a damned good question, and I didn't have the answer.

34

An unknown number of invisible Oblivion Guard were making their way from the elevator door to us. If my cloak hadn't been dispelled by Liem earlier, then I could fight them on their own terms. Or maybe I could turn their own dispel against them and even the odds, provided it wasn't a one-shot countermeasure.

I ran back to the kitchen and found the sigil pad Liem had used to activate the dispel. I traced the same sigil he had and hoped it worked. A bubble of blue magic erupted from the pad and spread through the penthouse.

The invisible guardians shouted in dismay as the enchantments on their cloaks fizzled out. They faded into view as they came around the corner into the kitchen. I counted six of them and most of them wore familiar faces. I'd fought alongside several of them in the war and trained with two of them. We might have once been on the same team, but I'd never been friends with any of them.

They recovered quickly from the surprise of having their cloaks dispelled and spread out to form a line across the doorway leading to the elevator.

"My old friend Ena!" I blew a kiss. "How nice to see you again."

Tisha was with them as well. "Where's Anair? Oh, that's right, I killed him."

She glared at me with narrowed eyes. "Always full of tricks, Cain. That is the only reason your pitiful human body survived the trials."

"Did you not hear?" Valen Hearthstone, a low fae stepped forward, brightblade glowing in her hand. "Erolith is his adoptive father. He did not earn his place in the guard. It was given to him."

Myrna rocked furiously in her chair. "Someone free me!"

A dagger flashed and caught Myrna in the throat. She gagged as blood clogged her airway, then slumped.

"Oops, did I do that?" Layla said. "Sorry."

Ena bared her teeth furiously. "You will die for that."

"Wow, this is such a touching reunion." I held my staff at the ready but kept the brightblade off. "Except I never served with any of you because you're from Alpha, not Prime."

"Technically true." Ena sneered and stared down her nose at me. "This exempts us from the twisted bargain you forced your queens into."

"We will make short work of you and your...ilk." Valen spat on the floor. "It is because of you that our worlds are infested with the eldritch. You are a traitor to your own kind."

Hannah bared her teeth. "You talk a lot of shit for someone who hides behind invisibility."

Ena whirled her brightblade. "I do not hide behind anything. Let Cain fight me in single combat, and I will end him with at least a small shred of honor."

I barked a laugh. "Is this like the time you bragged that you could best Torvin in a duel and he spanked you with his staff after disarming you in less than a minute? I'm surprised your ego survived the humiliation."

Ena's pale face flushed. "That was long ago. I was but a novice. Now I am a master."

I counted six guardians. There was no way in Hades they were going to give up a numbers advantage like that to indulge in single combat. Ena might be dead serious about fighting me, but she also wasn't stupid. The Oblivion Guard wasn't founded on principles of honorable combat. It existed solely to do the bidding of the high fae and to get the job done any way possible.

The open layout of the kitchen and den area gave them enough room to spread out and surround us despite the unconscious troll bridge snoring loudly in the middle of the floor.

Hannah stepped forward, eyes glowing softly. "Maybe I'll just kill all of you."

Valen sneered again. "You are no Esteri, little girl. We know that you have no control over your powers."

"Why don't you push me and find out?" The glow in her eyes flickered.

My mind was working furiously to figure out how to delay a fight long enough for Aura to get what we'd come for. Fighting six guardians in close quarters was a death sentence. Layla apparently had other ideas. She casually flicked her hand. Something too small to be a dagger flew through the air.

The guardians flexed defensively, but it didn't go anywhere near them. Instead, it embedded itself in Thog's beefy troll buttock. He twitched but didn't move. I wondered if she'd poisoned him so he wouldn't get up and join the fight.

"Oops that one slipped too. I'm just a klutz today." Layla shrugged. "So, do you cowards plan to fight Cain or are we going to sit here and listen to you brag all night?"

Hannah shot Layla a dirty look. "Shut up!"

I tried to change subjects. "Who's behind all of this anyway? Am I really such a high-value target for the queens?"

Ena stared silently at me for a moment. "Why haven't you tried to run? You're hopelessly outnumbered."

Valen's eyes flared. "They came for the data."

The gig was up. The three of us couldn't hold off six guardians unless Hannah's magic decided to come online. On the other hand, I hadn't gone through all this trouble just so these assholes could ruin it. As long as we kept things up close and personal their magic casters couldn't take potshots at us. I gave Hannah my gun. "Shoot any of them that try to flank us, okay?"

She took the gun and nodded.

I turned toward the guardians. "Well, Ena? Ready for our glorious duel?"

"No, I think not." She readied her blade. "Kill them."

Layla glanced at Thog. "What the fuck is taking so—"

Thog roared and lunged to his feet. "Monsters!" He ran at the guardians, arms flailing as if trying to fight off invisible attackers.

"Finally." Layla smirked. "That last dart was dosed with fear potion."

Ena and the others suddenly found themselves embroiled in a battle with a bridge troll who was drugged out of his mind. I took advantage of the confusion and darted toward the nearest guardian. He spun to meet my attack. Thog's elbow caught him in the back of the head and sent him reeling.

I blocked his clumsy off-balance attack and slashed off the top of his head. Brains sizzled and leaked out. He convulsed and fell to the floor, spewing brains everywhere. I pivoted to Valen and locked blades with her. She rolled away from the crazed troll to give herself space. I sidestepped as Thog's fist swung wildly and nearly caught me in the head. Ena rammed her brightblade into his gut, but it only enraged him.

That wouldn't last long though. Blood still trickled from the dagger wounds inflicted by Layla earlier. He'd probably bleed out before they managed to kill him.

Valen and I exchanged a flurry of blows. She was precise with her attacks and counters and refused to let me bait her into an overstep or mistake. I backed up, pulling her further from the others while Layla and Hannah attempted potshots with daggers and lightning rounds.

I'd never dueled Valen, but I'd seen her fight before. It didn't matter what her opponent threw at her, she remained patient, meticulously attacking and countering her opponent to wear them down no matter how long it took. I was already tired from my earlier fights and heavy reliance on ghostwalking to improve my positioning.

My body sigils had been drained of power by the dispel. I didn't even know if they were still intact or if I'd have to redo them, but I certainly couldn't draw on them to put me over the top in a duel.

Without brute strength or superior swordplay, I couldn't hope to break through her defenses before she whittled down my endurance. I cast a shield just behind her left ankle, hoping to trip her, but she knew that trick all too well and broke the shield with a slash from her brightblade. Her fingers moved in quick patterns as she cast spells of her own.

I read the patterns as she cast them. The first was a suffocation spell. I countered it with a dispel, then cast another spell to stop a blinding hex. We dueled with magic and swords at the same time. The effort began to wear me down as she knew it would.

Thog went down with a final roar, blood spurting from multiple wounds on his neck. Tisha was down, a dagger jutting from her throat. The odds weren't quite in our favor, but they were moderately better than before. I just had to do something about Valen before she wore me down.

Ghostwalking wasn't an option. It took a considerable chunk of energy every time I used it. Her relentless magic and brightblade attacks weren't difficult to counter, but every blow was nicking away at my endurance. This fight was happening on her terms, and I couldn't let it continue.

The best option was pretty bad, but I took it anyway. I backed onto the balcony, weaving between the patio furniture and garbage that had accumulated there. A smirk broke through her stony expression when she saw I'd backed myself into a corner.

"Well, Cain, you're not nearly as dangerous as they led us to believe." She spat over the railing. "It looks like Ena will have to duel your Alpha counterpart instead."

Her slip of the tongue caught my attention. "You and your friends are from Feary Beta."

She looked mildly annoyed. "Yes."

"And you think I'm responsible for the eldritch infestation of Gaia Beta?" I mimicked her spitting. "I'm afraid that's not on me."

"Even if it's not, you bear the blame for the Beast War and a great many other transgressions, not the least of which is sullying the Oblivion Guard with a human member."

"Aw, did the big bad human hurt your feelings?" I considered my next move and hoped it didn't end up with me plummeting to my demise. "I'll make sure to light a candle for you."

Her eyes narrowed. She kicked aside the deck table. Empty bottles clattered and smashed against the concrete. I flung a quick succession of spells at her. She contemptuously batted them aside with counter spells and marched toward me, determination on her face. I let her get two thirds of the way toward me before doing the last thing she expected.

I ran at her. A faint smile appeared on her lips as she braced herself for the final confrontation that would end in my death. Then I jumped over the balcony railing and out into the void.

Surprised flashed across her face as I dove into the night sky. I grabbed the rope dangling there and swung out and around to the other side of the balcony. I rolled inside and slid the door shut, latching it and trapping her out there. She could use the rope to climb to the roof, but it wouldn't do her much good.

Layla was fighting two guardians at once with Myrna's oblivion staff. Hannah was barely holding off another one with the brightblade taken from the other dead guardian. I drew a dueling wand and blasted Hannah's attacker in the back. He stumbled forward and Hannah rammed the brightblade through his chest.

Ena jumped away from Layla to let her comrade continue the fight and came at me, anger burning in her eyes.

"Valen didn't think you could beat me." I glanced at the sliding door. Valen was trying to cut the latch with her brightblade but wasn't having much luck cutting through the enchanted glass. "I guess she'll get to watch you die."

"You'll be doing the dying!" Ena charged.

Her comrade screamed in pain and went down as Layla disarmed her and rammed her own brightblade into her guts.

Ena stopped in her tracks, apparently realizing that she was all alone against three of us.

Hannah smirked. "Don't tell me you're having second thoughts now that the odds aren't two-to-one."

Layla activated the brightblade on the other oblivion staff and dual-wielded them. "Oh, this feels sexy." She slashed the humming blades through the air. "Does it look sexy?"

"It's mega-sexy," Hannah said.

"Oh, yeah." Layla blocked the door to the elevator hallway. "Let's make this bitch bleed."

"I knew you couldn't win a fair fight." Ena stalked toward me. "Coward."

"Funny how your definition of a fair fight is six versus three." I walked toward her. "Give it your best shot." I hadn't seen her fight in years, but with any luck she'd still make the same mistakes that let Torvin swat her like an annoying fly.

She gasped and went stiff as twin brightblades burst from her chest. Layla shoved the body off with a foot. "We don't have time to be pussyfooting around, Cain."

I shrugged. "Do you see me arguing?"

She turned off the brightblades. "These are fun. Maybe I'll keep them."

I went to the balcony door and slid it open.

Valen stood at the far end, brightblade glowing. "Come get me if you dare."

Layla dropped the oblivion staffs and drew daggers. "If you insist." She flung the daggers.

I cast a flurry of spells at the same time. Valen tried her best to block everything, but it was impossible. A dagger caught her chest, her shoulder, and finally her throat. She slid slowly to the floor, blood pooling around her.

"We are not the last coming for you, Cain." She struggled to breathe. "You will die in the end." She spasmed and went still.

Hannah grimaced. "Should I feel bad that we just gang-banged her?"

"No, you should not." Layla picked up the oblivion staffs. "Those fuckers were more than happy with the odds earlier. We just returned the favor."

Aura stepped onto the balcony. "What did I miss?"

"Everything as usual." Layla raised an eyebrow. "Did you get what we need?"

"I hope so."

I went back inside to the slate with the dispel enchantment. The wall around it was heavily damaged so it only took moderate prying to work it loose.

Layla stood beside me. "What are you doing?"

"I want to study this, so I'll have a way to dispel cloaks." The slate wasn't much larger than a poker card, so I slid it into a pouch on my utility belt.

"Cain, look at this." Hannah stood over Ena's corpse pointing to a spot behind the drow's ear.

I knelt and examined the tattoo there. It was a white wing filled with intricate sigils. I examined it with my scope. It glowed faintly, but the fae dispel had drained its power. It seemed that body sigils weren't completely wrecked by the fae dispel for some reason, but without a charge, they were useless.

"They all have the same tattoo," Layla said. "Well, all except for the troll."

"That wing looks familiar." Aura shook her head. "But I can't place it."

Layla snorted. "Must be the sign of the almighty God Hand."

The elevator dinged faintly from down the hall.

"Gods be damned." Layla bared her teeth. "Are we going another round?"

"Hell no." I ran to the balcony. "Go!"

Layla grabbed the rope and shimmied up. I closed the balcony door while the others took turns climbing the rope.

A body seemingly lifted itself off the floor. Eight guardians shimmered into view, one of them holding the body. Their gazes flicked toward me. Aura had just vanished up onto the balcony roof. I scrambled for the rope and climbed up after her. Layla reached the building roof by the time I joined Aura. Hannah was already making her way up.

Aura gave Hannah time to get halfway up, then gripped the rope and climbed up after her. I pulled the slack rope up from the balcony below so the guardians couldn't easily climb it. A pair of hands gripped the edge of the roof and a face appeared. A swift kick in the head sent them back down.

I grabbed the rope and clambered up after the others. It wasn't a long climb, but after all the fighting, my arms felt like lead. Black worms crept along my peripheral vision, seeking to squirm further into my brain. I pushed back, clearing my mind so I could make it out of this alive.

Layla grabbed my arm and yanked me up and onto the roof. Hers and Hannah's wings were already strapped on. I pulled up the rope, then grabbed my wings and buckled on the harness. I took out my phone and oriented myself toward PDK, then did a running jump off the edge of the roof.

I pulled the control cords and the wings flared, catching the air and gliding. We were on the opposite side of the building from the balcony, but I still felt exposed. I glanced back. Aura, Hannah, and Layla were airborne, and no one else had followed us to the roof. I steered around a nearby building to put it between us and the Sovereign just in case.

The mission had been bloody and far from perfect, but we'd secured the data from the Eclipse servers. I just hoped it had what we needed to help us put an end to this madness.

35

We landed at the airport half an hour later, further reinforcing my opinion that the clockwork wings, while nifty, weren't practical for zipping around town or for military use if that was what the Futurists intended.

I texted Elton to let him know we'd made it out alive.

He responded a moment later. *Glad to hear it. Let me know if you can help with Wanda.*

I didn't reply because I wasn't sure what I could do about that situation. Despite that, she might still be a valuable resource to help me level up a few notches.

After stowing the wings in Dolores' trunk, I drove us back to Sanctuary, taking my usual roundabout route to ensure that we weren't being followed. I couldn't stop thinking about all the dots marking locations Eclipse had recorded every time I'd been seen. I wondered if my circuitous route was working against me. Maybe they spotted me with traffic cams and used that data as well.

I used illusion to hide Dolores and my face, so I didn't see how they could do that, but with magic, anything was possible.

"I can't believe we pulled it off." Layla blew out a breath. "I was starting to see those worms again during the fight. I don't think the malgorth cleaned my brain entirely."

"Same." I glanced back at the others. Hannah had fallen asleep, and Aura was staring silently at a small memory stick. "What's on there?"

She blinked and looked up. "I didn't have much time to search, but thankfully they had a filtered dump folder where they put their prioritized items for the surveillance. I also found the demi dossiers and reports from people in the field who track down rumors to find or confirm their status."

Layla whistled. "How large is Eclipse?"

"It's much larger than I could have imagined. There was a directory of handlers and supervisors who work at the Sovereign, but I doubt there's any direct information about who works at the real headquarters." Aura tucked the memory stick into her pocket. "I copied their network logfiles to see what else their system connected to, but we'll have to trace the IP addresses as soon as possible before they have a chance to change them."

"You can do that?" Layla pursed her lips. "You're not a hacker."

"You're right, I'm not a hacker." Aura looked out the window. "But I have scripts programs that do the work for me."

"Good enough." Layla turned around and looked at the road ahead. "We stirred up the hornets' nest good tonight. Gods know what kind of reception we'll get when we storm their real head-quarters."

"They weren't ready for us tonight and we barely pulled it off." I tapped a finger on the steering wheel. "They've been tracking all of us. They've even narrowed down your home base to downtown Atlanta."

Layla growled. "Those fuckers are tracking me?"

I nodded. "They'll know we're coming this time, but we don't have a choice. I can't just pick up and move, because there's no other place like Sanctuary."

"It's literally your birthplace," Aura said. "Even if your birth was supposed to be a human sacrifice."

"They can line up an army of crab tanks in front of the building and I'm still going in." Layla held up a fist. "I'm not letting those nosey fuckers find out where I live."

Aura rolled the memory stick in her fingers. "The penthouse here was obviously used for a lot more than the one on Beta. I wonder if they have a similar office on Alpha."

"Nah, they probably relocated everything to their secret lair." Layla cracked her knuckles. "Or maybe everything is here on Prime."

Aura leaned forward. "Cain, we need to go to one of my secure locations my cybermancer set up for me so I can run the network trace. It's best if we do that now instead of later."

I slowed down. "Where are we going?"

She gave me an address in East Atlanta Village.

I rerouted us to the new location and parked behind a bar that was overflowing with patrons and loud music.

Hannah awoke with a start. "Are we home?"

"No, we're somewhere Aura can analyze the data." I opened my door. "Do you want to sleep in the car?"

She nodded groggily. "Let me know if you find anything." She spread out along the seat to lay down.

Aura led us downstairs beneath the bar and through a heavy steel door. Inside was a small basement space with four clean concrete walls that obviously hadn't been a part of the original building. A short rack of servers sat on a desk next to a monitor. Aura turned on the machines and startup messages flashed across the screen.

She put the memory stick into a red slot on one of the machines. "That's a secure slot. If any of the files have viruses, then it'll keep it from spreading to the rest of the network."

"I don't need technical explanations." Layla unfolded a metal chair and sat down. "Just do the work, elf."

I took one of the metal chairs and sat next to Aura so I could watch her work. She opened a logfile with a string of network addresses and started copying them into a new text file. Most of the addresses were repeats of the same one—probably the server or firewall at Eclipse headquarters.

Aura pointed to the repeating group of numbers. "I'm pretty sure this is the address we need to search for." She opened a program with a blank field and a map. She pasted the address into the blank field and clicked the start button. The program began running a trace, enumerating each hop it took across the internet. After its fourth hop there was a long pause and an error message.

No response to ping. Testing other protocols...

A moment later it went to the next hop and stopped. A blue triangle formed just north of the junction of Highway 400 and Interstate 285. The program continued working, narrowing down the size of the triangle until it locked in on a single building.

"Is that it?" I leaned closer.

Aura zoomed in for a street view and displayed a black three-story office building. A tall iron fence and gate with a security office guarded the property from intruders. "I think so."

A red warning flashed on the monitor. *Address pinged. Refreshing VPN connection to new country.*

I pointed to the warning. "Is that bad?"

"The system uses a virtual private network, so the address appears to be in a different country." She pointed to a series of numbers beneath the warning. "It's already cut off that connection and reconnected to a server in Russia so the address can't be traced." She shook her head. "Unfortunately, if Elektrode is tracing us, there's not much we can do."

"How is he so unstoppable?" Layla made a disgusted look. "If this computer is routing through a bunch of countries, then how can he keep finding it?"

Aura shrugged. "I have no idea."

It seemed like a good idea to keep things moving, so I interrupted before they continued on that tangent. "We have the address. What's next?"

Aura closed the tracing program and opened a database program, then navigated to a file on the memory stick and imported it. After it finished, she opened the database and displayed the data in a spreadsheet format. Inside was a long list names and other information.

"This looks like the data I used to receive when I was a handler." She scrolled along the row, pausing at the columns. "This is the handler's name and the ID of the asset assigned." She skipped several columns and stopped at another one. "This is the type of super being tracked."

I examined the column. "W for werewolf, V for vampire, and M for magic user?"

"Yeah." Aura pulled up a find window and searched for *D*. The first one appeared a few hundred rows down. "Here's the first demi in the database." She moved the mouse cursor over a number in the column next to it. "Terminated twenty-one years ago."

"The database only goes back twenty-one years?" Layla said.

Aura nodded. "They probably used paper files before then."

"What an inconvenience." Layla blew out a breath. "How current is the data?"

Aura hit a button and the view moved to the last row in the database. "It's current as of today." She opened another program. "There are more tables to the database. This will import and link them all together, so the data is easier to understand."

Layla frowned. "And this is useful why?"

"We can see all the demis they've been tracking and see if they're still killing them or doing something else." Aura clicked the button and the computer started working. Then she switched to another window with a file explorer and started going through other folders. "What I'm really hoping to find is a list of the primary players and other assets. Maybe they have gatekeeper demis who can move them around quickly. Maybe we can find out who the gods of chaos are. Maybe they have a list of all the guardians who are tasked with killing Cain and his associates."

I grunted. "You really think they'll have that information on there?"

"No, but it's worth checking." She continued opening folders and checking them one at a time. One folder contained nothing but images with numerical names. Aura opened a few. Most of the images looked like the ones found in dossiers. Several showed the same people after they'd been apprehended or killed.

"Nice family albums," Layla said.

"These images link to the database files. Once the program is done organizing everything, you'll see how it links together." Aura opened another folder and clapped her hands. "They kept a file on the original orders."

"As in the original kill orders?" I peered at the alphanumerical file names. "How do you know which is which?"

"These are concatenated dates and target names." She scrolled far down and stopped in a section. Halfway down the page was a file name with a series of numbers and *HannahEsteri* in it.

I jabbed a finger on the monitor. "That's Hannah's kill order?"

Aura opened it. It was a document formatted like a memorandum, short and to the point.

The Black Hand has decreed a termination by special order for subject code-named HannahEsteri. Subject location is unknown. A tracker shall be assigned to tag subject. Tracker's handler is Janice. Termination assigned to Handler Alpha for special cause. As a special duty case, the source information has been redacted and is only available for Tier One clearance personnel.

Below it was Torvin's signature.

"Why is a magical assassination organization so intent on acting like a nub corporation?" Layla blew out a breath. "Memos and databases are so blah."

"Written decrees and other tracking methods are common on Feary," I said. "Even the Oblivion Guard has a tracking system."

"Yeah, but this is so mundane." Layla shook her head. "So, I guess the juicy information is on their mainframe?"

Aura nodded. "I'm afraid so." She opened a memo about a werewolf. "As you can see, the normal order declarations are a lot different. They list the type of super, family members, and all sorts of personal information. The demi memos are heavily redacted."

Layla rubbed her eyes. "So, the only useful information from all the trouble we went through is the location of the real headquarters?"

"The whole reason we did this was to find the location of their headquarters." Aura switched to the database program to check on its progress. "Everything else is just icing on the cake."

"And now they'll know we're coming." Layla grinned. "They'll be overconfident with that knowledge."

"Maybe." I folded my arms over my chest. "We left them with a penthouse full of dead bodies. We're giving them a second chance to be ready for us."

"Well, we don't have a choice unless we want Elektrode to lead them to our front doors." Layla pressed her lips together. "Even if we move, they'll just find us again with all those surveillance cameras. I'm ready to end this once and for all immediately because I hate moving with a passion."

"That's the plan." I patted her shoulder. "We're not going to give them a chance to breathe."

"Finally!" Aura stared at the monitor. "The database finished compiling so I ran a search on demis. There are twelve others they discovered since Hannah, but the orders are only to tag and track them." She opened the folder with the memos, sorted by date, and scrolled down until she was near the bottom. One of the documents had a different title than the others. She opened it.

Special Order 13

Torvin's death has changed our mission parameters.

Special Order 3 stated: Status D subjects shall be terminated, and all information classified to Tier 1. Special Order 3 is hereby revoked and declared null and void. Special Order 13 shall supplant Special Order 3.

Information pertaining to status D subjects is declassified. Our goal now is recruitment and training for these subjects. As such, surveillance shall be increased to include more than supernatural hotspots and will be extended to encompass ordinary humans. The number of personnel on the Demi Task Force will be tripled.

Once a demi is identified and confirmed, a newly created Demi Recruitment Force will be responsible for onboarding them and securing their loyalty through whatever means necessary. If you have any questions, please notify your supervisor.

-Olfir Goldseed Golden Knight, Highborn Protector of Faevalorn, King of Sonfel (Unified)

I read the memo twice. "What in the gods' names is Olfir Goldseed doing writing memos? And what does Unified mean?"

Aura opened another special-order document and read through it. "The special order acknowledges the existence and sovereignty of the shadow courts. When an order is given by all living alts, then it's unified. If it's not, then they indicate which dimensions are adhering to the order."

I raised an eyebrow. "Shadow courts?"

"I think that's what the Prime queens call their counterparts in Alpha and Beta."

"Olfir sure has a lot of titles." Layla shifted in her chair. "I guess they look good on his resume."

"He's the son of Queen Solara and Arctus, brother of Queen Mayce." I looked at the order over Aura's shoulder. "Mayce had a daughter by Solara's brother Solus that was supposed to rule the combined court of Faevalorn, but something happened, and the child died. Rumor had it that there was a brutal conflict among the high fae to determine who ruled the combined court. Olfir was secreted away to Gaia where he served as a knight of the roundtable with King Arthur. There's more to it, but the real story is probably locked away in a high fae library somewhere."

Layla whistled. "Now that's a story I'd like to hear."

"There were formerly four fae courts, including autumn and spring, but there was a fae war that decimated them and brought about the need to create a neutral combined court." Aura scrolled through the files on the screen. "All of that information was suppressed and declared illegal long ago, but the stories were passed down through the ages by oral tradition."

"I was never privy to all those juicy rumors when I was growing up." Layla stood and stretched her back. "Staying alive was my number one priority."

Aura switched back to the database. "I've got locations on all the demis they tracked and tagged. Most of them were identified even before Hannah and scheduled for termination. For some reason, Hannah was moved up in the queue. Now those same demis are scheduled for recruitment."

I tapped the screen. "Go back to the memos."

"For what?"

"Just do it." Something I'd seen nagged at my mind, but I couldn't put my finger on it. Aura switched back to the folder. I looked at the file names and tapped on one that was just beneath Olfir's decree for Special Order Thirteen. "Notice how some of the file names are almost identical, except for this symbol?" There was a black diamond at the end of the file name.

She opened it. The identical order was inside. "Maybe it's just a backup."

"Scroll to the bottom."

She did and revealed another paragraph.

The Winged God has approved this order in full, but all data is to be screened and filtered by our people before being sent to the courts.

Aura smacked her lips. "Well, this just got a lot more complicated. The Handers are playing for two different teams and taking orders from someone besides their queens."

"Who is the Winged God?" Layla scrunched her forehead. "I can't think of anyone fitting that description."

"I'm sure any god could grow a pair if they wanted," Aura said.

"Yeah, but what god is known for wings?"

I took the mouse and opened another file with a black diamond. At the bottom was a paragraph with modifications to the original order, also approved by the Winged God. "Well, now we know why they call themselves the God Hand."

"Why not the God Wing if it's a god with wings?" Layla rolled her eyes. "These people need to come up with better names."

"Well, whoever this mystery god is, it looks like they're planning on recruiting these demis for their own purposes and the queens are taking a back seat." Aura blew out a breath. "And for some reason, we're caught in the middle."

36

"How many demis has the God Hand recruited?" Layla asked.

"Thankfully, only two, according to the notes. It hasn't been that long since Cain killed Torvin, and they implemented their new policies. I don't think they have enough personnel to take on the task, especially if they're doing it without the queens finding out." Aura switched to a record with extensive notes. "They sent a pair of former Oblivion Guard to recruit one girl, but they only freaked her out and nearly caused a major incident."

I grunted. "Those are the last people you want recruiting super-powered human kids. Most of them have zero personal skills and regard humans as subpar creations despite any godlike powers they might possess."

"It looks like they've recently started hiring humans to do the job, specifically those who deal with children regularly." Aura tutted. "Wow, they're desperate."

I raised an eyebrow. "I'm surprised they aren't simply abducting them."

Layla shrugged. "It's better to have them join willingly so they don't turn against you."

"The two demis that joined were recruited by elementary school teachers." Aura turned to give me a disturbed look. "They're hiring school teachers, for gods' sakes!"

"That's creepy, even by my standards." Layla stuck out her tongue and mimicked gagging herself with a finger. "I wonder why they're suddenly so intent on building an army of demis when they were happily murdering them not that long ago."

"The fae were probably convinced that demis were a major threat to their rule. Humans First saw them as a perfect weapon against the fae—Daphne, for example." The sun demigoddess had survived even though we'd killed all the Firster leaders. I wondered what trouble she was up to now. "When Torvin was banished from Feary, they saw him as the perfect candidate to keep slaughtering demis so they couldn't be weaponized by humans." I leaned forward in my chair. "But once the gods of chaos stepped up their plans and split Prime into multiple timelines, maybe they realized it was better to fight fire with fire."

"Makes sense," Layla said. "I've gotta admit that I'm confused as hell about who's on which side. Are the gods of chaos against the fae, or are they allied with them? Or are they allied with the Elder Things, or just some of them? Like, what in the hell is going on?"

Aura blew out a breath. "That's a good question. The gods of chaos want to upset the natural order so they can overthrow Zeus and other current rulers of the various pantheons. Maybe their efforts are indirectly helping the Elder Things, but they figure they can fight them off once they've taken over. Or maybe the Elder Things are in league with the gods of chaos and have a power-sharing agreement in place once the current order is overthrown. Or maybe they're throwing so much chaos into the mix that nobody knows which way is up."

"How do you reason with Elder Things?" Layla ran a hand down her face. "They don't think like us or the Elder Gods. They thrive on pure chaos and insanity."

Aura turned back to the monitor and continued scrolling through the memos. She opened one. "Special Order Fifteen. Terminate Cain

Sthyldor and recruit his ward at all costs. Failing that, terminate Hannah Esteri to prevent the Cult of Nyar from taking her."

I leaned over and read the special order. It was short and to the point. "Cult of Nyar? I thought they were wiped out by Joe."

Layla's eyebrows arched. "Joe, as in the guy who saved you from becoming a human sacrifice?"

I nodded. "There was a splinter group of Ekhsis who worshipped Nyar and the Elder Things. He slaughtered everyone, my mother included, to keep them from sacrificing me. Then he took me to the Ekhsis on Oblivion where I lived with another family until everyone there but me was slaughtered. That was when Erolith found me and adopted me."

Layla laughed mirthlessly. "You have a thing for surviving slaughters. No wonder you're so hard to kill."

"Maybe there are other branches of the cult," Aura said. "Maybe they aren't connected to Ekhsis."

"I mean, sure. There are cults worshipping Cthulhu and other Elder Things, so I wouldn't be surprised if there are human cults for Nyar." I paced to the wall and leaned against it. "Why do the fae think the Cult of Nyar want Hannah?"

Layla shrugged. "You had a nice conversation with Nyar while you were in Hel, didn't you?"

I closed my eyes and remembered everything, including the circumstances that drove me to temporary insanity and allowed him to speak to me. "He said, do not fear the Elder Things. Do not believe everything the Elder Gods say. We are two halves of a whole. We cry out for unity. Nurture the gift and all will be made whole. The universe will exist in the utter madness of complete harmony."

"Well, as usual, that makes no sense." Layla huffed. "Can't these assholes just give us straight talk for once?"

"He said something else." I concentrated and remembered it clearly. "Nurture the seed. Embrace the apocalypse. I heard him say that in my head when I tried to use Panoptes and nearly drove myself mad."

"I remember you mentioning that in your story." Layla puffed out her cheeks and blew out the air. "Seems pretty obvious now that Hannah is the seed."

"I thought maybe he meant something inside me." I closed my eyes and imagined the frightening wormlike specter that was Nyarlathotep. "I thought maybe he'd implanted a seed of insanity inside me. But it makes a lot more sense in light of this new information that Hannah might be the seed and he thinks I can grow her into what they want."

Aura nodded. "And it means his cult wants her."

Layla rubbed her chin. "There were some people asking about you in Voltaire's that night I decided to let you handle all this alone. They had these freaky worm tattoos on their necks."

"What is it with people and neck tattoos?" I pictured the winged tattoos on the Handers. "You would think that makes it too obvious that they're in a cult."

I thought back to the last day I'd been in Voltaire's. I'd seen several such people but hadn't given them much thought. Magic users were particularly fond of identifying with covens and other magical groups with their tattoos. I hadn't made the connection between the tattoos and Nyar because I didn't automatically connect worms to him. From now on I probably would.

This new information expanded the possibilities and created a world of new complexities to sort through. How was Hannah a seed? Did it have something to do with her parentage? The only people who could answer that were probably cult members.

I walked back to the chair and sat down. "Is there anything else about Hannah in there?"

"I'm looking." Aura scrolled to the bottom of the orders and shook her head. "Nothing that I can find." She switched to the database and pulled up Hannah's record. "There's also nothing in the notes."

An alarm flashed on the monitor. *Tracing detected. Alternating VPN connection.*

"Crap." Aura pulled out the memory stick. "I knew Elektrode would find us again."

The bank of monitors crackled with static, and a familiar thin face appeared, leering at us. "You never learn, do you, Aura?" Elektrode giggled as if so pleased with himself that he could hardly stand it. He wore the same pair of large headphones with a microphone that I'd seen in the recorded video Aura showed us earlier. He had a tiny pug nose, no chin, and smatterings of cheese dust around his lips.

Aura ran toward a rack and reached toward a yellow cable.

"I don't think so." Elektrode made a pattern with his fingers and the rack of servers crackled with electricity. "Touch it and you're dead."

Aura laughed. "I'm immortal you sack of shit."

He looked at us, apparently using the webcam mounted on the monitors. "Cain Sthyldor, I'm this close to finding your little hideout." He pinched two fingers together. "You are a hard man to find, but I'm the best."

"How much do you know about me, Elektrode?" I stared at him emotionlessly. "Do you know what happens to my enemies?"

He giggled. "Cain, you're a member of the old guard. You're a washed-up old schooler who thinks everything can be handled with a brightblade. I'm going to show you that I can kill you without ever having to smell your breath."

I folded my arms and looked unimpressed. "Maybe I'll eat a garlic-onion sandwich just before I show up and kill you. Maybe all it will take is my breath to finish the job."

Elektrode giggled madly. "Let's see how you handle this." He looked down. A keyboard clacked loudly. Then he made an unfamiliar pattern with his fingers. Aura's cell phone exploded in her pocket. Blood spattered, and she went down in a heap.

"What the fuck?" Layla took out her cell phone and threw it away from her.

I took out my phone and held it up. "Go ahead, Elektrode. Do it."

His eyes flashed with excitement and his keyboard clacked again. He made the pattern again and flicked the sigil toward us. I assumed it traveled somehow through his camera and out of the monitor here. I didn't have time to peer through my true sight scope to see.

My phone grew red hot for an instant. And then the reflective protections on it bounced the signal right back. Several monitors exploded. Elektrode recoiled in surprise. "Oh, you have protections. I like a challenge."

I'd hoped the spell would rebound back through the internet at him, but apparently, I needed to be a cybermancer to make that happen. I couldn't beat him at his own game, so I decided to end this. Besides, he knew our location and a swarm of Handers was probably descending on us right now.

I summoned my staff, switched to longshot, and blasted the yellow cable Aura had been aiming for. Elektrode vanished and the monitors went to static. I blasted the rack of servers for good measure and then knelt next to Aura. "Are you okay?"

She breathed raggedly. "I think I'm done for."

I examined the wound and concurred. "I can see your intestines."

"What did I have for lunch?" She managed a smile.

"Is the memory stick tagged? Can we take it with us?

She nodded. "I ran the scan program my guy gave me, and it came back clean."

"Good." I picked her up. She groaned in pain and passed out.

We returned to the car quickly. Aura was still breathing and bleeding, so I put her in the trunk on the protective rubber cover that kept the carpet from getting stained. There wasn't much I could do except let her die. I considered putting her out of her misery, but she seemed pretty close to dying all by herself.

Hannah was still peacefully slumbering in the back and looking like anything but an apocalyptic seed. Layla and I climbed into the front seats and stared blankly out the window for a moment. Then I remembered Handers might be on the way and accelerated away from the bar, leaving East Atlanta Village behind. I pulled off at a strip mall and scanned Dolores for trackers, then performed evasive routing per my normal protocol.

The long drive back gave me time to process what we'd learned from the stolen data. There was a lot going on that we didn't understand. It was also likely that neither the fae nor the Handers knew everything that was going on. Gaia was a pot of honey with so many hands jammed into it that nobody knew who was doing what.

And maybe that was the plan.

The gods of chaos wanted to tip the current world order. Nyarlathotep wanted the same thing, but for different reasons. The fae wanted to preserve their godlike status while the Elder Gods were too busy fighting in the Divine Realm to care.

The question was, how did I put the parts concerning me and Hannah to rest so I could finally drink my gods damned mangoritas in peace?

I couldn't rely on Zeus or his ilk, nor could I exterminate every last member of the Oblivion Guard from Alpha and Beta. I'd have to do this piecemeal and with great care. The first step was rearranging my bargain with the queens. The next step—well, I wasn't sure about that just yet. There were too many unanswered questions.

What I did know for sure was that I didn't want the Elder Things or their minions gaining a foothold on Gaia Prime like they had in Beta. I also didn't want the gods of chaos overthrowing the current gods in power.

I was no fan of Zeus, Odin, or any of the gods I'd met so far, but having Loki and his ilk pulling the puppet strings seemed like a recipe for disaster. Maybe it wasn't as bad as having an eldritch infestation, but it was right up there. Keeping the status quo was in my best interests.

It was extremely risky trying to meet with the queens, or any high fae for that matter. My run-in with Aeolus in the lands of the summer court had left the distinct impression that nothing I said or did would give them cause to ally with me. And even if they did meet with me, striking a fair bargain would take every braincell available to me. After all, they'd found multiple ways to breach the bargain I'd made with them even before the gods of chaos caused a split in the space-time continuum.

There was no limit to the number of loopholes the fae could find in any bargain, no matter how masterfully it was written and sealed.

The other option was to recruit some muscle of my own. Elton and his Monster Squad might be the perfect group to help me put an end to this mess once and for all. I mentally put that option at the top of the list. The only caveat was that I'd almost certainly have to rob another bank or two in order to afford their services.

The last possibility seemed the hardest by far, but it also might yield the greatest long-term results and protection. It would be extremely difficult to maintain and might even lead to other worse possibilities, but it was worth discussing with Hannah.

But first, I needed to sleep on this. I was too tired to think things through. When we finally arrived at Sanctuary, I woke Hannah, then went to the trunk to retrieve Aura. Her flesh was cool to the touch since she'd died somewhere along the way home. It wasn't long until midnight, so I put her bloody body on a blanket in the den and left it there. Then I dropped into bed like a sack of potatoes and fell asleep.

I WOKE up later than usual the next morning, but it didn't matter because no one else had gotten out of bed yet either. I cooked a dozen eggs and sausages so the others wouldn't attempt to cook anything in my kitchen. Layla had a habit of making huge messes and never cleaning up when she used my kitchen. Aura's body wasn't in the den. She'd probably gone into the guest bedroom with Layla after resurrecting.

Hannah dragged herself into the kitchen about fifteen minutes later, her black hair tied back in a ponytail, and a fluffy blanket in hand. She smiled. "Sorry I conked out last night, but I was done. Did you find out anything?"

"Yeah, we found out a lot." I served myself some more eggs. "The God Hand has gone from killing demis to recruiting them, and you're at the top of their list. You remember when I told you about Nyarlathotep talking to me during my time in Hel and then again recently?"

She nodded forehead pinched in concern. "Yeah, why?"

"Apparently you're the seed he was talking about. He claims

you're a key to unifying the Elder Gods and the Elder Things into perfect harmony and chaos."

"That makes absolutely no sense." Her nose wrinkled. "Why me?"

I shrugged. "Obviously there's something important about your parentage that we don't know. If we knew who your father was that might clear up a lot of this confusion."

Hannah blew out a long sigh. "Did we find Eclipse HQ? Are we going to raid them?"

"We have no choice. Elektrode killed Aura by blowing up her cell phone, and he pissed me off, so he's at the top of my hit list." I bit into a sausage. "I have a few plans I want to run by you."

Her eyebrows rose. "By me?"

I nodded. "Yeah. You're at the crux of this entire situation. The fae might know exactly who you are, and I intend to find out, either through violence or negotiation. I haven't decided which."

"Violence sounds great to me right now." She scowled. "I don't want them to kill you."

"That might be the feelgood route, but we don't have the resources to overcome the Oblivion Guard and whoever else they have guarding Eclipse headquarters." I put down my fork. "The first option is negotiating a truce and finding out if an alliance might work better. Then we work alongside the fae to stop the gods of chaos and the Elder Things."

"Ew! Work with the fae?" Hannah shook her head. "I don't like that option at all. Besides, the Handers might have their own separate agenda."

"Agreed. The next option is to talk to Elton and find out if his Monster Squad can help us overcome the odds."

"Ooh, I like that one." She tilted her head. "What else is on the table?"

"The last is arguably the hardest but might pay off in the long run, provided it doesn't blow up in our faces." I took a deep breath. "We take the list of demis in Eclipse's database and try to recruit the demis ourselves. Even if Elektrode finds the location of Sanctuary, we'll have the power to stop them."

Her eyes widened. "Wow, that would be crazy, especially for you, Cain. You can barely deal with just me sometimes. How do you expect to train a bunch of other superpowered kids? You're not Professor X."

"I know, but Cain Alpha does it somehow. Maybe I have it in me too."

She laughed. "That's a big if. You two might have been the same person at one point, but he has Cthulhu controlling demis like Esteri for him. You don't have that advantage."

"I'm aware." I forked another sausage and bit into it. "So, what do you want to do?"

She tapped a finger on her chin. "Recruiting demis is a long-term approach. We need something to work in the short term. For that, I suggest we hire Elton and maybe extend feelers to the fae queens for a new bargain. But we'll need a lot of leverage for the queens to want to bargain with you."

"That's as good a plan as any."

Hannah winced. "On the other hand, maybe we could recruit a couple of demis to help us in the short term." She threw up her hands. "Ugh, plotting and planning is hard when you're on a short time limit."

I held up a glass of orange juice as a toast. "Agreed."

"So, what do you think?" she asked. "Recruit demis, or hire Elton?"

"Both?" I shrugged. "We're up against some major power players so we need all the options we can get." I went to the guest bedroom door and knocked. "Aura, I need the memory stick."

Aura opened the door a moment later, bleary-eyed. "Can it wait? I didn't sleep well after resurrecting."

I shook my head. "No, because we've got an army to recruit."

ura's eyes widened after I told her the plan. "You want to recruit demis?"

"Yep." I watched her carefully. "You have a problem with that?"

She shook her head. "No, but that means we'll be working against agents of the God Hand. It means we'll be exposing ourselves to even more danger."

"Maybe, but I think it's the last thing they'll expect us to do." I held out a hand. "Give me the stick so I can make a list of candidates."

Aura sighed. "Fine. Give me a moment."

"Can't a girl get her beauty rest?" Layla shoved past Aura with a huff. "We were up all night."

"You stay up partying all night all the time," Aura shot back.

"Yeah, and then I sleep in."

Aura pointed straight down. "Well, there's an entire basement downstairs if you want to sleep late without being disturbed."

Layla hesitated as if about to answer, then shook her head and went to the kitchen table.

Aura stepped into the bedroom and picked up the memory stick from the nightstand. "Let's analyze this together so we can pick our targets more easily, okay?"

"Sure." I took the stick and went to my room for my laptop. I copied the database over to the hard drive and then pulled up the main window. Raw data filled the monitor. I looked at the various icons but couldn't figure out how to narrow down the list to just demis, so I took the laptop to the kitchen table and set it in front of Hannah. "Do you know how to work this thing?"

She stared at it for a moment. "Um, is this a spreadsheet?"

Layla tore into a sausage and laughed. "Not even the genius child can figure out how to work that? It's a database, Cain. Surely you've used them before."

I shook my head. "Not like this."

Aura entered the kitchen and took the laptop to another spot. She sat down, typed on the keyboard and then clicked the mouse. I walked up behind her and saw the short list of demis.

"Okay, how did you do that?"

"I ran a query and filtered out everything I didn't want."

I blinked. "That tells me nothing."

"I'll show you how to do it sometime if you want, but for now, is this all the information you want?"

"Yep."

"Good." She switched to a blank screen and started dragging and dropping boxes. "I'll make a report that resembles a dossier, complete with pictures and notes. Do you have a color printer?"

"Yes."

"Then go away and I'll tell you when I need it."

By the time I finished breakfast, Aura was ready for the printer. I set it on the kitchen counter and plugged it in. She hooked up the laptop and printed a stack of dossiers formatted almost exactly like the ones Eclipse used to send me.

Layla smirked as she watched me. "Cain, it's kind of cute watching you try to use a computer."

I shrugged. "It's not exactly my specialty."

Aura spread the printed files across the table. "Unfortunately, there's no information about parentage or powers for the demis, so we'll have no idea what we're walking into. Best I can do is organize them by location and then we can decide what order we want to tackle them in."

I picked up the dossiers for two that were separated from the rest. "Are these the ones they've already recruited?"

She nodded. "I don't know how successful the recruitments were since there's nothing in the notes that indicates whether the demis willingly participated or if they're being forced."

"Maybe we need to rescue them," Hannah said.

"Maybe." I put the files down and glanced at the others. "Work on that. I've got another project to tinker with."

"Just for the record, I think this idea is awful." Layla stirred her eggs with a fork. "I thought the original plan was to infiltrate the headquarters, eliminate Elektrode, and steal the main database so we know who else is involved."

"It wouldn't hurt to have godlike powers on our side when we do it," Aura said.

"You tried recruiting demis before and failed miserably." Layla chomped into another sausage. "Imagine being a single parent to a kid with superpowers. You've done everything to keep them safe and secret because if the government finds out what your kid can do, they'll lock them away and study them—and that's if they don't kill them while trying to bring them in. Now imagine some stranger shows up at their doorstep and says, hey, we want your kid to join our army." She whirled the sausage like a dagger in her fingers. "How successful do you think that approach is going to be?"

"When you put it like that it sounds really stupid." Hannah blew out a breath. "Maybe what we really need to do is just warn them that they're in danger and offer them a safe place to hide. Sanctuary is the perfect place for that."

Aura nodded. "I like that idea. We warn them that the God Hand knows where they live and offer them refuge if they want it. There's not much more we can do unless and until we earn their trust."

"We take the Professor X approach." Hannah clapped her hands.

"I like that idea."

Her analogy made me feel even more doubtful about this plan. I sure as hell didn't want to run a school for demigods out of Sanctuary, nor did I want to deal with the inevitable conflicts when the kids fought with each other. It was no wonder Cain Alpha kept his demis on an island in Lake Lanier, well away from anything valuable to destroy.

I picked up another dossier and read through the notes. This demi was a thirteen-year-old boy living with his mom and stepfather in Montana. They'd lived in Boston two years ago, but the kid started manifesting abilities and causing issues at school, so they'd relocated somewhere out of the way.

The other dossiers reported similar conditions for the other demis. Once their abilities manifested, that had led to the rumors which eventually reached the ears of interested parties. The parents had relocated further away from civilization in most cases, but by then, Eclipse already had their scents.

Recruiting demis was a solid long-term plan, but it would take a lot of travel, work, and trust to build a coherent fighting force. Maybe the best way to keep the God Hand from recruiting them was to finish this the old-fashioned way. With good planning, trickery, and a whole lot of killing.

"Look over the dossiers and let me know what you think. " I turned to Layla. "In the meantime, let's come up with a plan to end this on our own."

"Amen to that." Layla maintained eye contact as she gnawed on another sausage. "We've breached plenty of hard targets, Cain. We can figure this one out too, even if they know we're coming."

I went to my room and pulled the sigil slate with the fae dispel on it out of a pouch on my utility belt. I set it on my desk and summoned my staff, then examined it through the true-sight scope. There was nothing on the front of the slate, but the back was covered in intricate runes that had been engraved into the surface.

Some of the sigils were familiar to me, but many of them were three-dimensional and extremely difficult to reproduce. Like most fae enchantments, there was also no telling which sigils were necessary for the dispel to work. It was common for the fae to include fake sigils to prevent anyone from duplicating them.

The aura mode on my upgraded scope gave me insight that few could hope to have. Faintly glowing lines told me which sigils in the dispel were tied into the core enchantment. The ones without the glow were fake.

I propped the slate upright on the desk, then used a camera tripod to hold my staff in place so I could keep the scope focused on the slate. Using a pen and paper, I peered into the scope and started tracing the glowing lines.

By the time I finished some hours later, the core sigils were precisely recreated on paper. Using a fae text I'd liberated from their library just before abandoning the Oblivion Guard, I began looking for similar patterns so I could understand how to properly power them for an enchantment.

To those unfamiliar with fae texts, there seemed to be no rhyme or reason to the layout. One simply had to know that most were organized by elements and purpose. An enchantment this powerful was probably a combination of various elements bound together by a unifying sigil. I finally located one of the sigils under fire sign dispels and was able to narrow the search down for the others.

As suspected, the dispel was all-encompassing, meaning it affected earth, air, fire, and water in equal and devastating measure. It didn't include body, mind, and spirit runes which was why it didn't also obliterate the tattooed runes on my body.

Very few non-fae had access to fae-level enchantments. In fact, the majority of those with access were in the Oblivion Guard. It seemed highly unlikely they'd created this dispel just for little old me. And as the saying goes, the proof was definitely in the pudding.

At the very center of the runes was one pattern that hadn't been in the fae texts. That was because this rune wasn't fae level. In fact, it came from a much higher power. This particular rune was the one that tied the others together and gave them the power to dispel fae enchantments.

The rune in question was a small wing, nearly identical to the winged tattoos on the Handers. Judging from the power emanating from it, it was almost certainly a god-level rune. The God Hand had this dispel created so they could defend themselves against the Oblivion Guard.

I took a moment to consider what that meant.

The Handers truly were rogue guardians. They'd forsaken their pledges to the queens and were now serving the Winged God. They were trying to kill me so they could recruit Hannah for this mystery god. I had a feeling the queens didn't even know everything that was going on. This was definitely some god-level trickery going on here, and it reeked of the gods of chaos. But which of those gods had wings?

The sheer number of plans within plans was dizzying. I blew out a breath and tried to break it all down. It took a few minutes, but I managed to form a picture that made sense. Even so, it was still pure speculation.

My theory was that the Winged God, an agent of the gods of chaos, had been silently recruiting Oblivion Guard members from Beta and probably Alpha since Feary in both dimensions had been heavily impacted by events on Gaia. Those who'd had the closest ties to Torvin were the most likely candidates for recruitment. They were the ones who'd love to take a more heavy-handed approach to Gaia.

The Winged God had then made sure the queens discovered the loophole in my bargain. This ensured they would send the Oblivion Guard after me, meaning the Handers among them were free to kill me all while pretending to be following orders from their queens. This also enabled them to fully take control of Eclipse and its assets, all while keeping faithful members of the Oblivion Guard in the dark.

They were also probably silently recruiting more members from the Oblivion Guard, but with the knowledge that one day their true intentions would be revealed, leading to a civil war in the Oblivion Guard. So, the Winged God gave them a powerful dispel that would wreck fae enchantments, giving them the upper hand.

They'd installed the enchantment in Eclipse headquarters not because they thought I'd attack it, but in case of an attack by the Oblivion Guard.

It was a lot to process, but I felt confident that I was mostly right about everything. It meant there was another way to approach this problem, and it meant involving the queens. It also meant that I'd been given a new weapon in my arsenal—one that could help me achieve my goals. I just had to find the best way to use it.

The first test was to see if I could duplicate this enchantment. Simply drawing the patterns wasn't enough. If that was the case, then I'd have made my own oblivion cloak by now. Some fae-level enchantments were just too powerful for me to bind properly. The elemental sigils on this enchantment were no problem for me, but the god-level sigil might be another matter.

A fist pounded on my door. "Cain, are you still in there?"

I stood and stretched then opened the door. "What do you want?"

Hannah peered past me. "You've been in here for hours."

"I'm working on something."

"On what?"

I showed her the paper with the dispel enchantment. "A new weapon."

"I have no idea what that does, Cain."

"It gives us a fighting chance if we attack Eclipse." I checked the time and saw that it was midafternoon. My stomach rumbled, but I wasn't ready to take a break just yet. "I'll be out when I'm done."

Hannah sighed. "I'll be practicing downstairs, I guess."

"Good." I closed the door and went into my closet. I flipped up the table in the middle of the room. The floor rotated up with it, revealing a staircase. I descended into the maze of tunnels beneath Sanctuary, took a few turns, and entered my supply closet where I kept potions and other items kept in my utility belt.

One shelf held a supply of blank sigil slates. I'd procured them some time ago and used them to secure secret passages and doorways around Sanctuary. They were the best permanent method of locking down entrances because then I didn't have to manually refresh and power the wards on a regular basis. Even though that was their primary intended use, I'd discovered other creative ways to use them.

Inscribing them with more complex trap wards and other magic enabled me to have ready-made defensive or offensive spells I could deploy at a moment's notice. The only downside was their weight. Alone, they only weighed a few ounces, but by the time ten or more were stacked together, they added about a pound to my already heavy utility belt.

I grabbed a box of them and took them across the corridor to my work room. I booted up the computer on the worktable and powered on the inscribing machine linked to it with a cable. I took the paper with the sigils and ran it through my high-resolution scanner. Once the digitized image appeared on the screen, I imported it into the software for the inscribing machine and resized it to fit on a sigil slate. I clamped the slate to the table and positioned the inscribing machine over it, then ran the program on the computer.

The machine went to work tracing an exact reproduction of the patterns in a matter of minutes. Although it would have been great having it replicate the pattern directly from the original slate, the resulting inscription would have been useless. The core pattern for the enchantment needed to be inscribed first and then infused with magic to power it. Decoy sigils could then be added atop it without destroying the initial enchantment.

In cases like this, I had to strip everything down to the essentials for the spell to work. All those hours spent untangling the web had been unfortunate but necessary.

I took the completed sigil slate and laid it on another workbench. I went back into my supply closet. Using my finger, I traced a sigil on a slate securing an old, yellow refrigerator in one corner of the room. I'd repurposed the unit with a preservation enchantment to keep perishable items in stasis. A small rack on the top held dozens of tiny vials. I plucked a pair of them from the rack, one with a blue lid, and the other with a gold lid. Then I went back to my workshop.

I flipped the nearly finished slate over and inscribed a simple sigil into the other side. This pattern would serve as the trigger for the dispel enchantment. The vial with the blue lid contained pixie dust —a necessary ingredient in binding fae elemental runes. I opened it and sprinkled dust over the slate.

Then I opened the vial with the golden lid and hoped this was the secret sauce that would allow me to properly power the bindings. The crimson fluid inside was Athena's blood. When Baura had impaled her with Soultaker, she'd bled all over the sidewalk. It wasn't every day that I had the chance to procure the blood of a god, so I'd taken every last ounce I could.

I placed a few drops right over the winged rune and mixed it in with the pixie dust. The dust began to glow, and my fingers tingled with power. Focusing on the slate, I willed a steady flow of power through the pixie dust and into the patterns.

Athena's blood soaked into the winged rune. The pixie dust glittered and was absorbed into the other runes. I examined the sigil slate with my scope. The lines glowed faintly with power.

"Holy shit, it worked." It was the first time I'd tried binding a high-level sigil with Athena's blood, and I was pretty pleased with the results. It made me wonder if I could use the blood to make my own oblivion cloaks as well.

That experiment could wait.

Now that I had a fully charged slate, it was time to test it. I followed the tunnel for a distance until I reached a ladder leading up to a hatch. I traced a pattern on the sigil slate securing the hatch and pushed up. Above me, a small stump slid to the side to open the passageway. I'd found many such hidden hatches and doorways during my time mapping the tunnels under sanctuary. The Cult of Nyar had built in enough hidey-holes and secret exists to make a medieval castle designer blush.

I climbed out of the hole, followed a path through some trees, and emerged on a barren field pockmarked from explosions and littered with broken objects. My testing grounds were probably not appreciated by the local elemental Caolan had used to secure the acres surrounding Sanctuary, but it was a necessary evil. Testing new wards and other spells ensured they'd work when I needed them.

Large rings of various metals allowed me to contain spells that might otherwise expand beyond the confines of the testing grounds. Thankfully, I didn't have much need for anything with that big of a bang. Another section consisted of a tableau of gray granite with fae sigils permanently engraved in the surface. I went to those and powered each of the fae sigils one at a time using pixie dust. They glowed softly to indicate they had power.

One sigil was an alarm ward, another a frost ward, the next fire, and so forth. They were powerful defenses that I used around the property in case anyone miraculously made it through the outer walls. I'd engraved them in the stone long ago so I could test their effectiveness when they were properly rooted in the earth as most fae magic was. Now they would help me test the fae-level dispel I'd stolen from the God Hand. I knew the original dispel would do the trick, but this would ensure the copy I'd made functioned the same way.

Once I had most of the sigils powered, I traced the trigger sigil on the slate and tossed it onto the stone. There was a fifteen second delay built into the trigger, so I jogged back a distance and counted down. A bubble of blue energy bloomed from the slate and spread across the granite, snuffing out the fae sigil wards instantly.

The bubble continued to expand, crackling with energy, growing wider and marginally taller as it spread across the granite and out for another thirty or forty yards in radius. I backed up further as it continued coming toward me. The bubble fizzled and faded in a shower of sparks only feet away from me. Apparently, I'd given it a little too much juice for testing purposes.

I whistled. "I guess that works just fine." None of the fae sigils were glowing, but I went over and threw an area of affect spell over them just to see if anything triggered. Nothing did. I now had what was in effect a powerful dispel bomb that could not only take out the wards at Eclipse HQ, but also ensure any guardians inside didn't have the benefit of their cloaks.

After that all we had to do was survive what was sure to be an onslaught of the deadliest fighters in all the worlds.

38

I went back through the tunnels, to my room, and found the others at the kitchen table. Hannah and Aura were pinning dossiers to a corkboard that they must have found in my junk storage downstairs near the training room. Layla was watching a wildlife documentary on TV.

"Has anyone seen Fred?" I asked.

"Nope." Layla answered without looking away from the screen. "I could use another therapy session, though."

I certainly wanted one before we attempted infiltrating a building guarded by a small army of Oblivion Guard who might have other god-level defenses at their disposal. My episodes of insanity were fewer and farther between, but all it took was a microsecond for an enemy to remove my head or gut me.

Hannah pursed her lips. "So, what have you been doing all this time?"

"Weaponizing the dispel enchantment they used at the Sovereign." I went into the kitchen and started making a sandwich. My homemade bread supply was dwindling since I hadn't taken the time to bake some more. "It's not just a fae-level dispel, either. The binding rune in the center is the symbol of the Winged God."

Aura and the others stopped what they were doing and turned to me.

"That thing is a god-level dispel?" Aura whistled. "That's not concerning at all."

"Who in the hell is the Winged God?" Hannah leaned back. "Maybe it's an angel?"

"Angels aren't gods," Layla said. "I'm sure it'll be obvious once we get a visual. Let's just get a picture book of gods and look through them all."

"I did that with an internet search already. Nothing popped out at me." Hannah rapped her knuckles on the table. "How did you bind it?"

"I used Athena's blood."

"Oh, yeah!" She nodded in approval. "I'd forgotten about that."

"Well, at least something useful came out of getting murdered." Layla muted the documentary she was watching. "What's the plan for using the dispel?"

"We can blow up all the wards guarding Eclipse HQ and take out their oblivion cloaks."

"At which moment everyone in the building will know we're there." Layla huffed. "That's not much of a plan. Full-frontal assault isn't exactly our style. What else do you have up your sleeve?"

"Not much." I sliced honey-roasted ham and layered it on the bread. "I'm working on some ideas."

"Yeah?" She raised an eyebrow. "Care to share?"

"I'm considering a diversionary attack to draw them out of the building while someone infiltrates and steals their data." I looked at Aura. "Think you could manage to sneak in while they're after us?"

Her forehead pinched. "Um, there's a lot more to it than sneaking in. I'll have to locate the servers, access them, and then take the time to sort through terabytes of data just to figure out what to steal."

"I don't think we can divert their attention long enough." Layla shook her head. "Besides, we need to fuck them in the ass so hard they don't dare come after us again."

"With just the four of us?" Hannah pshawed. "That's impossible."

I put the finishing touches on my sandwich and took a bite since I had nothing else to add to the conversation. It would be insanely hard to hold the focus of everyone in that building while Aura sneaked inside. Hannah was right—four of us wouldn't be enough. We needed reinforcements.

While eating my sandwich I sent a text to Elton. *Need extra people for a raid on Eclipse HQ. Can you assist?*

He responded a moment later. *I'm pulling for you, but I'm not in the mercenary business anymore. I lost enough good people joining fights that weren't mine.*

I tried one more time. *Eclipse is recruiting demis. If we don't stop them, they'll soon be everyone's problem.*

He didn't reply for a while which gave me hope he was thinking about it, but then he replied. *Sorry, Cain, I can't. My old team is scattered and most of them wouldn't come back if I asked. Good luck.*

Would you at least help us identify and recruit demis before Eclipse gets to them?

Maybe. Get back to me if you survive.

It wasn't much of an answer, but it was better than nothing. I had another option but wasn't very hopeful it would lead to anything. I finished my sandwich then went back into my room and locked the door. I went down the secret staircase in my closet and followed a tunnel that led beneath my garage.

From there, I got in Dolores and drove toward downtown Atlanta until I reached an alley on the west side of town. A green X spray-painted onto the asphalt marked a safe planeswalking zone I'd identified years ago.

A file with precise GPS coordinates on my phone led to spots like these. They were handy on Gaia, but next to useless on Feary since there were no global positioning satellites over that world. I'd solved that issue by using lodestones inscribed with tracking sigils and buried them just beneath the surface.

I summoned my staff, concentrated on the veil separating the worlds, and slashed downward. The air bubbled out and swallowed me. The cold of absolute zero flashed across my skin for an instant, and then I stood in the forest just outside the walls of Faevalorn, the unified capitol of Feary.

Climbing over or breaching the wall was nearly impossible. The entire city was surrounded by a magical perimeter that prevented portals from working within the city. Only the fae could use them inside the barrier. Otherwise, I would have taken the time to map out transition coordinates somewhere inside.

The only way into the city was through the gates. Sneaking through wasn't an option, not even with illusion. There were always pixies watching the gates and they could see through basic illusion and fae glamour. The high fae would be alerted of my presence and then all my enemies would be notified of my location. Outsmarting or outrunning drow, ogres, goblins, and others who wanted me dead wasn't usually a problem, but this time around there were also the rogue Oblivion Guard I had to worry about.

Thankfully, I had at least one ally I could count on to help circumvent that. I pulled a sprig of pine from my utility belt and held it up. Rubbing it between my fingers, I said, "Tempest, I call upon thee." The sprig dissolved into pixie dust and floated away on the wind.

Now it was just a matter of waiting, so I sat down on a log and considered what I wanted to say to the pixie I'd rescued from the clutches of Firsters. Dusk settled over the forest before an answer to my summons arrived. A glowing orb flitted between the trees, flying zigzag patterns until stopping before me.

The orb was a small ball of light in the hand of a pixie. She landed lightly on the log next to me and the light glowed brighter to reveal her face. I nearly breathed a sigh of relief when I saw it was Tempest.

She smirked. "Expecting someone else?"

"You never know these days." I sighed. "Prime is infested with alts from Alpha and Beta, and most are trying to kill me."

Tempest's smirk faded. "I don't understand. You mentioned dimensions last time we spoke but didn't elaborate."

"There are variations of our worlds in a multiverse, but all of them are derived from the original universe called Prime." I told her how Loki and the gods of chaos caused a recent split in the timelines that resulted in the creation of Alpha and Beta dimensions, each one with a duplicate version of everyone that we called alts.

"And our alts have been invading Prime to replace us?" Her eyes flared. "This would explain so much!"

"Would it?"

She nodded. "There have been rumors of pixies vanishing only to mysteriously return days later slightly different than when they left. Perhaps they are being kidnapped by beings from the alt worlds and replaced with their doppelgangers."

I regarded her. "Are you the original Tempest?"

"Cain, I don't think I would betray you no matter which dimension I came from." She patted my arm with her tiny hand. "You saved my life."

I nodded. "Still, you can't be too careful."

Tempest pursed her lips. "I am surprised that you contacted me again since you said you wanted me to forget all about your kind deed."

"Turns out I need all the allies I can get." I shrugged. "I thank your cousin for giving me the sprig so I could summon you."

"I thought my services might be useful to you." She looked up at the wall. "Faevalorn is dangerous place for you."

"Yes, and it's even worse now that Oblivion Guard from other dimensions are trying to kill me."

She gasped. "But that would breach the agreement you made with the queens."

I shook my head. "No, they're exploiting a loophole. Guardians from other dimensions can attack me since I didn't make the bargain with their queens."

Tempest frowned. "You made the agreement with them well before the split in the dimensions. Technically Cain Prime made the agreement with the Prime queens. So even after the dimensions split, the bargain had still been made with you."

"That might technically be true, but they haven't suffered a penalty for trying to kill me."

She tapped a finger on her chin, gaze lost in thought. I let her think about it since pixies were nearly as skilled at bargaining as the high fae. She flinched a moment later, mouth dropping open as if realizing something to horrible to consider.

"What is it?" I asked.

"There is another possibility." Tempest shivered. "The alt queens are willing to violate the agreement to kill you since the punishment will only affect them and not the queens from Prime."

I rocked back as the implications struck me. "The queens from Alpha and Beta would willingly lose power to violate the agreement? But that would absolutely wreck the world order on their respective versions of Feary. Why would they risk that?"

"I don't know, Cain. Your death surely cannot be that valuable to them." Her eyes narrowed. "Then again, I could be completely wrong. Magic does not always follow technicalities. Perhaps they will not be penalized by exploiting this loophole."

"Either way it's extremely inconvenient for me." I pulled a small glass orb from my utility belt. "This contains a message for Erolith. Please get it to him. I'll wait here for the response."

She nodded uneasily. "I pray he is your Erolith and not an imposter."

"Somehow I don't think that will matter." I sighed. "Erolith is bound by duty, but he has defied it to help me in the past. I think even Erolith from Beta would want to help me."

"Then we will put it to the test." She cupped her hand and gathered glittering pixie dust in it, then pressed her hands together. There was a small flash of light and another pine sprig appeared. "Take this in case you need to summon me again Cain."

I took it and placed it in a pouch on my belt. "Thank you, Tempest." I tilted my head. "By the way, where does pixie dust come from?"

"You're asking if it comes from my ass, aren't you?" She rolled her eyes. "It's an aura, not an emission. Does that satisfy your curiosity?"

I nodded. "It does, thanks."

"Good luck." She took the glass orb from me and flitted away.

I knew it would take some time before Erolith responded, so I planeswalked back to the alley on Gaia and went to a nearby nub restaurant. I ordered a beer and some tacos to go, then took my food back over to Feary again. I mulled over strategies for attacking Eclipse headquarters while I munched on tacos and drank the beer.

I'd fought in large scale battles against various creatures from Feary, against humans, and against eldritch abominations, but my real strengths were in stealth and infiltration. The same could be said of most members of the Oblivion Guard. We weren't designed to be a standing army. We were supposed to be magical ninja assassins.

Operating against superior numbers wasn't necessarily an obstacle to any member of the Guard, but it certainly made things more challenging when going up against people with the same training. Even so, the same principles applied.

Know your enemy, their numbers, their strengths, and their weaknesses. Above all else, know who is giving the commands and whether cutting the head from the snake will eliminate the threat. The latter option wasn't realistic since the alt queens were probably the ones giving the commands. I didn't stand a prayer of killing even one queen, much less four of them.

I'd maneuvered them into a favorable bargain by instigating the Beast War, but starting another major conflict wasn't an option this time around, especially if they were willing to lose power simply to kill me. Was Hannah really so valuable to them that they would risk everything?

The Winged God probably wanted Hannah alive, whereas the queens most likely preferred her dead since she posed an existential threat to them if she was indeed the seed that Nyarlathotep spoke of.

It felt like I was back to square one going all the way back to when I'd first left the Oblivion Guard and was being hunted by the fae. Except this time, I had Hannah in the mix and no tricks up my sleeves to outsmart the fae.

Or did I?

The more I thought about everything that had happened, the more convinced I became that the queens of Alpha and Beta wouldn't lose power by killing me. If that was the case, they'd simply go straight for Hannah and ignore me. On the surface that sounded bad for me, but in reality, it meant I still had leverage.

It also led me to a conclusion I hadn't considered before. I'd previously believed that the Divine Council was being controlled by Hera, and that her jealousy was the reason they were assassinating every demi they could find. Then I'd met the goddess and learned it wasn't true at all. Torvin had been controlling the agenda of the Divine Council.

Peel away another layer and it was now obvious that Torvin wasn't the one truly pulling the strings. Back when I'd first rescued Hannah, I'd been summoned to the unified court in Faevalorn and both queens had personally given me an audience. Both demanded I hand over Hannah. When I hadn't, they'd left me to the tender mercies of my enemies outside the palace gates.

It seemed so obvious now in hindsight that the fae queens were the ones running the entire show. They wanted Hannah dead. They wanted me dead. They had motive and with their loophole, they now had opportunity.

I whistled and took a gulp of beer. "Gods be damned, I thought I was perceptive, but I never even considered that."

"Considered what?" Erolith faded into view. He sat on the log next to me as if abruptly appearing like that was as normal as a walk in the park.

I gave him a direct look. "What do you know and when did you know it?"

"I suspect you're talking about the plot to kill you and Hannah." Erolith ran his hand over the log and the wood molded itself into a table between us. Then he produced two glasses, a flask of drow brandy, and his pipe, setting each of them on the newly formed table.

I shook my head. "Are we turning this into a bonding experience?"

"Cain, I have been trying to reach you for some time."

"About my car's extended warranty?"

Erolith poured two fingers of brandy into each glass, then packed his pipe and lit it. "After you left Baura in my care, I had her taken away to a safe location. Shortly after that, I received a summons to appear before the queens at the unified palace."

"I'll bet I can guess why."

"I was promoted to lord and given holdings in the southeastern regions near Minos." His left eye twitched slightly. "This promotion relieved me of my command of the Oblivion Guard."

39

Learning Erolith was no longer the commander of the Oblivion Guard shocked me. I didn't know how long he'd been the spymaster for the fae, but it certainly had been for centuries, if not millennia. "They took away your command and gave you holdings in a place no civilized fae would want to live?"

He nodded.

"Holy shit, that's petty." I held up my glass. "Here's to being scorned by the queens."

He clinked his glass to mine and sipped the blue liquid. "The queens wished to send me a message. Even though I kept my relationship with you hidden for all these years, now they know and are punishing me for it. I can no longer protect you from the Oblivion Guard."

"How in the hell did you keep it secret from them for so long?"

"Because I raised you in a distant village far from Faevalorn, no one knew you existed." He lit his pipe and took a puff. "Keeping your existence secret for so long was not difficult. When you applied for the Oblivion Guard, no one suspected you and I had any relation."

"I didn't even know you were the leader of the guard." I snorted. "Keeping secrets is your specialty."

"That is correct, though I have been doing it for so long it is almost second nature to me."

"More like first nature." I rotated the glass in my hand. "How did they find out?"

"Unknown, though I suspect the number of encounters we've had recently piqued someone's interest." He puffed on his pipe. "They perhaps perceived my treatment of you as preferential and began to dig into your past. I thought I had covered your falsified origins quite well, but nothing is foolproof."

"They might have also discovered I'm Ekhsis and that linked them to you."

"Doubtful. Your survival was kept secret. No one knew we'd found you in the hidden Ekhsis village." Erolith gazed into the dark forest. "In any case, the queens now know. As is typical for them, they have not directly dealt with me, preferring instead to make me irrelevant by giving command of the Oblivion Guard to someone not tainted by disloyalty."

"Well, that's just dandy." I finished off the brandy and poured another two fingers. "I'd hoped to ask you for help with this, but now that's a moot point."

"Your message mentioned you needed help, though it was lacking details." He took another puff from his pipe. "Elaborate, please."

"Eclipse, the Divine Council, and a new organization called the God Hand are all connected. Torvin might have been publicly banished from the Oblivion Guard, but he never left the service of the queens."

"I know." He puffed on his pipe and held it out to me. "When you killed Torvin, you threw Gaian operations into disarray."

I scowled and refused the pipe. "You knew all this time that Torvin and his minions were assassinating demis for the queens?"

"It was something at the peripheral of my knowledge, but yes I was aware."

"I would ask why you didn't bother telling me, but you've never been forthcoming about anything."

"It seemed unimportant, and quite honestly, saving that girl seemed rash and ill-planned." Erolith held out the pipe again.

I accepted it this time and took a few puffs to calm down the anger building inside me. *This was just Erolith being Erolith.*

"Cain, I was unaware of the purpose of killing demis. Information recently came into my possession that sheds light on it."

"It's because of who Hannah is, right?"

He nodded. "One of my pixies discovered that very recently the queens were told that Hannah is of great importance to the Elder Things, namely Nyarlathotep. I don't know the source of this information, but the queens obviously deemed it credible. There was a prophecy that a seed of ancient power would destroy the current order and make the two halves whole. The queens assumed this seed would be in the form of a demi since the Elder Gods have ancient power. So, they demanded that they all be executed once identified. They created an organization for doing this and named it the Divine Council, then allowed it to be credited to Hera to divert attention from them."

"Gods be damned." I shook my head. "How long has this been going on?"

"The prophecy only came to light over a century ago, though my source was only guessing. It's possibly much older than that. The queens only discovered it relatively recently."

"Relatively recently by fae standards could mean anything."

"Nearly a hundred years ago," Erolith amended. "The Divine Council hid itself amongst the nubs by changing its nature. Eclipse is only the most recent iteration. Now that Hannah has been found out, it has gone from hiring freelancers to directly using former members of the Oblivion Guard."

"Former? More like rogue."

"Though they are attempting to kill you, they are not rogue elements."

"Actually, many of them are working for someone they call the Winged God, and they even have cute tattoos to prove it."

His eyebrows arched. "Winged God?"

I nodded. "These rogue agents are still pretending to work for the queens, but I have reason to believe the Winged God's agenda is much different than that of the queens. He or she wants to recruit demis, not kill them. They want me dead so they can take Hannah alive."

"The queens have distanced themselves so much, it seems not even they know the full extent of the plot within plots." He seemed impressed. "I suspect this Winged God is nothing less than a trickster god."

"We think the same thing." I decided to ask him about Tempest's hypothesis. "Do the queens know for sure that their loophole gambit won't be in breach of the bargain they made with me?"

"By attempting to harm you directly but with agents from Alpha and Beta, the queens meant to test the bargain. If these actions were in breach of the bargain, then they would have felt the strain on their power." He took the pipe back from me. "There was no strain. The technicality they discovered is sufficient to bypass the bargain."

"Well, that's the first good news I've heard tonight."

Erolith raised an eyebrow. "How is this good news?"

"Because it means I have leverage. I thought the Alpha or Beta queens were willing to sacrifice their power just to have me killed. If that's not the case, then it means they do have something to lose."

He watched me carefully. "It means they have free license to kill you."

"Alpha and Beta do, but not Prime."

"And this helps you how?"

I blew out a breath. "It means I need to figure out what leverage to apply and where to apply it."

Erolith looked at me expressionlessly for a moment, then nodded. "How can I help?"

"I want to infiltrate Eclipse headquarters on Gaia and steal valuable information that might provide me with leverage. I'd hoped you could help us overcome the odds with help from the Oblivion Guard, but even if you were still in command, that wouldn't be realistic." I watched his reaction, but his face gave nothing away. "They also have a cybermancer who's tracking us and trying to find my secret hideout."

"Eclipse does possess useful and even forbidden information." He tapped his pipe against his hand to knock out the used tobacco. "When Torvin was given his mission, he was essentially given complete control of operations. This enabled him to protect the queens by keeping them out of the loop. Since he was no longer under their command, it also gave him license to find and kill you. This carte blanche naturally led to Torvin abusing his power. I had no authority to stop him, but I did catalogue his most egregious offenses."

"Torvin was leading his own black ops organization without oversight?"

"Precisely. He had a trove of ancient fae texts converted digitally and stored on computers. Many of them were in the forbidden knowledge category, but he said it was necessary to help him hunt down all demis in a rapidly changing human world." Erolith considered the pipe for a moment, as if trying to decide if he wanted to smoke more. "There is knowledge within those texts that the fae queens absolutely do not want becoming public knowledge. Though they are masters of evasion, they cannot tell a direct lie."

I blinked in surprise. "That's the most negative thing you've ever said about the queens, at least to me."

"I have always had my reservations about other high fae, but I also believe in the greater good and my duty to preserve it." He shook his head sadly. "I am concerned about what is to come, depending on who they choose to take my place."

"Do you know how they're transporting people from one dimension to another?"

"I'm afraid not. Dimensional shifting beyond the power of the queens as far as I know."

"You know a lot, so I'm willing to bet you're right." I swirled the drink in my glass. "Maybe they have a gatekeeper demi with the ability to do that."

"Did you find any such demi in the information you stole?"

"They don't go into detail about demi powers in the redacted data-base we took. I assume the information will be in their headquarters." It felt strange telling my adoptive father about the theft, but since he was no longer the fae keeper of the law, it seemed I could tell him more than usual without worry. "Of course, now they know we're coming since we used their network activity to trace a location."

"And they are at this very moment preparing their defenses against you." Erolith pressed his lips together. "They are also moving their servers to a new facility in Faevalorn and placing them behind an aegis that blocks anyone except a select few from entering."

"They're that scared that we'll be able to breach their defenses?"

"They've underestimated you time and time again, Cain. I think they've learned their lesson."

I frowned. "Hang on, how do you know this?"

"I still have my eyes and ears everywhere, even within the walls of Eclipse."

It was a stupid question on my part. Of course, Erolith knew everything. "If you were still commander of the Oblivion Guard, would you be telling me this?"

"My oath would have prevented it, though I would have still offered indirect information." He took a sip of brandy. "My promotion relieves me of that oath."

"Gods be damned, you fae have the slickest tongues."

"I also know of this cybermancer you spoke of earlier. He has been trying to find your home for quite some time. Your recent spate of adventures have given him a great deal of locational information."

"Makes sense." I considered everything he'd said. "So, we've only got two days before those servers are moved? I guess we'd better get cracking."

Erolith decided to pile on. "In the meantime, they have sigil encrypted all their computers, making it impossible for anyone to steal the data without a sigil keycard."

I felt myself deflate. "You probably could have led with that since it makes any plans to steal their data moot."

"Yes, it's highly unlikely you could hope to steal such a card."

Erolith removed a metal card from his cloak and placed it on the log. "If you do manage to come into possession of such a card, it will also allow you to access their secured doors, meaning the only challenge would be slipping through the one hundred and forty-three Oblivion Guard patrolling the facility."

I blinked a few times. "Excuse me if I'm a little suspicious at how helpful you're being."

"I'm simply pointing out the obvious." A pack shimmered into visibility next to him. He placed it on the ground between us. "I still owe certain duties to the queens, so of course I cannot directly help you and must dissuade you from such a reckless course."

"Me?" I put a hand on my chest. "I would never do something so reckless and unplanned."

"I know. I hope we've averted a disaster."

"Well, thanks, Dad."

"You're welcome, son."

"I assume anyone guarding this facility would be from Alpha or Beta." I tapped a finger on my chin. "I wonder how many are with the God Hand and how many are loyal to the queens."

"That is something I don't know." A hint of disappointment crossed his face. "This Winged God is exceptionally skilled at hiding his moves and disguising his minions. It is something I will try to look into."

I didn't know how direct he would be with me, so I asked an indirect question. "Where would you move these servers if you wanted them to be absolutely secure?"

"I would keep them someplace like the Administerium." He took another draw of brandy. "No one can breach the aegis surrounding it."

I whistled. "That's one of the most heavily guarded buildings in Faevalorn besides the royal palace. Breaching it is mostly impossible."

"Indeed."

The Administerium was red tape central for all of Feary. Though the royal court might issue orders and decrees, the bureaucrats who handled all the paperwork operated in the Administerium, a tall black building that looked like the not-so-secret lair of a super villain.

Despite its importance, the fae had ordered it be constructed as far from the palace as possible while still keeping it within the walls of Faevalorn.

The dwarves, of course, had taken things to the next level, making an impregnable fortress that towered over the east side of the city like a cursed monolith. It was staffed by a variety of low fae, all of whom seemed to take perverse pleasure in red tape and legalese.

I'd only been inside a few times. The building was packed at all times of day with beings of all races, rich or poor, seeking audience with someone who could put a stamp on a piece of paper so they could comply with the law.

The interior was a literal maze, probably designed to drive people mad from trying to find the right department to visit. I suspected the fae took sadistic pleasure in subjecting people to such a monstrosity, because its existence seemed wholly unnecessary.

If Eclipse was relocating their data to the Administerium, our chances of getting to it were slim to none. "I assume it would make the most sense to relocate the servers there and not just the data."

He nodded. "Yes, since the Administerium currently has no nub computers that I'm aware of."

"Maybe we can get the servers while in transit."

"I doubt they will leave anything to chance during transport." Erolith turned his glass on the table. "If I were in charge, I'd assign a large complement of guardians to escort the cargo to the nearest mushroom portal which is approximately ten miles away."

"Then I guess we'd better get our asses in gear." I finished my drink and stood. "Thank you."

"For what?" He stoppered the flask and put it and the glasses into a satchel at his feet. "I simply came to talk with my son."

"It was a great bonding experience." Another question occurred to me. "Do you think they'll use your counterpart from Beta for any of their shenanigans?"

"My counterpart from Beta died trying to stop Baura." He tucked his tobacco pouch and pipe box into his satchel. "I only recently learned this information, but it came from a trusted source. I am the only Erolith remaining, it would seem." He glanced meaningfully at the bag he'd placed on the ground, then turned and vanished into the forest.

I picked up the bag and looked inside. What I saw warmed me from the inside out. I walked the few steps to my transition zone and slashed my staff downward. The air bubbled out, swallowed me, and took me back to Gaia.

Erolith's information painted a grim picture of our chances, but the keycard and knowledge of the enemy's numbers increased the odds. Not only that, but the bag he'd given me contained four oblivion cloaks. I didn't know how he could say he wasn't directly helping me without it being a lie, but the fae apparently had their own view of what constituted the truth.

Now we were armed with a sigil keycard, oblivion cloaks, and knowledge about what to expect. GI Joe wasn't wrong when they said knowing was half the battle. By the time this was over, I hoped to teach the fae a valuable lesson about trying to break a bargain even if they found a loophole in the contract.

We'd stirred up the hornets' nest. Now it was time to smoke them out.

40

I returned home and went back inside through the front door instead of my secret tunnel. It was late but the others were still up watching television.

Hannah did a double-take. "Cain, did you sneak out through your tunnels again?"

"Yep." I picked up the remote and turned off the TV. "I had a talk with Erolith. Eclipse is moving their servers to the Administerium on Feary in two days. Once it's there, we'll never get our hands on the data, and Elektrode will be free to track us to his heart's content."

Layla grimaced. "I'm not afraid of much, but the Administerium is something else."

"It's a black hole of despair." Aura blew out a breath and leaned back. "I'd try breaching the imperial palace before trying my luck at the Administerium."

Hannah frowned. "Um, what in the world is the Administerium?"

"Imagine if someone combined the DMV, the IRS, and every nub bureaucracy into one giant building that looks as if it was crapped out of the very bowels of Hades." I went into the kitchen and got a glass of water. "Even then you wouldn't understand the horrors of the Administerium."

"Why in the world do the fae need something like that?" Hannah looked flummoxed. "I thought they were all about nature, not paperwork."

"They're all about trickery and making people take bad bargains, so it's actually just a manifestation of their sick fantasies." Layla waved off the tangent. "How are we supposed to infiltrate Eclipse in two days' time?"

Aura winced. "Realistically, tomorrow is our best window of opportunity."

Layla snapped her fingers. "How about we nail them in transit?"

I shook my head. "Erolith said the convoy would be impossible to breach. The optimum time frame is within the next twenty-four hours."

"Impossible." Layla huffed. "I've heard that word before and we've made it possible."

I gave her a wry smile. "There are one hundred and forty-three guardians patrolling Eclipse headquarters."

She blinked. "Okay, that sounds impossible."

"Which is why we're not going to attack them."

Hannah groaned. "We're giving up?"

"I didn't say that." I showed them the keycard Erolith had given me. "I'd planned to use the fae dispel bombs to take down their defenses so we could get inside, but now we don't need to do that. All we need to do is give them a reason to leave the facility partially unguarded so we can slip inside and get what we want."

Hannah gave me an incredulous look. "Is this the part where you whisper a plan into our ears, and we tell you that it's a great idea?"

"Basically yes." I told them the outline of my plan.

"Not going to work." Layla got off the couch and went to the fridge. "Guardians from Prime will respond."

"No, they won't—at least not right away. Most of them are in Beta and Alpha guarding those queens since the ones from those dimensions are here. The majority of the Oblivion Guard are guarding Eclipse right now."

Layla plucked a beer from the fridge. "Well, why didn't you mention that earlier?"

"Because this is just the plan in a nutshell." I checked the time. "The biggest downside is that we have no time to flesh it out or practice. I'm not usually one for committing to a half-assed plan, but if we don't pull this off tonight, then our only other option is to methodically murder one-hundred plus guardians and hope that's enough to keep the fae off our backs."

"Sounds exhausting." Layla shrugged. "I'm in as long as I can personally castrate Elektrode."

Aura smirked. "I'll take one testicle, and you take the other."

"Deal." Layla knocked back the rest of her beer. "Let's do this."

I texted Elton. *Any possibility you can modify our wings for us tomorrow morning? We need them by tomorrow evening.*

"I have equipment stored at another safehouse that I'll need to get tomorrow morning," Aura said.

I nodded. "Hannah can take you after breakfast. I might have to meet with Elton."

Layla yawned and stretched. "I'm going to get my beauty rest."

"Me too." I went into my bedroom and locked the door. Instead of going to sleep, I went into the tunnels and to my workroom where I started duplicating sigil slates with the god-level dispel. By the time I finished binding the enchantments with Athena's blood and pixie dust, I was exhausted. I stored the dispel bombs in a satchel, went upstairs and went to sleep.

AFTER BREAKFAST, Hannah and Aura went to fetch the gear we needed for the data heist. Elton had replied to my text and was willing to make the wing modifications I wanted, so I got in Dolores and headed up to his place.

He was waiting in the hangar when I arrived with the bundles of wings. "So, you want the jet engines on the wings instead of the parachutes?"

I nodded. "We're going to need some speed for this operation."

A ghostly figure flickered into visibility next to him. "Hello, Cain."

I nodded. "Wanda. Maybe if I survive this, we can look into helping you."

"I'm sorry I can't help you, Cain." Elton unfurled a pair of wings and placed them on a large workbench. "I've been through too much. Lost too many people."

"Are others carrying on the work of closing portals?" I said.

He shrugged. "I wouldn't wish that kind of work on anyone, but I hope so. I just hope those dumbass bureaucrats don't fuck over anyone else like they did us."

"Maybe you can tell me more about your work after this is over." I leaned against the workbench. "Maybe we can find more like Wanda who can help me understand my origins and potential."

"I would like that very much," Wanda said. "Freeing other Enlightened would also reduce the number of portal events."

Elton stared at Wanda for a moment. "Yeah, we can look into that." He took the first micro-jet engine and latched it onto the back of the wings with metal clamps that fit perfectly.

I tried to wiggle the engine, but it didn't budge. "That looked easy enough."

He reached into a box and pulled out another set of clamps. "I welded a set for my wings, and figured I'd create more of them in case you decided to get the modification yourself."

"The mechanists could learn a thing or two about simple yet effective solutions like this."

Elton chuckled. "I wish I could learn how to make a pair of wings, but all I'm good for are simple clamps."

It took him thirty minutes to outfit all the wings. We went outside to the airstrip and tested each one to ensure everything held. I furled the wings and strapped them into the trunk.

Elton shook my hand. "I feel guilty for not helping you. It's not my fight, but—"

"I have the same philosophy myself." I shrugged and got into the car. "I decided to help someone once and now look at me."

"You helped Hannah?"

I nodded. "Now I hardly ever have time to savor my mangoritas."

"Mangoritas?" He frowned. "Sounds like something a college girl would drink."

"Then I guess college girls have good taste." I closed the door and drove home.

By the time I got home, Hannah and Aura were back from their errands, and Layla was in her underwear watching another nature documentary. We had lunch and then went outside to practice with our wings and to make sure the modifications were still functioning properly.

Then we went inside and fine-tuned the plans.

"Why are we waiting until two in the morning?" Hannah asked around midnight. "It's dark enough already."

"Because it's the dead of the night when most everyone is asleep." Layla grinned. "Even seasoned vets let their guard down a little at that time of night."

"It sounds made up, but whatever." Hannah held up her arm and touched the side of her smartwatch. "Synchronize watches in three, two, one, mark." She pressed the side of the watch. Nothing happened since it was already in sync with her phone.

Layla snorted. "Someone's been watching too many spy movies."

Hannah sighed. "In the good old days of analog watches, they always had to sync them before a mission. It's kind of sad that it's all done by computers now."

Layla smirked. "We can go get some old watches if you really want to."

I checked the time. "It's time to go."

Hannah pumped a fist. "I'm ready."

We went outside to the cars. Hannah, Layla, and I got into Dolores. Aura hopped in Hannah's clockwork car behind us. I drove toward Atlanta. Aura took another route and went north.

I parked in the alley right over the spot marked as my transition zone, then got out and slashed my oblivion staff downward. The air bubbled out. A blink later, I stood in the forest, Dolores sitting in the clearing behind me. Hannah and Layla were still inside.

Layla poked her head out of the window. "That look on your face tells me you didn't think that would work."

"No, I'm just concerned about driving Dolores through the forest." I climbed into the driver's seat. "There's not a lot of space for maneuvering."

Hannah leaned forward against the front seats. "Cain, it's pitch-black outside. "How do you even know where to go?"

Layla laughed. "Cain probably has ten different routes out of here."

"Six ways." I turned on the headlights and drove west. "There's a wagon trail just outside of the clearing, but it'll be a little tricky getting through the trees."

Dolores bumped across the grassy meadow until her headlights lit the trees at the edge. I navigated the narrow space between two oaks, then twisted and turned my way through the forest until I reached the rutted wagon trail. It circled northeast and met the stone highway a quarter of a mile later.

Despite the late hour, there was still some traffic since fae lanterns hanging from the trees lit the road and surrounding area almost as well as daylight. A farmer on an ox-drawn cart flinched in surprise as I pulled onto the main road and my headlights hit him in the eyes.

I turned off the headlights and gunned it down the stone highway. The great wall of Faevalorn rose above the trees less than a mile distant. Pedestrians and people on horseback lurched out of the way as I passed even though I was nowhere close to hitting them. The people here had seen plenty of steam-powered carts and wagons, but muscle cars were something you didn't see every day in the lands of the fae.

The highway branched ahead. I took a hard right onto the perimeter highway that followed the curve of the wall. It ran the entire perimeter of the city, intersecting the other main highways leading to the city gates at each of the cardinal locations. I pressed harder on the accelerator. Dolores roared to life and picked up speed.

Moments later, the highway leading to the western gate came into view. A monolithic black shadow jutted from behind the wall, a dark presence that cast dread into the hearts of all who had to enter. The Administerium was probably more feared by most than the dangers in all the wilds of Feary. That was why I planned to take perverse pleasure in what we were about to do.

I pulled off the perimeter road and took a rutted wagon trail a short distance into the trees. We got out and took our clockwork wings from the trunk and strapped them on.

Hannah looked dubious. "You're sure they don't have an invisible barrier to keep people from flying over the wall?"

"Griffins fly in and out of town all day." I checked the pouches on my utility belt to ensure I had everything. "We'll be fine."

Hannah looked at her watch. "We've got fifteen minutes."

I unfurled the wings and turned up the dial. The wings flapped and I rose into the air until was just over the trees. Then I pulled the cords and flew toward the wall. Layla and Hannah followed close behind me. Once we reached the wall, I braked and hovered in place, then turned up the dial so the wings would carry me straight up.

The wall was about a hundred feet high, so it took a moment for us to reach the top and glide over it toward the Administerium. I spoke into my headset. "Let me know when you're in position."

Layla and Hannah flew in opposite directions around the sides of the building and disappeared from view.

"Ready," Hannah said.

Layla spoke a moment later. "In position."

I pulled five sigil cards from my pouch. "Bombs away." I traced the trigger sigil on the first one and tossed it toward the building. I glided along the side of the building dropping the dispel bombs as I went. I'd increased the timers to two minutes to give us extra time.

Hannah and Layla flew back into sight just as the first bombs went off. Giant bubbles of dispelling energy bloomed around the Administerium, casting the night in blue energy as they rippled through the building. Wards flashed and fizzled. The safezone around the building crackled and died. There weren't many people near the building at this hour, but those nearby ran shouting and screaming away from the pandemonium.

"Gods be damned, I don't remember the dispel being that strong at the Sovereign," Layla said.

I grinned. "I might have infused the slates with a little more pixie dust than was absolutely necessary."

Hannah pumped a fist. "Hell yeah!"

It was impossible to tell if we'd knocked out all the magical power in the building since the windows were always black from the outside, but the warning trumpets and sirens going off told me that we'd done exactly what we'd set out to do.

Now there was just one step left, and it was the most dangerous. We ascended higher and higher until all of Faevalorn spread out below us, lights twinkling like a sea of fairy dust. Then we dove toward the center of town where the great towers of summer and winter shined majestically at the imperial palace.

The only indication of the barrier protecting the palace was a faint shimmer in the moonlight, a nearly transparent dome of powerful fae magic. As we neared the edge, we angled north. Layla and Hannah threw their remaining dispel bombs. I did nothing just in case this might be considered a direct attack on the queens.

Crackling blue energy expanded below, lighting the night sky. With a deafening boom, the barrier disintegrated into fiery streams of pixie dust. The response was almost instantaneous. Dark clouds erupted from the summer and winter towers, dust glittering in the sky behind them. I hadn't seen that many pixies in one place since the Beast War and I didn't want to stick around to talk.

"Gods almighty." Layla veered back around. "Let's get the hell out of here."

"Don't have to tell me twice!" Hannah reached for the red button on the wings control panel. "I hope Elton's jet engines don't blow up."

"I'm sure they'll work fine." I oriented myself back where I'd parked Dolores and pressed the button. "To infinity and beyond!"

Layla and Hannah pressed their buttons.

The miniature jet engines whined to life, growing louder until they screamed. I picked up speed gradually and then abruptly shot forward as the engine burned through all its fuel in a burst of speed.

The wings shuddered. The metallic feathers rattled violently as if everything was about to shake apart.

Layla's voice crackled over my comms. "Cain, your wings aren't locked into glide!"

I realized I hadn't pulled the control wires completely taut and corrected my mistake. The feathers locked together smoothly, and the turbulence faded. Within minutes we were back over the wall. The jet engines ran out of fuel, and we glided silently toward Dolores.

I spotted the small light orb I'd left as a beacon and dove toward the ground, braking slightly to slow momentum. The ground rushed up to meet me much faster than I'd expected, so I pulled up at the last minute to avoid reducing myself to tomato paste. I flared the wings and slowed, then dropped heavily to the grass.

It wasn't a perfect landing, but at least I hadn't broken anything.

Layla came to a running stop ahead of me. She took off her helmet and grinned madly at me. "That was fun!"

Helmet under one arm, Hannah appeared out of the darkness. "You're finally starting to sound like the old Layla again."

"I'm starting to feel like her too." Layla looked as if she wanted to say something more, then nodded toward the forest. "Let's get out of here before we get swarmed by pixies."

"Good idea." I furled my wings and jogged down the wagon trail to Dolores. We stowed the wings in the trunk, hopped in, and I navigated us back to the road. I hit the afterburner on the straightaway and we jetted down the perimeter highway.

After nearly obliterating an oxcart that unexpectedly pulled onto the road ahead, I slowed down. There was no sense in running over innocent travelers in our haste to get away. It was fine if the queens knew that I was behind the attacks tonight. In fact, it was all part of the plan.

Moments later, I pulled onto the transition zone, got out, and slashed my oblivion staff down, slicing open the fabric between the planes. The air bubbled out and took us back to Gaia. I took out my cell phone and sent a message. *Mission complete.*

Aura replied a moment later. *It's working.*

I hopped in the car and got us back on the road.

Layla gave me an expectant look. "Well?"

"It worked."

Hannah whooped and clapped her hands.

"Don't celebrate just yet." I stared grimly at the road ahead. "We've still got work to do."

Thankfully, the Eclipse building wasn't too far down the road, and traffic was light at this late hour. We arrived two minutes ahead of schedule. I pulled into the parking deck of a neighboring building, then we grabbed our equipment and headed into the small strip of forest nearby. I summoned my staff and surveyed the area with my scope.

I swept the building in normal mode and saw nothing, so I switched it to true sight. A lone aura glowed on the rooftop. Four more stood at windows inside. Five cloaked guardians in total on this side. I imagined there were others stationed at windows on the other sides as well, making for a grand total of around ten. It was a far cry from the one hundred and forty-three that Erolith had mentioned.

Which meant my plan was working perfectly so far.

41

The plan had been simple.

The guardians from Prime were covering the duties of their doppelgangers in Alpha and Beta. Most of the guardians from the other two dimensions had gathered here to guard Eclipse from me, meaning very few were in Faevalorn doing their primary job of guarding the queens.

Our attacks in the capitol had forced them to make a choice: stay and guard Eclipse or return to Feary and protect the queens and the Administerium.

By using the dispel bombs against their defenses, I'd given them the impression that a full-scale assault was coming. They knew what I was capable of because of the Beast War. For all they knew, I'd riled up the griffins, cecrops, and all the other formerly enslaved races and convinced them to march on Faevalorn to overthrow the fae queens.

That would have been a nearly impossible task even with an army at my back, but we could have done serious damage to the palace. Even though an insurrection wasn't realistic, it would have shaken the image of the fae as our untouchable overlords. That would have led to trouble, especially among those factions that most hated fae rule.

In order to preserve their image, an overpowered response was necessary. They'd recalled most of the Oblivion Guard from Eclipse to Faevalorn, leaving only a skeleton crew in place. The response was even better than I'd hoped for, and it meant whoever commanded the guard wasn't very good at their job.

Erolith never would have responded with such a kneejerk reaction. He probably would have seen the ploy for what it was and laid a trap. It was possible that the current commander had done the same and ordered all his people to position themselves behind thick walls to hide their auras from my scope, but I doubted it.

I consulted the diagram of the building that had been in the bag from Erolith. I'd memorized the layout, but it never hurt to look it over one more time.

I put on an oblivion cloak, another gift in the care package Erolith had given me. "Wish me luck."

Layla clapped my back. "Go get 'em bucko."

"Be careful." Hannah took my hand. "You sure you don't want me to come with you?"

"Positive. I need to be in and out fast." I activated the cloak and headed across the road. The parking lot around the building was small since there was an underground parking deck. I used my true sight scope to keep an eye on the guardians in the windows, but none of them reacted to my presence since the scopes on their staffs couldn't see through fae glamor.

I skirted around the side of the building and went to the steel door at the back. I pulled on it and it opened thanks to the tape Aura had put there to block the lock. The door inside led to the stairwell. Aura would have gone down to the first sublevel where Erolith had told us the servers were. I went upstairs to the third floor.

Once in the hallway, I scanned both ways with my true sight scope. A lone guardian stood at the window facing the back side of the building. He held his scope to his eye, looking back and forth for intruders. I went the opposite way, took a right at the next hallway, and found the door marked on the diagram.

This place looked like an ordinary office building, but there were no nameplates, no safety signs handing on the wall, and certainly nothing from a human resources department. The door had no handle because it only opened when the hand of the owner was pressed against it. I didn't want to leave any trace that I'd been here, so I took out my tools.

There was no lock to pick since a magnetic latch held the door closed. I slid a thin piece of metal with a sigil inscribed on it into the space between the door and the jamb, then willed power into it.

A small burst of magnetic energy countered the power holding the latch in place. The door swung open with a barely audible click to reveal a large, mostly empty room. A big metal cage with thick cables running from the top sat in the center of the room. I used my scope for a look around. There was only one aura, and it was in the center of the cage. Trip wards guarded the perimeter—simple spells that would sound an alarm and jolt an intruder with electricity.

Like a ghost, I flitted across the room, jumped over the trip wards, and sidled up to the entrance into the cage. The inside was full of monitors and equipment I couldn't make heads or tails of. A thickly padded chair supported a thin man who stared at the monitors in an almost catatonic state. He moved his fingers as if typing on an invisible keyboard, then stopped, tilting his head as if receiving information.

Elektrode wore the same thick headphones I'd seen during our conversation at Aura's safehouse. Data scrolled past on some of the monitors. Another monitor displayed a map with the triangulation graphics. He wasn't much closer than before, but it was close enough.

I hadn't expected him to be up this late. Erolith's diagram indicated that a bedroom attached to this office was where Elektrode spent most of his nights. I'd hoped to find him asleep in bed, but this would do. His headphones deafened him to my approach, and he was too focused on one of the monitors to see me coming.

Keeping low, I crept up behind his chair so I my reflection wouldn't show in any of the monitors. He never even saw me coming. I took out a small cannister and sprayed the mist in his face.

Elektrode's eyes flared in surprise. Head jerking toward me, he gasped, "Cain!"

I made jazz hands. "Surprise!"

He slumped. The area around his chair was littered with empty bags of cheese balls and candy bars wrappers. A garbage can overflowed with empty energy drink cans. Our boy was a total slob. The mouse and keyboard were on a tray attached to the chair. Both were shiny from finger oil and crusted in cheese dust.

No one ever seemed to clean in here, and it showed. That was good news because it meant few people ever checked up on Elektrode, opting instead to let him do his thing in private.

I pulled him out of the chair and put another oblivion cloak on him. I activated the enchantments and slung the invisible load over my shoulder. Using my scope with the other arm, I navigated past the trip wards and stepped into the hallway, closing the door behind me. The magnetic latch clicked.

I banished my staff and looked at my phone. Aura had texted me.

Tap secured. Ready to leave.

That had been one minute ago, meaning she was probably waiting at the back door. I looked through my scope to ensure the guardian at the end of the hallway was still watching the back of the building, then quietly opened the stairwell door and eased it shut behind me.

I made my way back to the first floor and found Aura waiting in position. She flinched when I deactivated my cloak and revealed myself.

"You have him?"

I nodded.

"Excellent." She activated her cloak. "I can't believe Erolith just gave you these."

"Don't get too used to having it." I activated my cloak then touched her to pair our cloaks so we could see each other.

She sighed. "You don't trust me with one?"

"Nope." I went outside, pausing to look for any cloaked patrols, then went back around the building. The cybermancer was skinny and light, so I had no problem jogging back to the parking deck where Layla and Hannah waited for us.

We deactivated our cloaks. I took the one off Elektrode and laid him flat on the concrete. Layla took the devices from my scan kit and ran them up and down his body. She rolled him over and repeated the process.

"Oh no, our boy has a dirty bum." Layla produced a slim blade and expertly sliced open his right butt cheek.

Hannah grinned. "I think you're enjoying this too much."

"Am I?" Layla slapped Elektrode's other bare ass cheek. "This little fucker almost found out where I live."

"We all know you live in a van down by the river," Hannah said.

"I told you that was our little secret." Layla squeezed the cut buttock and a tiny metal capsule slid out of the incision.

I knelt next to her. "You're well aware that my scan kit can disable those without minor surgery."

"Yeah, but this is more enjoyable." She crushed the capsule with the butt of the dagger. "There are a couple of sigil trackers on him too that you'll need to take care of."

Hannah wiped away the blood and stanched the blood with gauze and medical tape. "That's a lot of trackers."

"Yeah, because this guy is valuable and dangerous to them." Using my scope, I found the sigils. They were similar to the complex tracking sigils I'd used in the past to tag fugitives and assassination marks, meaning it would take a good thirty minutes to disable both of them. Thankfully, I didn't have to worry about that.

I reached into the car and pulled out a low powered version of the fae dispel. I carried him a hundred feet away, then activated the fuse on the sigil slate. I backed up a good distance and watched as a small blue bubble ran over the unconscious cybermancer.

A quick check with the true sight scope confirmed that the tracking wards were completely drained of power. As with my tattoos, the dispel didn't have a binding for body, meaning I'd have to remove them manually later.

I took the scan kit and gave him one last check before stowing him in the trunk next to the wings. "We're good."

Hannah giggled. "This is amazeballs. We did it!"

Aura slid into the back seat and turned on a laptop. She tapped on the keyboard and nodded. "The tap is working perfectly. Download in progress."

"Now all we have to do is convince the fae to lay off." Layla got into the front seat. "I don't know why, but that part seems a lot harder than everything else we've done."

Hannah scowled. "Fae assholes."

"The hard part is crafting the bargain." The first time around had required me to agonize over every single detail. Now I had to create what was essentially an amendment to the original, and this time I had to make sure it was foolproof against fae from multiple dimensions.

"Maybe you should've asked Erolith for bargaining advice," Layla said.

I shrugged. "I think this is a battle he expects me to win on my own."

"On your own?" Hannah laughed. "He gave you a keycard access to the Eclipse building, told you where everything was, and what to do. Without his help, that asshole in the trunk would have found the location of Sanctuary before we could do anything to stop him."

I drove out of the parking deck and onto the road. "He was just fired from a position he's held for ages. Since he's no longer bound by duty, he had no compunctions about helping me."

"Well, he handed you the keys to the kingdom." Layla shook her head. "It wasn't that long ago he was trying to arrest us on trumped up charges."

"He's nothing if not enigmatic." It had been one of the most pleasant meetings I'd had with Erolith since dropping a brain damaged Baura into his care. Maybe now that he was retired, we could connect in a more meaningful way, provided I managed to negotiate a solid truce with the fae. With their prized cybermancer and data, I had leverage that could probably buy me just about anything I wanted from them.

Hannah peered at the screen. "Are you downloading everything to that laptop?"

"No, it's going to another of my hidden facilities. Once there, it'll upload to the cloud so we can access it from anywhere without being tracked." Aura closed the laptop. "It's a lot of data, though, so it's going to take all night."

"As long as it gets me my life back." Layla blew out a breath. "Not being able to go to the bar for a drink is driving me crazy."

"I can make drinks," Aura said.

Hannah smirked. "I think Layla misses her orgy parties in her van down by the river."

"Those too." Layla stared out the window. "Nothing like the fresh odor of an orgy in the back of a van."

Aura grimaced. "Thanks for that imagery. And why do you keep talking about a van by the river?"

Hannah laughed. "You'll have to find that out for yourself."

Layla sighed. "We have oblivion cloaks and daggers. I still think we should've killed everyone in that building."

"Normally I'd agree, but we don't know which guardians are Handers and which ones are loyal to the queens." I glanced sideways at her. "And we didn't have enough time to go around the building looking for winged tattoos."

Hannah leaned forward and poked her head between he front seats. "Do you think Thog's kids are going to be all right?"

Layla barked a laugh. "I'm positive that bridge troll was lying about having kids."

Hannah sighed. "I hope so."

When we arrived at Sanctuary, I deposited the slumbering cyber-mancer into a cell in the basement and went straight to bed. I needed my mind fresh and rested so I could outline a bargain that would prevent the fae from hunting us and we could finally resume our lives.

. . .

FRED WAS WAITING for me when I emerged from my bedroom the next morning.

I went into the kitchen to make breakfast. "Where have you been?"

"Exploring." He looked up at me with big eyes. "Cain, I don't like being me."

I tossed bacon into the cast iron pan and gave him a look. "Didn't we have this conversation a few days ago? You've come a long way since being an octopus. Your speech is improving, and you can travel just about anywhere there's water. What's not to like?"

He waved his stubby arms at his body. "I am stunted. I can never improve this. I want to be tall and graceful like you."

"Maybe you're not exactly dexterous on land, but in water you're Aquaman."

His mouth tentacles quivered. "I am an ugly fish."

I sighed. "Fred, you're not ugly and you're certainly not a fish. Your father tried to use you for evil purposes, but you've overcome that. Now you're free."

"But what gives me value?"

I walked around and knelt next to him. "Fred, you're family."

Tears welled in his huge eyes. "Thank you, Cain. I thought my existence was a curse, but maybe it's a blessing. I just wish I could be more...human."

"You're more human than most." I lifted him up onto a stool at the kitchen counter then resumed making breakfast. I noticed Hannah standing at the door to her bedroom, tears trickling down her cheeks.

I cleared my throat. "What's wrong?"

"That's why I love you, Cain."

I raised an eyebrow. "My bacon cooking skills?"

She ran over and gripped me in a bone-cracking hug. "Because you love me, and you love Fred. Because you gave us a family."

I tried to pry her arms loose, but her godlike strength was too much. "You can let me go now."

Hannah giggled and released me. "And you always play the tough guy."

"He makes excellent bacon," Fred said.

"It's not exactly hard." I flipped the bacon and started mixing pancake batter.

"I want to know if the data downloaded." Hannah went to the guest bedroom and opened the door. "Get up, sleepyhead!"

Aura's exasperated voice replied. "It's six in the morning."

"Where's your laptop?"

Aura groaned. "Go away! I'll be out in a minute."

Hannah stepped back from the door. "Where's Layla?"

"She slept downstairs." Yawning widely, Aura emerged from the bedroom with the laptop. She set it on the table and opened it. She nodded a moment later. "Everything finished downloading. Now I just need to sort through it. This could take a while."

I finished cooking breakfast and laid out eggs, bacon, and pancakes. Aura nibbled on pancakes, but barely took her eyes off the computer screen.

"There's so much here, I barely know where to look." She blew out a breath. "The program I used created a virtual copy of their entire system and removed all their security protocols."

"Can we wipe their copy? I don't want them having that tracking data anymore."

"The program wiped their servers and fragged the hard drives." She looked up from the monitor. "Since I wiped the data from the computers in the Sovereign building, that means we have the only copy."

"Unless Elektrode made more backups," Hannah said.

Aura nodded. "He probably did, but we have him and they don't."

I stood behind her and looked at the screen. "I'll get that information from him one way or another."

"Ah, here's the main index." Aura clicked a button. "I've got to hand it to him. Elektrode did a great job organizing the data."

One of the categories in the long list caught my attention—*Demis.* "Click that one."

Aura did and an alphabetical list of names filled the screen. Hannah's name was there. She clicked on it and a dossier appeared. It looked nearly identical to the one Eclipse had given me when tasked with tracking her, but there was a lot of new information that had been added in recent months, including that she was now under my protection.

Hannah leaned in. "It's so creepy seeing my info in their database."

The layout resembled every nub database I'd ever seen. Name, date of birth, and even social security number were listed. I went to the one field I was most curious about—*Father's Name*. In place of a name was an enigmatic entry: *Shard*.

"Shard? What the hell does that meant?" Hannah huffed and looked down. "Why is it so hard to find my father?"

I thought back to my conversation with Wanda and knew there was only one thing it could mean. "It's because you don't have a father."

42

Hannah gasped. "How can I not have a father?"

"If this is correct—and that's a big if—then there's one way to interpret this." I sipped my coffee. "When the planet Ekhsis was hit by the Big Bang, Cha and Ord were killed. Shards of their beings rained down on the population, almost instantly giving godlike powers to humans and creatures alike. That was the genesis of the Elder Gods and the Elder Things." I shrugged. "Maybe they think your birth is related to a shard."

"There's nothing in the notes that clarifies it." Aura frowned. "All of that happened billions of years ago. Even if a shard somehow made it to Gaia, how did it impregnant Hannah's mother? Wouldn't it have just given her godlike powers?"

"I have no idea." I pressed my lips together. "Sorry, kiddo."

"Man, I was really hoping the fae had the answers." Hannah looked glumly at her pancakes. "It'd be nice to know who my dad is."

"I know. I know." I went back to my seat. "Unfortunately, that'll have to wait until we find our leverage against the queens."

"I'll find something." Aura went back to browsing the database.

While she was doing that, I went into my room and started

crafting a bargain that would leave the queens no wiggle room. The
original bargain forbade them from harming me so long as I abided
by fae law. I hadn't wanted that addition, but they'd refused to give me
free license to break the law as I wanted. I'd countered with another
clause saying they couldn't harm me if I broke the law but could
punish me by reasonable standards.

There had been a lot of back and forth and neither side had been
happy with the final bargain, but that had been a big win in my book.
Given the chance to craft any bargain I wanted, I would forbid them
or alternate versions of them from other planes or dimensions from
harming me or my acquaintances through any direct or indirect
action, or by proxy.

That was about as comprehensive as it got, but I'd have to have
something major to dangle over their heads to succeed with that. I
tinkered with various versions, imagining what clauses they might
want to add that would water down the language.

I'd been at it for hours, so I took a break from the document and
went down into the tunnels. I took a few memorized turns and then
pressed my hand against a stone with a slight discoloration. The wall
slid aside to reveal one of the hidden vaults I used to hide the few
relics I'd kept from the lost armory of Hephaestus.

It was likely I'd need a trump card to play in case the queens
decided to get nasty, and I needed to refresh my memory about what
all I had. I'd made a list with details for each item thanks to Noctua's
help.

A lot of the items gave the user godlike abilities, but the side
effects were often too harmful to warrant using them. Kind of like
how Panoptes could drive the wearer mad even before it was infected
by Cthulhu's gaze.

As I read down the list, one item caught my attention. *Winged
boots – allow the wearer to run at incredible speeds but burns through their
body's energy so fast that it could kill them.*

I remembered Layla wanting these boots until she'd found out
that part. I went to the shelf marked on the inventory list and looked
up at them.

"You've got to be kidding me." I hurried back up to my room. The sound of someone pounding on my door echoed into the tunnels, so I picked up the pace and climbed up the stairs into my closet.

"Cain, are you in there? We found something you'll want to see!"

I opened the door just as Aura cocked back her fist to knock again.

She blinked then took my hand and dragged me to the kitchen table. "This is big."

"Big enough to scare the queens?" I certainly now knew something that, if true, was already scaring me.

"Maybe." She showed me a screen with several paragraphs of text. The same word was highlighted in every instance. "Most of the orders were signed only by Torvin, but in many cases there was reference to commands from the Winged God."

"That's nothing new." I stared at the screen. "We already knew he was running the show in some instances."

"Or she," Hannah said.

I shook my head. "It's a male."

Hannah rolled her eyes. "You don't know that. Women can be supervillains too."

Aura ignored her and continued. "Torvin was following the queens' instructions but was also serving the Winged God. It looks like he would feed the queens information based on whatever the Winged God wanted him to do. The original command to kill Hannah came from him, not the queens. This is the god that was running the show, not Hera."

"That's not particularly surprising, given what we gleaned from the Sovereign database." I crossed my arms. "What's the big deal?"

"Take a look at this one." Hannah tapped her finger on the screen.

I read the paragraph below it.

There will be no interference in White House Springs. The others wish to attempt our gambit and turn the child against Cain, thus making it easier to recruit her to our cause. This command comes from the Winged God himself.

Hannah pouted. "Okay, fine, it's not a female god."

"No interference in White House Spring? What the hell are they talking about?" I cleared the search bar and typed in the town name for a search. There were several results.

The first was an order: *You are assigned to give this packet of information to the Firsters in such a way they will believe they acquired it through their own spies. You will monitor the situation and ensure they plan to carry out an attack against the Human-Fae Alliance meeting in White House Springs.*

The second one was a report from their agent.

The Firsters accepted the information. They are planning to attack the Human-Fae Alliance meeting at White House Springs.

There were several updates about the progress of the mission, including a list of high-ranking fae. Eclipse planned to have its own personnel onsite to help with the assassinations, but the third result changed the plan.

Cain is in White House Springs. All agents are to withdraw and await further instructions until we discover why he's there.

It seemed my appearance had thrown them for a loop. The next document was a picture taken of a scroll written on golden-threaded parchment.

Faithful servant, Cain's appearance was unforeseen and is not your fault, despite what the others have said. I am sending you this private message to assure you that your loyalty is appreciated.

The cabal has plans to nudge history in the right direction and turn the child against Cain. Ensure your people are out of the way and do not interfere as this is a delicate operation. Once this is done you will be granted free license to seek your revenge against Cain.

We will take the child into our fold and make her a member of the cabal. Loki has unfairly attacked and accused you but that is because he feels we are so close to our goals. You have always carried out my commands to the letter, and you will receive your gift, a winged bracelet that will make you as fleet of foot as I am.

Memorize the commands below, for this letter will burn to ash moments after you break the seal.

The bottom part of the image was illegible as it looked like it had started to burn just as Torvin took a picture of it with a cell phone.

The letter only confirmed what I already knew to be true, thanks to the winged boots. I shook my head in disbelief. "The Firster plot against the HFA was instigated by Torvin and the cabal, aka the gods of chaos." I connected the next dot. "They were already planning something, but once they found out I was there, they decided to change fate and turn Hannah against me."

Aura nodded. "It shows that your appearance was unplanned. Despite their careful plotting and planning, we showed up and threw a wrench into the operation. So, they came up with a plan to change fate."

"That would indicate they knew what was about to happen, but how can that be the case if our presence was unplanned?"

"Because you and Hannah are obviously linchpins of fate. They knew something momentous might happen and it would give them the chance they needed to interfere." Aura tapped a finger on the screen. "But that's not even the most surprising thing in that letter."

Hannah looked expectantly at me. "Cain, don't you see it?"

I'd known it from the moment I saw those winged boots. "Yeah, and it's bad. So, so bad." I bit my lower lip and stared at the image of the parchment. "The Winged God is the god of speed among other things. And it seems he's also the leader of the gods of chaos." I hesitated to name him but did it anyway. "It's Hermes."

Aura blew out a breath. "You concur with my theory."

"It's not a theory. I was looking at artifacts in one of my vaults and saw those winged boots from the armory that Layla wanted. The wings on them look identical to the tattoos we've seen. And the only major god of speed that I know is Hermes. That letter to Torvin was just icing on the cake."

"Oh, this is really bad." Hannah looked scared. "I thought Hermes was one of the good guys—or at least as good as a god can be."

"He's mainly known for being the herald of the gods and for speed, but he's also a trickster by some accounts, which would put him in the same camp as Loki." I sighed. "This means he's playing two sides against the middle."

"Isn't he fighting the war in the divine realm with Zeus and the others?" Hannah looked confused. "How does he have the time to do that and run around plotting their overthrow?"

"That's a damned good question." I stared at the computer screen. "Hermes is the one who chained Baura to her rock. It's obvious now that he intended for her to escape all this time."

Hannah looked shocked. "God, you're right!"

"They did a damned good job of screwing up the timelines when they interfered in White House Springs." I shook he head. "So much for divine intervention."

"Why were they there in the first place?" Hannah ran a hand down her face. "What was so important about riling up the Firsters so they'd attack that HFA meeting?"

"It seems as though they wanted to spark another Human-Fae War," Aura said. "I'm not sure why, but they obviously had a reason for it."

"It was to sow chaos, but I don't think another war would have done much to give the cabal a chance at overthrowing Zeus and the others." I tried to connect the dots and failed. "It would have diverted the attention of the fae, but not for long since the Firsters are just a fringe element these days. Maybe they had larger goals in mind and that was just the first step."

Hannah tapped a finger on her chin. "I think Hermes wants to end up as top god after all this is over. Loki and the others are just pawns to him."

"Loki isn't someone you use as a pawn," I said. "If anything, they're working as equals for now. If they achieve their goal, then I'm sure one of them would gladly betray the other for the top spot."

"But why?" Hannah groaned. "They're already gods for god's sake. Can't they just be happy with what they have?"

Aura laughed mirthlessly. "Of course not."

Hannah worked her lips back and forth. "Can we use this information to keep the fae off our backs? Or would they even care that Hermes is plotting against the current world order?"

"Oh, they'd care. But if we spill this secret, then Hermes will find out and then he'll operate openly, no longer taking care to hide his dirty little secret." I clenched a fist and pounded it on the table. "He'll bring down the hammer on us for sure."

"But he can't act directly against you unless you act against him, right?" Hannah didn't look convinced. "I mean, I guess Layla was killed just because she stumbled against Mars, so if that's all it takes, then we're not really safe."

"It's better if we find something else to use against the fae." Aura shuddered. "Cain is right. We can't risk forcing Hermes into the open. The fae are hard enough to deal with, and the gods of chaos—the cabal—are currently only indirectly operating against us. I don't want that to change."

"Me either." I stared at the computer screen.

A calculating look crossed Aura's face. "Or we could threaten to join Hermes if the fae don't make a bargain. If they agree, then you'll remain neutral to their interests."

I considered that for a long moment. "That's actually not a bad idea."

Hannah frowned. "But what if they call our bluff?"

"Is it a bluff, though?" Aura raised an eyebrow. "Maybe Hermes could offer us protection. Maybe it's time we stopped fighting these major powers."

"Yeah, but that would mean they'd use me." Hannah shook her head vehemently. "I'd have to be in their cabal and do what they wanted. It'd be like being enslaved to Cthulhu all over again."

I had, of course, considered that. Joining Hermes and the cabal was a non-starter, but the mere threat of it might work against the fae.

Hannah raised a finger. "We could bargain with Hermes and threaten to tell Zeus and the others what he's up to unless he protects us."

"Not a good idea." I shook my head. "If we use this information to protect us from the fae, then the fae will almost certainly tell Zeus. It's only of value so long as only we know it."

"Then include that in the bargain," Hannah said. "Tell the fae they can't reveal this information."

I closed my eyes and envisioned how the queens might respond to such a proposal. Was the threat of Hannah and I joining Hermes enough to make them agree to leave us alone?

I envisioned a dozen different ways this plan could come back to bite us in the ass. "This information is too dangerous to use as a bargaining chip. If Hermes is revealed, then he'll stop helping Zeus in the divine realm and further cripple them. They're already operating with a skeleton crew as it is. We don't need to offer the Elder Things another opening into the human worlds."

Hannah raised her hand. "Ooh, I have an idea."

Aura frowned. "And that is?"

"We threaten to release the entire database to the supernatural community on Gaia. There must be a lot of juicy information in those forbidden texts." Hannah grinned. "I'll bet they wouldn't want that getting out."

"Those forbidden texts also contain powerful magic that could be devastating in the wrong hands." I shook my head. "Evil assholes like Alistair would be unstoppable. We need to find a middle ground."

Aura huffed. "Well, I'm out of ideas. We could comb the database for weeks and never find something that's safe enough to use. It's only a matter of time before they find a replacement for Elektrode and eventually pinpoint your hideout."

"Releasing the entire database or even just the forbidden texts to the supernatural public would be a nuclear option." I drummed my fingers on the table. "It would be a bluff, pure and simple, and they'd know it."

"You're right." Aura groaned. "And if it became public knowledge that you have this information, then you'd have a lot more than just the fae trying to hunt you down. Alistair and others like him would do anything to lay their hands on this information."

"Then we're stuck? We did all this for nothing?" Hannah threw up her hands. "That sucks!"

"I'll keep looking. There's bound to be something we can use." She turned to Hannah. "Even if there's no usable blackmail material on here, this was still worth it."

I left them and went downstairs to check on our guest. I opened the door and leaned against the frame. Elektrode was huddled in a corner, face miserable. He looked up at me, hatred burning in his eyes.

"There's only one way you beat me, Cain." He pushed to his feet, black robes swishing. "You cheated."

"This isn't a video game, Elektrode." I gave him a dead-eyed stare. "Do you hate humanity, or are you just stupid?"

"Of course, I hate humanity." He sneered. "You have no idea who you're up against, do you? You think it's just me? Well, it's not."

"Are you talking about Hermes?"

He stopped talking, mouth open. "How did you—"

"I've met Loki, Hermes, and Zeus, just to name a few gods." I shrugged. "I've even been to Valhalla. If you think mentioning a god is going to strike fear into my heart, then you don't know much about me."

Elektrode blinked in confusion. "How did you go to Valhalla? You're alive!"

"I was Death for a while." I kept my face emotionless. "You should take some small comfort that there's an afterlife waiting for you."

His bravado fled in a heartbeat and his face blanched. "No, wait! I can tell you anything you want to know!"

"We've got the entire database, so I don't know what you could add to that."

"What do you want? I can give you anything!" He staggered back. "Um, you want powerful spells? Money? I'll even work for you!"

I chuckled mirthlessly. "What do I want?" I laughed a little louder for a slightly maniacal effect. "I want the fucking fae off my back." I pounded a fist against the wall. "I want Eclipse, the God Hand, and the Oblivion Guard to get out of my life so I can drink a gods damned mangorita in peace!"

He stumbled against the mattress and fell on his ass. "They want the girl."

"I'm aware. Hermes is playing the fae like a fiddle, using them to get her for himself." I crossed my arms. "The worst part is that he knows damned well what he's doing could open the floodgates for the Elder Things to infest Prime."

"I have faith in my master." Elektrode seemed to regain a little spine. "He will destroy the old world order and create a new one. Then we will squash the Elder Things and take their worlds."

I gave him a look of disbelief. "It's obvious he's fooled you too." Hermes had everyone dancing like puppets on his strings, even the queens. Even me.

It was time to stop dancing.

"If you want to live, you're going to tell me how you were homing in on my secret lair, and you're going to make sure all the data you gathered is destroyed so no one can use it again."

He melted quickly under my glare. "I want assurances."

"You'll get them." I stepped back out of the doorway, suddenly certain about what I had to do next.

"Where are you going?" He shouted.

I closed the door without answering.

We could dig for weeks like Aura said and come up with plenty of blackmail items to secure a new bargain with the fae, but they'd never stop looking for a way out, for a way to kill me. And that was because of one simple fact—they didn't know the truth.

I knew what I had to do.

"Cain?" Layla emerged from the practice room, sweat beading her forehead. "You look like you're determined to do something stupid."

I nodded. "Probably. Want to come?"

Her eyebrows rose. "Where?"

I told her.

She laughed. "Really? That's the best you could come up with after all the shit we've done?"

"I think it's all we need."

"You crazy son of a bitch." She clapped my shoulder. "I'm in."

I raised an eyebrow, waiting for the punch line.

Layla doubled down. "No, I'm serious. I'm really coming with you." She kissed me. "You're so cute when you're trying to figure me out."

"I'm always cute." I nodded toward the stairs. "Go get ready. I'll meet you in a moment."

She slapped my ass in passing and jogged upstairs. I went into the meditation chamber and procured the one thing I hoped would convince the fae queens that it was best to leave me alone. It was a gamble, but it was all I had.

Then I went upstairs and told the others my plan.

"Cain, don't you dare go!" Hannah gripped my arm. "They'll eat you alive."

"Maybe, but odds are this is the best way out." I mussed her hair. "You're a priceless commodity, kiddo."

Aura didn't look convinced. "On the surface it sounds stupidly simple, but maybe it'll work."

"Instead of forcing the fae into a bargain, I can lure them into an uneasy alliance." I shrugged. "It's worth a try."

"Your only collateral is me." Tears pooled in Hannah's eyes. "What if they kill you?"

"The entire point of killing me is to get to you." I squeezed her shoulder. "If they know they'll lose you forever, I think they'll resist the urge to end me."

"What about Elektrode?" Aura said. "Are we keeping or killing him?"

"Keeping for now. He's agreed to erase all copies of the data they were using to track down my hideout. If I don't make it back, you'll need to take the reins on that."

She sighed. "Great. One more thing to worry about."

Layla emerged from the guest bedroom, her hair wet from the shower. She wore her standard black yoga pants and athletic top. "How many daggers should I bring? Fifty?"

"As many as you want." I cracked my knuckles. "I have a feeling we'll need them."

Hannah hugged me. "Please don't die."

"I'll do my best."

Layla faked a hurt look. "What, no hug for me?"

Fred hugged my leg. "Be careful."

"I will, little buddy." I patted his head and freed my leg, then turned to Layla. "Let's go."

It was time to do or die.

43

Sometimes even the best laid plans lead nowhere. We'd stolen knowledge that could certainly be used to force the fae into a bargain, but the cost of doing so might lead to terrible consequences further down the road. I planned to try a safer route first. If that failed, then I could consider the nuclear options.

"Let's take a motorcycle to Feary this time," Layla said. "I want to roar into town in style."

"They'll shoot us off it before we reach the gate." I shook my head. "This calls for a more level-headed approach."

"We could wear oblivion cloaks."

"The pixies can see through the glamour, and the cloak wouldn't hide the motorcycle."

She huffed. "Fine."

I drove us into Atlanta to the transition zone near the wall of Faevalorn. I'd considered using my typical spot closer to Sanctuary and flying in on a griffin, but it was likely that the city was a no-fly zone thanks to the little stunt we'd pulled off last night.

After planeswalking us to Feary, I looked up and confirmed my suspicions. The sky above the walls was thick with pixies just looking for an excuse to smack a bitch. Layla and I walked down the wagon trail I'd driven Dolores on and got on the road leading to the gate. The line of wagons, people, and other beings waiting to get inside the city stretched as far as the eye could see.

"I think we stirred up the hornet's nest." Layla smirked. "What now?"

"Now we cut in line." I walked alongside the stone road, catching dirty looks from others as I walked past them.

"Hey, back of the line!" Someone shouted.

I waved a hand. "Official business coming through."

A pair of orcs stepped into my path a moment later, tusks glistening green with whatever disgusting meal they'd recently had.

The first one balled his fists. "Back of line, little man."

I looked him up and down. "I'm on official business."

"No, you not." He looked me up and down. "No uniform, nothing."

I summoned my staff and the brightblade hummed to life. "Is this official enough for you?"

His eyes widened and he backed up, nearly tripping over his companion. "Yes, guardian. Apologies."

I banished my staff and kept going. Naturally, the commotion drew the attention of the pixies. Three of them flitted down, dusting the line with a trail of pixie dust. They hovered in front of me, condescending glares on their faces.

One of them gasped. "It's Cain."

The others flinched in response.

"Cain?" One of the orcs tilted his head. "Sthyldor?"

"Great, now you've done it." I sighed. "I request an audience with the queens."

"An audience?" The first pixie's lips peeled back in a snarl. "Your filth has no place here! Send an alert. Have him arrested!"

"Sthyldor!" The orc roared and came at me. "You ruin my life!"

Layla grinned. "Is this that more levelheaded approach you were talking about?"

I gave her a dirty look and turned to face the oncoming orc. "Let me guess, you were a slaver." I summoned my staff. "And you want to die."

The other orc grabbed his companion and dragged him back. "Stop, Guga! He kill you!"

"Let me die!" Guga growled. "I was master but now I am beggar because of him!"

"Listen to your friend," I said. "Better to be a beggar than a corpse."

Guga bared his tusks in impotent fury, but finally relented and let his friend drag him back in line.

I started walking for the gate, only a scant thirty yards away while the pixies trailed behind us.

"You will halt!" the lead pixie said. "The guards have been called."

"Fine with me." I stepped up to the guards at the gate, my brightblade still lit. "I'm here to talk to the queens.

"I really wish we had that motorcycle right about now," Layla said with a sigh.

The guards looked in confusion from my brightblade to the pixies shouting at me. They were just ordinary city guards, both elves from the look of them, and this was far above their paygrade. They did what anyone would do in their situation and shouted for their superior.

One of them went to a building and knocked on the door. "Captain, please come out here!"

A low fae emerged from a building a moment later and looked down her nose at us and the pixies. Her eyes flared slightly when recognition set into her eyes. "Cain Sthyldor?"

"Why does everyone have to say my name like that?" I shook my head. "A hello, how are you today, fine sir would be much more polite."

"No one has manners these days." Layla shrugged. "Not even the fae."

"Arrest this man," the pixie demanded. "He is wanted for multiple crimes."

"Really?" I turned to her. "What crimes, exactly?"

She sputtered. "Too many to list!"

I turned back to the captain. "I'm here to see the queens. Simply tell them that should anything happen to me, the seed will blossom in the care of another."

The captain blinked. "What is that supposed to mean?"

"That's between me and the queens."

"Arrest him!" the pixie shouted again.

The captain flicked her gaze to the pixies. "You will quiet yourself, or I'll throw you in a cell."

The pixie looked outraged, but the city guard had jurisdiction.

The captain rang a bell. A moment later, a pixie flitted into view and hovered in front of her. "Yes, captain?"

"Carry a message to the palace. Cain Sthyldor requests an audience with the queens. He also sends this message: If anything happens to him, the seed will blossom in the care of another."

The pixie looked alarmed upon hearing my name and gave me a long look before flitting away toward the city center.

The captain waved over a group of guards. "Fetch a carriage, put them in it, and guard it."

They hustled to obey. A horseless pumpkin carriage rounded the corner a short time later and parked in front of us. Layla and I climbed inside and made ourselves comfortable for the wait.

It didn't take long for a pair of pixies to fly into view, one wearing the pale colors of winter, and the other in the bright colors of summer. They hovered in front of the captain and spoke with her in hushed tones.

The captain nodded several times then shouted a command. "Form up and escort the carriage to the palace!"

"Gods, this is going to take all day," Layla groaned. "I can run faster than this fucking pumpkin."

At first, I thought the guards planned to walk, but then they fetched horses and encircled the carriage. The captain took the lead. "Move out!"

The pixies flitted away.

I blew out a breath. "Unless I'm mistaken, things are about to get hairy."

Layla looked through the window, eyes scanning the nearby buildings as the carriage began to move. "What's our backup plan?"

"The horses."

We were on the main avenue leading to the imperial palace. The street was wide enough for three carriages to ride abreast, but the city guards had spread out across the road as if they owned it, causing foot traffic and other carriages to pull over to the side or divert to side streets. Like many old cities on Gaia, the buildings here connected to each other, leaving only a few alleyways here and there.

Layla pursed her lips. "You really think the Handers will try something?"

"Oh, I'm certain of it." I kept an eye out of my side of the carriage. "Gods only know how many pixies are working for Hermes and have rounded up their forces."

She pressed her lips together. "Should we warn the captain?"

"Won't do much good, but we can try." I leaned my head out of the window. "Captain, there's a possibility that we'll be attacked."

She cast a look of disdain at me. "There are many who want you dead, Sthyldor, but few who would go against the might of the city guard."

I glanced at the other guards. "The Oblivion Guard would."

She laughed mirthlessly. "Why would the Oblivion Guard attack us?"

"There are rogue agents who want me dead." It was a simplified version of the truth but trying to explain everything would only make her believe me less.

"You are the only rogue guardian I know of." She turned her gaze back to the road. "Quiet yourself. I am happy to let the queens deal with you."

A lone figure appeared in the middle of the street not far ahead. The lead guards continued moving ahead. "Out of the way! Official business."

A brightblade crackled to life in the hand of the person. "You will hand over Sthyldor now, or we will go through you to get him."

The captain stopped and spun her horse around, but another

guardian appeared behind us. Shops and homes lined the street. There were no alleys or side streets offering escape. One of the guards raised a horn to his lips and took a breath. A longshot blew out the back of his head before he could sound the alarm.

Layla pressed her back to the seat to keep her head out of view of the window. "The shot came from the roofs."

"Yeah." I dropped to the floorboard. "There's a bakery just outside. We can probably make it when the fighting starts."

"Leave the carriage," the captain shouted. "I will not die for Cain Sthyldor."

Layla grinned. "What fight?"

"Damn. Guess that captain doesn't have a big enough ego."

"She's not stupid." Layla put hand on the door handle. "Ready?"

"Let's go." I counted down from three on my fingers, then Layla opened the door and we dashed out and into the open door of the bakery.

A pair of longshots sparked off the stone road. One blew out the window to the bakery. The people inside shouted in alarm as we burst through. Layla headed for the back door, but I yanked her through the kitchen and into a side door leading into an alley.

Movement above caught my eye. I dodged left as a guardian landed next to me, brightblade whirling. He landed on a broken section of stone, causing him to stumble ever so slightly. Layla caught him in the throat with a dagger before he could adjust his balance. His brightblade rolled across the ground hissing as it touched a stream of spoiled milk leaking from the kitchen door.

I ran west through the alley to the next street over, then hugged the side of the building to keep out of sight beneath the awnings. Footsteps pounded across the roof above, but they were going toward the bakery. It seemed the other guardians didn't realize they had a man down in the alley just yet.

The sparse foot traffic on the narrow street wasn't enough to keep us hidden. I motioned toward the buildings on the other side. Layla nodded and we sprinted across the narrow road and into an alley leading to another major avenue. Someone shouted. We'd been spotted.

This road should have been bustling with traffic, but there were only a few pedestrians and wagons rolling down it since the normal traffic was on lockdown. Our only hope of reaching the palace alive was keeping ahead of our pursuers.

"I knew the motorcycle was a good idea." Layla scowled. "Maybe we can ambush them when they come after us."

"We have no idea how many are coming." I ran across the road and into another alley. It intersected with a service street running behind the buildings for this road and the next one over. It was narrow with plenty of awnings and overhangs to give us limited cover.

Layla wrinkled her nose at the smell. "You know how to show a lady a good time."

"There's a goblin bakery nearby that makes great rat pies."

She made a face. "You also know how to make a woman gag...the wrong way."

I paused to consider our options. We could keep running toward the palace, or we could turn around and give up. Having gone through all this trouble already, giving up seemed pretty lame. Running directly toward the palace, however, was too risky. They probably had horses and could easily reach the gates long before we did.

A middle option seemed best. I located a stone sewer cover in the alley and knelt next to it. "Give me a hand?"

Layla wrinkled her nose harder than last time. "I am not going into the sewers. The things that live down there are more dangerous than the Oblivion Guard."

"It's not that bad unless you go into the Deeps." I put a hand into one of the vent holes. "Just help me lift it, okay?" Unlike the metal manhole covers on Gaia, these things were large and made of thick stone. Even with my body sigils powered it would be hard to open one of these by myself.

She sighed, bent down, and helped me move the lid to the side.

The smell wasn't as bad as I'd thought, but my nose was probably accustomed to the foul odors from the garbage bins back here already.

With that done, I started running back toward the town gates. Layla gave me a puzzled look but followed. We continued for two blocks, then I cut left back to the avenue we'd run across moments ago. I scanned the rooftops with my scope. An aura glowed distantly on a high rooftop. From that vantage they could see this street and the next one over, but they were busy scanning the opposite direction.

A few pixies flitted over the rooftops, but they were all going back the way we'd come from, meaning our misdirection was leading them away.

"Smart." Layla looked up and down the road. "Circling back and around?"

I nodded. "They think we're going straight for the palace's main gate."

"Where else are we supposed to enter?"

"There's another gate on the opposite side of the palace. Hopefully it won't be locked down."

"I wish those damned oblivion cloaks weren't useless against pixies," she grumbled.

I walked casually across the avenue so the sudden movement wouldn't draw the attention of the roof sentry. We continued through the alley and over to the avenue where the captain's convoy had been ambushed.

Only the body of the dead guard and our abandoned carriage. remained. The captain and the others had hightailed it out of there. I considered the carriage for a moment, then climbed onto the driver seat, turned it around and then set it to automatically drive itself back to the city gates at top speed. It might work as a diversion, but I doubted it.

I scanned the rooftops and street, then hurried across the road to another alley.

We continued making our way laterally for three more blocks

before cutting back toward the palace. The streets were mostly empty and the skies in this area were clear of pixies. It took us the better part of an hour to make our way to the centrally located palace and the rear gate. This gate was about as wide as two carriages and rarely used except by high fae.

It was normally guarded by a contingent of city guards, but they were nowhere to be seen. I took a look through my scope and spotted eight cloaked guardians.

"Shit." I let Layla look through the scope. "We're not going in that way."

"Are they Handers?" she asked.

I nodded. "Almost certainly. They don't use Oblivion Guard for normal guard duty."

Our only way in was blocked.

44

The Handers had posted people at the palace gates as an insurance policy in case I evaded their ambush in the city. Even if I fought my way past them, there was no way for me to open the gates without a special seal.

Layla groaned. "What now?"

"There's one more place to try." I went into a backstreet and followed it for a distance until we came to a stretch of the road that I knew from mine and Layla's last narrow escape from the palace. I looked through the scope and verified there weren't any cloaked guardians nearby.

"Ah, I remember this place." She crouched and looked up and down the wide avenue that circled around the palace. "Do you think it works from this side?"

I zoomed in on the section of wall and found a small niche hidden behind illusion. "I believe it does." I ran across the road, put my hand in the hidden niche, and found the latch. A slab of wall slid back and to the side, opening a narrow corridor inside. We slipped through, and I closed it behind us.

We were on the palace grounds with a hedge maze between us and the road leading to the entrance. Normally the fae peace seal granted protection to anyone on these grounds, but since I'd blown that to hell last night, all bets were off. I had no way of knowing if the fae had repaired the damage I'd done last night, and I couldn't exactly stop and ask someone.

Then again, maybe I could. I summoned my brightblade and started hacking a path through the hedge maze. Ordinary blades couldn't so much as put a dent in the tough branches, but a brightblade worked just fine. It didn't take long to reach a clearing where a pair of cecrops were lounging on benches.

Suddenly alert, they sprang to their feet, fangs bared, barbed tails twitching. I was about a heartbeat away from a lethal injection of poison, so I gave them a moment to get over their surprise before offering the snake women a curt bow. "Dusana and Morgina, I am pleased to find you well."

Dusana blinked in confusion. "Liberator? Why are you destroying our hedges again?"

"I'm in need of your help."

Morgina hiss laughed. "It seems you are always in trouble, Liberator."

Layla grinned. "Always."

The pair had helped me and Layla escape from the palace grounds by the very same secret opening the last time we'd been here for an audience with the queens. "Has the safe zone around the palace been restored?"

Dusana shook her head. "The entire ring was dispelled. It was quite a shock to all of us who work on the palace grounds. Such a thing has never happened as far as we know."

"My bad." I shrugged. "I did that to get the attention of the queens and now I'm on my way to an audience with them."

Dusana and Morgina hissed in amusement.

Morgina tilted her head, forked tongue flicking. "How can we help, Liberator?"

"Can you escort us to the braided road? I know there's a centaur in here somewhere and I don't feel like disturbing him."

"How do you not go insane with boredom just hanging out in this maze?" Layla asked. "Even on a busy day there can't be that many idiots who leave the braided road to wander through here."

"We read a lot of books." Dusana's tail coiled behind her. "I am particularly fond of romance novels."

I banished my staff. "I know a bridge troll who might have some good recommendations."

Layla frowned. "Who, Durrug?"

Morgina sighed with pleasure. "Ah, you know my husband?"

I did a double-take. "You're Durrug's wife? I knew he was married to a cecrops, but he never mentioned her name."

"Yes, though our work schedules often keep us apart for days." She smiled sadly. "I think we enjoy romance novels because we long for each other's rough caress."

"That's sad." Layla patted her back. "Maybe you ought to get different jobs."

"Durrug enjoys his work immensely, and though mine is somewhat boring, the benefits of working for the imperial palace are quite good."

"Indeed," Dusana said. "We must ask you to not destroy our lovely hedges the next time you visit. It traumatizes the gardeners."

"Sorry." I glanced at my handiwork. "I'll just call your names next time."

"Yes, please do."

Layla ran her hand along Morgina's green, lightly scaled skin. "Wow your skin is so soft. Do you moisturize?"

"Naturally." Morgina hissed in pleasure. "Maiden's milk works wonders."

I didn't even want to know more about that.

Thankfully, Dusana was already walking back into the maze. "We will lead you to the braided road."

Moments later we stood at the edge of the road. True to its name, it was braided from strands of platinum and gold, signifying the unity of winter and summer here in the unified capitol of Feary. We normally would have entered through the massive alabaster gates down the road to our right. Then again, there was nothing normal about me visiting fae royalty.

"Thank you for your help." I gave them a curt bow. "I'll tell Durrug I finally met his wife."

Morgina grinned, showing her fangs. "Please do. He is quite fond of you."

Layla snorted. "Durrug is fond of Cain?"

"Yes. We would not have met if Cain hadn't started the Liberation War." She touched my hand. "May venom give you strength."

"May your enemies feel your sting, Morgina." I patted her hand and started down the road. Layla had been right. Morgina's skin was very soft.

Layla watched the pair return to the maze and then jogged to catch up. "I'll never get over how weird you are, Cain. For a loner you sure do have a lot of friends."

"They're not friends."

A pair of giant polar trolls watched us from a frozen cave in the winter wasteland to the right of the braided road, ready to spring on us if we dared step off the path. Unlike their smaller kin, they had little intelligence and couldn't be reasoned with. Only the enchantment on the road protected travelers from their gentle affection.

Layla noticed them too. "Is anyone ever stupid enough to leave the path?"

"There have been a couple of incidents."

"The fae are okay with people getting ripped apart by polar trolls or poisoned by cecrops?"

I turned to her. "We're just ants to them."

"I'd daresay you're more than an ant to them." She smacked my butt. "Let's hope they don't decide to kill us."

"They can't directly harm me or order me to be harmed."

"Yeah, and how'd that work out last time we were here?"

"Not great," I admitted. "But desperate times call for desperate measures."

"Yeah."

The palace was only a hundred yards away, its crystal dome

glinting in the sunlight. A pair of pixies, one in golden garb, the other in platinum, flitted down the road toward us. They didn't hide their astonishment at seeing us alive.

"The court is probably full of pixies from Alpha and Beta, so don't trust them." We didn't have the protection of a fae seal granting us safe passage to the palace, and since I'd knocked out the safe zone around the palace, there really was nothing keeping us from being attacked here.

Layla grunted. "Who's to say the queens are the ones from Prime?"

"Pride," I said. "There's no way the queens from Prime would allow what they perceive as inferior copies to pretend to be them."

"I can see that." She watched the incoming pixies. "So, um, how dangerous are pixies?"

I chuckled. "Is that fear I hear in your voice?"

"Of course not. I just don't know what to expect." Layla gave me a curious look. "And you never told me what happened between you and the pixies of Evanor."

"It wasn't fun, I can tell you that." I considered summoning my staff but decided to see how things went before instigating a fight. "Pixies are fond of rooting spells to immobilize their foes so they can pummel them with frost or fire, depending on which court they're from. They also have blinding spells and plenty of other tricks up their sleeves. I trained against them, so I know their tells. If they attack, I'll shield and you counterattack, okay?"

She pursed her lips. "Simple enough, I guess."

The pixies hovered about thirty yards away and regarded us coldly.

"Declare yourselves," I said. "Am I speaking to pixies of Prime, or of another world?"

They exchanged glances, and I knew their answers. Pixies in the colors of summer shimmered into view over the gardens to our left while those in the black, grays, and whites of winter appeared over the ice maze to our right.

"Those little fuckers were just a distraction." Layla gritted her teeth. "How many pixies did you fight in Evanor?"

"A lot." I gave the pixies in front of us a frosty glare. "I hope you're here to escort me to the throne room, because I really don't want another pixie massacre on my conscience."

"Another?" Layla hissed from the side of her mouth. "I really need to hear this story."

The winter pixie scowled. "You have nothing of value to say to the queens. Leave the palace grounds at once."

"Ah, I get it." I pursed my lips. "You never told the queens I was here, did you? You thought the guardians from Alpha and Beta would kill us before we ever got here." I looked around at the pixies moving in on us from all sides. "Tell me, who is your true master?"

"We follow the one who will restore the fae to true glory." The summer pixie looked down her nose at us. "The queens have lost their way."

This was worse than I'd suspected. It meant the queens had lost control of those who should be their most loyal subjects. "Does this treachery run all the way through the Oblivion Guard as well?"

"It is not treachery!" she shrieked. "It is the will of the gods!"

"Uh, oh." Layla tsked. "The gods are dead, remember?"

I looked around at the encroaching circle of pixies. "All of you follow the gods of chaos, then?"

"We are all of the same mind," the winter pixie said. "Leave the palace grounds or face our wrath."

I resisted drawing my weapon. "Tell me, have the pixies from Prime completely lost their minds as well, or are they still loyal?"

"They have not seen the worlds under their domain ravaged by apocalypse weapons. They are not faced with the fact that their existence is but a shadow in a timeline that never should have existed, but for you, Cain Sthyldor." The summer pixie's eyes glowed yellow. "We of the shadow worlds will do what is best for all of faedom throughout the worlds."

"Well, at least this makes me feel better for what I'm about to do." I cracked my knuckles. "You will escort me to an audience with the queens, or I will clear the path myself."

"You will drown in your own blood," the summer pixie said.

"And freeze in it," the winter pixie added.

I summoned my staff and the brightblade hummed to life. "Very well. Let the contest commence."

I barely had the words out of my mouth when pixies from either side cast root spells. The ground beneath our feet glowed with sigils and brambles and frozen thorns began to sprout. I cast a counter-spell, striking a sigil across the ground. The brambles and thorns turned to dust before they fully formed.

The summer pixies were already cocking their arms back in unison, prepared to launch another barrage. The winter pixies were just a split second behind them, so I couldn't do anything about them. A fan of daggers streaked through the air toward the winter pixies, throwing them off their stride before they could get the spells off.

I'd come prepared with complex counters and cast a reflection shield just as the summer pixies released a combination of root spells and fire orbs. The shield bounced back all but two fire orbs before it collapsed. I deflected the fire orbs that made it through with my brightblade.

Reflected bramble spells sprang from the ground beneath their casters, snaking around them even though they were hovering ten feet off the ground. Fire orbs rebounded at the pixies who originally flung them. They scattered in all directions. The brambles caught those who strayed too near, wrapping firmly around arms and legs.

One winter pixie lay dead in a pool of blood, a dagger protruding from his eye. Bubble shields surrounded the others to protect them from Layla's deadly aim. With most of the summer pixies temporarily hindered by their own spells, I turned to the lead pixies.

"One last chance. Surrender, or die."

They vanished behind cloaks. I flung a sigil slate with a low-powered fae dispel on it. A blue bubble expanded, dispelling their cloaks just as the winter pixie blew on her hand as if blowing a kiss. A cloud of frost billowed from her palm. If that cloud hit me, it would freeze my lungs and give me a lethal case of frostbite.

There was no way to reflect such a powerful elemental spell, and we had nowhere to run, so the only option was to counter it. I deactivated the brightblade and spun my staff, then thrust it out to cast a gust spell. The burst of wind threw the frost cloud back at the pixies. They dodged nimbly out of the way. Another winter pixie howled in pain as Layla's dagger pierced her bubble and cut her leg.

Layla dodged a flurry of ice daggers and hurled tiny blades of her own back at them. "Like my enchanted daggers, bitches?"

Determined to escape the circle of death before the summer pixies escaped from their brambles, I fired a modified longshot at the lead winter pixie. She was too busy dodging her own frost cloud to see it coming. The shot hit her chest and electricity crackled across her skin. She flopped to the ground like a rag doll. The lead summer pixie shrieked in despair.

I rolled forward, fired another shot at the summer pixie, but she juked it easily. That was fine, because she wasn't my primary target. I scooped up the unconscious winter pixie and held my staff against her throat.

"Cease your attacks, or she dies." I shouted.

The winter pixies turned their focus from Layla to me. Layla backed up to join me, more daggers ready to fly. The lead summer pixie balled her fists in impotent fury.

"Layla, hold her." I gave her the winter pixie.

She gripped her around the chest and held a dagger to her throat. "What are you doing?"

I examined the unconscious winter pixie with my scope and found the faint lines of a wing tattoo on her neck. I was beginning to think that these tattoos were something more than just a simple way of declaring a person was in a gang. These tattoos had power.

I knew why scores of pixies had abandoned their queens, and it wasn't just because they were angry. It was because they'd declared absolute loyalty to their new master, Hermes.

45

It was no small matter for pixies to abandon their queens. They like the high fae, had a strict hierarchy. When your leaders told you what to do, you did it. Even though the high fae didn't like it, the gods were still in that hierarchy. These pixies had been convinced to skip a link in the chain of command.

I didn't think it would work, but I tried to bargain with the lead summer pixie anyway. "Take us to the queens or your friend dies."

She stared darkly at me. "I will make no bargains with you, human filth. Kill them!"

"Hold, Petal!" One of the winter pixies raised a fist. "Ifri is unconscious and unable to perform her duties. It is my duty as her second to take command."

"Yes," another winter pixie said. "Nori has a say in this matter since Ifri cannot speak for herself."

"Then speak!" Petal raised her hands. "Command your subordinates to kill them!"

Nori frowned. "But he will kill Ifri if we do. He has proven himself a capable warrior. Perhaps we should avoid more bloodshed and take him to the queens. They can deal with him."

"No." Petal bared her teeth. "They cannot be allowed to reach the queens."

It suddenly became clear to me that not every pixie here had declared allegiance to Hermes. Judging from the uncertain looks on the other summer pixies' faces, they were also unsure about killing us and sacrificing Ifri.

I took the chance to speak. "Your leaders have been compromised —they have abandoned the queens and declared loyalty to the gods of chaos." I tapped Ifri's tattoo. "This rune on their flesh binds them to their service. This cabal of gods is working against the queens. Would you also betray your rulers and join them?"

Nori blinked. "A rune on their flesh? What nonsense is this?"

"It makes sense," a summer pixie said. "Petal would never take these matters into her hand. She would tell the queens and defer to them. This entire episode has been most irregular."

"Kill them or suffer banishment." Petal's eyes glowed. "Do as I command."

"You need to subdue her," I said. "If you examine her neck, you'll find a faint tattoo in the shape of a wing."

"A tattoo?" The summer pixie looked bemused. "And you claim this is the rune of chaos gods?"

"It is." I nodded at Petal. "Look on the back of her neck."

"No!" Petal flourished her hands in a pattern and orbs of fire streaked in all directions.

I threw out a series of shields to block them. I felt my hand grip Petal, restraining her arms, even though my hand was nowhere near her. It seemed my newfound telekinetic ability had decided to stop in and say hello. I tried to sense my exact emotions and state so I could finally identify the trigger, but Petal's struggles made it difficult to concentrate.

"Restrain her!" the summer pixie said. "Clearly, Petal is not herself!"

Another summer pixie looked uncertain. "Are you serious, Raya?"

Raya dodged a fireball. "Yes! She just tried to burn us with fireballs, you fool."

The other summer pixies gripped Petal's arms and held her fast. My telekinetic grip vanished, and I was back to normal.

Raya examined the back of Petal's neck. "There is a tattoo in the shape of a wing. The patterns within are complex. It is indeed a god rune."

The other pixies gasped as they saw it. The winter pixies approached to examine her and seemed just as dismayed. Finding out your leaders were traitors was traumatic, especially for pixies.

Raya bared her teeth. "I thank you, but also hate you for showing me this truth, Cain Sthyldor."

"You were being manipulated. I hope that now we can cooperate." I nodded at Layla. "Give them Ifri."

"I'm not giving up my insurance." Layla scowled at me. "Besides, they hate you, Cain."

"He is vile human filth," Nori said. "But in this case, he is correct. We are being manipulated to betray the best interests of the queens." She turned to Raya. "Let us escort Cain and summon the queens. They can deal with him as they see fit."

"Agreed." Raya looked at Layla. "Be gentle with our sister. She is a traitor, but you may not mete her justice. That is also for the queens to decide."

The other winter pixies picked up the corpse of their dead comrade, tears in their eyes. They bared their teeth in anger at Layla.

"We will not forget this," one said in cold fury.

Layla bared her teeth back at them. "Hey, blame yourself for blindly following a leader into a fight you couldn't win. You attack me, and I'm in it to win it."

Nori regarded Layla with a cold look that clearly indicated this matter wasn't settled. "Let us go to the palace."

Layla handed over the unconscious Ifri and the summer pixies subdued Petal to stop her struggling. Then they led the way toward the palace. A winter and summer pixie flew ahead to send word to the queens that I was coming.

I took the chance to get some answers. "Nori, which dimension are you all from?"

"Beta." She shivered. "Gaia is overrun and the other worlds are feeling the dire effects."

"Who hatched the idea to use beings from the other dimensions to kill me as a means to bypass our bargain?"

She didn't so much as look back at me. "That is something you must ask the queens."

"These are the queens of Prime we'll be seeing, yes?"

"The queens of Prime safeguarded their rule with bargains to prevent the queens of the other dimensions from asserting their dominion here." Nori clenched her tiny fists. "Do you know what it is like to discover you're nothing but a shadow of your real self?"

"You're as real as the pixies from Prime," I said. "Your timelines diverged greatly from Prime, but that doesn't mean they're not worth fighting to preserve."

"So you say." Raya spun in the air to face me while still flying backwards. "How are we supposed to overcome the infestation on our Gaia? The power of our queens wanes more every day as the natural power of that world is consumed by the eldritch."

"Time to fight back while you still can." I shrugged. "If the queens avoid fighting, then Feary will die a slow death with Gaia."

"I agree!" A dagger of ice formed in Nori's hand. She twirled it and tossed it into the air. "This is what we were preparing to do until the queens turned their focus on you." The dagger fell to the stone road and shattered. "I wonder how many of our people have betrayed the queens."

"Probably not many," I said. "Hermes would target leaders so he could control you without having your direct loyalty."

"Our hierarchy is strict." Nori sighed. "He exploited our strength and turned it into weakness."

Layla barked a laugh. "Blindly following commands isn't a strength."

I wondered if the tattoos had been a choice, or if maybe Hermes had forced them onto these pixies. Maybe the queens could remove the tattoos and find out.

I looked up at the palace dome. One side glowed with sunlight while the other was crusted in ice and snow. Turrets towered high above the dome, an equal number on each side for winter and summer. A pair of guards looked alarmed at our procession as we approached the entrance, but they let us in without comment.

The interior was unchanged from the last time I'd been here. Sunshine refracted off the summer side of the crystal dome hundreds of feet above, casting rainbows on a sparkling waterfall. A small stream wound its way through lush gardens, and bees buzzed among flowers as tall as trees. Butterflies of every kind fluttered about the massive atrium. Multiple species of birds and other lower animals wandered about the miniature paradise.

On the winter side there was the usual amount of ice and snow. Where the stream crossed the braided path from summer to winter, it was frozen solid. Ice bees tended to frost flowers and snowy white butterflies flitted about. My favorite part of the winter side continued to be the little penguins waddling around a pond.

The braided path continued into another chamber, this one filled with craggy trees and sand that glittered like flecks of gold on the summer side. An arid tundra of sparkling crystals presented an equally beautiful view on the winter side. Each consecutive chamber had its own theme, but I was surprised to see that the third atrium in had changed.

One side was a forest, the leaves red and yellow with their autumn colors. The other side was bright and green, glistening with fresh rain and the smells of spring. The two courts had never paid such a homage to their forgotten brethren, and it made me wonder what had changed.

Layla noticed. "You look surprised, Cain."

"Why are autumn and spring represented here?" I asked the pixies.

"Only the queens can say," Raya replied.

We arrived in the throne room. The queens weren't there, of course. They would never arrive before someone and wait for them. The only time they were already here was if they were holding joint court, a very rare occurrence that only happened once per year when the seasons were in balance.

There had been slight changes to this room as well. Instead of the braided wood on the summer side and the ice on the winter side, there were now four patches of land, each one with a small tree, its leaves indicative of a seasonal phase. To see all four fae courts represented in the throne room was even more shocking than the chamber dedicated to autumn and spring. The queens weren't just paying lip service, they were putting all four courts in the seat of power.

I looked around. "What in the hell is going on here?"

"Only the queens can say," Raya replied.

"You're absolutely no help." I stopped at the end of the braided path where a small circle of woven platinum and gold marked where petitioners were to stand.

Nori cried out, "A visitor seeks audience with the queens. May we have the honor of your presence?"

Strands of fire twisted and whirled in the yellow sunlight while glittering ice and snow performed a dance of its own in white frost light. A glowing throne of gold coalesced on the left and a throne of icy platinum solidified on the right.

The air rippled and bubbled to the sides of each throne.

A woman in a billowing yellow dress, hair as golden as the sun, face more beautiful than humanly possible appeared on the left. Another woman in white, with long, platinum locks appeared at the same time on the right. Her face was beautiful, but cold. The woman on the left was dark and tanned, while her counterpart was pale as ice.

The queens moved without hesitation to their thrones, sitting down and regarding me disdainfully, though not as much as they might have in the past. Though they were absolute masters of manipulation, there were minute cracks in their royal facades. They had the looks of beings who expected unconditional loyalty and yet were steadily losing control of their subjects.

Mayce, queen of winter, wasted no time getting to the point. "What have you done to our worlds, Cain? We have felt the unraveling of the very fabric of the universe since your last visit here. Why can you not simply die and let us set our worlds back on course?"

Solara, queen of summer piled on. "The Beast War would have been preferrable to the abominations you've spawned. Now the eldritch have overrun a shadow Gaia and threaten us with annihilation. You are a cancer upon our very existence."

I waited to make sure they were finished, then stated my case. "I assure you that all of these things you accuse me of are far outside my power. What you are faced with now is due to the eternal war between the Elder Things and the Elder Gods. Except now, a faction of gods from many pantheons have formed a cabal in an effort to overthrow the current order so they can rule the human worlds." I weighed my next words carefully, but there was no avoiding them. "My queens, if I am so powerful, then you are admitting that I, a lowly human, have risen above you."

The pixies hissed in unison, some of them spitting.

"Leave us!" Mayce flicked her hands to shoo them away. "We will continue this conversation in private."

"But my queens, we have other matters to discuss!" Raya pointed to Petal. "Our sisters are bear the rune of these chaos gods! They have forsaken you and now serve the cabal."

"I notice you didn't mention you know who," Layla muttered. "How long before they figure out what that wing represents?"

"I don't know, but there was no way around this," I muttered back.

Mayce's eyes tightened at Raya's declaration. "Explain."

"There are tattoos upon their necks. They bind these pixies to the chaos gods." Raya bowed deeply while hovering in the air. "We know we are but shadow versions of your pixies, but if this affliction is widespread, it might affect our Prime versions as well."

"Bring the afflicted to me." Mayce motioned them forward.

The pixies deposited Nori and Petal at the feet of their respective queens and backed away. The queens examined the necks of the pixies for a moment before anger washed over their faces. They turned to each other and conferred in soft tones. They must have used a blur spell because I couldn't read their lips or understand anything they said.

Layla leaned over and whispered. "I guarantee you they know what the wing means."

I nodded. "Probably. But it also means they won't tell anyone else about it. The secret will be safe."

Solara turned back to them. "We may be able to help them, but not now. Keep your sisters asleep and confine them to a chamber."

Nori and Raya bowed, then the other pixies recovered their unconscious leaders and left the throne room by the way we'd come in. Then it was just me, Layla, and the most powerful fae in all the worlds.

I was already wishing I hadn't gotten out of bed that morning, but now there was nothing to do but forge ahead and state my case. "You want me dead, and that's totally understandable. A lot of people would like to see me dead, and they all have their reasons. I now know why you took such a keen interest in Hannah when I last met with you and it's not because she's a regular demi. She's something else. Something extraordinary. And she scares you."

The queens had great poker faces, but the twitches in their eyes told me I'd hit a tender spot.

I continued. "You think killing me will allow you to take control of her, but I can assure you that's not the case. She and I have a family bond now. If anything happens to me, the seed will blossom unhindered and with a new master."

Mayce smiled coldly. "I think she will be happier with us. We are willing to leave you alone if you simply hand over the girl."

"What better place would there be for her but to live in eternal golden summer?" Solara smiled warmly. "We only want what is best for the girl because that will allow us to preserve our worlds."

"Besides, there is little evidence the girl has developed very much since being in your custody." Mayce raised a frosty eyebrow. "Let us assure you that we have nothing to do with the current threats against your life. Those decisions were made by our shadow selves, and they are not subject to the bargain you made with us."

"Yeah, funny how that loophole works." I shrugged. "Well, if you don't believe me, maybe you'll believe this." I removed a mason jar from my satchel. In it was a bit of potting soil and a single white flower I'd retrieved from the meditation chamber. A gentle nimbus glowed around the petals, giving it a peaceful aura. The soil was all over the place in the jar due to all the fighting and running, so I opened the lid and carefully pulled it from container.

The queens stared at the flower, faces twisted in revulsion and fear. What they saw now had completely broken their carefully guarded facades. Because this flower hadn't been created by a god. It wasn't natural to this world or any human worlds.

It had been created solely by Hannah.

46

The exposed roots of the flower squirmed as they sought sustenance. There hadn't been much for it to thrive on in the stone floor of my meditation chamber, but these flowers somehow found a way to survive. I dropped it onto the frozen tundra beneath the winter tree. The flower shivered with anticipation as it suddenly found soil that was rich with nutrients even though it was freezing cold.

It shuddered and began to grow. White bulbs formed along the stem, blossoming not into flowers but into mouths of sharp teeth. Some of them disgorged humanoid babies that screamed and cried as they crawled across the frozen ground, only to turn brown, wither and die seconds after birth. Some turned to pixies with petal wings. The creatures shrieked like banshees until they, too turned brown and died, spiraling to the ground like leaves.

"Enough!" Solara flashed forward and burned the flower to ashes with a burst of flame from her hands. "You have defiled this court with an abomination!"

"I have proven to you that Hannah will turn into a monster if you take her from me. She will infect both courts and turn Feary into a dead world." I stood my ground despite being uncomfortably close to someone who could incinerate me with a flick of their hand. "She can also become something wonderful if you give me a chance to train her."

Shaking with anger, Solara glared at me.

Mayce rose and walked down to us. "What is she, Cain?"

I blinked in surprise. "I thought you knew."

"We know she is a seed of destruction." Mayce regained some of her calm. "She will be our downfall."

"She is also a seed of creation," Solara said. "It is equally likely she could be our salvation from the Elder Things."

"There are beings who wish to manipulate her into becoming our downfall." I looked at the ashes of the flower. "Nyarlathotep, for one. The cabal of chaos also wishes to steal her and use her for their own gains, but I think their efforts will only end with an eldritch invasion. We are at a crossroads, my queens. The fate of Prime hangs on your next decision."

I'd never seen the queens look outright shaken, but they weren't hiding anything now. They knew if they forcefully took Hannah to either court, she could inadvertently destroy their natural order. I let the disappointment show on my face as well, because I'd hoped they knew exactly what Hannah was.

The meditation chamber had been full of Hannah's flowers. They'd grown from the walls, the floor, and even the ceiling. But they usually died within a week. The ones she'd created in fertile soil burned themselves out in minutes. It was a good thing, too, because they would have infested the world already.

We'd seen similar flowers growing in the hidden Ekhsis city on Oblivion, but they'd been normal. None of them had teeth or spawned flower children. I needed to take Hannah to Wanda and find out if these pale flowers had been common on Ekhsis. There had to be a connection somewhere so I could finally have definitive answers on Hannah's origins.

Maybe Hannah was a seed of Ekhsis. There were simply too many ways to interpret such a vague term.

Solar and Mayce conferred with each other, shielded by their privacy magic. I felt certain they were discussing killing Hannah and me and being done with this. But they knew the risks if they failed as they had before. Hannah might go berserk and end everything. I might escape and make them pay dearly.

"Cabal of Chaos?" Layla grinned. "That's a nice name."

"Yeah, it's not bad." I smirked. "CoC for short."

She snorted. "Sounds about right." Her grin faded as she turned to look at the ashes of the abominable flower. "You know what I don't get? Why hasn't Esteri demonstrated these abilities before? She just shoots death lasers out of her face."

"I had a conversation with Cain Alpha about that before." I recovered my mason jar from the ground and brushed it off. "We think Esteri went down a path of complete destruction after she thought Cain betrayed her. She doesn't even know how to calm her mind enough to create anything. It's also possible that since she's still on Cthulhu's leash it's stunted her development."

"Thank the gods." Layla sighed in relief. "This kind of power is scarier than anything I've ever seen before, and I've seen a lot."

"You and me both." I put a hand on her shoulder. "Thanks for having my back."

She raised an eyebrow and looked at me sideways. "You're too sentimental sometimes."

"No, I just recognize a good thing when I see it."

"I'm a good thing?" She laughed sarcastically. "Just stop talking, Cain. I don't want to go back down that path right now."

"What path are you on, Layla?"

She worked her jaw back and forth. "Damned if I know. Ever since you jailbroke me from Soultaker I've been listless."

The queens turned toward us, faces once again set in stone.

Solara spoke. "We agree that the child should stay in your custody. She should be trained to control her dangerous powers that they might benefit us against the eldritch and others who would end the natural order of the worlds that we have maintained for so long."

"We will set aside a special place for you and the child to live so we can monitor this training," Mayce added. "You will no longer need to live in hiding because we can protect you. This will be beneficial for all involved."

"Mhm." I rolled my eyes. "Can you protect me from the Cabal of Chaos?"

"Loki and the others will not be able to find you."

I decided to say what they already knew. "What about Hermes?"

They stared at me blankly for a moment before Mayce responded. "What does Hermes have to do with this?"

I couldn't tell if they were messing with me or not. "Surely you already figured it out."

They looked at each other and then to me. "Explain."

"You truly don't know, do you?" I whistled. "The winged tattoo is a symbol of Hermes."

Faces stony, they still managed to look like deer caught in the headlights.

I kept going since I'd already given up the secret. "Hermes is the leader or one of the leaders of the cabal."

"We truly did not know," Solara said. "The shadow queens and their minions were in charge of all Gaian operations, so perhaps they know the truth."

Mayce scowled. "If they kept that from us, then I will be most vexed."

"You intentionally covered your eyes and ears so your shadow courts could kill me. They in turn are being manipulated by Hermes and his cabal." I let that sink in for a moment. "All of your ill-conceived actions nearly unleashed the very thing you're trying to prevent."

"Hold your tongue, human." Mayce looked ready to freeze me into an ice statue. "That is no way to speak to your rulers."

I held out my hands. "Are you the rulers, or is Hermes?"

"Hermes." Mayce stated the name in disbelief. "He is a Greek god and one in good standing with the others. Why would he take the path of Loki?"

"He was a trickster god in eons past." Solara narrowed her gaze. "Perhaps he grew bored of the current order and seeks excitement.

Perhaps this has been a plan of his all along. He is often mistreated and looked down upon by the others."

Mayce directed a frosty glare my way. "You are certain this winged tattoo is his?"

"I'm absolutely certain. There are certain artifacts like winged boots and helmets that give the wearer incredible speed, just like Hermes."

Solara pursed her lips. "This information must remain between us. If Hermes realizes we know his true intentions, then it will bring him into the open. That could be disastrous for those fighting in the divine realm."

"I'm glad we agree on something," I said. "This secret must go no further." I considered weaving it into the bargain but decided the queens' self-interest would keep the secret safe.

I posed a corollary question. "How is Athena these days?"

"She is completely mad." Mayce shivered. "The mightiest warrior of the Greeks has been shackled and put to sleep by Zeus since she is just as likely to attack allies as she is enemies. Now only Mars, Zeus, and Hermes fight on the front lines. The others are busy fighting invaders on other fronts. If we reveal Hermes, then they will be down another god in the eternal war."

I'd learned from Artemis that the eldritch were constantly exploiting back doors as ways to bypass the front lines of the war in the divine realm. She and others hunted those invaders to prevent infestations. The Greek gods couldn't afford to lose Hermes on the frontlines.

"Are there other places like the Dead Forest on Feary?" I looked back and forth at them. "Other eldritch infestations that you've allowed to grow here?"

"There are other blights in the land, yes, but not by our choice." Solara seemed uncomfortable admitting it, but it seemed they were being unusually forthright today in light of the revelations about Hermes and their traitorous pixies. "Once a land is despoiled, it is out of our control."

I waited for more clarification, but she left it at that. "You have armies you could marshal. Why not do that and eradicate these blights?"

"Because they have not grown in some time, and it is safer to just leave them alone." Frost vapors drifted from Mayce's fingers, as if she wanted to use them on me, but she continued. "Some of these blights are not eldritch in nature."

Layla frowned. "Then what are they?"

Mayce didn't so much as look at her, but she answered. "Some remain from old wars we have tried to purge from memory."

I looked pointedly at the spring and autumn trees. "Some of them come back to haunt you, don't they? There's a reason for the presence of autumn and spring within this throne room, isn't there?"

Solara managed to look slightly ashamed for a moment. "We mistreated our kin because they were weaker than us. There is no solstice for their seasons, no peak strength. We thought them unnecessary and because of that, excluded them. This led to wars, death and mass exterminations. This is why some lands of Feary do not exist on any maps, because we have hidden them that our shame might not be revisited."

"Our brethren were not all dead as we thought," Mayce said. "It seems our past has come back to haunt us, and we are trying to make amends before another war weakens our worlds while we are under threat of eldritch invasions."

"Holy shit." I ran a hand down my face. "You realize this is no coincidence, right? This has the fingerprints of chaos all over it."

"But which chaos?" Mayce said. "Eldritch, or our very own gods?"

"I'm willing to bet both." I blew out a breath. "And the problem is, our gods of chaos don't seem to care that they're risking total annihilation."

"This is why you must bring the girl here and train her under our protection." Solara held out her hands imploringly. "We can hide her even from Hermes."

"This is the bargain, Cain Sthyldor." Mayce crossed her arms and placed the full weight of her gaze on me. "Accept it, or there will be dire consequences."

"No."

The queens stiffened and all emotions vanished from their faces.

Mayce stared at me coldly. "We are being more than generous to someone who is a traitor and insurrectionist."

"No, you're trying to control me and Hannah and that's not going to happen." I maintained eye contact even though every fiber of my being was buckling under the weight of their gazes. "We do this my way, or you can take your chances letting the shadow queens try to kill me. They haven't done very well so far, have they?"

They remained silent for a long time.

Solara finally spoke. "He is this way because he is not of our worlds. He and the girl are both alien infections that should not exist here."

"Was I supposed to hear that?" I asked. It was a startling revelation to find out that they knew my true nature.

"It is the truth." Mayce's lips curled with disgust. "You are a relic from a failed world."

"Actually, I'm a relic from the first successful world." I maintained my air of defiance. "And that brings me to another point—Erolith."

"He is paying for his crimes." Solara's eyes glowed with power. "That he would aid you, a creature who is every bit as alien to us as the eldritch is beyond our reasoning."

I resisted the urge to call them some choice names and chose reason instead. "The Ekhsis existed before the Elder Gods or the Elder Things. That world was the genesis of our gods and the gods of alien worlds. Erolith is a brilliant strategist. He knew that the only way to beat the eldritch in the long term was with power that existed long before they did. He saw the potential in me to be a champion of this world if only you'd allow it."

I was making this up as I went along, but it sounded like something Erolith would do. I was probably eons away from ascending into someone who could defeat gods. Hell, it was something I didn't even want to think about. I just wanted to drink my damned mangoritas in peace. But it was obvious those days were behind me.

One way or the other, I was now in the clutches of beings far more powerful than me.

The anger in their eyes faded, though not entirely. It was evident they also thought this was something Erolith would do. He was high fae, but he was not like them. He had chosen a path of service to the realm and put duty above self-interest.

I hammered my point home with one final statement. "Erolith is devout in his service. Do you really think he could ever do anything to betray his queens?"

The anger completely left them. Though their expressions didn't change much, it was obvious they realized their mistakes. It was also obvious that they were probably too proud to admit to it, meaning Erolith might be forgiven, but it was unlikely they'd reinstate him unless and until they had good reason to do so.

"Individual choice has its risks and rewards, but if you can just get out of my way, I think you'll be pleased with the results." I cleared my throat. "Let me and Hannah make our choices. Leave us alone."

They remained silent.

I kept talking. "Do that, and we'll do what we can to clear other eldritch infestations like we did with the Dead Forest. Make a bargain with me to ensure my safety from the shadow queens and their minions and let today be the start of a cleansing that will see Feary and her queens on a path to the proper natural order."

"I do not like you, Cain Sthyldor." Mayce twirled frost vapors from her fingertips. "But you make sense."

"You will be our unlikely champion," Solara said. "But no one except us and our shadow selves will know. You will still have enemies and threats to you that we will not protect you from. You will be entirely on your own against the agents of Hermes and his cabal."

I nodded. "I would rather face all the dangers of the world as a free being than live in utter security as a bird in your gilded cage."

Mayce smiled. "Perhaps I like you a little after all."

Solara smiled as well. "He is troublesome, but a worthy adversary."

"Perhaps it is because he is not truly human." Mayce nodded as if that was the correct answer.

"Can we get past this lovefest and make a deal?" Layla said. "I'm getting hungry."

The queens ignored her. "Let us hear your bargain, Cain Sthyldor."

"First, I need to know something." There was a lot I needed to know, but this was important. "How are the guardians from the other dimensions traveling back and forth?"

Mayce looked as if she didn't want to answer, but she relented. "The shadow queens from Beta were given a device that allows it. A pixie said it was a gift that would allow them to seek their revenge on you, Cain Sthyldor. With it was a message detailing the loophole that could allow them to kill you and take control of the girl."

"Perhaps this pixie was an agent of Hermes." Solara grimaced. "I don't know how else a pixie would have laid hands on such a device."

I groaned. "A device as in a Tetron?" I suddenly knew where Baura had sent it and why. It was an insurance plan in case I defeated her. It also confirmed that she'd been working with Hermes, because there was no other way she could have convinced a pixie to deliver a device or a message unless that pixie was under his control.

It also made me feel that I wasn't a complete moron compared to her. Hermes had helped Baura immensely. He had somehow provided her with that open portal just so she could lure to me to Beta for an easy kill.

Mayce observed me. "What do you know of this, Cain?"

I told them. "Baura left a fake Tetron in place of her real one so I wouldn't know it was gone after I defeated her."

"Baura?" Solara frowned.

"The mad elf who destroyed Gaia Beta with apocalypse weapons. She sent the shadow queens the Tetron along with the plan to defeat me. I suspect Hermes helped her with that plan."

Mayce looked doubtful. "An elf did this?"

"She had apocalypse weapons from the lost armory. I also think she had alliances with Hermes and probably even eldritch like Nyarlathotep."

"That fucking elf." Layla laughed mirthlessly. "Even after she's been brain damaged and defeated, she has a backup plan to kill you."

"Yeah, but there's no telling how many of her plans came from Hermes or others in the cabal." I felt a little better knowing I hadn't been completely outsmarted by Baura. It wasn't much, but I'd take it.

Solara and Mayce exchanged looks, then turned to me.

"It is obvious we must do whatever is necessary to stop this, but Gaia Beta has given the eldritch a firm foothold very close to our worlds." Solara sighed. "The infestation must be purged before it manages to spread here."

"Yes, and we believe the girl can help," Mayce said. "The shadow queens of Beta have lost considerable power as the infestation destroys the natural order."

I cracked my knuckles. "Then let's bargain."

47

Bargaining directly with fae queens is normally enough to make anyone go insane. Hell, bargaining with any high fae is a torturous process unless you don't care about being ruthlessly manipulated into a terrible deal.

Thankfully, I had experience and the willingness of the queens to do what I wanted—for the most part at least. But there was one major piece to the puzzle once we arrived at the final bargain.

The shadow queens had to agree as well.

As separate entities who were technically of equal power to the Prime queens—though they would never admit that—the other queens had to seal the bargain with me as well. Otherwise, they and their minions could continue to directly come after me.

They had a process in place whereby a pixie controlling the Tetron would travel among the dimensions at regular intervals to convey messages to the so-called shadow courts and vice versa. She arrived near the beginning of the bargaining process and immediately left to deliver the messages to the two shadow courts. She arrived with the other four queens not long after I'd sealed the bargain with the Prime queens.

I really wanted to inspect them for tattoos but doubted any of the

fae queens would accept the rune of Hermes on them. The Prime
queens had already inspected the messenger pixie to ensure she was
loyal.

I'd expected the queens to look identical, but the ones from Beta
were scarred and weary looking, as if they'd fought one too many
battles and lost. The ones from Alpha looked nearly identical, but
they also seemed much more tired and worn down. The loss of power
in their dimensions had taken a toll.

None of them looked happy to see me.

"What is the meaning of this?" Solara Beta asked at once. "Why is
he in your presence?"

"We have sealed a bargain with him," Solara replied. "We now
require the rest of you to seal it so we can begin the road to
recovery."

"Recover?" Mayce Beta's hair was buzzed almost to the scalp and a
scar ran across her left eye. "This man holds the seed of our
destruction!"

"I gotta admit that Mayce Beta looks badass," Layla murmured.
"Damn, I want a scar over my eye."

"Hemlock wears an eyepatch," I reminded her.

"She's a fucking poser."

The Alpha queens chimed in with their displeasure as well. I sat
back and thoroughly enjoyed watching the fae queens bicker and
argue like middle schoolers. It was clear the shadow queens didn't
think they were any less worthy than the Prime queens, but it was
also obvious that they'd lost significant power due to the destruction
of the natural order in their respective dimensions.

The mechanists had done quite a number on Gaia Alpha. Gaia
Beta, of course, was quickly turning eldritch.

"Silence!" Solara Prime thundered after a protracted argument.
"Mayce and I hold supreme power and we will wield it against you,
much as it pains us to do so. We will assume control of your worlds if
you leave us no choice."

"We control the Tetron." Solara Beta raised her chin in defiance.
"You cannot reach us without it."

I rose and bowed deeply toward the Prime queens. "I have a Tetron that my queens can borrow so none may defy them."

"This is an outrage!" Mayce Alpha cried. "I will freeze him into an ice statue and put him in my garden."

"No." Mayce Prime's voice was calm, quiet, and deadly. "I will kill any of you who oppose this bargain because it is the only thing that will save the natural order on all our worlds. Can you not see that we are being manipulated by the gods of chaos? By Hermes himself? With the power of the girl behind us, we can restore natural order and avoid destruction."

"She's right." Solara Alpha slumped. "I feel the weariness of my wounded worlds weighing heavily on my powers. I fear if we don't enlist the girl however we can, we will simply cease to exist, and the eldritch will rule supreme."

"The gods are fighting an unwinnable war in the divine realm," Solara Prime said. "We are the only ones who can save Gaia and Feary. You saw how the gods in their hubris destroyed Oblivion. Now we are watching it happen all over again right beneath our noses. They are fighting a war on two fronts and don't even realize it."

The Alpha queens briefly conferred, then nodded. "We will seal the bargain."

The Beta queens looked angrily defiant.

"Do not test our resolve, Beta." Mayce gave them a look so cold it made me shiver.

Their defiance melted beneath her frosty gaze.

"We think you are wrong," Mayce Beta said. "I will be the first to remind you when our worlds are beyond repair."

Mayce Prime took her hand and patted it. "And I will be the first to remind you when we salvage what is left and rebuild better than before."

Layla tutted. "Family drama. Gotta love it."

I recited my bargain to them. In a nutshell, it protected me and any Cain in any dimension from any queens existing now or in the future. That was to protect me and my alts if more splinters occurred in the timelines.

Solara Alpha looked impressed. "The Cain of our world resorted to brute force to protect himself. You, however, have used logic and trickery that is impressive for a human. I can see the training Erolith imparted in you has borne fruit beyond even our imagining."

It sounded like a long, backhanded compliment, but I took it. "Thank you, my queen. However, if I'd had a brute force option, I might have considered it. Fate delivered Cain Alpha a small army which I do not presently possess."

"There is yet another problem," Mayce Beta said. "Many of the Oblivion Guard who were trying to kill Cain by our orders have abandoned us. With this new information you've given us, we now see they serve new masters, namely Hermes and his Cabal of Chaos. We have no control over them."

"Then I'll just have to be careful." I shrugged. "It's nothing I'm not used to."

"Very well." Solara Prime stood. "Let us adjourn and pray this is an auspicious start to our partnership. Our worlds are at stake and higher powers wish to hinder us for their own gain. Let us navigate these waters better than we did the last time."

"Agreed." Mayce idly drew crystal shapes in the air. "Keep us apprised of your progress Cain. We will have the first offensive ready to go within the month."

I wasn't entirely pleased with that aspect of the bargain, but it had been necessary to win their agreement. We were going to help clean Beta of the infestation by any means necessary, and I was the one in charge.

"There are still pixies and rogue guardians in the city that will try to kill me," I reminded them. "I request your aid departing the city."

"We will portal you wherever you wish to go," Mayce said.

"How does that work, exactly?" I'd always been curious to know how the fae could open gateways to just about anywhere.

"It is beyond your means, I'm afraid."

Despite our new bargain, I didn't want to give them the location of my transition zones, so I said, "Just outside the southern gate is fine."

"As you wish." She traced a pattern of frost in the air and slashed her hand through it. The air bubbled. Layla and I stepped up to it and it swallowed us whole. An instant later we stood outside the city gates in front of the long line we'd bypassed earlier.

Those at the front of the line gawked as we appeared through an ice gate that only high fae could utilize. They moved well out of our way, probably assuming we were fae ourselves even if our demeanor didn't support that.

We enjoyed a peaceful walk back to the transition zone where I took us back to Gaia. Things had gone about as expected, but I'd shouldered some heavy responsibilities to ensure our future. I was once again in the service of the queens, but this time I was in charge of my destiny.

This time I planned to do better.

After arriving back at Sanctuary, Layla stopped outside and stared at the church. "You think it's safe to go back to Voltaire's yet?"

"The queens agreed to actively hunt down the traitors and purge them from the Oblivion Guard. Hopefully the Handers will be too busy getting their asses handed to themselves to worry about us."

"Excellent." Layla grinned. "I'm going to force the elf back to bartending so I can pretend all of this never happened."

"Good. I've got something to take care of. Tell the others I'll be back later."

She raised an eyebrow. "What else could you possibly have left to do except heavy drinking?"

"I need some answers." I got back in Dolores and headed for the airport. I hadn't gotten far when a woman stepped into the road in front of me, her face a mask of frustration. I pulled to the side of the road and got out. "Hello, Ithia. I'm glad you decided to save us both some time."

"You were really going to fly straight out to confront Alistair just to get my attention." Fate stated it as fact since she'd probably read my intentions in her loom of fate. "I'll answer your question, but there are reasons why I didn't simply swing by to tell you."

"Because it would break your loom?"

"It would risk more splinters in the timeline, and you know how much I hate those."

"How's Garrick and Chronos these days?"

She blinked, taken off guard by the unexpected questions. "They're fine. Garrick has been spending a lot of time with Yuki, to the detriment of his job, but I'm certain he'll get back into the swing of things soon enough." Fate cleared her throat. "As to your question, there were forces in place to keep you from ever meeting Elton. I discovered outside interference from another fate deity and simply did what I needed to do to return things to normal. I can't tell you anymore about why for reasons you know all too well."

"I suspected as much." I crossed my arms and leaned against Dolores. "I assume you also know about the Cabal of Chaos and their true leaders."

"Unfortunately, yes. I only found out when you did because I've not kept as close an eye on other threads since you're so keen on breaking the rules."

"Why didn't Hermes create a splinter timeline when he held open that portal for Baura?"

She pursed her lips. "You're fishing. I'll bite, but only this once. It's imperative that you turn back around, go home and enjoy a brief respite, because your thread is full of uncertainties."

"Duh." I laughed mirthlessly. "I promised to help the fae clean up Beta. That certainly doesn't bode well."

"Hermes has children who are demis. Unlike other gods, he claims his as his own and keeps them close. They have various aspects of his abilities, one of which is opening dimensional gateways. That is why Prime is filling up with alts from Alpha. Aldus Bergstrom is just one example of that."

"I knew there had to be someone like that out there." I thought about the possibilities. "Is that who helped Eclipse move around their demi assassins?"

"Yes." She touched my arm. "Pray you never meet a child of Hermes. Many were raised without a mother and lack human perspective. Be careful, Cain."

Fate sparkled into dust and drifted away on the wind.

"Well, shit." I'd suspected Hermes had demi children, but I hadn't expected that last part about him keeping them close. This did not bode well for my future.

I got back into Dolores and sat there. A moment later, Hannah drove past in her clockwork car. She hit the brakes and backed up. Layla rolled down the passenger window.

"This is where you were going, Cain?" She laughed. "I mean, I guess it's better than fighting monsters on your first day."

Aura opened the back seat window. "Why are you just sitting here?"

I shrugged. "Just counting trees."

"Well, we're going to Voltaire's."

Hannah looked excited. "She's going to make me a mangorita!"

"Guess I'll meet you there." I turned on Dolores. "It's time we had a night of heavy drinking."

"Even the girl?" Layla grinned. "Oh, this is going to be fun."

Hannah hit the accelerator and the clockwork car lurched forward at a leisurely pace. I watched them go for a moment then pulled onto the road.

I'd enjoy all the mangoritas I wanted to the fullest today, because the future was full of monsters.

BOOKS BY JOHN CORWIN

Join the Overworld Conclave for all the news, memes and tentacles you could ever desire!

https://www.facebook.com/groups/overworldconclave

Or get your tentacles via email: www.johncorwin.net

Fan page: https://www.facebook.com/johncorwinauthor

CHRONICLES OF CAIN

To Kill a Unicorn

Enter Oblivion

Throne of Lies

At The Forest of Madness

The Dead Never Die

Shadow of Cthulhu

Cabal of Chaos

THE OVERWORLD CHRONICLES

Sweet Blood of Mine

Dark Light of Mine

Fallen Angel of Mine

Dread Nemesis of Mine

Twisted Sister of Mine

Dearest Mother of Mine

Infernal Father of Mine

Sinister Seraphim of Mine

Wicked War of Mine

Dire Destiny of Ours

Aetherial Annihilation

Baleful Betrayal

Ominous Odyssey

Insidious Insurrection

Utopia Undone

Overworld Apocalypse

Apocryphan Rising

Soul Storm

Devil's Due

Overworld Ascension

Assignment Zero (An Elyssa Short Story)

OVERWORLD UNDERGROUND

Soul Seer

Demonicus

Infernal Blade

OVERWORLD ARCANUM

Conrad Edison and the Living Curse

Conrad Edison and the Anchored World

Conrad Edison and the Broken Relic

Conrad Edison and the Infernal Design

Conrad Edison and the First Power

STAND ALONE NOVELS

Mars Rising

No Darker Fate

The Next Thing I Knew

Outsourced

ABOUT THE AUTHOR

John Corwin is the bestselling author of the Overworld Chronicles and Chronicles of Cain. He enjoys long walks on the beach and is a firm believer in puppies and kittens.

After years of getting into trouble thanks to his overactive imagination, John abandoned his male modeling career to write books.

He resides in Atlanta.

Join the Overworld Conclave for all the news, memes and tentacles you could ever desire!
https://www.facebook.com/groups/overworldconclave
Or get your tentacles via email: www.johncorwin.net
Fan page: https://www.facebook.com/johncorwinauthor
Website: http://www.johncorwin.net
Twitter: http://twitter.com/#!/John_Corwin